SECRETS & SONS

JACQUELINE DIAMOND

began her career as an Associated Press reporter and television columnist in Los Angeles, and has interviewed hundreds of celebrities. Now a full-time fiction writer, she has sold sixty-three novels that span romance, suspense and fantasy. Though she was born in Texas and raised in Nashville and Louisville, home is now Southern California. Jacqueline received her fifty-book pin from Harlequin at the 2003 Romance Writers of America National Conference in New York.

AMANDA STEVENS

Born and raised in a small Southern town, Amanda Stevens frequently draws on memories of her birthplace to create atmospheric settings and casts of eccentric characters. She is now the author of over thirty novels, the recipient of Career Achievement awards in Romantic/Mystery and Romantic/Suspense from *Romantic Times* magazine and was a 1999 Romance Writers of America RITA® Award finalist in the Gothic/ Romantic Suspense category. She currently resides in Texas.

JACQUELINE
DIAMOND

AMANDA
STEVENS

SECRETS & SONS

HARLEQUIN®

TORONTO • NEW YORK • LONDON
AMSTERDAM • PARIS • SYDNEY • HAMBURG
STOCKHOLM • ATHENS • TOKYO • MILAN • MADRID
PRAGUE • WARSAW • BUDAPEST • AUCKLAND

ISBN 0-373-23023-0

SECRETS & SONS

Copyright © 2004 by Harlequin Books S.A.

The publisher acknowledges the copyright holders of the individual works as follows:

HIS SECRET SON
Copyright © 1999 by Jackie Hyman

A MAN OF SECRETS
Copyright © 1996 by Marilyn Medlock Amann

This edition published by arrangement with Harlequin Books S.A.

® and TM are trademarks of the publisher. Trademarks indicated with ® are registered in the United States Patent and Trademark Office, the Canadian Trade Marks Office and in other countries.

www.eHarlequin.com

Printed in U.S.A.

CONTENTS

HIS SECRET SON
Jacqueline Diamond

Chapter One

Joni Peterson was removing her TV dinner from the microwave oven when the phone rang. Reaching for the plastic container with pot holders, she let the answering machine pick up.

"Hi, it's Joni! If you're calling me or Jeff, please leave a message!"

She wasn't surprised when the caller hung up.

Through the kitchen window, she could see the twilight fading across her patio and small backyard. A crisp October breeze ruffled her roses and the brush on the hill beyond.

Near the edge of the dense woods above the house, a neighbor's gray-striped cat prowled, then vanished into a shadow. Seconds ticked by, but there was no further sign of it.

When she bought the house last year, Joni had relished the privacy. Now the remoteness of the place made her uneasy.

A few drops of steaming sauce from the fettuccine Alfredo plopped onto the back of her hand as she set the plate on the table. Instinctively, Joni lifted the burned spot to her mouth to take away the sting.

Maybe she should have grabbed the phone. It might

have been her eight-year-old son, Jeff, calling from his friend Bobby's house half a mile away to tell her he'd forgotten something for his sleepover.

But if it had been Jeff, he would have left a message, she told herself firmly. Besides, he spent the night at Bobby's so often that he kept an extra toothbrush and sleep shirt there, so what could he need?

She scooted into her chair and picked up the newspaper to read while she ate. As usual, she'd barely had time to glance at it in the morning before leaving for her job as public relations assistant at Viento del Mar Community Hospital.

The phone rang again. Joni picked it up. "Hello?"

A click, followed by a dial tone. Darn him! The man knew exactly how to irritate her. Although she'd signed up for Caller ID, the man had his number blocked.

So far, he'd been careful. The calls hadn't been frequent enough to spark any action by the phone company. The other harassment—roses cut from her bushes and left on the porch to wither, a pair of sunglasses taken from her unlocked car and set on her patio—wasn't threatening enough to concern the police, an officer had told Joni when she called.

No one was going to arrest Lowell Peterson for anything less than a major crime. As the owner of Peterson Printing, one of the largest companies in the central California town of Viento del Mar, her ex-husband wielded a lot of power.

As she rinsed the plastic tray and tossed it in the recycle container, Joni kept expecting the phone to ring again. Where was he calling from anyway? His home? His car?

The shadows deepened on the hill behind her house.

On the patio, a breeze rattled the loose pedal on Jeff's bike. She made a mental note to tighten it and to remind him to put his bike in the garage. Maybe she should put it away now, but there was no rain in the forecast. A night outside wouldn't hurt it.

Joni retreated to the den, their combination guest room and electronic haven. Kneeling by the video rack, she picked out an old favorite, *The Sound of Music.*

As she stood up, she found herself face-to-face with a group of photos on the wall. The largest, taken three years ago, was a formal portrait of her, Lowell and Jeff. She'd hung it there in an attempt to keep her son's life as normal as possible.

The photographer had posed them on risers so that the gap in heights wouldn't be so apparent. Even so, Lowell had a commanding presence. Tall and blond, with a piercing light blue gaze, he'd swept Joni off her feet when she was a nineteen-year-old clerk and he was the son of the company's owner. Five years her senior, he'd already been pushing for a dynamic expansion of Peterson Printing.

Studying his photograph, she could feel the excitement of being singled out by him. Her amazement at discovering the intensity of his interest had enabled her to hold her head high on their early dates, even though she knew she didn't fit in with his country-club friends.

Joni wasn't sure what he'd seen in her. She'd been described as interesting-looking, with her high cheekbones and slightly crooked nose, but never beautiful. Certainly it hadn't been her rather boyish figure that attracted him.

How much had she really loved Lowell, and how much had she been awed by him? It was a bit late, Joni told herself ruefully, to worry about that.

Slipping the video into the VCR, she sat back to enjoy Julie Andrews and the Rodgers and Hammerstein songs. Half an hour later, she realized to her relief that the phone hadn't rung again. Maybe Lowell had better things to do tonight than make a pest of himself.

She was immersed in the movie when the wind picked up loudly enough to be heard over the TV. Storm coming, she thought absently. The forecasters had been wrong, as usual.

A crash from outside set her heart racing. The metallic jangle reverberated down to her bones.

The bike! It must have blown over. "Oh, for goodness' sake," Joni grumbled aloud. The last thing she felt like doing was going out into the nippy air and hauling Jeff's bike to the garage. Yet if a storm really was starting, the patio's cover wouldn't offer much protection.

Joni turned off the VCR. In the service hall by the back door, she pulled on an old sweater and stuffed her feet into a pair of canvas slip-ons. As she let herself out, she flicked on the patio light. Its glow penetrated no more than a few feet into the gloom.

"Here, bikey, bikey." The wind tore away her feeble attempt at humor. Moist and chill, it blasted through the sweater as if it were a cobweb.

She should have remembered to bring a flashlight, she thought, but going back inside was silly. She wanted to get this chore finished as quickly as possible.

In the faint light, the patio chairs stretched grotesquely. Unable to distinguish between shapes and shadows, Joni banged her thigh against the glass table. She let out a couple of swearwords she would have suppressed had Jeff been home.

Wind gusted against her back, bringing the first drops of rain. Strands of shoulder-length hair whipped free of her bun and scrambled around Joni's face as if attempting to flee.

By the time the breeze quieted, her eyes were adjusting to the dark. She could make out spoked tires and twisted handlebars lying on the concrete a few steps away.

Another blast of wind hit, and something arced through the air. As Joni dodged, she recognized the object as the hummingbird feeder she'd filled this morning.

The glass globe had been a Christmas present last year from Lowell's grandfather, Herb, who doted on Jeff and remained Joni's friend. It was a beautiful feeder, but if she hadn't moved so quickly, the darn thing would have beaned her.

Near the garage, a shoe crunched on concrete. The hairs on her neck stood on end.

"Who is it?" Beyond the patio, she couldn't see a thing.

"It's me."

She recognized the tenor voice and the footsteps coming toward her, firm and confident, with an occasional scuffing noise as if he were impatient to be moving faster.

A tall shape loomed into the porch light. She stared in dismay at her ex-husband.

No wonder he hadn't made any more phone calls. He'd come to confront her in person.

"Joni, are you all right?" A frown creased the face worthy of a men's magazine. Strong, symmetrical, rugged.

Lowell wore a designer suit and an open-collared silk shirt. What the well-dressed man wears to stalk his ex-wife, she thought furiously.

"What are you doing here?" Rain misted her face and the wind tugged more hair from its knot. On the hillside, bushes swished.

"It's not what you think." He stopped a dozen feet away.

"What is it I supposedly think?"

"That I've been harassing you."

"So here you are, sneaking around my patio after dark," she retorted. "Obviously, this disproves the whole idea."

"Where's Jeff?" he asked abruptly.

Joni's alarm deepened. Why did he want to know? Was he planning to attack her? If he thought their son was home, he might not risk it. "Asleep," she said.

"No, he's not. I saw you come home alone."

He'd been watching her. Goose bumps crept along her skin. "Lowell, please leave," she said. "Jeff's at Bobby's house. They'll be bringing him home any minute."

He eased forward. The hunter, not wanting to startle his prey. One large hand reached toward her arm.

"Joni, surely you don't believe I would—"

A blast of chill air ripped away the rest of his words and a thrashing noise from the slope made Joni turn sharply. As she did, something bashed into the side of her head with a crunch.

The world spun madly and her mind filled with pain beyond enduring. She barely felt her ribs hit the spokes of the bike as she fell.

Chapter Two

Joni's head ached and her side throbbed. The patio was a jumble of dim light and confusing, lumpy shapes.

She wondered if this was a dream. Then she became aware that she was soaked and profoundly chilled.

She ought to go inside. She had to move.

Her numb hands flexed with difficulty. In her right palm, she discovered, lay something slender but hard. When she gripped it, it felt like the haft of a kitchen knife.

"Hello? Are you here, Joni?" The voice with a Chinese accent belonged to her neighbor, Celia Lu. From the sound, she was walking up the rise from her yard.

Joni tried to answer. All that came out was a grunt.

A flashlight beam swept through the mist. "Hello, anyone?" Celia called. "Who is here?"

This time, Joni managed to prop herself up enough to catch the light in her eyes. Pain sliced into her head and she fell back.

"You are hurt?" Celia hesitated at the edge of the patio. A childless woman in her fifties, she had moved next door about six months ago. Lonely during her husband's absences on business, she came over frequently to chat. "I call for help?"

Joni hated to involve the police or paramedics. In view

of Lowell's prominence, the incident would be sure to make the newspaper. But she couldn't handle this alone. "Yes, please," she whispered.

"Someone else is here? I hear noises. A shout."

"Lowell. I guess he's gone." But why would he leave her here, injured?

Celia played the flashlight across the patio. It wavered and stopped on a dark shape. Her mouth opened and out came a high-pitched needle of sound that went on and on.

The scream merged with the throb in Joni's head, pulsing at the same frequency. Consciousness shattered into a thousand shards, and silence returned.

WHEN JONI AWOKE, two men wearing light blue jackets knelt beside her, one holding an umbrella while the other checked her pulse. Brightness turned the patio a violent white against a rippling silver curtain of rain.

Her clothing was soaked with a sticky substance that Joni recognized as hummingbird nectar. Her head must have smashed open the feeder.

To her right, she glimpsed figures bending over something. There were three people: a uniformed officer, a man in a plaid sport coat who scribbled on a pad, and a woman taking photographs.

"What happened?" she muttered, and caught a startled look from the paramedics.

"Detective!" one of them called. "She's awake!"

The man in the plaid coat continued making notes. "Yeah, yeah, I'll be right there."

When he moved, Joni saw a crumpled shape on the ground beyond. A portable floodlight picked out disarrayed blond hair and the expensive weave of a gray suit jacket marred by a dark stain.

"Lowell?" she asked.

The detective skirted some broken glass and crouched beside her. "Mrs. Peterson? I'm Detective Terry Mac-Dougall."

All she could murmur was "Lowell—is he all right?"

"I'm afraid he's dead," the man in the plaid coat said.

Joni didn't hear whatever he said next. A rushing noise filled her brain, a combination of dizziness and disbelief.

Lowell? Dead?

Their divorce two years ago had been bitter, following Joni's discovery that he was having an affair. That had been the last straw after years of his sarcasm and domination.

And yet he could be warm and funny, especially with Jeff. Lowell had been a towering figure in her life. She couldn't accept that he was gone forever.

Right after she left him, he'd harassed her a few times with phone calls and petty vandalism. That had soon stopped, though. After Joni asked for only reasonable child support and agreed to generous visitation rights, Lowell had even apologized.

A few months ago at his request, they'd begun having dinner together occasionally to discuss Jeff and reestablish a friendly relationship. It had lasted until a few weeks back—when the harassment resumed. Lowell denied being behind it, but the actions were exactly the sort of thing he'd pulled right after they separated. Joni just wished she knew why he'd started in again.

Now he was dead, and she might never know. Even though she'd felt anger and resentment, she'd never wished Lowell any harm.

His death would hurt people she cared about—Jeff and his great-grandfather, Herb. It was going to affect a lot of other people, too, in ways she couldn't even begin to think about.

The police detective was kneeling next to her, waiting with a look of strained patience, and she caught him glancing at her right hand.

Hadn't she been holding a knife? It was gone now; maybe she'd dreamed it.

"You...found—"

"We're keeping the knife as evidence, Mrs. Peterson," the policeman said. "Would you care to make a statement?"

"I didn't kill him," she said, and saw in his face that he didn't believe her.

Lowell must have been stabbed, she thought. But he was so strong. Who could have done this?

The detective asked her to describe what had happened. After she did, he asked her the same questions again, as if trying to trip her up.

She didn't understand why he seemed so accusing. It *was* odd, awakening with a knife in her hand, but even if somehow she'd wielded it, she would only have done so in self-defense.

What did the man think she had to gain by murdering Lowell? As he excused himself to confer with the photographer, his voice gave her a clue. He used that pseudorespectful, subtly mocking tone that some people adopted when addressing the rich.

He thought she'd done it for the money.

Lowell's wealth, including the ownership of Peterson Printing, would presumably go to Jeff. And therefore, until he grew up, to Joni. She didn't want it, but she doubted the detective would believe her. On TV, people killed for money all the time. Maybe some did in real life, too. But not her.

The police would be even more suspicious if they learned that Jeff wasn't Lowell's biological child, but she hoped the medical records would remain confidential. Besides, to Joni, the boy *had* been Lowell's son.

She just wished she could remember exactly what had happened tonight. If she could explain how she came to be holding the knife, maybe she could convince the detective of her innocence. But her mind remained a blank. As she'd told MacDougall, she recalled exchanging a few words with Lowell, and then nothing.

Finally, the policeman gave the paramedics the okay to remove her. They fitted Joni with a cervical collar to protect her head and neck, then gently lifted her onto a gurney.

As they rolled her to the ambulance, she saw Celia standing on the sidelines, staring at her with mingled horror and fascination. It gave her the bewildering sense of being some stranger in a newscast instead of her ordinary self.

The doors closed and the ambulance jolted forward, sirens screaming. Joni's mind began to fade.

At the hospital, she slipped in and out of consciousness most of that night and early Thursday morning. She felt the needle pricking her hand to start the intravenous tube. She heard the diagnosis: a concussion and bruised ribs. She listened to carts rattling by in the hospital corridor and voices on a distant intercom, but still she remembered nothing of what happened to Lowell.

The nurses seemed solicitous, bringing extra pillows and laying a cool cloth across her forehead. Joni's public relations duties included interviewing staff members for the in-house newsletter. Apparently, she'd generated some goodwill, or perhaps, as she hoped, they were this kind to all the patients.

Later that morning, she finally came awake. The first thing she did was to call Bobby's mother, Kathryn Owens.

"I'm so sorry," Kathryn said earnestly. "I heard on the radio what happened. But the boys don't know."

"If you or Fred wouldn't mind driving Jeff to Herb's…"

Joni hated to impose. Over the past few years, the Owenses had done her more than their share of favors. But her son needed someone close to give him the awful news about his father, and the best person was his great-grandfather.

"Of course we don't mind. Jeff knows the address, doesn't he? And we'll stop by your house and pick up some clean clothes for you." Her friend knew where Joni hid a key. "You'll need something to wear when you leave the hospital."

Joni started to thank her, but Kathryn waved it away. "I know you'd do the same for me."

"Of course," she said. "But I hope you never need it." Thank goodness for friends, Joni thought as she hung up. Without them, a single mother could scarcely survive.

Around noon, she heard raised voices in the hall and recognized the gravelly tones of her boss, Basil Dupont. The nurse was refusing to let him in until the doctor gave the okay for visitors. He in turn refused to leave a potted plant until he could deliver it in person. For a public relations director, Basil had a remarkably dour personality.

Finally, he went away, taking the plant with him. She dozed again, awakening when the nurse came in with the clean clothes Kathryn had dropped off. The woman also carried a large flower arrangement in a vase. "A man brought this while you were asleep," she said, and handed Joni the card.

"Get well soon," read a masculine scrawl, followed by a signature. Charlie Rogers, her son's soccer coach. That was sweet, Joni thought.

The last time she attended a practice, he'd come over afterward to talk and seemed on the verge of asking her out when the Owens family stopped by. He'd been kind to come and visit her, Joni thought, but, all the same, she was glad she hadn't had to make small talk.

By late afternoon, her mind cleared enough for her to sit up and read the newspaper. On the front page was a photograph of her and Lowell that had been taken five years ago at a charity concert. In happier times.

Rain pelted against the hospital window. The dark mood suited Joni as she studied the reporter's words, trying to let reality sink in.

Printing company owner and country-club board member, Lowell Peterson, was found fatally stabbed on the patio of his ex-wife, whom he was suspected of harassing. The police have declined to release information about the murder weapon, but unconfirmed reports say a kitchen knife was missing from the cutlery block on the kitchen counter.

Although rain has destroyed much of the evidence, police say it appeared that the former Mrs. Peterson confronted her husband and an altercation ensued. Mrs. Peterson sustained a concussion and bruised ribs.

The cuts on Mr. Peterson's hands and arms are believed to indicate his attempts to fight off the knife attack...

All the pieces fitted. Except that Joni hadn't taken a knife when she went out to the patio.

It was possible, however, that she had left it on the glass table a few nights ago while barbecuing. She couldn't be sure she'd brought the knife inside.

Could she have killed Lowell and not remember it? Joni

didn't want to believe it, but especially after suffering a head injury, she couldn't completely disregard the possibility.

The newspaper ran a lengthy biography of Lowell. His honors during high school. The student offices he'd held at nearby University of California, Santa Barbara. His prominence in the community.

Joni stared at her former husband's chiseled features in the photograph. Once upon a time, he'd swept her into the clouds. Unfortunately, she'd had years to sink back to earth under the weight of his critical, controlling behavior.

Two years ago, she'd hit the ground with a thud. It had taken one phone call from Kim DeLong. Until then, Joni had refused to believe the gossip about them. Kim had been Lowell's high school sweetheart, but they'd drifted apart in college. After marrying, then divorcing a banker in San Francisco, she'd returned to Viento del Mar a year earlier.

Judging by Kim's maliciously gleeful tone, she'd enjoyed calling Joni to crow about her affair with Lowell. She'd also enjoyed rubbing salt in the wound by saying that Joni had never been the right woman for him.

When confronted, Lowell had admitted the affair and, furious about the phone call, dropped Kim immediately. Her bitterness was loud and abusive.

Joni pushed the memories aside. Kim and the divorce now seemed almost trivial compared with Lowell's death.

How was Jeff taking it? And what about Herb? The realization that she might have caused that dear man the worst kind of pain—the loss of his grandson—made her feel even more despondent.

Another thought sent terror prickling along Joni's spine. What if she were convicted of murder and sent to prison? She'd never even seen the inside of one except in films, the kind where prisoners were beaten and humiliated. How could she survive in a place like that?

And Jeff. What if he lost both his parents? Who would take care of him?

There was no other family but Herb, who was seventy-seven and had a heart condition. Joni's own father had deserted when she was just a child. Her mother, a hard-working waitress, had died of an aneurysm shortly after Joni turned eighteen.

Jeff's only other close relative was Lowell's brother, Dirk, whom she had met briefly at her wedding and at her father-in-law's funeral two years later. She remembered little about him except that he had bright blue eyes, like Jeff's, and seemed eager to get away from Viento del Mar.

At Lowell's request, Dirk had reluctantly donated sperm, but his only acknowledgement of Jeff was to send a small present each Christmas, usually an article of clothing that might have been chosen by his secretary. "Uncle" Dirk didn't even acknowledge the boy's birthday.

She and Lowell had discussed the possibility of some-day telling Jeff the truth. Joni believed a child had a right to know his own background, but Lowell had been so un-comfortable with the subject that she'd put it aside for later.

If she kept the secret too long, though, there was always the danger that Jeff might learn or suspect that he'd been lied to. Rather than risk damaging his faith in her, Joni meant to tell him the story when the time felt right. But not now.

A tap at the door interrupted her reflections. "Joni?" came a warm male voice.

Despite his gray hair and a few age spots, Herb Peterson retained the erect stature and classic face that had once made him a popular figure in Viento del Mar society. The years had put a sparkle in his blue eyes and lent a curve to his mouth, and the sight of him always raised Joni's spirits.

Today, though, there was a redness around his eyelids and a tightness to the way he held himself. She could see that he had been mourning.

"Please come in." She gave him a quavery smile.

"The nurse said you could have visitors. Jeff's down the hall looking at babies through a window," he said. "I thought it might be best if you and I spoke alone."

She wished she knew the right thing to say. "Herb, I'm so sorry about Lowell. I honestly don't remember what happened."

"Did he attack you?" His voice broke painfully.

"He admitted he'd been watching me," she said. "Then he took a step toward me. After that, I don't remember anything."

Herb remained on the far side of the room. "I have trouble accepting that my grandson was capable of stalking you. Let alone trying to harm you."

"I don't think he did, and yet he must have," Joni said. "It doesn't make sense, does it?"

"No, it doesn't. By the way, I caught a reporter trying to sneak in here. I told her I'd complain to her paper if she bothers you again."

"Thank you."

The town's newspaper and radio station were both owned by a local businessman who was an old friend of Herb's. The man couldn't ignore a major news story, but he would keep his staff within reasonable bounds.

A movement near the half-open door caught Joni's eye. She rolled her head on the pillow until she saw her son edging into the room. He wore his new navy pullover and tan Sunday-school pants, and his brown hair had been tamed with a comb and water. The extra tidy appearance only emphasized his unaccustomed pallor and the dark circles beneath his eyes.

"Hi, sweetie." She was grateful when he ran to her, even if his hug did make her ribs ache.

"Be careful, Jeff. Your mom's been hurt." Herb rested a hand atop his great-grandson's shoulder.

"What did you tell him about…about…?"

"He understands that his Dad's gone to heaven," Herb said. "We stopped by the church and prayed for him on our way here. I also asked the minister to officiate at the service."

Joni hadn't given a thought to the funeral. As Lowell's ex-wife and suspected slayer, she doubted she would have any say about the matter anyway. "That's fine. When will it be?"

"I've scheduled a memorial service for Monday afternoon," Herb said.

"Jeff?" She gazed into the storm-blue eyes of the little boy who, despite a trace of gangliness, still seemed like her baby. "How are you feeling? Scared? Sad?"

"I miss Daddy," he admitted in a whisper. Although Lowell had rarely played with his son as a baby, he and Jeff had begun spending more time together since the divorce. "Do you think the police are wrong? Maybe he's not really dead but, like, in a coma."

"I'm afraid not, honey." Joni understood how he felt. She still imagined Lowell must be alive somewhere, out of sight. Working at the plant. Playing racquetball at the club.

"Maybe he could come back," Jeff persisted. "They could clone him. Like Mr. Spock on *Star Trek*."

"That's make-believe," she said.

"I know," Jeff conceded.

He understood, Joni thought, at least on an eight-year-old level.

"When are you coming home, Mom?"

"The doctor said I might be able to leave tomorrow."

"I want you back today," the boy said.

"There could be some delay...." she began hesitantly. "Legal matters." She didn't know how to explain the possibility of her arrest. It might be more than Jeff could bear. Maybe more than she could bear, too.

"No, there won't," Herb said. "I've got the name of one of those top lawyers from Los Angeles. If anybody gives you a hard time, we'll talk to him."

"Herb, I can't afford that."

"I can," he said. "And I will. Don't you worry, Joni. Nothing can ever make up for losing my grandson, but I know in my heart you aren't to blame."

"Thank you," she whispered.

"It's a simple fact," he said. "No need for thanks."

The room fell silent. On a distant intercom, a woman's voice summoned a doctor to the delivery room.

Then Joni heard a noise in the hall that sent her heart slamming into her throat. It was irrational. A trick of the imagination.

Lowell's footsteps.

She knew that sound so well. The well-muscled weight of him. The confident step. The slight scuff as if he were kicking the ground out of his way.

She'd been listening to people come and go along the linoleum all day. Hospital personnel, patients, visitors. None of them had sounded remotely like Lowell.

The steps headed in their direction.

"That's Daddy." Jeff gave her a confused look, then ran toward the door.

Herb caught him by the arm. "Jeff, wait!"

"It's him!"

The newcomer stopped right outside, blocked by the partially closed door. Even though she knew that it couldn't possibly be Lowell, Joni found herself holding her breath.

The door swung open.

His hair was darker then Lowell's, and his eyes a deeper blue. But he had the same broad shoulders, the same arrogant stance.

To her surprise, she felt a shiver of the awe that used to run through her eleven years ago, every time Lowell stopped by her counter at the print shop. This man radiated an intense masculine power, perhaps even more strongly than his brother.

"Dirk," Herb said. "You got here fast. I just sent the message last night."

"I was in the Silicon Valley on business," said the man, giving his grandfather a rueful hug. "I'd been planning to head down this way tomorrow. Lowell and I were going to get together for the first time in years. Now we'll never have the chance, will we?"

As he turned toward Joni, his words seemed full of accusation. He paid no attention to Jeff.

In all these years, hadn't he ever been curious about the boy he'd fathered? What kind of man was Dirk Peterson?

In the past, it hadn't mattered. Now, it mattered tremendously. Because, Joni realized with a jolt, he might be in a position to take Jeff away from her.

Chapter Three

With a bandage wrapped around her head and her hair limp against the pillow, Joni didn't look much like the girl Dirk remembered from years ago.

She'd made a striking bride with her unusual bone structure and large hazel eyes. Her shy way of ducking her head had been countered by the athletic buoyancy with which she moved.

The impression of vulnerability mixed with resilience had lingered in Dirk's mind as he returned to the Los Angeles university where he'd been earning a business degree. But he'd been too preoccupied with his own unresolved adolescent rage and with deciding on a career to give much thought to the woman who married his domineering brother.

A few years later at his father's funeral, Joni had appeared very young in her black suit. But Dirk hadn't paid her much attention; he'd been suffering deep regret at the realization that he and his father would never have a chance to be close.

His sister-in-law looked older now, and less impressionable. In her expression, he read sorrow and determination.

She'd only grown more alluring, even in bandages, he reflected unwillingly. She reminded him of a kitten that had survived to maturity, gaining a few scars but developing a self-contained silkiness along the way.

He suspected she would always hold part of herself back. That had been his impression when he first saw her, dancing with his brother at the country club a few nights before the wedding. It had been Lowell who pulled her closer, Lowell who whispered in her ear, and Joni who shifted her face subtly away.

What had her motives been in marrying his brother, and then in divorcing him? Was she an opportunist? A manipulator? Or simply an intriguing woman with hidden depths?

Dirk had to remind himself that this wasn't his battle to fight.

The hell it wasn't. Lowell had been his brother even though they'd come close to hating each other in their younger years. Correction: Dirk had come close to hating the older sibling who delighted in taunting and belittling him.

There'd been one night when he'd nearly killed Lowell himself. It was just before Dirk went off to college, and even now he could taste the hot fury as he'd slammed his fist into his brother's jaw. Thank goodness someone had pulled them apart. But after that, they'd both known enough to keep their distance.

Now, when they'd finally been on the verge of reestablishing their relationship, maybe even doing some business together, the chance had slipped away tragically—ripped away forever by the woman lying in front of him.

The silence lengthened. Dirk roused himself to offer, "I hope you're feeling better."

"The doctor says I'll be fine." She had a low, sensuous voice. "I was lucky."

Judging by her bandages, she must be in a lot of pain.

That she refused to make a show of her discomfort fitted his impression of her reticent nature.

He needed some answers, though. And the sooner the better. "It would help if I knew exactly what my brother did. It's hard to mourn him properly when I have so many questions."

"I wish I could remember." Joni's eyes fixed on him earnestly. Brown flecks stood out against the green.

"The police said you have amnesia about the moments just before you were knocked unconscious. That isn't unusual."

Sometimes, he knew, amnesia could result from the brain's lack of time to transfer impressions into long-term memory before blacking out, in which case the information was lost forever. Other times, trauma made the victim repress the incident, in which case she might have a chance of remembering.

"You talked to the cops?" she asked.

"I don't like getting my information secondhand," Dirk said by way of confirmation.

After reading the newspaper this morning, he'd called the detective, who grudgingly answered a few questions. The police considered the case open-and-shut and, perhaps as a result, their work had been sloppy.

Dirk had taken some police-science courses in college and later undergone antiterrorist training while working for an overseas security agency. Even his current highly successful company, which developed new businesses in emerging economies, required attention to security.

He objected to the way the crime scene at Joni's house had been muddied with footprints. Furthermore, her clothes, on which the blood spatter might indicate where she'd stood during the stabbing, hadn't been collected until they'd been removed at the hospital. By then, spilled hummingbird nectar, rain and careless handling had smeared everything.

The officers had talked to the neighbors immediately adjacent, but they hadn't canvassed beyond that. Someone else might have noticed a jogger or an unfamiliar car but, without being questioned, wouldn't connect it to the case.

Despite the flaws in the police work, however, Dirk didn't doubt their conclusion. Lowell had been stalking Joni and she'd fought back.

The only issue that might have to be resolved by a jury was whether Lowell had presented an imminent threat to her life. Or had she simply seized the excuse to get rid of him?

"Did they tell you anything that wasn't in the paper?" she pressed.

He shrugged. "Not really." It was the truth, as far as it went.

"I'm not sure we should discuss this in present company." Herb tilted his head toward the boy, then changed the subject smoothly. "I apologize for calling your secretary, Dirk. I would have preferred to talk to you in person, but no one answered at your Rome apartment."

"That's because I'm hardly ever home. I'm the one who should apologize for not giving you my cell phone number," Dirk said.

He spent much of his time traveling. His company worked with venture capitalists and businesses seeking to expand into emerging nations. Using the Internet, contacts and financial sources, Dirk would identify locales with underutilized natural and human resources, and with reasonable political stability.

He then visited the sites, met with local officials and business people and prepared a report on the suitability of establishing manufacturing, mining, distribution or other operations. Depending on the client's needs, Dirk and his staff sometimes helped negotiate licenses and locate head-quarters.

The work was exhilarating and highly profitable, but he shouldn't have let it become so all-consuming. He'd last seen his grandfather four years ago, when they'd spent several days together in Athens after Herb took a cruise of the Greek islands. Since then, contact had come mostly via Christmas cards.

Now he noticed a few more wrinkles on his grandfather's forehead and a bit of thinning in the gray hair. The man hadn't lost an ounce of his steely directness, though. "I'll take that cell phone number before you forget, grandson."

Dirk smiled. "You bet. I want us to get together a lot more often." He pulled out a business card and wrote the number on the back.

"You walk like Daddy," said the boy who stood next to Herb. "I thought you were him."

"You must be Jeff." Dirk bent and shook his hand solemnly, admiring the child's composure. It had to be tough on the boy to lose his father and to see his mother injured this way.

He was glad Lowell had been able to have his own son after all. Dirk hadn't been happy about his brother's demand that he donate sperm, but he'd been working on a dangerous assignment in central Asia and agreed to leave a specimen in case he was killed. When Lowell tersely notified him six months later that the sperm hadn't been needed, the news had come as a relief.

He wasn't ready to be a daddy. He wasn't even sure he was ready to take on the responsibilities of an uncle, but the circumstances left him no choice.

"Are you going to live here now?" Jeff asked.

"Just while I put some things in order," Dirk said.

"Who's going to take me to ball games?" Tears glistened in the little boy's eyes. "Daddy bought season tickets."

"Ball games?" Viento del Mar didn't have any professional teams. "Where?"

"Lowell sometimes took him to Los Angeles," Joni explained. "On their weekends together."

"I'll do it." Herb's fierce expression forestalled any attempt to point out that he was in no condition to be making a round-trip drive of more than four hours. "Don't you worry, Jeff."

The baseball issue could be handled later, Dirk decided. It was time to cut to the chase.

To Joni, he said, "I spoke to the family lawyer this morning. Are you aware that, in his will, Lowell left the printing company and the house half to me and half in trust for your son?"

Her lips formed the word. "No."

"The rest of the estate goes into a trust fund for Jeff," he said. "My brother named me as trustee."

"Who's going to run the company?" Herb asked. "I nearly drove myself into an early grave when I was in charge, and even so, I wasn't half the manager my son was, or Lowell, either. I'm not about to pick up the reins now."

"I can get it in shape to sell," Dirk said. "Or I can hire an executive to run it. Either way is all right with me. I think Jeff's mother ought to have some say in the matter."

Joni's long lashes drifted down, and she forced them up with a visible effort. "I can't make any decisions right now."

"It can wait," Dirk said. "Your first priority is to get well."

He wondered at the impulse he felt to protect her. He'd been aware all morning, through his meetings with the detective and the lawyer, that he'd been looking out for her interest as well as his nephew's.

Now the pallor of Joni's skin and the suffering in her gaze galvanized him. He wanted to reassure her that he would take care of everything so the tension could ease from her body and that lovely mouth would curve invitingly.

Yet he couldn't be sure she hadn't deliberately killed his brother. And even if he were, he didn't want to encourage her to depend on him. He wouldn't be staying in Viento del Mar long enough to do more than tie up loose ends.

"Call me in the morning and let me know what time they're releasing you," Herb said. "We'll pick you up."

Joni shook her head on the pillow. "I'll take a cab."

"Don't be ridiculous!" Herb said, bristling.

His grandfather must care a great deal about this woman, Dirk thought in surprise. Even Lowell's death hadn't shaken their bond.

"I'm not being ridiculous," Joni said. "You know me, Herb. When I'm hurt, I'm like a wild animal. I hole up and lick my wounds." She gave a small shrug. "I just need some time alone."

"You've spent too much time alone after my grandson—" Herb glanced at Jeff "—did what he did with Kim. I won't let you bear this by yourself."

"You can come over later," Joni said. "I'll call you after I've gotten my bearings. I promise."

Herb grumbled but gave in. "I reserve the right to spoil my great-grandson rotten in the meantime."

"By all means." Warmth suffused the woman's face,

and the entire room seemed to glow. Whatever else might be true of her, she clearly loved her son.

Dirk glanced at the boy. This was not only his nephew but, except for Herb, his only close relative.

He could see his brother in the boy's build, but that didn't explain Dirk's pang of recognition. With a jolt, he realized the boy reminded him of himself. The troubled deep blue eyes. The unruly hair, darker than either Lowell's or Joni's.

No, not himself, he thought sternly, but his mother. Tina Peterson, who had died of lupus when he was twelve, had been the source of Dirk's dramatic coloring. In Lowell, those genes must have skipped a generation.

Herb clapped a hand onto the boy's shoulder. "We'll let you get some rest, Joni. See you tomorrow."

"Bye, Herb. Jeff, I love you." Her gaze flicked toward Dirk. "It's good to see you, although I'm sorry about the circumstances."

"So am I." He let the older man and the boy precede him through the door.

He disliked leaving Joni in the hospital unguarded. Yet if she had slain his brother for her own advantage, the person she would most need guarding against was Dirk himself.

"Join us for supper?" Herb asked as they descended in the elevator.

"Sure," he said. "At the club?"

"Our special club," his grandfather replied. "Follow us."

Outside, the clouds were clearing. In the twilight, Herb's bright red sports car whipped out of the parking lot ahead of the blue rented Volvo.

Dirk had chosen the solidly built car out of habit, after years of working in developing nations where the dangers ranged from gun-wielding rebels to vicious potholes. He had to smile at the way he and his grandfather had reversed the traditional roles. Herb had youthful fervor to spare.

Herb and Jeff's "club" turned out to be McDonald's. The boy ordered a Happy Meal but barely ate half, then wandered dispiritedly toward the brightly colored play area.

"Usually he runs so fast he's a blur," Herb said. "He seemed to take the news okay about his father, but I know he's hurting."

"Want to leave?"

"We need to talk first." His grandfather cleared his throat and leaned forward. "I want you to clear your brother's name. I don't believe he attacked Joni."

"I thought you liked her." Dirk speared a French fry.

"I more than like her. I love that girl." The older man swallowed hard. "She's like the daughter I never had."

"Either she murdered Lowell, or he tried to murder her," Dirk said. "I can't clear one without condemning the other."

"There has to be some other explanation," Herb insisted.

"The police will—"

"This is Viento del Mar!" Herb smacked his cup onto the table so hard it sent droplets flying. "What do they know about investigating a homicide? Besides, you're the only one who can get inside Lowell's head. Try to figure out what he was doing and thinking this past month, why he would resume harassing Joni just when they were on good terms again."

Dirk wanted to help, but he couldn't deliver the impossible. "Grandpa, I'm not a mind reader."

"Maybe he had a mental disorder or was taking some

medication that affected his behavior. There has to be a reason!''

Dirk was on the verge of protesting the urgency of returning to business when something stopped him. It might have been the pinched look on his grandfather's face. It might have been the notion that, in spite of their longstanding antagonism, he owed his brother something.

But fundamentally, it was the realization that the main reason he itched to leave Viento del Mar was that, since the moment he'd returned, the old anger and pain had closed around him like a vise.

Dirk had never been able to please his overcritical father, Donald. In his father's view, he wasn't athletic enough; he was too intellectual; he picked the wrong friends.

Glib and popular, Lowell had adopted his father's attitude. At the country club, at school, in front of friends, he never missed a chance to put his little brother in his place.

With his rebellious streak, Dirk had maintained a tough exterior. Inside, there were moments when he ached so much he could hardly breathe. The worst times were when he needed his father most. After his mother's death. After the breakup of his first intense teenage love affair. Whenever he felt vulnerable, that was when Donald tried hardest to reshape him and Lowell was at his most supercilious.

Well, Dirk wasn't a kid anymore. This request meant a lot to his grandfather. It was time to face down the old emotions and defuse what was left of them.

That he might also be helping Joni shouldn't have affected his decision. But when he pictured her lying in the hospital bed, pale and injured, Dirk understood how helpless she must feel. He just hoped he wasn't giving her too much benefit of the doubt. There was no sympathy in his heart for liars and schemers.

"All right," he told his grandfather. "I'll do the best I can. But you may not like what I find."

"As long as it's the truth," Herb said, "I'll take it."

HOSPITAL POLICY REQUIRED that departing patients be wheelchaired to the front door by a volunteer. On her way out on Friday morning, Joni had intended to stop by the public relations office to collect her undelivered plant, but it was out of the way and she hated to inconvenience the volunteer.

She hoped to return to work on Monday. If Basil gave it a good watering today, she told herself, the plant should survive until then.

As planned, she took a cab home. It was a clear, crisp day, and the driver, a man in his fifties, maneuvered the hospital's steep drive so carefully that the car barely jounced.

Joni's ribs and head didn't hurt much, thanks to a last dose of hospital painkillers. The doctor who removed her bandages that morning had given her a prescription, which lay unfilled in her purse.

She didn't want to take any medication that might blur her thinking. If it were possible, she needed to recall those final moments of Lowell's life. She needed to clear her name, not only with the police but with Dirk, as well. For some reason, it mattered very much what he thought.

He had the same brooding intensity as his brother, but there was a gentleness about him that touched her. Several times, she'd even imagined she saw concern in his expression.

She knew better, however, than to yield to her instinctive physical response to the man. He possessed the same magnetism that had drawn her to Lowell, and look where that had led.

The route home took them past Peterson Printing. It lay a couple of miles east of the hospital along San Bernardo Road, one of the town's two main streets. The original one-story building in front didn't look like much. Signs advertising photocopying and low-cost faxes plastered the front window through which Joni could see the counter where she'd been working eleven years ago when she met Lowell.

A stand of trees partially masked the much larger building in back. Inside could be found the massive presses that thundered day and night, the bustling art department, the layout and typesetting computers, the photoreproduction and engraving equipment, the binding facility, the warehouse and loading dock and, of course, the offices.

The local newspaper was printed here. So were wedding invitations, magazines, books, advertisements, corporate annual statements and other orders from around the region. She could almost hear the roar of the presses and smell the tang of the ink. It had been exciting to work there, especially after she learned desktop publishing and was promoted from clerking. Although she'd given up college after marrying, Joni had continued at her job until Jeff was born.

Lowell would have preferred that she spend her days swimming and playing tennis at the country club rather than working. He'd disapproved of her in other ways, too: her lack of style, her shyness, her tendency to get disheveled while playing with Jeff.

Nothing that came naturally to Joni seemed to please him. In time, she'd realized that even when she did win his acceptance, it was only temporary. To survive emotionally, she'd had to stop caring about his opinion.

The cab turned into Canyon Acres, the meandering development where she lived. Because of the uneven terrain, the homes were widely spaced below the forested hills. Some of the lower slopes blazed pink with bougainvillea, while each house sported its own emerald patch of lawn.

"Say, wasn't there a murder out here?" the cabbie asked as he turned into Joni's cul-de-sac.

She didn't want to reveal too much to a stranger. "Somewhere around here."

"You be careful, lady." He pulled into her driveway and stopped. "You want me to walk you inside?"

Her stalker was dead. What did she have to fear? "No, thanks," Joni said.

"I'll wait out here while you take a look around." The man had a kind face. "You wave at me out the door, and I'll go."

"Thank you." A surge of relief caught Joni off guard. She hadn't realized she would feel this nervous about returning to the scene of the tragedy.

Maybe it hadn't been such a good idea to come home by herself. Still, although she knew most people would have opted for companionship, she had grown up spending time alone and needed a certain amount of solitude to feel complete.

Joni paid and got out of the cab. Thank goodness the police had brought her purse to the hospital Wednesday night after locking the house, she reflected as she took out her keys.

On the porch, she scooped up two newspapers and plucked a bill from the mailbox. As she unlocked the door, she listened for anything amiss, but heard only the hum of the refrigerator.

She checked the living room, the den and the bedrooms. Drawers stood partially open and cushions had been tossed aside by the police, to whom she'd given permission to enter the premises. Detective MacDougall had told her that he'd tried to minimize the mess.

In the kitchen, she found masculine footprints smeared as if someone had tried to wipe up mud with a paper towel. Too stiff even to contemplate washing the floor, she returned to the front and signaled the driver.

After he pulled away, Joni changed from the slacks and blouse that Kathryn had brought into jeans and a rose-colored sweater. Then, gathering her courage, she went out the back door.

Chapter Four

Sagging yellow police tape surrounded the patio. Against a support beam leaned Jeff's bike, the front spokes indented where Joni had fallen on them. She wanted to put it away but decided not to enter the crime scene.

Someone had collected the broken glass, and yesterday's heavy rain must have washed the blood off the concrete. The glass table stood sideways to its usual position; the small barbecue grill remained close to the house, by the back door. Brown patches staining the edges of the narrow lawn were the only reminder of the tragedy that had taken place here two days before.

Snatches of memory came to her from that night: the wind and the darkness, the gash of fear when Lowell confronted her. Was it possible she had stabbed him? Could a person commit such a violent act and not remember it?

In high school, she had refused to dissect a frog because the idea of cutting into an animal, even a dead one, distressed her. Could she have cut down a man?

Joni tried to recapture the tactile sense of the haft in her hand, but she couldn't. The only way she could picture herself using a knife was against a cutting board.

Trembling, she retreated inside. At least she'd gotten through this first agonizing visit to the backyard. Surely her anxiety would fade with time. If not, she could sell the house. But that would mean a disruption for Jeff, and it would be expensive. Regardless of what anyone might think about her wanting to get her hands on the inheritance, she intended to preserve every penny for her son.

Twinges of pain crackled through her ribs. In the bathroom, Joni took a couple of over-the-counter pain pills and forced herself to confront the bruised face in the mirror.

Dark circles made half-moons beneath her hazel eyes, and her skin had a raw pallor, as if she hadn't slept in a week. Although she'd never been vain, Joni applied some cosmetics to cover the worst damage.

Bending forward, she fought an onrush of dizziness as she brushed her shoulder-length blond hair into its accustomed bun. The brush grazed the swelling on one side, and she winced.

At least she no longer looked as if she'd put on fright makeup for Halloween, she decided, and dampened her bangs so they would lie straight. Next, she headed for the kitchen to fix some coffee.

Joni had read yesterday's newspaper at the hospital, so she chucked that one into the recycle bin. Opening today's edition, she sat down to face the worst.

A follow-up story offered no new information, just sorrowful reactions by leading citizens and employees at Peterson Printing. As for Joni herself, a hospital spokesman—her boss, Basil—reported that she was recovering.

Gee, she was in good condition. That should come as welcome news to her rib cage.

She skimmed the rest of the newspaper, stopping to read a short article about the soccer league. A group picture of volunteers included Jeff's coach, Charlie Rogers. How normal they all looked. And what a nice change it was to read about something that didn't involve Lowell's death.

Charlie wasn't a bad-looking man, she decided as she studied the photograph. He'd been thoughtful to bring the flowers, but she felt no particular attraction to him. In fact, she hadn't been attracted to anyone in a long time, not until yesterday.

Into her mind leaped an image of Dirk, probing and intensely masculine. In the hospital, his nearness had made her sharply aware of her own femininity. She'd had to force herself not to drink in the rugged length of him, the tanned skin and thick, barely tamed dark hair. Not to let her gaze linger on the sturdy hands as they tapped impatiently against his thigh.

With a start, Joni realized she had been disappointed when he left without touching her. He hadn't brushed a wisp of hair off her forehead or even shaken her hand. She wanted him to touch her. This stranger. This man who held the power to devastate her world. She must have been alone too long, she reflected with a sigh.

Her glance returned to the newspaper photo. Soccer. Tomorrow was Saturday, which meant Jeff must have a game. She needed to call Kathryn to confirm the time and place.

Joni pressed a rapid-dial button on her phone, preset to the Owenses' number. On the third ring, Fred answered. He ran his life insurance business from a home office.

"Joni?" he said when he heard her voice. "Are you out of the hospital?"

"So rumor has it."

"Kathryn or I would be happy to bring you some lunch," he offered.

"No, thanks. But I do need to know about the game tomorrow."

"Eleven o'clock at the high school," he said. "Do you want us to take Jeff?"

"Thanks, but I want to keep things as normal as possible for him." She brushed aside the thought that it would be a relief not to have to attend. "Or maybe I should keep him home till he's had more time to adjust. What do you think?"

There was a pause while Fred weighed his answer. She knew how much he valued sports; if it hadn't been for a knee injury, he might have played professional baseball himself.

"If he strongly doesn't want to go, I wouldn't force him," Bobby's father said at last. "But otherwise, kids do their grieving in bits and pieces over a long period. Keeping him home might even delay his adjustment."

"That's what I think, too," Joni agreed. "Thanks, Fred."

"If there's anything you need, just call."

After she hung up, she sat in the kitchen trying to settle her uneasy spirits. What was it that kept nagging at her as if she'd left some business unfinished?

Through the partly open blinds, she regarded the rosebushes below the retaining wall that separated her narrow yard from the hill. One branch hung limply, probably broken either by the police or by Lowell himself.

On the slope above, just past a yellow-flowered bush, a squirrel scampered across a large gray rock. It was a peaceful, almost idyllic scene.

What could she have overlooked? There must be some clue about what had happened, something that would jog her memory.

Joni studied the calendar hanging beside the refrigerator. Halloween was next Thursday. It would also be her thirtieth birthday, not an occasion she looked forward to with much joy.

Especially with a possible murder charge hanging over her head.

Determined not to brood, she carried her cup to the sink. As she set it down, she caught sight of the cutlery block with its telltale empty slot. Joni's stomach clenched. She should put the blasted thing out of sight. But right now, she couldn't bring herself to touch it.

Grimly, she opened the dishwasher and set her cup in the top rack. The thing was nearly full, so after pouring some detergent into the dispenser, she turned it on.

Outside, clouds dimmed the sunlight. Weariness came over Joni so swiftly that she barely managed to stagger to the den before collapsing on the couch. She felt light-headed, perhaps from the delayed effects of hospital medication or from the injury itself. Before she knew it, she was asleep.

In her dreams, her mind must have been working. When she awoke, she had a sharp, disturbing realization of what she had missed.

The dishwasher.

Groggily, Joni stumbled to her feet and went into the kitchen. Finished with sudsing, the machine was rumbling into a rinse cycle. Heedless of the spray, she yanked it open. A second later, the water was automatically cut off.

Her gaze went first to the cutlery rack in the bottom, but there was nothing unusual about the welter of forks and spoons and butter knives. Her throat tightening, Joni pulled out the top rack.

There it lay, barely noticeable behind a row of glasses. The carving knife missing from her block.

She had laid it flat because it was too long to fit with the regular cutlery. It was such an ordinary sight that it hadn't even registered in her conscious mind, and the police must not have thought to check the top rack.

The weapon they'd found in her hand wasn't hers. Whom did it belong to, and how had it gotten there?

Numbly, Joni set her find on the counter, then closed the dishwasher. It sluiced back into action.

Water on the floor was turning the policemen's dried footprints into a muddy mess. From force of habit, she grabbed a rag from beneath the sink and knelt to wipe it up. The routine act of scrubbing freed her mind to absorb the significance of her discovery. She hadn't killed Lowell.

The knowledge came with a flood of relief. She hadn't deprived Herb of his grandson, hadn't cheated Jeff of his father and hadn't taken the life of a man whom, in spite of everything, she still cared about.

She hadn't killed him, but someone had. Someone who was walking around, unsuspected. Someone who had tried to pass the blame off on her.

Would the police believe her story? A person could probably pick up a similar knife at a thrift shop or garage sale, not to mention any department store. If only she hadn't washed the darn thing, it would have been easier to prove that her own knife had been sitting here for two days with food on it.

She tossed the rag into the sink and Joni sank into a chair at the table. She was too lost in thought to notice that a car had stopped in the driveway. Only when the doorbell rang did she jerk back into the present.

It might be Herb and Jeff. Or the mail carrier with a package. Or…

The killer. He could be anyone.

The bell shrilled again. She didn't move.

Someone tried the knob. In disbelief, Joni heard it turn and the door creak open.

She must have forgotten to lock it after she waved to

the cabdriver. "Herb?" she tried to say, but the words stuck in her throat.

The visitor didn't call out. It was strange the way he walked into her house unannounced. She heard masculine footsteps marching through the hallway. Crossing the den.

Maybe she should run for the phone or grab a knife or…

It was too late. Someone was coming through the kitchen door.

DIRK FOLLOWED Terry MacDougall through a rabbit warren of desks and cubbyholes to a partitioned bay brightened by a view of the police department parking lot. Files, foam cups and While You Were Out messages littered the desk.

"Sit anywhere," the detective said.

Aside from his own swivel chair, two mismatched highback seats crammed the small space. Computer printouts filled both of them. Dirk looked to see if the man was joking, noted that he wasn't and shifted a stack of papers onto the floor.

"You understand," the detective went on, "that department procedure won't allow me to tell you much."

Dealing with the authorities in Viento del Mar wasn't much different from negotiating with officials in a Third World country, Dirk mused as he sat down. The main differences were that he doubted Detective MacDougall expected a bribe and there were no naked electrical lines snaking along the wall.

"As you know, I've cleared this with the chief," Dirk said. "He seemed sympathetic to my position."

MacDougall regarded him with open cynicism. In his late fifties, the man had thinning, light brown hair and a few acne scars left from adolescence. He'd spent a lot of years on the force, Dirk guessed, and even in a small town had probably seen too much for his own good.

"Of course he did. The Petersons own one of the biggest companies in town, as I'm sure you reminded him." Idly, the detective adjusted a triptych of photographs facing him. His family, Dirk assumed. "I suppose you think your brother's death rates special treatment."

"'Special treatment' meaning what? I don't expect you to blow my nose for me or wipe the widow's tears. I also don't expect you guys to be in a hurry to name a suspect so you'll look good in the newspapers." Seeing anger flare in those pale eyes, Dirk added, "Nothing personal, Detective."

MacDougall shrugged. "Seems pretty obvious what happened. The only question is, was she really in fear of her life? That's the D.A.'s job to decide."

"Is that your idea of detective work—to settle for what seems obvious?" Dirk demanded, and immediately realized he'd gone too far. "I'm sorry. I realize you're the professional here. But I don't think you can write this case off that easily."

The other man quirked an eyebrow. "Mind if I ask why you're so keen on helping your sister-in-law?"

No point in explaining about his promise to Herb. Dirk doubted the detective would take kindly to the idea of his conducting a private investigation.

Yesterday afternoon, he had questioned his brother's doctor about any mood disorders or medications. No luck there, not even a referral to a counselor during the divorce. Lowell would have considered it a weakness to seek help with his emotions.

Earlier today, Dirk had gone through his brother's office at the plant but found nothing that hinted at Lowell's state of mind. The police had already searched there as well as

Lowell's house, his car and his club locker, but so far as Dirk knew, they hadn't found anything.

He planned to talk to his brother's friends at the country club, especially Kim DeLong, who he understood was bitter that Lowell had ended their affair instead of marrying her. It wasn't an interview he looked forward to.

"She isn't just my sister-in-law," Dirk said. "She's also my nephew's mother. Even if Joni is eventually cleared, what will the strain and publicity of a trial do to Jeff in the meantime? I think subjecting either of them to unnecessary prosecution would be reprehensible."

"Are you so sure it's unnecessary?"

"Think about it, Detective," he said. "There are no witnesses, and it's medically credible that Joni doesn't remember what happened. Even if she did stab my brother, which is by no means proven, doesn't the evidence point overwhelmingly to self-defense?"

"I'd say a jury should decide that for themselves." MacDougall watched him intently.

"These aren't cardboard figures on a TV show," Dirk pressed. "My sister-in-law has been through a lot already. So has my nephew. A trial isn't exactly a minor stress, and it could last a long time. I don't think that's a step to be taken lightly."

"What are you asking me to do?" The man fiddled again with the photo frames. Dirk glimpsed one of the shots, a middle-aged woman posing with two teenage girls. So the detective *did* have a family.

"Don't be in a rush to go to the D.A.," he said. "Talk to people around the neighborhood. Look into whether anyone might have had a grudge against my brother or my sister-in-law."

MacDougall grimaced. "I hate to tell you this, Peterson,

but I don't think we're going to get any new evidence in this case."

"Maybe not, but what's your rush?" Dirk challenged. "If you miss anything, it could prove highly embarrassing. I should think you'd want to cross every *t* and dot every *i*."

A sigh escaped the other man. "Fine. I'll hold off for a few days while we do some more legwork. That's the best I can offer."

"Good enough." Dirk stood, and they shook hands.

The other man's grip was damp but firm. He handed over a card. "That's my home number. Don't use it unless you have to."

"Thanks."

On his way out, Dirk passed Communications and heard a dispatcher summoning an officer to the scene of a two-car collision. It made him wonder what his life would be like if he'd yielded to impulse in college and switched his major from business to police science.

Still angry at Lowell after their knockdown fight and largely alienated from his father, Donald, Dirk had considered breaking with his family's expectations and pursuing a career in law enforcement. He'd taken some courses in the field and found he liked the subject but disliked the prospect of being confined to routine police work.

He'd stuck with business. Then, during his senior year, a buddy in Dirk's martial arts club told him of a firm recruiting for overseas security work.

On impulse, Dirk went with him to the recruiter's presentation and got hooked. He'd signed up immediately after graduation, working as a bodyguard and, later, as a consultant assessing security needs for American businesses.

He didn't regret the decision, although the work had

been more grueling and less romantic than he'd imagined. It was during those years that he'd identified a need for his present consulting business, and had capitalized on the knowledge and contacts he'd acquired.

Dirk only wished that either he'd never met Elena or that he could have saved her. Maybe she would have died even if she'd never fallen in love with him. But that possibility didn't make it hurt less. He couldn't help her now. Regrets accomplished nothing, Dirk reflected, and pushed them aside.

After leaving the police station, he stopped for a hamburger, then drove to his grandfather's condo. There he found Herb washing the lunch dishes and looking tired after a morning of playing with Jeff.

Joni hadn't called yet, but brushing aside any objections, Dirk insisted on driving his nephew home. The boy collected an overnight bag and got into the front seat. After fastening his seat belt, he sat up straight, arms wrapped around the bag. Jeff had the strong Peterson jaw, Dirk noticed, and Joni's well-defined mouth, but the innocent gaze of a little boy.

As he started the car, he wondered what they could talk about. Dirk had dealt with officials from Beirut to Bangkok, but eight-year-olds were another matter. Until now, Jeff had been nothing more than a name and a picture on a Christmas card.

"What grade are you in?" he asked.

"Third." The boy stared through the windshield.

"What are you studying?"

"Cursive."

"They teach cursing in school?" Dirk turned left from Canyon Vista onto San Bernardo Road.

"No, that's writing instead of printing!" The boy must have seen his smile. "You're being silly, aren't you?"

"I'm trying."

"That's funny," the boy said.

"Then why aren't you laughing?"

"I mean, it's funny that you made a joke," Jeff explained. "Dad never made jokes, just Mom."

Lowell wasn't known for his sense of humor, Dirk had to admit. "Do you expect me to be exactly like your father just because I'm his brother?"

"I don't know," Jeff said wistfully. "I don't have a brother. If I did, I think he'd be like me."

"You can never tell." They went by the printing plant and crossed the bridge over Viento del Mar Creek. Following the map his grandfather had drawn, Dirk passed the high school and turned into the Canyon Acres development. "Can you help me find your street?"

"Sure." The boy proceeded to give clear directions, sounding very grown up.

Dirk wondered why he felt so intrigued by his nephew. Maybe it was because, with his bright turquoise eyes, Jeff seemed almost a mirror image of what Dirk had been like at his age.

"I wonder who that is." Jeff pointed to a maroon sedan parked in a driveway. Startled, Dirk realized they'd reached Joni's house, which was set partway up a hill.

He parked by the curb. "You don't recognize it?"

The boy shook his head, then indicated the open front door. "Mom never leaves the door like that. Flies could get in."

Disquieted, Dirk slid from the car. Jeff hopped out beside him. He didn't want to call the police without good reason. Still, the situation didn't look right, and with her injuries, Joni was especially vulnerable.

He couldn't leave Jeff in the car while he investigated, though. The safest place would be with him.

"Stay behind me," Dirk said, and the boy obeyed. In single file, they walked toward the house.

Chapter Five

The footsteps grew louder. Whoever had invaded Joni's home was in the den, almost at the kitchen....

The lanky figure of her boss appeared in the doorway. "There you are," he said.

"Basil!" Joni nearly chuckled in relief, except that the sallow skin and shadowed gray eyes of the public relations director evoked solemnity rather than amusement. "You didn't have to do this."

"The staff would never forgive me if I didn't give you this." He held out a purple chrysanthemum plant.

"Thanks. It's lovely," she said. "I'll just set it on the table." He handed it over without speaking.

With his long silences and elliptical comments, Joni's boss wasn't exactly Mr. Personality, but she liked him. And she respected his ongoing struggle as a recovering alcoholic.

She knew it was up to her to keep the conversation going. "I heard you trying to get past the nurse at the hospital. She certainly put her foot down."

"She was just doing her job." Expressionless, he gazed around the kitchen.

"I'm going to try to come back to work on Monday."

"That would be fine."

Seconds ticked by on the wall clock. Before she could think of anything else to say, Joni heard a rapid, light tapping at the back door. With relief, she recognized the knock as Celia Lu's.

"My neighbor." She went to answer it. After a moment's pause, Basil followed.

"You are home!" The dark-haired woman patted Joni's shoulder and edged by her into the utility hall. "I come in? Oh, who is this?"

Joni made introductions. Basil gave Celia's hand a perfunctory shake and the two stood eyeing each other like a pair of dogs both trying to stake out the same territory.

"Joni needs to rest," Basil growled at last.

"I think, if she needs something, maybe I can help!" Celia chirped. Ignoring the man's fidgeting, she plied Joni with questions about the hospital and the doctor's orders and the police investigation.

They sat in the living room, listening to her account of what had happened, but she had nothing new to offer. If a third person had been involved, Celia hadn't seen him.

On the street, a car stopped. Joni had her back to the window and didn't realize anyone was approaching the house until Celia said, "It's your son. And a handsome man! Do I meet him before?"

"I certainly haven't," Basil growled. "Who is that?"

Joni turned and, through the translucent curtain panels, watched Dirk edge toward the house at an angle. A tan turtleneck sweater and tailored dark blue slacks emphasized the muscular contours of his chest and the slimness of his hips.

With the light behind him, he couldn't see them, Joni realized. "It's my brother-in-law."

Even if she hadn't known Dirk was trained to handle danger, it was obvious from the tight positioning of his arms and body and his repeated, quick scans of the area. Behind him, Jeff mimicked Dirk's movements, even cocking his head the same way. It was as if the two had spent years together.

"I didn't know," Celia said. "Lowell had a brother?"

"He lives overseas." Irrationally, Joni was glad Dirk had come. Just the sight of him made her feel safer.

"I'll be going, then." Basil stood up. "Don't let the chrysanthemum sit too long before planting. It'll get root bound."

He stomped outside, passed by the startled Dirk with barely a nod and headed for his car.

"A strange man," Celia said. "I hope he does not visit often."

"He won't need to. I plan to go back to work as soon as I can." Joni reached the front door as her son bounded up the steps. She caught him in a hug, which he accepted with less wiggling than usual.

"What was Mr. Dupont doing here?" Jeff asked from below her chin. "We thought it was a stranger! Why did you leave your door open? Oh, hello, Mrs. Lu."

Somehow Joni got through the next few minutes, making introductions and polite conversation until Celia reluctantly departed. Jeff wandered into the den to play video games.

Throughout the encounter, Dirk's eyes swept the living room as if it held a secret that he intended to extract from it. Concentration gave his face the intensity of a wolf's.

"You can't find my decor all that interesting," she said when they were alone.

"What?"

"I got most of this stuff at a thrift shop," Joni pointed out. "What's so fascinating?"

The corners of his mouth twitched. "I always inspect my surroundings. It pays to be alert."

"I know you do business in emerging nations, but surely they can't be that perilous! Not people's living rooms anyway."

He shifted on the balls of his feet like a wild creature uneasy at finding itself indoors. "Exposed electrical wires can kill. So can a snake in search of a dry place to sleep."

"What fun," Joni said dryly. "We don't have to contend with any of those threats around here, thank goodness."

He started to laugh, then sobered. The amusement evaporated from Joni's mood, too, as she realized the irony of her remark, given what had happened to Lowell.

That reminded her about the knife. She was accustomed to keeping her own counsel, but she didn't have enough experience to evaluate how she should handle this situation. Besides, Dirk of all people had a right to know the truth about his brother's slaying.

"I want to show you something," she said. "I need your advice."

"Mine?" A dark eyebrow quirked.

"Dirk, I don't know much about evidence. Or murder investigations."

He regarded her assessingly. "Are we playing helpless, Joni?"

The man certainly knew how to irritate her! "Is it playing coy to need a second opinion?"

She hadn't realized he was moving toward her until his muscular frame halted only inches away. "You could be trying to win me to your side. It's an old tactic, Joni. Ask my advice, and I may start to feel like we're allies."

There was no point in beating around the bush with this man. "If we aren't allies, what are we?"

He grinned. "That's more like it."

"More like what?"

"The attitude I would expect from the woman who kicked my brother out when he did her wrong."

"I didn't kick him out," Joni admitted. "I kicked myself out. Otherwise, why would I be living with thrift-shop furniture while he kept the mansion?"

"You could have fought for it. Most women would have." Dirk reached out and brushed a long wisp of hair from her cheek. His touch was gentle and oddly possessive.

Joni wanted him to touch her again and wished she didn't. In her confusion, she spoke more forcefully than she'd intended. "I never felt comfortable in that house anyway. It belonged more to his housekeeper than it did to me."

"You might have insisted on a settlement. After all, you were the injured party," he pressed.

"Lowell provided for Jeff," she said.

"Yes, I know. He bought this house for him," Dirk said. "That was the only way you would accept it."

"You do very thorough research," she conceded.

"I hope so. Now show me your evidence."

There was no hint of indulgence in his tone, which was fine with Joni. She liked directness in a man. Even brutal honesty was better than manipulation.

Maybe that was why she'd put up with Lowell as long as she had. At least she knew where she stood with him even if that place wasn't particularly elevated. Or, rather, she'd believed she knew where she stood until the day Kim called.

"It's in the kitchen." She led the way, keenly aware of Dirk's heat radiating against her back.

The man had a gift for dominating his surroundings.

Dirk might be less flashy than his brother, but he had more real strength.

No wonder the two hadn't gotten along. Lowell could never bear to be upstaged.

"There." Joni indicated the knife on the counter.

Dirk's lips pursed as he studied it, mentally measuring its size and design. "Where did you find it?"

"In the dishwasher." She clicked her tongue. "*After* I ran it. Stupid, huh?"

"The police should have checked."

"They probably did. It wasn't in the cutlery tray; it was half-hidden under some glasses. I didn't notice it myself until too late."

He scowled. "It's sloppy work, nevertheless."

"Maybe so, but that doesn't change the facts," she said. "Now that the knife's been washed, I'm going to have a hard time proving it's been sitting here all this time, aren't I?"

"Are these the only knives you have?" He indicated the cutlery block.

"No," she said. "I picked up a few odds and ends when I was living in an apartment, right after the separation."

"Where are they?"

She opened a drawer. "Here. But the police probably checked it when they went through the house."

As Dirk shifted past her, she caught the scent of expensive soap and, beneath it, a hint of something feral. Without warning, prickles of desire ran along her skin and her nipples stiffened.

Joni didn't want to feel anything for this man and yet she found his nearness intensely pleasurable. So pleasurable that she had to back up several steps for her own peace of mind. From the den came the pings and screeches of a video game. The reminder of her son's presence brought her down to earth.

Dirk examined the contents of the drawer without handling anything. "Most of them are different makes, but there's a paring knife that's the same."

"It's the department store's house brand," she said. "Lots of people have them."

"So the murder weapon could have come from the drawer even if it didn't come from the block," he reasoned.

"I didn't have another knife that size," she protested, then had to add, "I don't think."

"You're not sure?"

"Not one hundred percent. But if I were in a hurry, I would've grabbed one out of the block, not poked around in a drawer."

His gaze returned to the knife on the counter. There was a long pause; she could almost see wheels turning inside his head as he mulled over the implications of this discovery. She tried to hold still, to give him time to think, but her head felt suddenly light. It had been foolish to remain standing this long, Joni realized as she caught hold of the counter to steady herself.

Dirk grasped her arm. "Have you eaten lunch?"

His face tilted down, his well-defined mouth inches from hers. At close range, the contrast between his thick dark hair and shocking blue eyes struck her as intensely sensual. If she weren't careful, she might lift her mouth and taste him.

Taking her by the shoulders, Dirk steered her to the table. Blurrily, Joni noticed that, by the wall clock, it was 1:35. "I had coffee."

"That's a great lunch. What do you plan to have for

dinner—iced tea?'' He opened the refrigerator and peered inside.

''I forget to eat sometimes,'' she admitted.

He removed a loaf of bread, a package of turkey slices and some condiments. ''You don't think much of your-self, do you?''

''What is this, instant psychoanalysis?'' Joni said, bristling. ''Lots of people forget to eat.''

''Lots of people don't also marry my brother.'' Pulling out a cutting board, Dirk set to work. ''I loved the guy—hell, when I was a little kid, I practically worshiped him—but he could be a real pain. Herb told me how he put you down all the time.''

She rested her chin on one palm. ''We were a mis-match. I guess when he proposed, he saw something in me that wasn't there.''

''He knew exactly what he was getting when he mar-ried you. Mustard?''

''Yes.'' She nodded distractedly. ''What *was* he get-ting, since you seem to have it figured out?''

''A beautiful woman who thought so little of herself that she would put up with his arrogance,'' Dirk said. ''Exactly what he needed, and not an easy combination to find.''

''I'm not beautiful,'' Joni protested. ''And I'm not a pushover, either. I didn't put up with his playing around.''

''Kim DeLong forced the issue by phoning you.'' Dirk layered tomato and lettuce onto the sandwich and sliced it into two triangles. ''Is this enough food?''

''Plenty.'' As she accepted the plate, Joni discovered that she was ravenous. The glass of orange juice that Dirk handed her disappeared almost as fast as the sandwich.

What he'd said about Lowell rang true, although it

bothered her that this stranger had more insight into her marriage than she did. Still, Dirk had known his brother a lot longer.

"About the knife." He straddled a chair next to her. "You'll need to give it to the police as soon as possible."

"Even though it won't do any good?"

"It could help your lawyer create doubt about your guilt," he suggested.

His words echoed through her mind with eerie unreality. Legalistic maneuverings sounded so foreign to her ordinary life. "Do you know if they're going to file charges?"

Dirk tapped one finger on the surface of the table. "I hope not."

"Because you think I'm innocent, or to spare Jeff?" Joni caught her breath. Why had she brought up the delicate subject of their son?

"Herb asked me to find out what really happened, for Lowell's sake," he said quietly. "And I guess for Jeff's sake, too."

Jeff's, but not hers. "Does Herb think I might have killed Lowell on purpose?"

"My grandfather loves you," Dirk said. "Therefore, he believes the truth will exonerate you. He lacks confidence in local law enforcement, and I don't blame him."

"He asked you to investigate this yourself?" she asked. "How will you do that?"

"Discreetly." Leaning back, he propped one long leg on a chair. "I've started going through Lowell's papers and talking to people, trying to determine his state of mind and why he would attack you. But this business with the knife makes me wonder."

"Wonder what?" she asked.

"Wonder if I'm taking the wrong tack." His air of

concentration deepened. ''The assumption has been that you killed Lowell, and the question is what he did to provoke it. Whether he forced your hand, and if so, why?''

''But now?'' His answer mattered more than she could say. More, perhaps, than she could bring herself to admit.

''If you were calculating and devious, you might've gone out today and found a duplicate knife.'' Dirk was assessing the possibilities as if she weren't there. Joni supposed she should be offended, but instead she welcomed his objectivity. ''Considering that you just got out of the hospital, that seems unlikely unless you have an accomplice or you bought the knife in advance. In either case, you would have planned a better alibi.''

''So, by default, you think somebody else did it?'' she asked with a touch of irony.

''Did they?'' Cobalt eyes fixed on her. ''You ought to know, Joni.'' He reminded her of a detective holding himself apart from the scene. Yet she had the feeling he was leaning toward her side.

''The murder weapon wasn't my knife.'' Her head still felt woolly, but at least it had stopped spinning. ''I didn't take a knife outside, of any shape or size. Dirk, I didn't even know anyone was out there. I went out to the patio to put Jeff's bike in the garage.''

''Why didn't you tell that to the police?'' he asked. ''Reading the report, I got the impression you went outside to confront Lowell.''

''I said I went outside and found Lowell there.'' Details of the interview eluded her. ''At least, I think that's what I said. I was so dazed, I'm not sure how I phrased it.''

''So you wouldn't have had any reason to take a

knife.'' His jaw worked. ''Except that you *were* being stalked.''

''By Lowell,'' she said. ''I think.''

''You're not sure about that, either?''

''I never actually saw him or heard his voice on the phone,'' she admitted. ''But it was exactly the same stuff he pulled after I moved out.''

''You're sure it was him the first time?''

''He admitted it,'' she said. ''Once we resolved the issues in our divorce, he apologized.'' Something else occurred to her. ''Wednesday night, he did confess that he'd been watching me. He said he saw me come home alone.''

''Did he say why or for how long he'd been doing it?'' Dirk asked hoarsely.

She shook her head.

''Did my brother ever hit you? In all the time you were married?''

''No.'' She might have felt intimidated by Lowell's world and in awe of her powerful husband, but she wouldn't have tolerated physical abuse.

Dirk was absorbed in his speculation. ''So what we have is someone harassing you, and my brother watching the house, then coming forward to talk to you. You smack your head into the hummingbird feeder and wake up holding a knife. In the meantime, someone has stabbed Lowell to death.''

''Unless I've blocked something out, which is what the police seem to believe.''

''That's what I assumed, too, until now,'' Dirk said. ''Think hard, Joni. Does anyone have a grudge against you or Lowell?''

''Not that I know of. Except Kim, maybe.''

"Any man who's shown you undue attention? What about your boss?"

"Basil's always been kind of strange," she admitted. "But I don't think he's dangerous."

"How long have you worked for him?"

"A year and three months, roughly. I got a job fairly soon after the divorce." Her system must have absorbed energy from lunch because Joni felt stronger now. "He's never asked me out, but he's never come over here before, either."

Dirk took a small notebook from his pocket and jotted in it. "Any other men?"

She thought of Charlie. "Jeff's soccer coach brought me flowers at the hospital, but I didn't get a chance to talk to him. He's never behaved in a threatening way. I hardly know him."

"What about women?" he asked. "A rival at work? Or anywhere else?"

"Well, Mrs. Wright never seemed to care for me very much." That was the Petersons' longtime housekeeper. "I don't think I lived up to her notion of the right kind of woman for Lowell."

"She doted on my brother," Dirk said. "She certainly wouldn't have killed him."

"So there we are," Joni said. "Back to me with an unidentified knife in my hand."

Dirk put the notebook away. "And the possibility of a killer on the loose."

"But if someone wanted me dead, he—or she—had every opportunity to kill me that night," she noted.

"Maybe he didn't want you dead. Maybe he wants you for himself."

The shivering came from deep inside. Being stalked by Lowell had seemed annoying but only a little scary. The possibility that there might be some madman who believed he could possess Joni aroused a deep and chilling dread.

"You're cold." Dirk leaned toward her protectively.

"No. I'm scared." But she wouldn't let herself panic. She needed to understand the killer so she could figure out who he might be. "If he...wants me, why try to frame me for murder?"

Dirk considered for a moment. "From the profiles I've read of stalkers, a man like that might be trying to punish you. It's all part of his need to take control of your life. Herb said you and Lowell were getting friendly again. That could've set him off."

"But if I were in prison, he couldn't have me."

"Maybe he doesn't think that clearly. Or he might've assumed you'd get off on a plea of self-defense."

The possibility of a psychopathic stalker was almost worse than the fear that she'd stabbed Lowell and blocked it out. "This is so bizarre."

"I could be wrong. There might not be such a man at all." Dirk's tone was noncommittal. "Just to be on the safe side—do you have a security system?"

She shook her head.

"It didn't occur to you that installing one might be a good idea?" His dark eyebrows arched questioningly.

"I didn't believe Lowell would hurt me." In retrospect, Joni wished that she had paid more attention to her ex-husband's protestations of innocence. After talking to Dirk, she was almost certain now that whoever had made those phone calls and committed the vandalism, it hadn't been Lowell but someone else. Someone deadly.

"I don't suppose you keep a gun in the house?"

"Not with an eight-year-old running around. I'd rather

something happened to me because I didn't have a gun than have my son get hurt because I did," she asserted.

Dirk's expression softened. "You have that mothering instinct full force, don't you?"

"Of course." She refrained from wondering aloud how he could have so little in the way of fatherly instincts. Men were different from women that way, she supposed. Maybe he realized that a globe-trotter was in no position to raise a child. Or perhaps he'd distanced himself so completely that he didn't think of Jeff as his son.

"Where are your Yellow Pages?"

She blinked at the sudden request. "In the drawer under the phone."

"You're going to get a security system, today if possible." He stood and strode toward the phone. "I'll pay for it."

"Thanks. I'd be grateful." Until now, a household alarm system had sounded like more nuisance than it was worth and the cost would have strained her budget. But she could see that she needed one.

Dirk spent the next twenty minutes on the phone, trying to find a company that would promise immediate installation. Finally, he yielded to the inevitable and made an appointment.

"It's a good system," he said after hanging up. "They'll wire all the windows as well as the doors. Unfortunately, we can't get it installed until Wednesday."

"That sounds so far off."

"It's the soonest anyone could come. I'll sleep here until then." He wasn't asking; he was telling.

"Sleep here?" Joni stared at Dirk as he paced to the window to look out. He had a well-developed build, a bit more compact than Lowell's, and a cocky way of holding himself. This strange, alluring man intended to live in her house for the next five days? "I don't think so."

"What are you worried about—gossip?" he challenged. "As if people weren't already running off at the mouth? Besides, I'm your brother-in-law."

"Ex-brother-in-law."

"Joni," he said, "there's no way I'm leaving you here unguarded."

"Mom?" Jeff wandered through the kitchen doorway. "What are you guys talking about?"

"Your uncle wants to move in for a few days," she said.

"To watch over you." Dirk gave the boy a smile. "If you don't mind."

His little face lit up. "Really? Would you? That would be nice, wouldn't it, Mom?"

Joni's spirits sank. She didn't want her son becoming too attached to Dirk and complicating an already difficult situation. "I don't think it's a good idea."

"Please." Where had that worried frown come from? Jeff seemed to have grown suddenly older. "Dad died right outside. Uncle Dirk knows how to protect us, don't you?"

"I won't let anything happen to either of you." The man set one hand on his son's shoulder. For the first time, Joni noticed that they had matching indentations in their left cheeks.

"I'll sleep better if he's here," Jeff pleaded.

Joni swallowed her objections. Dirk's reassuring presence would help her son through these next few days as he absorbed the fact that he would never see his daddy again. It might help her, too.

"All right," she conceded. "He can stay until we get our security system installed."

"Thanks, Mom," Jeff said, and then, no doubt parroting a phrase he'd heard on television, added, "You won't regret this."

Dirk chuckled. "I certainly hope not."

Joni hoped not, too.

Chapter Six

Both Jeff and Joni retired to bed early. With the house quiet, Dirk went into the kitchen and cleaned up the remains of their fast-food dinner.

Detective MacDougall had come by earlier to collect the knife and interview Joni about it. Dirk couldn't tell from his reaction whether he believed her story, and Joni seemed too exhausted to care.

After grilling her, the man had spent several hours examining the contents of kitchen drawers, the dishwasher and refrigerator, then prowling the patio. Finally, he'd removed the yellow tape and departed with the knife.

In the den, Dirk went to work hanging his clothes in the closet and tucking his underwear into the only drawer in an end table. Cramped quarters, but he'd certainly stayed in worse.

When he'd stopped by the Peterson estate that afternoon to retrieve his belongings, Mrs. Wright had frowned in disapproval at learning that he was moving to Joni's house. After working for his family for twenty years, she was taking Lowell's death hard.

She'd softened after Dirk pointed out that he was staying there for Jeff's sake. But was he really? he wondered as he opened the couch into a bed.

Joni had asked his advice about the knife, but beyond that, she didn't seem to think she needed help. He had a feeling she wasn't used to leaning on anyone.

Damn it, he wanted her to lean on him. Or at least to spend more time with him. He wanted a chance to discover the side of herself that she hid from the world.

Those brown-specked green eyes had a way of confronting him boldly, then flicking shyly away, that made him itch to find out what she was thinking. To touch her skin and feel the silkiness of her hair and surprise her in a hundred subtle ways.

He wondered how Joni would react if he took her in his arms. Whether her mouth would yield beneath his and her body come alive. Whether her hands would grip his shoulders as he eased open the buttons on her blouse...

Great idea, Dirk told himself harshly. If he made love to Joni, then what?

He hated staying in one place for long and backed off at the first sign of anyone trying to rein him in. That was how life had shaped him, and it was too late to change his character now.

During his last year in security work, he'd become involved with a bodyguard named Elena. A beautiful woman with white-blond hair and a crackling sense of humor, she had a black belt in karate but was growing tired of constant travel and danger.

By that time, Dirk was considering leaving the security firm to start his own business. When an entrepreneur for whom he'd consulted offered him a chance to join a new venture, Dirk decided to invest his savings and go for it.

Elena announced she was ready for marriage and children. Dirk wanted those things, too, someday. But, excited about his new challenge, he asked her to give him more time.

His new firm had brokered computer services in a country carved from the former Soviet Union. Dirk worked day and night, setting up a system that matched local companies with experts from around the world. His consultants could do anything from putting together a firm's hardware system to custom-designing its software.

Once the company was running smoothly, Dirk sold his share for a large sum. He'd identified another business opportunity, this one in central Africa, and proposed it to a group of venture capitalists. That led to establishing his own consulting company.

For the first time in his life, he felt in charge and powerful. Like someone his father would have respected.

Tired of waiting, Elena took on another assignment in South America. The man she was protecting turned out to be the target of drug dealers. He died in an ambush of machine-gun fire. So did she.

Remembering the day he'd received the news still felt like a punch in the gut. Dirk had loved Elena, and he'd failed her.

Maybe he hadn't been honest enough, with her or with himself. Maybe he wasn't cut out to be anyone's husband.

In the five years since then, he'd always seemed to need another mountain to climb. Just thinking about some of the projects he was juggling made the adrenaline start to pump.

Joni didn't strike him as the type to want a short-term affair, and Dirk didn't intend to hang around Viento del Mar for long. The best thing he could do would be to watch over her, strictly as a friend, until she recovered her health.

That, and find out what had happened to his brother.

As he went into the hall bathroom to stow his shaving kit, Dirk heard steady breathing from Jeff's bedroom.

Joni's door was closed, and he guessed she would be asleep by now, too.

His watch showed five past eight. It was at about this hour two nights ago that his brother had been slain.

If he walked through the scenario from Lowell's perspective, trying to view it with his brother's eyes, he might gain a better understanding of what had happened. Experience had taught him that even the smallest details could change the big picture.

First, Dirk decided, he had to set the scene as it had been that night. Remembering the description from the police report, he switched on the rear porch light. Leaving the kitchen and den illuminated, he donned a windbreaker, picked up a flashlight and went outside.

Lowell's car had been found around the block, parked out of sight. No one recalled seeing any other strange cars in the neighborhood, although he wasn't sure the police had talked to all possible witnesses.

MacDougall had speculated that Lowell must have watched the property from behind, on the slope, although the rain had destroyed any evidence of where he'd waited. Lowell had been wearing a thin suit, though, so he hadn't come prepared for a lengthy stakeout.

Dirk decided to start in front. His brother must have arrived from that direction at some point. Besides, for security reasons, it was important to get a sense of how the area looked after dark.

He descended the sloping driveway, past his rented sedan. Down the street, a car turned into a driveway, its headlights cutting a swath through the darkness before shutting off. Somewhere a dog barked, once, twice, and then stopped.

Darkness fell, deep and layered. There was no street-level illumination, and clouds blocked the moon. Even through the windbreaker, Dirk could feel the October chill.

Standing in front of the house, he scanned the neighborhood. All the structures were one story; from seeing them in daylight, he recalled that they were stucco with wood trim, designed to blend with the environment.

On Joni's side, the houses sat against the perimeter of the development, with only woodlands beyond. On the opposite side of the street, the residences were half-hidden on rolling lots.

Just beyond Joni's place lay a cul-de-sac. Because of the curvature and an intervening stand of trees, the end house was some distance away and at an angle that made it unlikely the occupants could see much of her front yard, let alone the back.

Turning, Dirk scrutinized Joni's house. Light glimmered from the living room, while the thin front curtain allowed a glimpse inside. All he could see, though, was a framed print on the wall. Not enough to satisfy anyone intent on observing her. A watcher would have to choose a position behind the house all right.

According to Dirk's research, the woods stretched for miles, crossed by a few hiking trails. Only someone who knew the area could have come that way by night.

Lowell had never been the outdoor type. In addition, although he could be impulsive, his temper usually subsided with time. He might not be quick to forgive, but he wasn't the type to calculate a slow-burning revenge, either.

Yet he admitted he was watching Joni. Why?

Hands jammed into his pockets, Dirk trudged up the driveway. He didn't want to believe that his brother had threatened her, any more than he wanted to accept that she had killed him. So far, however, nothing but the existence of a second knife indicated a third party might have been involved. Until he found more evidence, he must not let wishful thinking affect his judgment.

Joni reminded Dirk a lot of himself in his younger days, when he'd had to weather his father's faultfinding and Lowell's frequent digs. He, too, had built up a cautious exterior and learned to hold his feelings inside. Most of the time anyway. That didn't mean she was like him in other ways. Even Herb had some doubts about her, or why would he have pressed Dirk to begin this investigation?

At the top of the driveway, he followed a concrete walkway behind the garage. Stopping short of the diffused glow from the porch light, Dirk surveyed the patio. Even in moonlight, it was full of shadows, and the sky had been overcast on Wednesday. Joni had said she didn't realize anyone was there until the last minute, and he could believe it.

Dirk turned his attention to the slope, or what little he could see of it. It would be almost impossible to descend in the dark without making a racket. Besides, Joni had said Lowell came from this side, near the garage.

There was nowhere to hide, this close to the house. Swinging around, Dirk headed for the short drop that divided Joni's yard from the neighbor's. As he neared the divide, the leaves of a thick shrub grazed his face. He pushed them aside, then realized as they rustled and swayed that what he'd assumed was a bush was instead a long branch.

With his flashlight, Dirk traced it backward. The branch and several others arced outward from a tree located a short ways uphill, on the property line.

What had appeared to be a dense plant was instead a canopy formed by overgrown branches. In the space he had assumed would be filled by a thick trunk, there was room for a man to hide.

This cover stood no more than a dozen long strides from Joni's back door. From here, through the rear windows, Dirk could have seen anyone standing at the sink or sitting at the kitchen table. He could also see the street and any cars that might come up the driveway.

He shone his flashlight inside the blind, at the ground. When something glistened, Dirk knelt to check it out.

Just a piece of quartz, he found to his disappointment. Then, still crouching, he spotted the heel print.

It was a faint impression, but deep enough for him to see the kind of tread that came from an athletic shoe. The night Lowell died, according to the police report, he'd been wearing smooth-soled Italian leather.

Dirk trained the flashlight closer. The shallow print showed no sign of rain damage. It must have been made since Wednesday night.

His arms prickled. Someone had been watching the house yesterday or today. Watching Joni. And Jeff. And him.

Detective MacDougall must have gone home for the night by now. He wouldn't appreciate being rousted at this hour for anything less than an emergency, and this didn't qualify. But Dirk vowed to call the man first thing in the morning.

He wondered if Lowell had discovered the blind, or if he'd waited for Joni, oblivious, only a few feet from a hidden observer. It was an unnerving possibility.

To complete the survey, Dirk retraced his steps toward the patio. The dusty light globe glared into his eyes, blocking his vision as it would have done to Lowell in his final moments of life. His brother could have made out Joni's figure on the patio, but he couldn't have seen much beyond that. The slope to his left and the lawn and trees beyond the patio were blotted out.

And, of course, he wouldn't have seen someone approaching from behind. From the leafy hideout.

In the woods, a coyote howled, its wail bouncing and echoing. The sound made Dirk jump. Annoyed at himself, he crossed the patio, skirting the heavy glass table. It took several seconds before his night vision returned.

From a reverse angle, he surveyed the scene. The patio. The slope. The trees above, black against a charcoal sky.

In the woods, he spotted a pinprick of light.

Dirk stared at it in confusion. For a moment, he thought it might be a safety light, but why only one? Besides, it wasn't large enough to provide security.

Then it moved. Gripping the flashlight, he aimed it up the slope, but its beam wasn't strong enough to penetrate that far. The light vanished. Did the intruder realize he'd been noticed?

Instinct urged Dirk to give chase, but the other person had a head start and knew the terrain. A newcomer would likely reap nothing more than a twisted ankle. Worse, he would leave Joni unguarded.

There was no proof, of course, that this person had any connection to Wednesday's tragedy. Anyone who lived in the area might be taking a walk.

But only a fool ignored patterns, and one was definitely taking shape here. The second knife. The footprint inside a hiding place. The light on the hill.

The odds had shifted. It seemed less and less likely that Joni had been the one who wielded the murder weapon. Or that his brother had been her stalker. More likely, Lowell had appointed himself as lookout to nab the prowler in the act. A prowler who was still free, his existence not even suspected by the police.

To keep his promise to Herb, Dirk would have to expand his scope. Instead of a narrow probe into Lowell's state of mind, he was now looking for a killer who might be anyone.

JONI AWOKE SHORTLY AFTER nine o'clock on Saturday morning. She couldn't remember the last time she'd slept this late.

From the den came the chatter of a cartoon show. Outside, a car turned into the driveway. Dragging herself to the window, she spotted a light brown sedan with Detective MacDougall at the wheel. What was he doing here?

Moving stiffly, she pulled on some clothes, brushed her teeth and ran a comb through her hair. After downing some aspirin, she went into the den.

"Uncle Dirk's in the backyard," Jeff announced from where he sat watching TV.

"Is the police officer with him?"

"I guess so." He showed no further interest. Normally, her son was underfoot when anything happened, peppering the grown-ups with questions.

"Jeff?" she said. "Do you feel all right?"

"I just don't want to go outside." His hunched shoulders revealed more about his anxiety than any words could have.

Joni gave her son a hug. He'd lost his father and, on top of that, had to deal with the fact that the death had occurred under their noses. She wished she could make the pain go away, but children, like adults, needed time to grieve.

"I love you," she said. "Everything's under control, honey. Okay?"

"Okay." He returned his gaze to the screen, obviously uncomfortable with talking about his feelings.

In any case, Joni needed to find out what the detective was doing. She wouldn't be much good to her son if she went to prison. Between her house and the neighbor's, she found Dirk holding up a heavy branch for the detective, who was inspecting the ground. Behind MacDougall stood Celia, watching with lively interest.

"What's going on?" Joni asked.

Three faces turned toward her. "Your brother-in-law has discovered a possible hideout for our stalker," Mac-Dougall said. "Only problem is, there's no evidence anyone's used it."

"There was a heel print here last night." Dirk brushed a lock of dark hair from his forehead. "Someone's erased it. And I saw a light moving in the woods."

"You came out here last night?" she asked.

"I figured I might learn something if I retraced Lowell's steps," he said. "Apparently, I was right."

Celia hugged herself. Although she was neatly dressed in an embroidered blouse over black pants, her tangled hair indicated she'd dressed quickly. "You saw someone on hill? What time?"

"About eight-thirty," Dirk said. "He must have seen me discover the blind."

Joni's hands went cold. If it were a casual hiker, he wouldn't have erased the footprint. There really *was* someone watching her house.

The detective looked up from making notes. "This does put a different slant on things, although it's too bad we don't have the print. You say it was some kind of athletic shoe?"

"I couldn't be sure which brand, but it was that type of tread."

"Lowell never wore his Nike shoes outside the health club." Joni barely managed to keep her voice steady.

"I don't believe my brother could have left that print.

It showed no rain damage.'' Dirk's concerned gaze met hers.

He'd shaved this morning and put on a V-necked navy sweater over a crisp tan shirt and pressed jeans. It seemed unfair that anyone could look so well put together this early on a Saturday, she reflected irrelevantly.

''Have you seen any prowlers, ma'am?'' the detective asked Celia.

''No, but I keep my blinds drawn after dark,'' she said. ''Especially when my husband's away.'' He had departed the previous week for a monthlong business trip to Taiwan and Singapore.

MacDougall checked the area. Then, accompanied by Dirk, he stomped up the slope to the edge of the woods. Leaving Celia to trail them, Joni went inside.

Judging by the crumb-covered plates in the kitchen sink, her son and Dirk had already fixed toast for breakfast. Since Jeff was afraid of burning himself, Dirk must have toasted the bread for both of them.

A mother excelled at detective work when it came to figuring out household behavior, she thought wryly. Too bad she couldn't do the same for a murder.

As she fixed herself a bowl of cereal, Joni reviewed what Dirk had discovered. The footprint and the way it had been wiped clean, together with the knife, dispelled any lingering doubts. She knew with absolute certainty that she hadn't stabbed Lowell.

She was glad Jeff wouldn't have to grow up with the knowledge that his mother had killed his father, even in self-defense. And whatever Lowell might have done in the past, it repelled her to think of wreaking such violence on a man she'd once loved.

But now, Joni thought grimly, she had to deal with the

frightening prospect that remained. A murderer had been on her property last night.

She was grateful that her brother-in-law had security training. And that he cared enough about the truth to keep searching for it when the police had been ready to accept her guilt at face value. She wondered whether his support had anything to do with his being Jeff's biological father. In truth, his motivation no longer mattered. She was just glad he was here.

"Mom?" Jeff wandered in, holding a stuffed dragon named Yoshi. To her knowledge, he hadn't carried it out of his bedroom in months, but now, apparently, he needed the reassurance. "Don't I have a soccer game?"

"Oh, my gosh!" She jumped up. "I'm not supposed to bring the snacks today, am I?"

"You brought granola bars last week," her son reminded her.

She sighed. "Oh, right. Where would I be without your memory?"

"Panicking," Jeff said tartly, and went off to change clothes.

The prospect of attending the game lifted Joni's spirits. She needed something normal to hang on to, and what could be more normal than kids' soccer?

She was sitting on the edge of the opened couch in the den, lacing her tennis shoes, when Dirk came in. Outside, the detective's car rattled away.

"Find anything?" she asked.

His mouth twisted. "Nothing. No pun intended. By the way, I trimmed back the branches as far as I could with the tools from your garage. I don't think anyone will be hiding there for a while."

"Thanks," Joni said. "Dirk, your help means more than I can say."

"That's why I'm here." The flimsy sofa bed sank as he sat beside her. "It's why you have to put up with my dishes in the sink and my shaving kit in the bathroom."

"I don't mind. Not at all." It must be the light-headedness from her injury, Joni thought, that made her so aware that she was sitting next to an incredibly desirable man. His spicy scent pervaded the sheets and surrounded her like a cocoon. She ached to curve against his broad chest and feel the strength of those muscular shoulders. To cup his well-shaped head in her hands.

A bed. A man. What would it feel like to lie here with him?

She didn't intend to find out. Life was too complicated already.

Down the hall, she could hear Jeff clomping about in his bedroom. The boy could make more noise fishing his shin guards and spiked shoes out of the closet than Joni could make dropping an entire stack of pots and pans. Well, almost.

"Something going on?" Dirk raised an eyebrow.

"Soccer game," she said.

"You're into that?" An indentation flashed in his cheek as he smiled. "Do you realize that soccer moms have become legendary?"

"I'm not much of a soccer mom," Joni confessed as she retied one shoe. "I hid in the back when they asked for someone to make the team banner."

"Didn't they catch you?" he teased.

"No, but Jeff's best friend's mother volunteered." Joni sighed. "I had to spend a whole Sunday afternoon helping her cut out pieces of felt and glue them together. It looks pretty good, no thanks to me. Kathryn's the talented one."

"Where do they hold these games?" he asked.

"It depends on who else needs the fields. Today we're

playing at the high school." Joni stood, trying to convince herself that she didn't feel the other shoelace working its way loose.

"This should be interesting." Dirk uncoiled from the low bed.

"You're coming?"

"Whoever's been watching you is most likely an acquaintance," he said. "I need to get to know your friends."

Jeff trudged in, wearing shorts and a jersey in the team colors of black and silver. "Are you coming, Uncle Dirk?"

"I wouldn't miss it."

The boy straightened as if an invisible burden had been lifted. "Great!"

The two of them walked ahead of Joni through the house. Their sturdy gaits had the same boyish swing, she noticed with a pang.

They took Dirk's car. It was a pleasure, Joni discovered, to get away from the house.

As sunshine flooded through the windshield, an oldies song bounced from the radio. In the back seat, Jeff danced in place. Amused, Dirk kept glancing at the boy in the rearview mirror.

Being together, the three of them, felt like the old days when she'd been part of a two-parent family, Joni mused. She hadn't realized how much she'd missed that sense of completion.

But a deep uneasiness refused to let her enjoy the good mood for long. As they turned left from Canyon Acres onto San Bernardo Road, Joni remembered what Dirk had said earlier. *Whoever's been watching you is most likely an acquaintance.*

In the bustle of getting out the door, she hadn't given

his assertion much thought. Now it struck her with painful clarity.

The stalker might be someone they would see at the game. The coach or his assistant. One of the parents. A soccer-league official.

Until this case was resolved, she couldn't trust anyone. She had to stay on the alert, even among friends. Or perhaps, as Dirk had indicated, especially among friends.

Chapter Seven

Cars filled much of the high school parking lot. It was a quarter to eleven, Joni saw from her watch, and pregame practice had started half an hour ago. Jeff had missed that, but at least he'd attended practice last Wednesday. And he was here for the game.

"I didn't realize soccer was so popular." Dirk angled his rental car between a van and a station wagon. "There are quite a few cars here."

"There are two teams with about a dozen kids on each, so it does get crowded." A synchronized cheer drifted from the nearby gymnasium. "Also, it sounds like the cheerleaders are practicing today, too."

"This whole scene reminds me of a sixties TV show about middle America." Dirk cut off the engine. "It's another lifetime, if not another world."

"You grew up here," Joni pointed out. "It shouldn't seem *that* strange."

"After watching *Melrose Place* in Nairobi and *The Brady Bunch* in Bombay, dubbed into the local languages, it's hard to view America the same way," he said.

"There's Coach!" Grabbing his soccer ball, Jeff waved to Charlie, who was shading his eyes on the playing field. The coach waved back.

"Bobby's here." Joni pointed to the Owenses' white minivan, distinguished by the black and silver racing stripes Kathryn had painted along the side.

"Bobby, I take it, is a good friend?" Dirk asked his nephew.

"The best!" Jeff loped ahead of them across the black-top, and on the field his friends cheered his approach.

"We should have been here early for practice," Joni admitted as she walked beside Dirk. Her head and ribs ached dully. "I hope that, under the circumstances, the coach will understand."

"Whether he understands isn't important," he said. "Joni, I know these are familiar surroundings, but this situation isn't normal. You can't afford to let your guard down. You have to imagine we're in a foreign country where we don't know whom to trust."

Was that possible? she wondered as they passed a group of three team mothers, one with a baby in a stroller, the others shepherding toddlers. Exchanging startled glances, the women turned away without greeting Joni. They'd always acted friendly before, but until now, she reflected, she hadn't been suspected of killing anyone.

"I guess I might as well be in a foreign country," she agreed sadly.

On the playing field, Jeff joined the other boys milling around. As his assistant herded them into line, the coach turned to stare at Joni.

She waved. "Thanks for the flowers!"

He nodded, but his half smile vanished as he turned his attention to Dirk. Was she imagining it, or was that a look of hostility?

Tapping her companion's arm, she asked, "Do you know him?"

Dirk glanced at the coach. "Not that I recall. Did he grow up around here?"

Now that she thought about it, Joni recalled hearing that Charlie had moved to town a couple of years ago. "I guess not. He seems to have taken a dislike to you, though."

The man on the field turned abruptly away. "Temper, temper," Dirk murmured. "You said he's been paying attention to you? I need to have a talk with that guy."

To their left, a silver-and-black banner displayed a soccer ball and the slogan, "Win, Raiders!" Across the field, a blue-and-white banner proclaimed, "Sting 'Em, Hornets!" In both sets of bleachers, parents were spreading out their blankets.

"Friendly rivalry?" Dirk asked.

"Most of the time," she said. "Some of the parents get carried away. Did you ever play when you were a kid?"

"One season of Little League," he said. "That was the popular sport back then."

"Lowell had a couple of trophies," she recalled. "He encouraged Jeff to go out for soccer."

"My brother was a star." Dirk spoke without rancor. "Maybe I could've been, maybe not. What I couldn't take was my father standing on the sidelines screaming at me whenever I made a mistake. How well did you know Dad anyway?"

Donald Peterson had been the hard-driving head of Peterson Printing when Joni went to work there. To her, he'd remained a distant, intimidating figure until his death from a heart attack two years after her marriage.

"Not well," she admitted. "I was grateful he didn't object to Lowell's marrying me."

"Knowing my father, he saw you as suitable material to carry on the line," Dirk said. "An obedient wife who wouldn't put her career or her social life ahead of having children.''

"I never considered it that way." It hadn't occurred to Joni that a lack of accomplishments might be viewed as an advantage. "Oh, there are the Owenses! Let me introduce you."

From halfway up the bleachers, Bobby's parents greeted her warmly, a welcome contrast to the other parents' reactions. When she introduced Dirk and explained that he was staying with her, Kathryn's immediate response was "I'll bet that makes Jeff feel safer!"

"Jeff isn't the only one," Joni confessed as they took seats on her friends' blanket.

"But surely there's no danger to you now." Worry creased Fred's round, pinkish face. Of average height, he played basketball several times a week to battle his tendency to put on weight. "I don't mean to be insensitive, but with Lowell gone—"

"We're not certain my brother was the one stalking her," Dirk said.

"Really?" Kathryn glanced in alarm from him to Joni. "You mean there's been more harassment?"

"No." Joni didn't feel like going into detail about the footprint in the blind and the knife in the dishwasher. "There are a few pieces that don't fit."

"If you'll excuse me, I'm going to try to talk to the coach before the game starts." With quick, sure footing, Dirk swung down.

"Someone should warn him that Charlie's never in a mood to chat at game time," Kathryn sighed, finger combing her short brown hair.

"What does he want to talk to Coach about?" Fred asked.

Joni didn't want to reveal that Dirk was conducting his

own investigation; if word ever reached MacDougall, he'd be furious. "He's taking an interest in my son. I don't see how it can hurt."

"Perhaps not," Kathryn said. "As long as he's realistic. He might mean well, but no one can replace Jeff's father."

"He isn't too much like his brother, is he?" Fred added in concern. "I mean, he's living in your house, Joni. What if he gives you a hard time?"

"It's only until I can get an alarm system installed," she said. "Besides, believe me, I would never allow a man to treat me the way Lowell did ever again."

Below, Charlie brushed off Dirk's attempts to talk and marched onto the field. Dirk remained in place, watching the coach and the players.

Color and movement in the parking lot distracted her. Joni noticed a group of cheerleaders in orange-and-purple costumes scattering to their parents' cars. A few, probably sisters of soccer players, headed toward the bleachers.

Among them prowled a tall woman with a sculpted face and long, dark hair as silky as a model's. She was, as everyone knew, the volunteer cheerleading coach. She was also the woman who had broken up Joni's marriage.

Kim DeLong, dressed in a black silk blouse and matching leggings, strode toward one of her society friends in the opposing bleachers. Halfway there, she paused to stretch like a cat, the movements displaying her curves to maximum effect.

Men gawked. Some of the women frowned, but Joni knew that none of them would dare reproach the woman. From her father, Kim had inherited a large share of the town's commercial real estate and a leading position in society, and she was known to be vindictive.

Kim and Lowell had been a golden couple all through high school. Because they were five years older than Joni, she hadn't known them then, but she'd seen their pictures in the newspaper. They'd been shimmeringly beautiful and mind-numbingly rich.

During college, the two had dated for a while. Then an older man, a banker from San Francisco, won Kim away. She'd married him after graduation, reportedly breaking Lowell's heart.

He'd quickly recovered and married Joni. When Kim divorced her husband half a dozen years later and moved back to Viento del Mar, Lowell hadn't shown any interest.

Only after Kim called to brag about her conquest did Joni learn that, according to gossip, the raven-haired woman had set her sights on Lowell from the day she returned. Maybe, the busybodies said, he'd been dissatisfied with his wife; he had certainly criticized her enough. Joni suspected he'd also been flattered by Kim's pursuit and too self-centered to consider what it meant to break his marriage vows.

On the field, the game began, but she found it hard to concentrate. Seeing Kim brought back unpleasant memories and in addition her over-the-counter pain medication was wearing off. Her ribs throbbed and she had to grip the seat more than once until her head stopped spinning.

At first, Jeff played carelessly, without his usual spirit. After a while, though, he got caught up in the game and even scored a goal. From her spot, she could see Dirk studying the crowd and knew he must have noted Kim's arrival. But he spent most of his time calling out encouragement to Jeff.

Kathryn had implied that Dirk might be trying to take Lowell's place. Neither the Owenses nor anyone else, even Herb, knew the truth about Jeff's parentage, but Joni supposed her friend's speculation might not be entirely wrong. Even though she no longer believed Dirk would seek custody, he seemed to be drawing closer to his son. If he did want an ongoing relationship, it would mean spending more time in Viento del Mar.

With a start, she realized that the prospect pleased her. She felt more comfortable talking with Dirk than she ever had with Lowell, and his physical nearness brought a new awareness of her own femininity.

Her husband had been classically handsome but remote. Dirk, on the other hand, made her breath come faster every time she glanced at him. In a visceral, intensely personal way, she wanted him.

Disturbed, Joni stared down at the man pacing beside the field. The last thing she needed was to let herself become vulnerable to him. Losing Lowell had hurt badly; if she ever allowed herself to fall in love with Dirk, how could she bear to give him up? This time she knew in advance that she couldn't keep him. Only a fool would set herself up for that kind of loss.

A murmur from the bleachers roused Joni into the present. Coach Charlie, who had bent to pick up a soccer ball, had split his pants up the back seam. Judging by his red face, he didn't find the incident funny.

"Those uniforms aren't made very well," Kathryn said. "How embarrassing."

"The problem is, he's put on weight," Fred observed. "Don't blame the pants."

After muttering a few words to his assistant, the coach marched toward the parking lot. Joni hoped he had some extra pants in his car; the game was a close one, and the kids needed his guidance. Sure enough, by the end of half-time, he returned in a fresh pair of sweats. For the rest of the game, however, Charlie let his assistant do the strenuous bending.

"I can't understand why the man's let himself go," Fred

commented. "He ought to be in shape. After all, he teaches exercise classes."

"Is that what he does for a living?" Charlie was one of the soccer league's best volunteer coaches, but Joni had no idea of his regular occupation.

"No," Kathryn said. "He works for a plumbing service— Oh, I can't look!" She covered her eyes as an opposing player stole the ball from Bobby right in front of the Hornets' goal.

Instantly, Jeff darted in and stole it back. With a fierce kick, he knocked the black-and-white orb past the goalie and into the net.

The crowd cheered. Below, Dirk raised both fists in triumph.

"Don't worry, dear." Fred patted his wife's hand. "Joni's son saved the day."

The game ended a few minutes later, 4-to-3 in favor of the black and silver. The Raiders lined up to call "Good game!" to their rivals. The Hornets returned the sentiment but without enthusiasm.

Teaching sportsmanship was one of the goals of the soccer league, but Joni wasn't sure the lessons stuck very well. Especially not with some parents. Right now, in the stands opposite, a father was chewing out a tearful little boy who had missed an easy goal. She winced at a mental image of Donald Peterson yelling at a childish Dirk.

Lowell had tried the same tactic once, but the boy had indignantly ordered his father to stop being so mean. After a moment's stunned silence, Lowell had apologized. She wondered whether it was an innate character trait or the result of being an only child that had given Jeff the nerve to fight back.

Dirk, on the other hand, had withdrawn from the sport. He didn't shrink from confrontations anymore, though, she decided, watching him pace across the field toward Kim DeLong.

She supposed he wanted to question the woman about Lowell. It made sense, but that knowledge didn't stop a twinge of jealousy at seeing Kim straighten her shoulders and greet him with the calculated smile she reserved for good-looking men.

People crossed the stands in front of Joni, blocking her view. "Need help?" Fred, shifting a cooler to his other hand, offered an arm.

"I sure do." Shakily, she held on to him as they followed Kathryn down from the bleachers. "You're a lifesaver."

"That's what friends are for." At ground level, he bent to give Bobby a hug. "Terrific game!"

"Yeah!" The boy beamed. "Hey, Mrs. Peterson, can Jeff come home with us?"

"Please?" her son chimed from beside his friend. "We want to work on our Halloween costumes."

"Oh, that's right, it's next Thursday." Joni hadn't even considered what her son would wear.

"We both want to be Wishbone." The boys loved the spotted dog who acted out canine versions of classic stories on PBS.

"Both of you as one dog?" Fred raised an eyebrow teasingly.

"In *The Prince and the Pooch,* he's twins," Jeff explained.

Starting to nod her understanding, Joni nearly lost her balance. Kathryn caught her shoulder. "You need to rest, so let us take Jeff for a while. Anyway, I need to measure the boys for their costumes. I've got some old material that might work. Do you want us to drop you at home?"

The dizziness passed. "I'll wait for Dirk."

"We'll bring Jeff by later, then." After making sure Joni could stand unsupported, her friends departed to stow the boys, soccer equipment and other gear into their van.

Maybe she should have accepted their invitation to go home, Joni thought. She knew she'd overextended herself so soon after leaving the hospital. But she wanted to find out what Kim was saying to Dirk. And to see for herself how he reacted to Viento del Mar's resident siren.

By the time she traversed the grass, most of the parents had left. Only a few of Kim's friends lingered nearby, none of them willing to meet Joni's gaze.

Kim's voice grew louder as she spotted the newcomer. "As I said, I don't believe there ever was any harassment. I think she made it up and then lured him there so her kid could get his money."

From Dirk's tone, Joni could tell he was straining for patience. "I wish you would try to remember what Lowell said the last time you talked to him. Whether he'd received any threats or was suspicious of anyone."

"What's the point?" At close range, the sunlight picked out a few strands of gray in Kim's hair, but she was still a stunning beauty. "The police know who killed him and so does everybody else. The only question is, why haven't they locked her up yet?"

Joni could feel her cheeks flaming, but she stood her ground. "Sometimes what 'everybody' knows is wrong," she said evenly. "If you really cared about Lowell, you'd help his brother find the truth."

Rage glittered in the woman's eyes. "If *I* cared about him?" she snapped. "I was the great love of his life. Ask anybody in this town. He only married you on the rebound. We may have made a few mistakes, Lowell and I, but we belonged together."

Joni didn't want to argue the point. "Then I should

think you would want to make sure the guilty person gets convicted.''

"The guilty person *will* be convicted!'' A pom-pom pin heaved atop Kim's bosom, its orange-and-purple fringe quivering. ''He would've come back to me eventually, but you couldn't stand that, could you? You cheap, social-climbing little tramp!''

Her pitch had risen, and Joni realized the ugly words might carry as far as the parking lot. She checked in that direction to make sure Jeff hadn't heard.

The only person visible was Fred, who finished stowing gear in the rear compartment, slammed the hatch and gave Joni a thumbs-up. The gesture of support eased her embarrassment but only slightly. Kim's friends were exchanging knowing glances. It was clear they relished this attack on someone they'd long viewed as an interloper.

''I'd be careful whom I was calling cheap, if I were you.'' Dirk's low, furious response brought a shocked stare from Kim. ''Do you think my family appreciates your having an affair with my brother and then calling his wife to brag about it? That's not exactly high-class behavior in anybody's book.''

Kim's mouth tightened, but she appeared to be weighing her response. Not so much because Dirk had spoken the truth, Joni supposed, as because his family also ranked at the top of the town's social hierarchy.

''You want to make me the bad guy? Suit yourself.'' Turning, Kim told her friends, ''See you later,'' and headed for the parking lot. The others, subdued, collected their children and departed.

''Thank you.'' Joni's throat caught as she gazed at Dirk.

He touched her waist, sending darts of pure pleasure streaking through her. ''That woman had it coming. I don't excuse my brother's adultery, but she's never shown a moment's remorse for the harm she did you and Jeff. Even Herb despises her although he's too polite to say so.''

She tried to keep her tone light. ''Gee, I thought you were my personal knight in shining armor, and instead you were just defending the family honor.''

A smile flashed across his lean face, but he sobered quickly. ''It's the same thing, Joni. You're part of the Peterson family. Herb and I both think of you that way.''

The glow of her gallant rescue dimmed. Not that she minded being considered a Peterson, but Joni realized she'd been hoping for a more personal response. She ought to be grateful that she hadn't received one, she reminded herself. She needed to keep her distance.

''Jeff went home with the Owenses,'' she said. ''So I can rest.''

''Have you known them long?''

The man didn't trust anyone! ''Three years, since the kids started school together,'' she said.

''I'm glad to see they're sticking by you.'' He guided her away from the stands. ''Let's get you home, shall we?''

The sudden tensing of his body sent a spurt of fear rushing through her. Joni braced for danger until she saw the reason for his reaction.

Red liquid smeared the hood of his blue car, spattering the windshield and dripping onto the bumper. It appeared that someone had tossed a can of paint onto the hood and fled. She saw no scrawled slogans or messages.

The nearby parking slots were empty. With a shake of his head, Dirk bent to check the pavement, possibly for footprints.

''I can't imagine who did this,'' Joni said. ''We've never had vandalism at a game before.''

''I doubt this is a random act.'' He circled the sedan.

"If it were, it's likely that paint would've been thrown onto other cars, and someone would undoubtedly have called the police."

"Do you think Kim did it?" Joni asked dubiously. "She was angry, but I have trouble imagining that she carries a bucket of paint in her car."

"The coach was out here for a long time after he ripped his pants," Dirk said. "He didn't look as if he liked me very much, either."

"Could be a lot of people." She sighed.

Pulling a tissue from his pocket, he spit on it and rubbed the paint. The tissue came away streaked with pink. "It's water soluble, which means it might wash off. I'm sure the car rental company would appreciate that."

"Aren't you going to report it?"

Dirk pulled his cellular phone from his pocket. "I doubt it'll do much good, and you need to rest. But I suppose we'd better."

Joni nearly regretted making the suggestion by the time the police got through. Although one of the officers let her sit in his car, it wasn't much more comfortable than the bleachers, and MacDougall spent an interminable amount of time taking samples and looking around the lot.

Worse, he didn't find anything useful. No telltale athletic shoe print, nothing to link the incident to anyone specific.

"We'll have the lab test the substance," the detective said, "but I'd say it's some kids pulling a prank."

Dirk didn't look satisfied, but he held his tongue.

Finally, the police departed and Joni sank wearily into the front seat of the rental. At least the windows remained clear enough for Dirk to drive. As he slid behind the wheel, she said, "By the way, I appreciated how you encouraged Jeff."

"He's a good kid."

In her concern over the paint, she'd almost forgotten the game's exciting climax. "He even scored the winning goal."

"I'm just proud of him for doing his best."

The way Dirk's mouth quirked reminded Joni so sharply of her son that she reached out to cup his cheek. When she pulled her hand away, it retained a lingering impression of firm skin with a hint of masculine roughness. "You remind me so much of him sometimes," she explained.

"Of Lowell?" He backed out of the space.

"No, Jeff."

Dirk pulled into the street, sitting stiffly erect. Finally, almost as if asking a question, he said, "He has our mother's coloring."

Joni supposed she should drop the subject. With Lowell, she'd learned to navigate a conversation as though it were a minefield. Some subjects, such as her own impoverished background and his relationship with his brother, had been guaranteed to put a chill in the air. From Dirk's reticence, she gathered that Jeff's parentage was similar forbidden ground. Well, she was tired of circumspection. They needed to get the subject out in the open.

"Why are you in such denial about it?" she asked.

"About what?"

He was deliberately being obtuse, which confused her. It was uncharacteristic of Dirk. "About Jeff. Being his father, I mean."

He slammed on the brakes. They'd reached a stop sign, but that didn't explain the abruptness.

"What?" As the word exploded from his mouth, amazement transformed his face.

He hadn't known. At the realization, Joni's stomach tightened. How was this possible? What on earth was going on?

And what sort of Pandora's box had she just opened?

Chapter Eight

"You do remember donating sperm, don't you?" Joni's words echoed in Dirk's ears.

He felt as if he'd stepped into an alternate reality. Could Jeff be his son after all? "Yes, but Lowell said it wasn't needed."

Behind them, a car honked. He tapped the gas and turned onto San Bernardo Road.

Joni clasped her hands so tightly the knuckles whitened. "He told you Jeff was his?"

"It isn't true?"

"I can't believe—"

"I had no idea—"

They both stopped. After a moment, Joni said, "There's no question about it. Once the doctors found he was sterile, Lowell never darkened their doors again. I went by myself for the inseminations."

"They couldn't have found some way to use his sperm?"

"He never provided any more," she said. "It was as if he wanted to put the whole thing out of his head."

"Jeff's my son," he said wonderingly.

"It never occurred to me that Lowell would lie to you," she admitted.

Dirk drove in silence as he tried to absorb this startling news. Finally, he said, "Do you think Lowell...that he held it against Jeff?"

Joni picked a loose strip of blush-colored polish from one fingernail. "Not that I could tell. He wasn't the type to change diapers or push a stroller, but I think he loved our son. Since the divorce, he'd made a real effort to spend time with him."

Dirk's mind surged with more questions, many of them difficult to put into words. One took shape at last. "Who else knows?"

"No one," she said. "Donald was already dead, and we saw no reason to tell Herb."

"What about Jeff?"

A slight shake of her head rippled her hair. She'd worn it loose today, in a long blond pageboy that made her look like a teenager. "I do want to tell him eventually, but I have to find the right way and the right time. I don't want to confuse him."

Confuse him? Dirk thought wryly. How about confusing an adult male who was trying, painfully, to absorb an impossible fact?

He had a son. A child. His own offspring.

He'd known this was possible, of course, when he made the donation, but he'd figured a child would belong to him only in the most abstract sense. In real life, any issue would be Lowell's, legally and emotionally.

Now Lowell was gone. And Dirk wasn't merely an uncle anymore. This revelation had changed everything in his universe.

They pulled into Joni's driveway. As he exited the car, Dirk scanned the area for danger and was even more relieved than usual not to see anything amiss. One crisis at a time was plenty.

In the kitchen, Joni heated soup and rolls for lunch. "I guess I dropped a bombshell, huh?" she said. "I assumed you knew."

"A reasonable assumption," he admitted. "What on earth was my brother thinking when he made up such a story?"

"That you would never find out, I suppose." She carried their soup mugs to the table. "If Lowell were alive, you wouldn't have."

"Lies have a way of being found out, don't they?" he said. "I'm glad you want to tell…Jeff the truth." He couldn't say the words "our son." Jeff had been Lowell's son for eight years, and that bond would never, and should never, be entirely broken.

As he ate, Dirk was struck by the casual intimacy of the scene. He was sitting across a kitchen table from the woman who had borne him a child.

From her scattering of freckles to the unaltered boyishness of her body, there was something intrinsically honest about Joni. Wispy bangs fell across her forehead as she curled in the chair, regarding him with mingled sympathy and wariness.

He relished being able to read her moods, at least some of the time. For a man who had learned early to hide his own feelings, her emotional openness came as a relief.

"How would you like to handle this?" he asked.

"Breaking the news to Jeff, you mean?"

"Not exactly." He buttered a roll, paying so little attention that he buttered his index finger, as well. "You know my work is overseas, which puts quite a distance between us. Would you like me to come home for holidays, that sort of thing? We could work out a schedule, something you and Jeff could count on."

"Dirk, I never meant to impose on you." Sunlight

streaming through the window intensified the green depths of her eyes. "You're free to go on as before, if you like."

"That hardly seems fair to Jeff."

"He likes you, and I think a relationship with you would help him as he grows," she said. "But I know you only agreed to be a donor because Lowell pressured you. As far as I'm concerned, you have no obligations."

No obligations. That was what Dirk had always wanted—a life filled with nothing except what he took on voluntarily. He'd realized in retrospect that he hadn't postponed marrying Elena simply because of business opportunities. He hadn't been able to face committing himself permanently to satisfying someone else's needs. The prospect was like being locked inside an airless room, the way he'd felt growing up beneath his father's thumb.

Jeff was different; he hadn't had any say in the arrangements made by grown-ups, and he could hardly be expected to meet his own needs. Besides, being around the boy was more fun than Dirk would have expected.

"I owe him something," he said. "Whether I chose this situation or not, I'm the only father he's got left."

Joni gave him a ghost of a smile. "Herb would enjoy seeing you more often, too. Sure, some kind of holiday schedule would be fine."

"We can work it out over the next few days."

"Great."

They finished their meal with no further discussion. Afterward, Dirk checked the premises again, made sure Joni locked the door behind him, then set off. He had a lot of ground to cover in his investigation and he couldn't afford to delay.

First, however, he paid a visit to Viento del Mar's only car wash. While soapy water cleaned the red paint from his hood, he called one of his assistants in Rome and went over the progress of a new business shipping medicinal herbs from Indonesia to France. He had completed the initial work and turned over day-to-day operations to a manager. Nevertheless, he kept an eye on his projects to make sure everything ran smoothly.

All traces of the paint were gone by the time he tipped the attendant. Whoever had thrown it had either intended more to annoy than to harm or had simply seized whatever paint was at hand. The killer, or someone acting on impulse?

The route to the Peterson estate took Dirk past the Viento del Mar Country Club. From the road, he could see part of the golf course and, behind a stand of trees, the red-tiled roof of the main building.

As a young man, he'd enjoyed having access to a swimming pool, weight room, racquetball courts and other facilities. He'd paid little attention to the gossip, the social climbing or the snobbery.

Now he realized how uncomfortable the setting must have been for Joni, especially after Kim returned from San Francisco. Nevertheless, as Lowell's wife, she might have taken her place if she'd shared the in crowd's values.

But she hadn't. Thank goodness.

He turned from the main road onto winding Pioneer Lane. It snaked through a canyon, working its way upward through heavy brush. A couple of miles along, he angled onto a private driveway. Palm trees lined the route to the one-story Spanish-style mansion. With its courtyard, tile-covered fountain and arched entryway, it reminded him of a Moorish palace.

Behind it lay tennis courts, a five-car garage and a guest cottage used by the three full-time staff members. Since Lowell's death, the main house was unoccupied; Herb had moved out long ago, seeking a more convivial atmosphere in town.

In his will, Lowell had left the house equally to Dirk and Jeff, but neither was ever likely to live there. Dirk hoped he could sell the place to a family that would make good use of it. A family with children...

Unbidden, an image popped into his mind of Jeff sailing a toy boat in the fountain while Joni watched, laughing. How could Lowell have been foolish enough to let them go?

He parked in a shaded turnaround. As he got out, a portly woman in a flowered shirtwaist dress hurried down the front steps. From her stiffly coiffed hair to her polished pumps, there was no mistaking the redoubtable Mrs. Wright.

The housekeeper had nearly reached her station wagon when she became aware of him. She halted abruptly, lost her grip on her purse and snatched it halfway to the ground. "My goodness! You startled me!"

"Sorry." He gave her a friendly grin. "I didn't mean to."

Hired during his mother's final illness when he was twelve, Mrs. Wright had made sure Dirk was ferried to and from school and had a lunch packed each morning. She wasn't the type to get personally involved, and he hadn't wanted her to.

"We're glad to have you back." Composure recovered, she spoke with her customary dignity. "You should tell Cook if you're planning to stay for dinner."

"I'm not moving back," he said. "I need to go through my brother's papers."

"I see." Her expression remained impassive.

"Off to run errands?"

"So to speak." The frown lines deepened in her forehead. "I hope you don't expect me to account for every minute of my day."

Somewhat taken aback by her frostiness, Dirk tried to reassure her. "Considering that you're on the premises almost all the time, certainly not." Mrs. Wright shared the three-bedroom guest house with the groundskeeper and his wife, the cook. "Take as long as you like."

With a nod, she departed. As he let himself into the house, Dirk wondered why Mrs. Wright had become so defensive when he'd only been making conversation. He also wondered why she'd taken a dislike to Joni. Had his sister-in-law's open, frank personality unsettled the housekeeper? Or did Mrs. Wright have something to hide?

He really ought to be careful about becoming paranoid, Dirk chided himself. The housekeeper had always kept her private life to herself.

Even if he hadn't known how much she cared about Lowell, Mrs. Wright was overweight and probably in her sixties. It would take more imagination than he possessed to picture her lurking in the woods at night, let alone overcoming Lowell on Joni's patio.

Dirk paced along a hallway past the oversize, sunken living room. Dark woods and sparse Mediterranean furniture created a cool impression, warmed by colorful throw pillows and wall hangings.

He thought of Joni living here, sharing breakfast with Lowell, bringing home Jeff as a baby. If she'd made any changes to reflect her personality, however, they'd been removed long ago.

Bypassing a large den and another hallway, he reached the master suite. This had once been his parents' room and then Lowell's, but thanks to the efficient Mrs. Wright, it appeared as impersonal as the public rooms. No hairbrushes bristled on the dressing table. In the entertainment corner, the CDs and laser discs stood neatly in place. Whatever mess the police had made in their search, Mrs. Wright must have cleared it.

Dirk slid open one of the two double closets. Inside, Lowell's clothes hung neatly, the suits and shirts in cleaners' bags, the athletic clothes pressed and placed on hangers. Everything was so tidy, he detected not even a trace of aftershave lotion.

In the second closet, he found two tuxedos in garment bags and rows of expensive leather shoes on racks. Dirk checked for jogging shoes that might have left the tread he'd seen, but there were none.

An office opened off the bedroom. At one time, it had served as his mother's sewing and dressing room, but wood paneling and office furniture had transformed it into a man's hideaway. Inside, Dirk found a desk, a wooden filing cabinet and a leather couch. A top-of-the-line computer and a printer-fax-copier covered the desktop.

Through the blinds, he could see the patch of lawn where his grandfather had long ago erected a swing set and a play fort. They'd been removed during his teen years, but it seemed a shame that Lowell hadn't replaced them for Jeff.

Easing onto the swivel chair, Dirk turned on the computer and searched its memory. Lowell's penchant for organization simplified the job: files from the printing company were grouped in one directory, games in another. The large number of entertainment programs mostly featured a sports theme. Even the preprogrammed Internet sites turned out to be either business or sports related.

After determining that the files held nothing relevant to his investigation, Dirk switched off the computer and went through the desk. In the top drawer, he noted neatly laid-out pens, pads, a stapler and two pairs of scissors. Below that, he found a few receipts and the latest quarterly reports from mutual funds.

The filing cabinet yielded income-tax forms, financial statements, insurance information and routine correspondence. Nothing useful there, either.

The family's safe had been placed, not very cleverly, behind a painting. After opening it with the combination the family lawyer had given him, Dirk found only a duplicate of Lowell's will alongside a few other legal documents.

With a sense of frustration, he closed it and replaced the painting. What had he hoped to uncover anyway?

Some detail that would help clear Joni, he admitted silently. Or at least something that might sway MacDougall's mind.

But what? If there'd been a bitter dispute of the kind likely to inspire murder, it could hardly have been kept secret in this town. And had Lowell received any threats, he would've turned them over to the police or his lawyer.

The bathroom proved equally sterile; even the cord to the electric shaver was fastidiously coiled. Returning to the bedroom, Dirk sifted through the nightstand but found nothing unusual.

There were some items of jewelry in the top drawer of the dresser, along with neatly folded underwear and T-shirts. The second drawer contained an electric blanket in such pristine condition that it might never have been used. The bottom drawer was empty.

Irrationally, Dirk wished some hint remained of his brother's presence. Whiskers in the sink. A magazine open on the nightstand. Mismatched socks in the drawer.

It was as if Mrs. Wright had removed any sign of Lowell's individuality, he thought with a flash of resentment.

The memorial service wasn't even scheduled until Monday afternoon. What was her hurry to tidy up?

But then, he recalled, she'd always dealt with stress by throwing herself into her work. When his mother died, the closet and bathroom had been cleared right after the funeral. He supposed a psychologist might say that such compulsiveness was a way of regaining control when her world went topsy-turvy.

Returning to the top drawer, Dirk examined the jewelry. Those items should go to Jeff, he determined, so he removed a dress watch, a couple of gold tie clasps and a set of silver cuff links. He was about to close the drawer when he decided to feel around the back of it one more time. In a corner, his hand brushed something velvety, and he pulled it out.

It was a small black jeweler's box. Inside, two large diamonds winked from a pair of crescent earrings. A crumpled piece of stiff white paper was wedged to one side. Smoothed out, it proved to be Lowell's business card. A message in his brother's jagged writing said, "Kim. No hard feelings. L."

On the back, in a different hand, was scribbled, "You can't buy me off. You'll pay, but not in money." There was no signature.

So Kim had returned the peace offering with a threat. That was hardly incriminating enough to make her a suspect, though, Dirk reflected as he tucked the velvet box into his pocket. Any woman who'd been dumped might write a note like that.

A glance through the rest of the house uncovered nothing more of interest. His time would be better spent at the printing plant, where round-the-clock shifts worked all weekend. Dirk had a lot of people to interview and documents to examine, especially relating to a publishing venture his brother had planned.

Even if he couldn't learn anything useful about Lowell, he needed to put the place in order. For Jeff's sake.

For his son.

BY THE TIME THE OWENSES dropped Jeff at home, Joni had awakened from her nap and started dinner. Dirk wouldn't be eating with them; he'd phoned to say he'd grab a sandwich at the plant.

"What are we having?" Jeff asked as soon as Bobby and his mother drove off. Fred had already left for his regular Saturday-night basketball game. "Oh, good, spaghetti! Mom, you should see our costumes. I mean, they're not done yet, but Mrs. Owens has this pattern…"

He chattered on while Joni stirred the sauce. The pattern did sound perfect, and thanks to Kathryn's skill with a sewing machine, the costumes would probably turn out better than anything they could buy at a store.

Joni did her best to return the Owenses' kindness by writing press releases for Kathryn's garden club and editing the scripts Fred used when calling insurance prospects. Also, last summer, she'd tutored both boys in spelling, a subject given short shrift by their school curriculum.

Still, she would never be able to do as much for the Owenses as they did for her. Whisking Jeff away from the soccer field today, for example. Thanks to them, he hadn't heard Kim's cruel words. *He only married you on the rebound.…You cheap, social-climbing little tramp!*

None of it was true. Lowell hadn't married her until two years after Kim took her heart to San Francisco. He'd had plenty of time to recover. As for social climbing, anyone who knew her realized how laughable that accusation was.

But a lot of people didn't know her. They made assumptions or they listened to the grapevine.

Dirk's accompanying her to the game might have set their tongues wagging in yet another direction, she supposed. Well, that would pass soon enough when he returned to his work and left Viento del Mar behind.

The prospect of only seeing him once or twice a year left a hollow feeling in her stomach. Or maybe, Joni told herself firmly, she was just hungry.

She set plates of spaghetti and salad on the table. Jeff ran to wash his hands, then scooted his chair close to the table and tucked into the food. Watching him eat, Joni wondered if other people had noted the resemblance to Dirk. She was glad he'd agreed to remain a part of Jeff's life even if it was only for special occasions.

While Jeff cleared the table, she loaded the dishwasher. At his request, she let him mop off the table, although he used so much cleanser that she had to dry it with a towel.

After the nightly ritual of toothbrushing and reading together, she kissed her son good-night and went to watch TV. But she quickly tired of it. Besides, it made her uneasy not to be able to hear any noises from outside.

All day, Joni had avoided thinking about Dirk's discovery of a footprint and a natural blind so close to the house, but in the lengthening silence, she could no longer avoid it. She was still being stalked, probably by the same person who'd murdered Lowell. He might even have been at the soccer game and splashed the paint on Dirk's car, although that act seemed petty compared to murder.

In her anxiety, Joni peeled another strip of polish off a fingernail. She decided to give herself a manicure. Glad to find something to do, she went to the dressing table in the oversize master bathroom and pulled out her manicure set. Soon the piercing scent of acetone filled the air.

Working on something concrete helped focus her thoughts. *Scrub off the polish.* The stalker wasn't some faceless monster. He or she had a name, maybe a job. *Rub hard, all the way to the cuticle.* If she ran through the possibilities systematically, maybe she could figure out who it was. It must either be someone she knew or someone who'd seen her and developed a fixation. A store clerk, a deliveryman, an orderly at the hospital.

She pictured Charlie earlier today, scowling at Dirk. She'd met the coach when soccer practice began in August, not long before the harassment started.

Charlie made a natural suspect. He'd shown an interest in Joni. And he'd been absent today long enough to have splashed paint on Dirk's car. He was also a relative newcomer to town, with no family here.

Yet Joni couldn't help wanting to give him the benefit of the doubt. She knew how it felt to be an outsider and the subject of other people's unwarranted assumptions. Besides, she'd known Charlie such a short time, it was hard to imagine his growing so possessive as to become homicidal.

When she was finished doing her nails, she turned on the hair dryer, impatient to have them set. A noise from Jeff's room, however, made her switch off the dryer.

The sound came again, a crunch or a scrape. Not from her son's room, but from outside, on the patio.

The stalker.

Anxiety billowed through her. She could barely think.

She should call the police. But…Dirk. Maybe it was Dirk.

He might've come home and decided to walk around the murder scene once more. Contacting the police would not only make Joni look foolish, it might make them less likely to respond in the future.

Taking a deep breath, she moved down the hall. In the utility room, she turned on the outside light and peered through the glass panel. All she could see was a circle of weak illumination.

Then, a twitch of movement—and a gray-striped cat strolled into view. It lowered its head to sniff at something. Curiosity satisfied, it ambled to her rose bed and squatted. Darn that animal! If it wanted to relieve itself, it should use the woods.

Grabbing a broom and a flashlight, Joni hurried out. "Beat it, buster!" For a moment, the cat held its position, regarding her with glowing eyes, then fled.

Joni scanned the yard and called Dirk's name a couple of times before walking to where she could see the driveway, but his car wasn't there. The noise she'd heard must have come from the cat.

About to go inside, she remembered that the animal had been sniffing something, so she trained her flashlight on the patio.

The beam stopped on a dark patch near where she'd fallen Wednesday night. She could have sworn there'd been nothing there earlier today.

Joni edged closer. The patch appeared to be thick, even gooey. Beneath the light, it glistened a dark reddish-brown. Like blood.

It took a moment to register something even more frightening: a swish of leaves from the direction of the blind, then a hard thumping as someone rushed toward her.

A scream welled deep inside, but Joni's throat clamped shut. All that came out was a rasping breath, as if she were strangling.

Chapter Nine

Joni's hands tightened on the broomstick. Fighting tremors of fear, she braced herself with the bristles held straight in front of her.

Into the light eased a slim figure, a woman with straight black hair above an oversize green sweater. "It is me." Celia Lu halted a few feet shy of the broom.

Joni lowered it. "You startled me!" Her breath came shallowly, and her chest constricted. The symptoms of panic refused to abate even though danger no longer threatened.

"Where is your brother-in-law?" her neighbor asked. "Is he not here?"

"He'll be back soon." Feeling suddenly weak, Joni grasped the edge of the glass table. "There's something on the patio. I think it's blood."

Celia produced her own flashlight and inspected the ground. "How disgusting!" She fumbled with something next to the house.

Joni didn't realize what her neighbor was doing until water from a hose swished across the patio. "Wait! Stop!"

The flow halted. "What is wrong? I am cleaning it for you."

"Celia, what if that's human blood? The police might be able to trace the DNA or something."

The older woman stared at her for a moment or two until comprehension dawned. "You think it is killer? I assumed…an animal, perhaps?"

"It might've been left here as a threat," Joni said. "Someone splashed red paint on Dirk's car earlier today."

Celia shuddered. "I am glad I locked my back door. Quickly. We go inside."

It was only when they'd reached the security of the kitchen that Joni began to think clearly again. A stalker might have made that mess, but the cat *had* left dead animals on the patio before. Perhaps this time a large one had managed to drag itself away. She hoped it survived.

"It is good your son sleeps soundly," Celia said. "Or does he stay at a friend's house?"

"He's here." Joni listened but heard no noise from Jeff's room. "That kid could sleep through a nuclear bomb."

"That is healthy, I think."

"Would you like some tea?" Receiving a nod, Joni put the kettle on. While they waited for it to boil, she asked, "Aren't you afraid to go wandering around in the dark, considering what's happened?"

"I forget about danger." Only a fine web of lines near her eyes hinted that Celia must be near fifty. Her habitually unruffled demeanor contributed to the impression of agelessness. "When my husband is not home, I like company. Besides, I hear a rumor that I wished to ask you about. I do not like to rely on—what do you call them? Third parties."

"A rumor?" Joni couldn't imagine where Celia would pick up gossip about her. But she supposed her neighbor must know other families, some of whom had children at Jeff's school. "What kind of rumor?"

"From the soccer game today." Celia, who as a matter of custom had removed her shoes when she entered the house, perched on one of the kitchen chairs. "That snooty Mrs. DeLong. She was very insulting to you."

"One of your friends overheard?" Joni steeped tea bags in two cups and carried them to the table. "Most people had gone by then."

"My friend—a lady I know from church—caught only a few words. Thank you. Is there any sugar?"

"Of course." Joni provided it, along with a small tin of cookies that she kept for company.

"Delicious," Celia pronounced. "No one likes Mrs. DeLong. She has a very poor character."

Joni wondered to what extent her neighbor had dropped by to seek company and to what extent she was fishing for more gossip to carry back to her friends. It was an uncharitable speculation, she decided, and dismissed it.

Natives of Hong Kong, the Lus had fled before its return to Chinese rule. Mr. Lu held a position with an American bank, so they hadn't suffered economically, but the cultural differences and the isolation must have been stressful.

"If you don't mind my changing the subject," Joni said, "why did you decide to move to Viento del Mar?"

"Perhaps it was foolish. My husband has a long commute. He works in Santa Barbara." After two cookies, the lid was returned to the tin, though not without a certain wistfulness on Celia's part. "He often goes overseas, so he let me pick our home. My cousin lives in town, so I chose here."

Joni hadn't been aware that the Lus had relatives in the area. "I don't think I've met your cousin, have I?"

Celia made a face. "He is a busy man, a dentist. I

thought his wife and I would be friends, but she has no time for me. All she wants is for me to baby-sit. I would be glad to do it, but only if we are friends. I am not her free servant!''

Despite the fierce words, Joni could see the sadness in her neighbor's eyes. No wonder the woman sought company; she'd chosen an out-of-the-way place to live in the hopes of being among family, and instead she was often alone.

If Celia hadn't come by Wednesday night, there was no telling how long Joni might have lain dazed in the storm. ''Well, her loss is my gain, as we say.''

Her neighbor puzzled over the saying for a moment. ''I think that is a compliment.''

''Definitely.''

A smile warmed the usually serious face. ''Do not worry. I will watch for this intruder. And if I hear that stuck-up Mrs. DeLong say bad things about you, I will call her many bad names! In Chinese.''

Joni laughed. ''Thank you.''

By the time Dirk came home, the two of them were watching an *I Love Lucy* rerun and laughing out loud. He looked tired but relieved to see her feeling well, and there seemed no point in telling him about the blood, or whatever it had been, until morning.

LYING IN BED ALL NIGHT, knowing Joni was only a few dozen feet away, set Dirk's body throbbing.

He'd been struck by her natural sensuality last night when she came to the door with her face aglow from watching a comedy. Warm light seemed to shine from within, and he'd become intensely aware of the softness of her skin and the slimness of her body in the clinging jeans and T-shirt.

Exhaustion from a long evening of evaluating the printing company's financial status had made it easy to fall asleep. The problem came when Dirk awoke about two in the morning and, en route to the bathroom, heard her easy breathing.

The house radiated Joni's essence. It brought out, almost painfully, the demands of his own masculinity. He nearly walked down the hall and opened her door to watch her as she slept. Only the knowledge that it would be an invasion of privacy held him back.

Dirk wasn't sure what he wanted or expected from this woman. To go to bed with Joni and then leave would hurt her. And, possibly, him, as well.

He knew what he was: a modern-day adventurer. The prospect of a home and family tantalized him, but the wildness of his own nature would never allow him to stay in one place for long.

Why was he suddenly yearning for something he couldn't have? Perhaps, he decided as he tossed sleeplessly, it was a reaction to Lowell's death. A sense of the past slipping away, of human connections vanishing.

Yet he'd just discovered the greatest human connection of all. He had a child.

The worst thing he could do, Dirk reflected, would be to dally with the boy's mother. Their son needed them both.

He finally dozed, only to be yanked from unconsciousness as Jeff bounced into the den. Prying one eye open, Dirk groped for his watch, then sat up sharply. "Eight o'clock? We'll be late for church."

The Petersons traditionally attended Viento del Mar Highlands Church. The service had started at nine o'clock ever since he could remember. Although Dirk wasn't religious, the church was as much a social as a spiritual center for the town's movers and shakers. Furthermore, he knew Herb expected them to attend.

"It's seven." Jeff clicked on his video-game system.

"Eight," Dirk grumbled.

The boy pointed to the digital display on the VCR. It read 7:02.

"It's wrong," Dirk said. "This watch keeps time in every zone around the globe. It doesn't vary by more than one minute per year, and it beeps if the battery runs low."

"Does it also beep when we go off daylight savings time?" Joni asked from the doorway.

The last Sunday in October. He groaned. "I forgot."

"I nearly did, too," she admitted. "I woke up last night and adjusted the time in my room and Jeff's. The VCR resets itself."

"We're not late for church after all," Jeff said. "Aren't you glad?"

Dirk supposed he was.

They ate waffles from the freezer served with plenty of syrup. "Sometimes I make pancakes from scratch," Joni said apologetically as Dirk helped Jeff cut his food. "I'm just not up to it yet."

"Still hurting?" Dirk regarded her with concern. "Maybe you should stay home for a few more days."

"I'd rather not, but I do tire easily." She finished a bite of breakfast. "Lowell's memorial service is at four o'clock tomorrow, isn't it? Maybe Jeff and I should both stay home."

To Dirk's surprise, the boy shook his head vigorously. "Can't you pick me up after school?"

"You're ready to go back?" he asked.

The boy gave him a puzzled frown. "Yeah, sure. They're having pizza for lunch. Besides, Bobby and I always play handball at recess."

The boy's reaction seemed odd, but perhaps he lacked the perspective to realize how permanent death was. At age eight, Dirk supposed he'd have been worried about missing pizza and handball, too.

He glanced at Joni for her reaction. "Do you think it's wise?"

She regarded her son thoughtfully. "If he stays around here, he'll only mope. It's best for him to stick with his routine."

Dirk supposed she was right. He found it easier to deal with his grief by taking action, and Jeff, too, might feel better if he kept busy. "Does he ride the bus?"

"Usually I drop him off on my way to the hospital," Joni said. "The day-care center picks him up afterward, and I collect him there when I finish work."

"I'll drive him in the morning," Dirk said. "You stay home."

To his relief, she agreed. Although only a fading purple bruise remained visible along her temple, Joni's fragile air brought home the fact that she'd been seriously hurt. By the time she applied makeup and dressed for church, however, she gave no sign of being ill. In fact, Dirk thought as he helped her into his car, his sister-in-law was likely to turn heads.

She'd chosen a smoke-gray suit with a dark green blouse that made her eyes glint like emeralds. Freshly washed and fragrant, her blond hair had been twisted into a knot, leaving a fringe around her face.

Jeff wore a navy blazer, a white button-down shirt and tan pants. He looked, Dirk realized with a start, like a miniature version of himself.

When they reached the church, they found quite a few cars already there. Another family entered the large, hushed foyer just as they did. Sideways glances and a deliberate turning away made it clear that they were snubbing Joni. Anger simmered inside Dirk. If he and Herb were willing to give her the benefit of the doubt, who were these people to pass judgment?

As the newcomers disappeared into the sanctuary, a door opened from the adjacent multipurpose room. Out came Mrs. Wright, who started when she caught sight of the new arrivals.

"Mr. Peterson!" The housekeeper, who had joined the church years ago after attending with the family, regarded him anxiously. "Have you seen Mrs. DeLong?"

"Kim?" He hadn't realized the two were even acquainted. "No, why?"

"She's chairman of the hospitality committee." Mrs. Wright gave Jeff a brief smile before continuing. "She was supposed to bring doughnuts for the reception after the service, but she's not here."

The hospitality committee was the domain of the town's social set, with an occasional addition like Mrs. Wright to handle any work the others found tedious. "Anyone can have a flat tire," Dirk pointed out.

"Yes, but she *does* have a car phone." The woman shrugged. "Well, there's nothing I can do about it now." She marched off, still without a word to Joni.

"Boy, that's awful," Jeff said.

If the housekeeper's attitude was affecting his son, Dirk would have to speak to the woman about it. "What is?" he asked cautiously.

"They don't have any doughnuts. I like the jelly ones best. What about you?"

"Chocolate," Dirk said. "Joni?"

"Lemon filled." She chuckled. "For once, I hope Kim shows up."

Inside, Herb had saved seats near the front. When Jeff

ran to his great-grandfather and hugged him, Dirk could see tears glistening in the old man's eyes.

Throughout the service, the room seemed to bristle with undercurrents. Even the minister, a young man who'd been hired after Dirk moved away, made a reference to their shared grief at the loss of a valued friend.

The reception afterward proved short, due to the absence of refreshments. Kim DeLong had not arrived.

"It isn't like her," Mrs. Wright clucked as she poured punch into paper cups.

Kim's friend from the soccer game fussed over a centerpiece of dried flowers. "She did say she hadn't found a costume yet for the Frightful Nightful." That was the country club's annual Halloween party. "Maybe she decided to make a shopping trip to L.A."

"And forgot about the doughnuts?" the housekeeper sniffed. "She should have called someone."

Jeff kept darting to the hallway in hopes of witnessing the arrival of the pastries. At his insistence, Joni went with him to peer out the front door.

Herb steered Dirk into a corner. "What have you found?" he asked without preamble.

"I don't think Joni killed Lowell, and I don't believe he was stalking her. But I haven't got a clue who is."

"Is? Present tense?" His grandfather's brows knitted in alarm.

"Very present tense." Dirk described the duplicate knife, the footprint in the yard and the red paint on his car.

"What do the police think?"

"I've persuaded them to hold off filing charges for the time being," Dirk said. "But I don't think they're eager to complicate their case."

"If their evidence isn't airtight, the lawyer I'm going to hire will mop up the courtroom with them," Herb growled.

Dirk chuckled at his grandfather's ferocity. Despite his heart condition, the man would go to any lengths to defend his family.

When Joni and Jeff returned, they invited Herb to picnic with them at Del Mar Park, but he declined. "Just be careful," he said in parting.

An hour later, Dirk and Joni had changed into casual clothes and were finishing their take-out fried chicken at a picnic table while Jeff scampered off to play. He didn't know the other two children at the playground, but soon they were all running and whooping together.

"He makes friends easily," Dirk observed. "He's more like Lowell than me in that respect."

"Or me, either. I think he takes after Herb," Joni said. "Listen, I need to tell you something."

He listened to her description of the blood, or whatever it had been, on the patio. "Did you look out there this morning?"

"There was a trace of brown along the edge of the patio, but it might have been left from Wednesday," she said.

"It didn't appear to be red paint?"

"Too brown and too thick."

"Since we're playing show-and-tell, I'd like you to see this." From his pocket, Dirk pulled out the black velvet jeweler's box. He'd been carrying it with him, uneasy at leaving it anywhere else. "Lowell's kiss-off gift to Kim."

Joni read the note. "Everybody knew she was furious. It's the kind of threat people make all the time."

"But usually not to people who get killed," he pointed out.

Sunlight played across her face as she rested her chin on one palm. In contrast to earlier this morning, a healthy pink flushed her cheeks, and threads of reddish-gold glinted in the hair that had pulled loose from its knot.

"Kim would certainly have a motive to harass me. But I can't see her overpowering Lowell."

"Not to mention that the shoe print I saw in the blind was man-size," Dirk noted. As the events at church this morning ran through his mind, he added, "By the way, was Mrs. Wright always this chilly toward you?"

"She used to acknowledge me, but not by much," she said.

"Any idea why you two didn't get along?"

"It wasn't so bad right after we were married. Then a couple of years before the divorce, I stepped on her toes, I guess." Joni pursed her lips at the memory. "I asked her where she went in the middle of the day. She would leave for several hours, two or three times a week."

"Did she tell you?"

"No, she blew up. She said no one had ever questioned her integrity before," Joni said. "I didn't mean to criticize. It just struck me as odd."

He recalled how the housekeeper had bristled yesterday when he asked if she was running errands. "What did Lowell say?"

"He told me Mrs. Wright was like a member of the family and she could come and go as she pleased." Joni's voice tightened as she recounted the rebuke. "Do you think I was out of line?"

"Considering you were her employer, I wouldn't say so. If she'd made special arrangements with Lowell, he should've advised you." Why *had* the woman been so touchy anyway? And where did she go?

Jeff and the other children jumped onto the swings and launched themselves into the air, whooping with glee. Eight years old. Dirk couldn't even remember how it had felt to be that age. He wondered what his son had been like as an infant or a toddler. When he took his first step. On his first day at school.

"I've missed so much," he said.

"You found more than the police did." Joni reached across the table to pick a leaf off his hair.

The touch of her fingers heated his scalp. "I meant about Jeff, not the investigation. Like his birth. And birthdays. All the special times I wasn't there."

"If you'd known he was your son, would it have made any difference?" she asked.

Dirk had to admit the truth. "I suppose not. I did what my brother asked, then put it out of my mind. Maybe that was noble or maybe it was selfish. Nothing I can do about it now."

"June seventeenth," she said.

"What's that?"

"His birthday." She smiled. "We'll be expecting you next year."

"I wouldn't miss it." At the far edge of the playground, a shadow moved in a thicket of tall bushes. Under the circumstances, Dirk was on permanent alert. "Any idea who that might be?"

Joni followed his gaze. "I can't tell."

"What's on the far side of those bushes?"

"A soccer field. We practice there on Wednesday afternoons, in fact."

If any teams were using the field now, they'd be making plenty of noise, Dirk thought. He heard nothing beyond the three children on the playground.

"I'll go check it out." Forcing himself to pretend disinterest, he strolled toward the field.

The shadow shifted as he approached, then vanished. Quickening his pace, Dirk loped into the thicket. A branch snagged his sweater, and by the time he tore free, he could see a man's figure vanishing across the small slope that separated the low-lying park from the street beyond.

Dirk broke into a run. He had no reason to connect this onlooker to Lowell's murder, but he'd feel better if he knew who the guy was. By the time Dirk topped the rise, he saw nothing but an empty sidewalk, a residential neighborhood and a scattering of parked cars.

He had left Joni alone at the picnic table. Suppose the intruder doubled back? Unwilling to risk searching for the man, Dirk returned to the playground.

"No luck," he said.

Shivering, Joni wrapped her arms around herself. She'd worn a lavender sweater, not heavy enough for the cool October breeze.

"We could go home," Dirk suggested.

"No. Jeff's enjoying himself. He needs to release some of his grief and tension."

He wasn't going to let her catch cold no matter how cautious he intended to be, so Dirk sat beside Joni and drew her against his chest. Her trembling eased, even as fire ignited inside his own body. "Better?" he asked gruffly.

"Much better," she whispered.

They nestled together, watching Jeff and his new friends play pirates on a jungle gym. As heat flowed between them, the floral scent of her shampoo proved a heady perfume.

Just sitting there, his arms wrapped around her, was an intensely sensual experience. It was a rare beautiful moment as they silently watched their son play.

An hour later, Jeff's friends scampered off to join their parents. Reluctantly, Dirk conceded it was time to go.

"Maybe we can see them again sometime," Jeff said.

"Andy and Maggy come here almost every Sunday. Could we come back next week, Mom?"

"We can try," Joni said.

"Uncle Dirk?"

"If I'm still—yes, sure." He wouldn't be gone that soon, would he? Dirk tried not to think about all the Sundays after that. The other afternoons that would pass as Jeff grew, the thousands of moments he wouldn't share.

At home, to spare the front carpet from Jeff's sandy shoes, they went to the back door. Dirk, watching for any sign of the stalker, noticed a brick askew in a built-in planter alongside the house.

"Did you do that?" he asked, pointing.

Joni stopped. "Oh, my goodness. That's where I hide the spare key!"

"Jeff? Did you move that this morning?"

The boy shook his head.

Joni bent to examine the brick. "Don't touch it!" Dirk said. "There might be fingerprints."

"I want to know if the key's here!" Dropping to her knees, she pulled the brick out and scooped up a small object. "Thank goodness!"

Could there be some innocent explanation for the loose brick? "When's the last time you took it out?"

"I can't remember," Joni said.

"Thursday." They turned toward Jeff. "Mrs. Owens took it out," he explained. "Remember, I had to get some stuff to sleep over at Grampa's house."

"That's right. She brought me clean clothes, too." Joni's voice quavered as she added, "But the brick wasn't like this yesterday or I'd have noticed."

"Who else knows about the key?" Dirk asked.

"Just Herb."

And anyone who's been watching the house from the

blind, he thought grimly. "I'll get someone at the printshop to come out and change the locks. For the time being, please stop hiding a key."

"Don't worry," she said fervently.

He insisted on going inside first, listening, watching, feeling for changes in air pressure. The only thing he noticed was a slow, creeping sensation on his skin. Dirk had learned to trust his gut feelings, and they were shouting, *Intruder!*

"If it's the stalker, I'm sure he's left some indication he was here," he said. "He'd want to flaunt himself."

Joni turned to Jeff. "You stay right here in the hall while we look."

"Not by myself!" he protested.

"Both of you go into the kitchen and wait by the phone," Dirk said. "Be ready to call 911."

He poked through the house, every sense on edge. Even ordinary noises seemed sharper and the smells harsher than usual. However, no drawers had been ripped open and nothing appeared damaged. But there was a final test.

Thanks to his years in security work, Dirk always made small folds in the edges of his clothing that would fall open if they were disturbed. He opened the end table in the den and examined his clothing without moving it. The folds were gone.

Someone had poked through his things. At the discovery, the hairs bristled on the back of his neck.

As Dirk straightened, he noticed a hint of orange beneath the table. On closer inspection, it revealed itself to be a small ruffled ball of orange and purple. Squatting, he plucked it from the carpet. It was instantly recognizable as a fringed pom-pom pin, the kind Kim DeLong had been wearing the last time Dirk saw her.

Chapter Ten

Detective MacDougall brought a crime-scene crew to the house. Joni wasn't thrilled about the mess they made, but she was glad that at least he was taking the break-in seriously.

Or so she hoped until he reported that the investigators had found nothing aside from the pom-pom pin. They could only assume that the intruder must have worn gloves and put plastic bags over his shoes.

She could read the unspoken tag line in his eyes. *If there really was an intruder.*

"I'm afraid we don't have a lot to go on," the detective growled as the team finished its work.

"What did you learn about the red paint?" Dirk asked.

"It's a brand the hardware store sells, although they don't remember anyone buying that shade recently," MacDougall said. "Too bad your neighbor hosed down the brown stuff on the patio. We couldn't find anything to test."

They stood on the front porch, watching for a machinist who worked the weekend shift at Peterson Printing. Dirk had arranged for him to rekey all the locks as soon as the police finished.

"What about the pin?" she asked. "And the threatening note Kim DeLong wrote to Lowell?"

MacDougall's face had a pouchy look, possibly from being called out three times on a weekend, or maybe from frustration. "The booster club sells those pins at games. As for the note, it doesn't prove anything."

She hated to admit it, but he was right. Their evidence didn't add up to much.

"I have one more question for you," MacDougall went on. "I didn't realize yesterday, Mr. Peterson, that you were staying on the premises. Don't you think that raises certain questions about your objectivity, if nothing else?"

She saw a muscle jump in Dirk's jaw. The detective's implication was unfair, and yet...

Since Dirk moved into the house, she'd been subliminally aware of him even when they were apart. The low timbre of his voice echoed in her bones; she awoke with vague memories of dreams filled with caresses and whispers. In the shower, when she passed the creamy soap across her skin, she could almost feel his presence, watching, touching, helping.

Could she be objective? Could he?

"My nephew and his mother are being stalked on the same property where my brother was murdered," Dirk retorted. "Until we can get a security system installed, I'm staying. Unless you're offering to post a round-the-clock guard?"

"We're a small department. We don't have that kind of manpower."

"Or I could move them both to the Peterson estate," he said. "Joni?"

Until these latest developments, the desire not to uproot Jeff had tipped the balance in favor of staying here. Now that someone had invaded the house, she wasn't sure.

Joni pictured the meandering mansion in its isolated setting. There would be plenty of room for them, but they'd have to contend with a hostile housekeeper, keys floating around in the hands of servants and no neighbors close enough to hear a scream.

She supposed she could move to a motel, but that idea didn't appeal to her, either. Flimsy doors, people coming and going outside and nowhere for her son to play.

"I'm staying put," she said. "This stalker will find me no matter where I go."

Dirk accepted her decision as if he'd expected it. To the detective, he said, "Will you talk to Mrs. DeLong about her pin?"

MacDougall stiffened. "I'm sure that will be part of the investigation."

He wasn't going to dig very hard, and Joni knew why. The detective didn't believe there was a stalker. In his mind, she had killed Lowell, and now she or Dirk, or both, were trying to plant doubt about her guilt.

Dirk must have been thinking along the same lines because after the police left and Jeff went to his room, he said, "I'm afraid that once MacDougall talks to Kim and she denies everything, he's going to turn his evidence over to the D.A."

"You think they'll charge me?" she asked numbly. "Why?"

"Because people don't like to repeat their mistakes," he said.

"What do you mean?"

"I've been doing some research on the Internet." Dirk led the way into the living room, where he stood at the window watching the driveway below. "Trying to get background on everyone who's relevant to this case. That includes the D.A."

From his tone, she suspected she wouldn't like what he'd found. "What did you learn?"

"A few years ago, he declined to file charges in a self-defense case," he said. "The suspect was a former boxer. He said his wife came at him with a knife and he punched her too hard.

"A few months later, they found out he'd previously killed a girlfriend under identical circumstances in another state and gotten off with the same excuse. By that time, he'd disappeared. There was a big stink about letting a murderer get away with it."

"So the D.A. won't back off unless I have ironclad proof I didn't do it." Joni's spirits sank. She didn't even feel strong enough to go back to work yet; how was she going to face a jury?

"Herb's got a top-ranking lawyer in mind," Dirk said. "If you like, I'll engage him right away so he can put his investigative team to work."

"I can't deal with any more people right now." Joni wrapped her arms around herself protectively. "You're the only help I want."

He rubbed his hands lightly along her shoulders. The friction lit a flame deep within her. "I may be doing you more harm than good. Now that he knows I'm staying here, MacDougall's going to discount anything I come across."

"I don't care. I'm glad you're with me." Tears threatened to shatter her composure, but she forced them back. "Dirk, I'm barely holding myself together. I don't know what's wrong. I'm not usually a wimp."

"You've been operating on automatic since Wednesday night." His fingers feathered along her neck beneath her loosened hair. "The trauma is catching up to you."

"Just don't leave. I don't care what MacDougall thinks."

"I'm not going anywhere." He moved closer, curving around her, lowering his face to hers. In another heartbeat, their lips would meet.

Outside, a vehicle downshifted as it ascended the driveway. A Peterson Printing van, she saw from the corner of her eye.

Unwillingly, Dirk released her. "We seem to have the world's worst timing. Tell you what. Tonight, I'm building a fire in the fireplace. Got any hot dogs?"

She smiled. "There's a package in the fridge."

"Any long skewers?"

"Not only that," she said, "I've got marshmallows."

"A woman after my own heart." The words lingered in the air as he went to meet the machinist.

THERE WERE MORE LOCKS than Dirk had realized—front door, back door, the door between the house and the garage, plus a side door from the garage to the yard.

The workman adjusted them all and handed him a set of keys. "I hope that takes care of the problem, Mr. Peterson."

"I'll see that you're paid extra for your time," Dirk said.

The man, a grizzled fellow who appeared to spend most of his spare time outdoors, shook his head. "I don't need no extra pay," he said. "What I want, like most of the guys, is for you to keep the company in the family."

"We haven't made a decision about that." Dirk wasn't surprised to learn that the staff had been speculating about the future. Their jobs might be at stake after all. "Unfortunately, there won't be anyone in the family who could run the place until Jeff grows up."

"Unless, well, unless you was to stay on." The man braced himself against his van. "I don't guess it's as excitin' as what you regularly do. But your brother was talkin' about startin' up his own publishing imprint. We was lookin' forward to seein' what he'd do."

"He mentioned it to me on the phone recently, as a matter of fact." Lowell, his voice brimming with enthusiasm, had suggested they work together on lining up big-name experts to write high-tech and business-oriented books, then market the imprint internationally. It sounded feasible, but Dirk assumed the publishing project had died with Lowell.

His own specialty was establishing new projects in developing nations, not running them day to day. He only stuck around until a company got off the ground.

He knew better, however, than to cut off his options. "It's still up in the air," he said. "Thanks for your input."

"Any time, Mr. Peterson." After a firm handshake, the man climbed into his van.

As he drove away, Jeff came out of the house dribbling a ball. "Hey, Uncle Dirk, want to play handball?"

Dirk felt he could use a workout, and it was a good chance to spend time with his son. "Sure."

Whacking the ball against the garage door and chasing it soon had him breathing hard. A lot harder than Jeff. Considering that the kid had run all over the playground earlier that afternoon, his stamina was impressive.

"You're quite an athlete," Dirk observed as Jeff returned a difficult serve.

"Dad says I take after him."

The ball flew into some bushes. Dirk loped over and collected it. "Lowell was a good sportsman."

"Yeah." The little boy drooped, and Dirk realized his

use of the past tense had been a reminder of Lowell's death. "I'll never be as good as him, though."

Dirk put an arm around his son's shoulders. "I don't see why not. Being an athlete runs in the family. Did you know my father was the star of the high school basketball team?"

"No," the boy said, "I didn't."

Donald had died in his mid-fifties, before his only grandson was conceived. Unlike Herb, he'd refused to obey the doctor's orders to diet, exercise and quit smoking.

"Your great-grandfather was a ballplayer, too," Dirk said. "Herb led his team to two basketball trophies. I bet you could, too, if you wanted to."

The child's face brightened. Such keen blue eyes and such an open, joyful expression. Joni had done a wonderful job of raising him.

With a pang, Dirk wondered whether Herb's proximity and his own occasional visits would be enough masculine support to guide the boy into manhood. Even if they were enough for Jeff, did he himself really want to miss these years with the only son he might ever have?

He refused to yield to impulse. The worst thing he could do was to promise more than he could deliver.

"Want to play some more?" Jeff asked.

Dirk gestured toward a pile of logs. "How about helping me build a fire instead?"

"Could we really?"

"I promised your mom we'd have a wienie roast for dinner," he said. "We'll have to be careful not to set the house ablaze, though."

"We can roast hot dogs in the fireplace?" The boy whooped. "Dad would never have gone for something like that!"

"Your dad probably had more sense than I do," Dirk muttered, but he was human enough to enjoy the compliment.

INSIDE THE GRATE, sparks snapped and leaped from a log. On the brick hearth lay blackened skewers, testament to a merry meal of hot dogs and marshmallows.

Joni lay back among the cushions she'd pulled from the couch. Jeff had gone to bed half an hour ago while, nearby, Dirk watched the fire through half-closed eyes. Her sense of contentment wouldn't last, she knew. That made her treasure it all the more.

"A penny for your thoughts." Lying on the carpet, she could feel Dirk's baritone voice ripple through the underlying boards.

Half-formed ideas sprang out before she even knew what she intended to say. "I have the oddest feeling that everything will come to a head by Thursday."

"Thursday?" he echoed. "Halloween?"

"Also my birthday," she admitted. "The big three-oh."

"Ah." Dirk stretched lazily along his cushions. "I remember my thirtieth birthday. Some friends took me to dinner in Rome."

"That sounds glamorous."

"Rome is more friendly than glamorous," he said. "We had a traveling party, from the restaurant to a nightclub, picking up more people at every stage. People we knew, or thought we knew, or who said witty things in passing, or who laughed at our jokes. I felt like a college student again."

Through the fire tangoed filaments of red and yellow, blue and black. "I never had that kind of carefree experience," Joni admitted. "I wish I had."

"I needed it." Dirk knit his hands behind his head. "I had to get away from here."

"Why?" she asked. "I know you and Lowell didn't get along, but he would never say why."

"Dad pitted us against each other," he said. "I guess it was his way of trying to spur me to be the kind of kid he wanted me to be, and I was too stubborn to yield. Lowell sure enjoyed needling me."

"He could be very cruel." She'd learned that all too well from her own experience.

"When we were little, I adored him." A touch of bitterness laced his words. "So when we were teenagers and he began taunting me, I supposed he must be right, that I really was inferior. It hurt so much that I couldn't deal with it, so I hid my feelings. I didn't even fight back."

"Not ever?" she probed.

"Not until my senior year in high school," he said. "Lowell came home from college and found out I'd taken up boxing. I was doing well at it, too, which galled him."

"Did he box?" Joni recalled a scar alongside her ex-husband's eye; she'd asked about it, but he'd brushed the question aside.

"No, but he didn't like seeing me succeed at sports. I guess it threatened his position as the brother who was better at everything," Dirk said.

She waited, hoping that he'd go on. After a moment's reflection, he did.

"One afternoon at the club, he and some of his friends started giving me a hard time," Dirk said. "Mostly it was Lowell. Calling me names, shoving me. He challenged me to a boxing match. I knew my coach wouldn't approve, but I'd had enough."

"You two fought?" she asked. "Where?"

"We found an exercise room that wasn't being used," he said. "Put on the gloves and went at each other. Lowell lacked experience, but he was bigger than me."

"He won?" Joni hugged her knees. She could almost see the two brothers squaring off; hear the catcalls of Lowell's friends; smell the fighters' sweat.

"He landed more blows than I did although they didn't do much damage," Dirk said. "He told me I was a loser and I'd always be a loser. I told him to quit acting like a jerk and that I'd had enough. When I started to leave, he suddenly swung around and socked me in the gut. I wasn't expecting it."

Joni flinched. "He cheated?"

"He wanted total and absolute victory, and I wouldn't give it to him, so he took it any way he could." Dirk grimaced.

"Were you badly hurt?"

"I could hardly breathe. Then I got mad," he said. "I've heard of people seeing red, but I never knew it could be literally true. Well, it is. I felt this rage, years and years of it that had been bottled up. I don't remember what happened, except that I attacked him with everything I was worth."

"So that's how he got the scar," she guessed. "Next to his eye."

Dirk nodded. "I might've hurt him even worse if his friends hadn't pulled me off. I got loose and went at him again until Lowell had to turn tail and flee. He hated me for humiliating him, and I figured he owed me an apology. That was fifteen years ago."

"I'm sorry you never had a chance to reconcile," Joni said. "Lowell must've realized that was the biggest mistake he ever made."

"No, it wasn't." Dirk's blue gaze burrowed into her. "His biggest mistake was falling in love and then being too stupid to hold on to the most precious thing in his life."

The intensity of his stare held her motionless. It flooded her with a delicious sense of her own femininity, a sensation Lowell had all but destroyed when he rejected her to have an affair.

She could scarcely breathe, and she didn't know why until she realized that she wanted desperately for Dirk to hold her. A voice inside warned that she shouldn't yield to this weakness. She didn't care. Wasn't it worth the risk to have something precious even if she couldn't keep it?

Whatever lay ahead, Joni couldn't think about it now. The only reality was the sheen of firelight on Dirk's bronzed skin and the inviting warmth of his smile. Without conscious intent, she shifted toward him.

He met her halfway, one hand catching her waist, the other cupping her cheek. Their mouths came together, tongue to tongue. They sank onto the pillows, their legs entwined. After holding back for so long, she arched wildly against him. Wherever they touched, pleasure sprang up, so powerful it ached.

His shoulders rippled beneath her hands. His mouth caught hers again, ravaging and teasing. Her breasts yielded beneath the hard pressure of his chest, and her nipples sprang erect, daring him to take more.

She'd always felt her rangy, boyish body was awkward. But not with Dirk. Angles melted and what had been stiff became molten; she dissolved into him.

His breathing roughened as his hands slipped beneath her sweater. He pulled it up, and fire licked across her breasts as he tasted them. Desire took tangible shape, the shape of flames. Hungrily, Joni loosened Dirk's belt, wanting all of him.

His movements stopped. She felt his head brush her chest, the hair tickling her sensitized nipples. When he pulled away, a chill rushed to take his place. In the flickering light, Dirk sat up. His face was flushed, and he was breathing rapidly.

Joni knew the moment had passed. There would be no more lovemaking, and yet her body defied her with its need. How could she gather her scattered, overheated molecules back into their ordinary shape?

"I can't begin to tell you how difficult this is." Raw emotion layered his voice. "Joni, don't ever think I don't want you. But I would only hurt you."

"How can you be so sure?" she asked.

"I loved a woman once." His voice sounded far away. "I wasn't there when she needed me. She was a bodyguard, like me, and she got killed."

No wonder he gave the impression of nursing a darkness inside. "It couldn't have been your fault."

"If I'd been the right kind of man, she wouldn't have gone on that assignment," he said. "And I'm still the same man I was then, Joni. I have the same needs, and they'll take me away from here."

She wanted to argue that she didn't care, yet she knew it wasn't true. Maybe in time he would change, but she wasn't foolish enough to count on that. She had a child to take care of, and a community to face that already thought the worst of her. The last thing she needed was a dead-end love affair.

He reached for her hand. "It's time we went to bed."

"I wish that were an invitation," she couldn't help saying.

"So do I."

Her body hummed defiantly as he helped her to her feet and put the cushions away. Joni collected the skewers and took them into the kitchen.

They'd gone to the edge tonight, she thought. She couldn't help wondering what lay beyond it.

It was hard to accept that she might never find out.

ON THE AFTERNOON of Lowell's burial, clouds glowered over the Viento del Mar Memorial Park, which was located on the far side of downtown, west of Canyon Vista Road. The planned memorial service had been changed to a funeral at the last minute when the coroner released his body.

Joni wasn't sure whether, as Lowell's ex-wife and suspected killer, she ought to attend. Jeff needed to be there, however, and she wouldn't let him go without her. To wear black seemed presumptuous, so she chose a navy outfit. She and Dirk collected Jeff at school and met Herb at the memorial park.

People filled the chapel and spilled out the rear and side doors. The size of the crowd surprised her until Dirk explained that he'd given the printing staff time off to attend, and Herb added that he'd notified the local radio station.

Inside, flowers covered the dais and the gleaming closed casket. As she walked along the aisle, Joni saw heads turn and heard whispering. The Peterson Printing employees were keeping their expressions neutral. But the country-club set was a different story: tight mouths, narrow eyes and loud voices.

"How dare she come!"

"What a lot of nerve!"

"I'm surprised they haven't locked her up yet!"

Dirk tucked Joni's hand into the crook of his elbow. She guessed from his angry expression that he was weighing the effect of these remarks not only on her, but also on Jeff.

Fortunately, Herb was filling the boy's ears with a running commentary on the types of flowers. Joni doubted her son even heard the rude remarks.

It surprised her not to see Kim DeLong among the

mourners. It wasn't like the woman to miss a chance to make her presence felt. A few hospital workers had come, including Basil. Even Detective MacDougall had arrived, lingering near the side door where he could survey the assembly. She wondered whom or what he expected to find.

Dirk escorted her to the front row, which was reserved for family. Already seated there, in a black dress and black hat, Mrs. Wright stiffened when she caught sight of the newcomers. The housekeeper nodded to Herb and Dirk, then resumed facing straight ahead.

Ten minutes later, the service began. Joni registered vaguely that the minister talked about Lowell's dedication to the community and his love for his son.

Jeff squirmed, trying to see the other mourners. At eight years old, he couldn't be expected to grasp the implications of a funeral.

Dirk stood up to say a few words about his thorny relationship with his brother and how they'd hoped to reconcile. Herb spoke about how Lowell had been changing and reassessing his values. No one mentioned the circumstances of his death.

Joni knew that Dirk had contemplated speaking out on her behalf, but she'd urged him not to. This was a time for people who had known Lowell all his life to come together in celebrating and mourning him. It was not a court of law in which to present her defense.

The burial was to be private, and after the service, only she, Herb, Dirk, the pastor and Jeff went to the grave site. Joni was grateful to be away from the disapproving gazes of so many people.

The newer section of the cemetery had the peaceful air of a country garden, with low trees scattered over its rolling lawns. Memorial plaques lay flat on the ground, in contrast to an older section, where headstones towered.

Lowell's marker wasn't ready yet; there was only the hole for the casket. With so little time to make arrangements, they hadn't lined up any pallbearers, so a couple of cemetery workers transported the casket from the chapel and lowered it into the ground.

"Is Daddy really in there?" Jeff asked.

"Just his body," Herb said. "His spirit is free."

"Is he here?" The boy gazed around hopefully.

Joni exchanged troubled glances with Dirk. She wanted Jeff to feel that his father was close by but not to have unrealistic expectations.

"His love is here," Dirk said after a moment. "For you." He ruffled Jeff's hair.

With the casket in place, Dirk tossed down the customary handful of earth. The pastor read a passage from the Bible, and then it was over.

Joni felt grateful for the leaden sky as they walked back to the car. A sunny day wouldn't have felt right.

In the parking lot, one figure stood waiting for them—the detective. From the set of his jaw, he didn't have good news. Joni wondered if he were going to arrest her. Couldn't he at least wait until they left the cemetery?

When they came closer, MacDougall said, "I don't suppose any of you have heard from Kim DeLong?"

Heads shook. "I didn't see her at the service," Joni said. "I wondered where she was."

"No one's seen her since Saturday afternoon," the detective said. "She disappeared right after she talked to the two of you."

Chapter Eleven

"Are you implying a connection, Detective?" Dirk demanded.

MacDougall's pouchy eyes barely blinked. "Not necessarily. One of her friends saw her get into her car and drive off. We assume she arrived at home since her car is there. But she isn't."

Joni remembered a comment at church. "Could she have gone out of town?"

"Possible but unlikely." The man studied each of their faces in turn. "Unless someone gave her a ride." The nearest public airport was more than twenty miles away in Santa Barbara.

"We hope Mrs. DeLong turns up safe," Herb said dryly, "but right now, we've just buried my grandson. If you have nothing further to add, Officer, we'd like to leave."

"Sorry about the timing." But MacDougall didn't look sorry.

Dirk glared at the man's back as he departed. "I wonder how hard he's tried to find Kim. The police around here aren't terribly thorough."

He exchanged glances with his grandfather. "Well?" Herb prompted.

"I guess I'd better put in some calls to people who might've seen her," Dirk said. "I ought to be able to track down some of her friends from San Francisco. Also find out whether she's used a credit card the past couple of days, although I'm sure the police have already done that."

"I wouldn't put it past the woman to hide out just to get attention," his grandfather muttered.

Joni thought about the pom-pom pin Dirk had found in her house. Was it possible Kim had gone off the deep end and was lying in wait?

It would almost be a relief to be able to give the stalker a name and a face. Yet she had a hard time seeing Kim DeLong in that role. Kim might be vicious, but she was no monster.

"I need to use the computer at the office," Dirk said. "Herb, would you take Joni and Jeff home?"

"And join us for dinner?" Joni added.

"With pleasure." Gallantly, the older man offered his arm. "Then I will trounce this young hotshot at one of those video games."

"The heck you will!" Jeff cried, clearly looking forward to the prospect of defeating his great-grandfather.

Dirk's eyes met Joni's over the boy's head. The tenderness she saw there reminded her of what had happened the night before. And, even more forcefully, of what he hadn't allowed to happen.

She suspected Dirk planned to stay out late deliberately to avoid a repeat. Well, he needn't worry. He'd made the limits clear, and she intended to honor them.

ON TUESDAY MORNING, Joni returned to work with a sense of relief. The familiar smell of antiseptic at the hospital, the crackle of the intercom and the blandness of the decor helped restore her equilibrium.

Dirk hadn't found any trace of Kim DeLong yesterday. The woman's unexplained absence added yet another puzzle and made Joni long even more for her normal, predictable routine.

"What do you plan to put in next month's employee newsletter?" Basil asked, emerging from his office just as she reached her desk. It apparently never occurred to him to inquire after her health; social graces were not his strong point. "We're behind schedule."

Joni didn't mind her boss's gruff manner. At least, here in the office, she felt safe. "I'll have a list of ideas on your desk by lunchtime." She hoped the staff members had e-mailed her some suggestions while she was gone. In the last newsletter, she'd urged them to do so.

"Also, we need to plan the Christmas party," her boss went on. The public relations team, which consisted of the two of them plus a part-time secretary who was off duty today, was responsible for organizing the affair.

Because nurses, orderlies, technicians and doctors worked around the clock, the party had to overlap two shifts. A small budget made the planning especially tricky.

"I think we should concentrate our efforts this year," she said. "One special tree instead of a lot of cheap decorations. Also, let's skip the party favors and put the money into hiring an outside caterer."

"Food Services will be insulted!"

"Food Services deserves a holiday break too, don't they?" she countered.

"I'll consider it," Basil said, and trudged away. The time change and the early darkness were making him even gloomier than usual, she noted.

Joni sat down to check her e-mail and found, as she'd hoped, a long queue. Food Services proposed on article on how to avoid going overboard on holiday calories; she made a note to follow up on it.

One of the custodians suggested a profile of his dog, Patches, which had placed third in a Frisbee-catching contest. Joni set that one aside, to use only if she were desperate.

She pulled together the best suggestions and printed them out, then opened her accumulated mail and interoffice envelopes. After that, she went over a press release Basil had left for her to expand and edit concerning the acquisition of new imaging equipment.

It lacked details, which she would need to research herself. He'd indicated the press release should go out today, and when Joni checked her watch, she was surprised to see it was already midmorning.

She spent the next hour in the radiology department, learning the ins and outs of the new equipment. Finally, she had enough details and quotes to round out a feature-style release.

At lunchtime, she returned to the office, grabbed her brown bag and headed for the cafeteria. The route took her by the temporary dialysis unit, which had been relocated while the hospital's renal center in a separate building was being remodeled.

As she passed it, two women emerged. One, a heavyset, elderly woman, was Edith Owens, Fred's mother. She had suffered kidney failure the previous year as a result of diabetes.

The other was Mrs. Wright.

The housekeeper's mouth dropped open at the sight of Joni, then snapped shut. She brushed past, making no attempt to explain. Not that there could be much doubt what she was doing there. No wonder the woman disappeared for hours at a time! She must be undergoing dialysis several times a week.

Joni wanted to reassure her that the Petersons would never penalize her for a health problem. But perhaps pride, or an intense desire for privacy, explained her reaction rather than concern about her job.

"Goodness," Edith said, staring after Mrs. Wright's rapidly departing back. "I wonder what got into her."

"I don't think she wanted me to know about her... condition," Joni said.

"It's nothing to be ashamed of!" Bobby's grandmother said. Joni frequently ran into her at Fred and Kathryn's home; the woman had become close to her daughter-in-law. "Dialysis may be an inconvenience, but it keeps us alive."

"I guess everybody takes it differently." Joni smiled. "I'm on my way to lunch. Care to join me?"

The older woman sighed. "I have to be so careful about what I eat and drink these days that it's easier to dine at home. But thanks for the invitation."

The cafeteria was a dark, low-ceilinged room with an uninspired selection of food. Not recognizing anyone among the diners, Joni bought some soup and a carton of milk, then sat at a table by herself.

So Mrs. Wright had to undergo kidney dialysis. If only she'd felt comfortable confiding in her employer, so much unpleasantness could have been avoided.

Troubled, Joni didn't pay much attention as she finished her soup and pulled her sandwich from its bag. Then something tickled her hand.

She glanced down. A couple of strands of purple and orange were dangling from atop the sandwich bag. For several confused moments, she tried to figure out how they'd gotten there. Jeff often left toys, rocks and other miscellany lying around. Could these bits of fringe have stuck to the sandwich bag by accident?

Purple and orange. The detective had taken Kim's pom-pom pin as evidence; there'd been no fringe left, as far as Joni knew.

She'd left her lunch sack unattended in her office for about an hour this morning. Someone must have entered and placed the strands inside.

If she was right, the stalker had been in the hospital. He had walked into her office. He had touched her lunch.

Her first impulse was to throw the thing in the trash, but she stopped herself. Detective MacDougall might not find this any more convincing than the pom-pom at her house, but perhaps she ought to report it.

Still debating what to do, she dropped the sandwich into the sack. On her way back to the public relations department, she found herself studying everyone she passed, wondering which of them might have done this.

On the threshold of her office, Joni experienced a profound uneasiness. What if the killer had come back while she was gone? Was she going to find some other indication of his presence?

Then she saw the message blinking on her computer screen, indicating an e-mail. That reminded her that she'd forgotten to log off when she left for radiology; but then, she'd never had reason to worry about anyone invading her space.

With a heavy feeling, Joni approached the computer and clicked on the e-mail. Onto the screen flashed a message: "Kick that jerk out of your house or the same thing will happen to him that happened to his brother. I'll be watching."

She stared at it numbly. Who had done this? Why couldn't he leave her alone?

Something Dirk had said came back to her, about the killer wanting to possess her. And to punish her for becoming friendly with Lowell. Was that what this beast was doing—punishing her for letting Dirk move in?

Forcing down her alarm, she checked the tag line and time. The e-mail bore the name Peters and had been sent an hour ago, which meant it had arrived while she was in radiology.

Bernice Peters was the secretary to the hospital's finance director. Fumbling for the phone, Joni dialed her extension.

"Finance director's office."

"Bernice? This is Joni Peterson."

"Hi! Welcome back!"

"Listen, I got a strange e-mail that was sent from your terminal," she said. "Did you see anyone lurking around your office an hour ago?"

"No, Mr. Drummond and I were both in a meeting with the administrator," the secretary said. "Oh, my gosh, I didn't think to log off. It's never been a problem."

The finance office was situated along the hospital's main corridor, with a stream of patients, staff and visitors going by. Easily accessible, although also easily observed. The killer had taken quite a chance. He must have a good excuse for being in the hospital and figured he could bluff his way out if questioned.

Mrs. Wright came to mind. She'd been there, but the scenario didn't fit with Joni's impression of the older woman.

Kim DeLong served on the hospital's governing board; her father had been one of the institution's original investors. Under normal circumstances, she could easily have done this. But she'd been missing since Saturday.

The perpetrator was probably too smart to have left fingerprints in Bernice's office, but Joni had to report this.

She didn't realize how deeply she'd been disturbed until she picked up the phone to call the police and saw her hands were trembling.

DIRK COULD HARDLY SIT still all day Tuesday. A restlessness nagged at him as he placed one phone call after another to his associates abroad; pounded on the computer keyboard; prowled through the printing company's offices.

He needed answers. And he needed relief from his own turmoil.

His old foe, self-doubt, whispered that he was failing Joni. That he wasn't smart enough or quick enough to save her from this darkness closing in around them. That he had barely been strong enough to rein in his own desires.

On Sunday, when they fell into each other's arms, he'd wanted to take her ten different ways. To open himself to her, demand more of her than she'd ever given before and let the fire consume them both.

It was more than physical desire. He'd kept aloof from any real attachment for so long that he hadn't realized how much he ached for intimacy. Returning to Viento del Mar had unleashed a lot of demons: along with self-doubt, an aching need to belong to someone, a wild passion that impeded rational thought.

This time, however, there was a real demon. A killer who possessed an uncanny ability to counter their movements and to prowl freely, unobserved. To taunt them.

Dirk's searches on the Internet yielded frustratingly inconclusive tidbits. Celia Lu's husband had been investigated on suspicion of smuggling Chinese artifacts, but these consisted of so few items that they were most likely personal possessions not intended for sale. Customs authorities had declined to prosecute.

Three years earlier, Basil Dupont had been convicted of

drunken driving but had remained clean ever since. As for the soccer coach, even this small town had four residents named Charles Rogers, two of whom lived in the same apartment building. Dirk left a message at the soccer league's office requesting the man's driver's license number. Since most of the league officials knew the Peterson family, he hoped they would cooperate.

Kim DeLong hadn't used her credit card since Friday. None of her old friends would admit to having heard from her, either.

By lunchtime, Dirk began to wonder if he were coming down with a fever. His body felt hot, on the edge of exploding.

He took a walk to burn off energy. After a few blocks, he passed the hospital and wondered how Joni was feeling. But he didn't want to disturb her at work.

At the intersection of Canyon Vista and San Bernardo roads stood a real-estate company. Impulsively, Dirk went inside and talked to a Realtor about selling the Peterson mansion, noting that he preferred a buyer who would retain the present staff. The man promised to draw up paperwork for a listing.

The prospect of putting the house on the market gave Dirk a small sense of relief. That and the walk helped dispel his tension, and that afternoon he was able to focus on the material his brother had left regarding the new publishing venture.

Lowell had acquired one manuscript already. Wondering whether Joni might enjoy editing it, Dirk thumbed through the typed pages. *The Post-Millennial Boom: Beyond the Internet,* written by an Australian computer whiz, speculated about evolving technologies that would revolutionize international business dealings. Dirk found it fascinating.

By the time he finished, several hours had passed. His mind hummed with possibilities, both for marketing this book and for commissioning others. This line could be sold around the world via the Internet from a base right here in Viento del Mar.

But he couldn't stay. The town was too confining and too full of ghosts from Dirk's past for him ever to live there again.

On the drive home, he saw that the cloud cover had thinned, permitting a streaky pink sunset. However, the radio forecast called for rain later in the week. By prior arrangement, he picked up a pizza. Finding himself the first one home, he changed out of his suit and sat down to watch the business news on PBS.

"The market apparently got the pre-Halloween jitters today," the announcer began. "It was definitely a trick rather than a treat for investors…"

Thursday would be Halloween, Dirk recalled. It was also Joni's thirtieth birthday. What kind of gift could he give her? Something special, but not excessive. Something brother-in-lawish, he thought with a trace of irony.

Into his mind popped an image of the velvet jewelry box his brother had given Kim. Diamond earrings hardly seemed appropriate under the circumstances, however. A gold watch? Too impersonal. A hair ornament? Too ordinary, he mused.

The perfect gift lay just out of reach in the back of his mind, taunting him. Well, he would figure it out by Thursday, Dirk told himself.

The *whir* of the garage door announced Jeff and Joni's arrival. As soon as he saw her pale, drawn face, he knew something was wrong.

"I'm just tired," Joni responded to his questions, but

he sensed she didn't want to talk in front of the boy. "I'm going to rest."

"I'll bring you dinner on a tray later," he said.

Unaware of the undercurrents, Jeff chattered as he ate. His P.E. instructor, he informed Dirk, had tested the third graders for fitness, and he'd been the second fastest runner in his class.

"Good for you!"

The little boy let out a long breath. "I wish I could tell Dad."

He touched the little boy's hand. "Wherever he is, I'll bet he's proud of you."

Jeff smiled, but he didn't look convinced.

Afterward, Dirk helped him go over his math homework. Jeff had a quick mind but tended to be careless; once he added where he should have subtracted and he forgot to carry a number while multiplying.

"Accuracy is vital," Dirk said. "Suppose NASA miscalculated and they sent a rocket to Jupiter instead of Mars? They might run out of fuel."

"They should carry extra gas just in case," Jeff proposed.

"It would be easier to do the math right in the first place."

The little boy wrinkled his nose. "Yeah, okay."

Being able to help his son, even for that little bit, gave Dirk a sense of satisfaction. Long after Jeff went to bed, it continued to warm him.

He cleaned up the kitchen and then checked on his son. Jeff had fallen asleep with *Charlotte's Web* propped on his chest. Smiling, Dirk set the book aside and switched off the lamp. He lingered there, drinking in the peaceful sight of the little boy sleeping.

When he withdrew, he saw that the door to Joni's room

stood ajar. Inside, a light was on. It was time to keep his promise of bringing her dinner.

In a kitchen cabinet, he found a wooden tray with snap-open legs. Dirk reheated some pizza, added a few sprigs of parsley to dress it up and poured a glass of mineral water. He would've liked to complete the picture with a rosebud but didn't want to stumble around outside in the dark trying to pick one.

Humming, he carried the tray through the house. Without a free hand, he couldn't knock, but he bumped the door a couple of times with his knee. When Joni didn't answer, he shouldered it open and went in.

The bedroom was empty, but the door to the master bath stood ajar. "Joni?" he called. "I've brought dinner."

"In here!" Her voice had a refreshing lilt. "It's okay. I'm decent."

Curious, Dirk edged inside with the tray. The room was larger than he'd expected, with a spa set into an alcove beneath a rippled window.

Amid a light froth of bubbles, Joni reclined in the water. She wore a Hawaiian-print swimsuit, ruffled at the bust and clinging to her slender midriff. Blond hair wisped from its knot atop her head, creating a halo around her face. In the rising steam, her skin appeared creamy and moist.

Dirk could feel his muscles tightening. Getting a grip on himself, he set the tray on the edge of the spa.

"I'm glad to see you're relaxing." He couldn't resist adding, "Do you always wear a swimsuit in the tub?"

"No, but it occurred to me, with all that's been going on, I should be prepared to get out in a hurry." Her mouth twisted wryly. "Anyway, this looks terrific. Thank you."

Dirk sat on the edge of the spa. He knew it would be prudent to leave, but they needed to talk. "You were upset about something earlier."

She finished a bite of pizza. "At work, I got an e-mail threatening your life if you don't move out. I tried to call you, but you were out and you must have had your cell phone switched off."

"The battery died," he said. "I didn't realize it until later." He'd found a replacement in Lowell's desk.

It shouldn't surprise him that the stalker knew he was living here, but the confirmation disturbed Dirk. While they were fruitlessly sorting through clues, this man had been watching them.

"Did you call MacDougall?"

"Yes, but the computer it came from had been left unattended, and there weren't any suspicious fingerprints."

"It was interoffice? The message was sent from within the hospital?"

She nodded grimly. "There's more. Whoever did it came into my office while I was in another part of the building. He—or she—left a couple of strands from a pompom in my lunch bag. I gave those to the police, too."

Mentally, Dirk turned over this information. The fact that the stalker had physically invaded Joni's workplace was disturbing.

Could it be a co-worker? A patient? "You didn't notice anyone in the building who seemed out of place?"

She frowned. "I did see Mrs. Wright. It turns out she's a dialysis patient. That must be where she's been going several times a week."

No wonder the housekeeper had been so touchy. With her reticent nature, she'd resented even innocent questions about her whereabouts.

"I hope she's all right," Dirk said. "You don't think she's responsible for the e-mail, do you?"

"I checked, and she was hooked up to a machine at the time it was sent," Joni said. "Kim could have written it, but she's still missing. Besides, I keep getting the feeling it's a man.''

''Why? Because of the footprint in the blind?''

''And that comment you made about the killer trying to punish me for making friends with Lowell. That sounds like a jealous man.'' Without warning, a tear slipped down her cheek.

Reaching out with the tip of his thumb, Dirk gently wiped away the drop. ''What is it?''

''I wish I'd given Lowell the benefit of the doubt,'' she said miserably. ''He was trying to protect me, and I accused him of being the stalker.''

''I can't blame you, not when he'd done the same thing before. The tragedy is that he died just as he was learning some important lessons.''

Dirk wished, more than ever, that he'd had a chance to talk to his brother one more time, heart to heart. To know him as the human being he'd finally become.

''I should've seen that he'd changed.''

''You're the one who made him grow up,'' Dirk said. ''He was lucky he found you, and in the end I think he was smart enough to realize it.''

The expression on her face was so wistful that, without stopping to consider, he leaned forward and brushed his lips across hers. When he drew back, her gaze smoldered at him.

''Do that again,'' she said.

''I'm not sure we should—''

One slim, wet arm reached out and pulled him forward. When his mouth met hers, Dirk lost track of where he was, of everything but the increasing pressure of their lips.

His tongue traced her teeth and probed deeper. A sudden intake of breath told him she was responding with an intensity that matched his own.

When she came up for air, Joni said, "Take your shirt off."

"Why?"

She gave a low chuckle. "Because I'm dripping all over you."

He felt a surge of recklessness. "I like wet clothes." Without stopping to consider, he slid into the tub beside her, blue jeans, polo shirt, socks and all.

It was a strange feeling, squishy and naughty. Joni's laughter tickled across his nerve endings. "I can't believe you did that!"

"Neither can I." Dirk started to laugh, too. Beneath his good humor, however, he could feel himself responding to Joni's half-naked presence. Eve must have been like this, he thought. Ripe and tempting, and scarcely aware of it.

He knew he ought to drag himself away while he still could. Then he realized that he couldn't. Maybe he was selfish, or maybe crazy, but an exquisite hunger raged inside him that only Joni could satisfy.

"I thought I was modest, but this is ridiculous," she teased. "Taking a bath with your clothes on!"

"As long as it doesn't get in the way," he said, and gathered her in his arms.

In the water, she seemed to float onto his lap. Her legs tangled with his, and suddenly Dirk could no longer bear the confinement of clothes separating them.

Chapter Twelve

Joni's self-consciousness yielded to a languorous delight. Being held by Dirk, so close and yet protected by their clothing, allowed her to luxuriate in the sensations tingling through her body.

The barriers between them blurred. Even through the fabric, she could feel his reactions almost as if they were hers.

His hard muscles made her keenly aware of her own softness. Of the fiery need to be touched, on her face and breasts and hips. To be filled by him.

Curling against Dirk, Joni inhaled his musky fragrance, enhanced by the effect of water. When his mouth sought hers again, she danced her tongue along the edge of his lips, relishing the way his grip tightened around her.

She had never before experienced this combination of desire and comfort, of complete trust. If only it could last forever, the passion rising but never requiring fulfillment. Perhaps, tonight, anything was possible.

As Dirk explored her mouth, his hand slipped the strap from her shoulder. Warm water caressed her bare breast, and his mouth followed. Once, in some other life, she had felt clumsy and boyish. Now, beneath his kisses, her natural voluptuousness blossomed.

When he caught the erect nipple, a profound yearning lashed Joni. Her breasts swelled with desire as he slid down her other strap.

Avidly, she feathered her hands across Dirk's shoulders, prizing their sculpted firmness. She wanted to touch him freely, to cherish his masculine beauty, to be some wild, sensual creature with no fear of consequences.

Hungrily, she helped him pull the wet shirt upward. As he lifted it over his head, she angled forward and brushed her nipples across his bronzed skin.

With a moan, Dirk caught her hips to his. His masculine hardness indented her, a warning and a promise.

Joni wanted this moment, this treasure. No other reality existed.

Dirk's breathing rasped as she unsnapped his soaked, clinging jeans and lowered the zipper. The other night, he had stopped her at this point. This time, the prospect would be unendurable.

She tugged the denim down his thighs. He was hard, all right, but acquiescent, leaning back in the tub so she could wrest the jeans free.

As she tossed them aside, powerful hands caught her swimsuit and worked it down her rib cage. Stripping her, Dirk found the sensitive inlets of her waist and navel, then the crease between her thighs.

Joni craved everything at once, all of him touching all of her. Yet she remained kneeling, motionless, as he found her most sensitive point and stroked it.

"Dirk," she whispered. "I want…"

"I know." His voice vibrated close to her ear.

He knelt before her in the water, and now they *were* in contact at every point. Merging seamlessly, yet still not one.

His hands caught her derriere and lifted her. For one

moment, Joni felt weightless and suspended before he shifted her against his groin and eased himself inside her. His vibrant masculinity extended her. A joy as pure as flame shot through Joni.

His movements began slowly, subtly, and then the rhythm intensified. She augmented his fluid music with a seductive counterpoint that spurred him on until his eyes narrowed in pleasure.

As his mouth probed hers, his movements speeded into an erotic dance. Why had she never realized she was capable of such sweet sensations?

Tightly, she pressed into Dirk, teasing and summoning him. He rocketed into her, lifting her, thrilling her. Passion exploded into ecstasy as the last shreds of control burst.

Joni soared with him, scarcely aware of the water around them. The world filled with colored lights, playing across her skin and glowing within her.

A wave of pure satisfaction made her so buoyant that Joni clutched his shoulders to anchor herself. She had the impression that they hovered above the pool, snatched from ordinary time and space into a realm of their own.

At last they subsided together, spent but luminous. She nestled against Dirk, not wanting to talk, just to feel his rapid breathing and know that he, too, had experienced something special.

It occurred to her, too late, that they should have been more careful. She'd already had one child by this man; she knew he was potent. But then, with a twinge that might almost be disappointment, she realized it was the wrong time of the month.

It didn't matter. The experience they had just shared was something she would always treasure no matter how empty the future might be.

DIRK STRUGGLED to understand this mad joy soaring through him. What had happened between him and Joni had elevated him to a new level of awareness.

The physical pleasure might be extreme, but even stronger was the profound sense of connection. They had forged a link whose implications he couldn't yet grasp.

Still, he couldn't afford to indulge in romanticism. The world would not stay on hold. In fact, he suspected that reality was due for a crash landing any minute.

Slowly Dirk drew into himself. When he did, he realized he was sitting in a tub of cooling water, with his wet clothes slopped onto the floor and Joni half-asleep against his shoulder.

From experience, he knew all too well how easily what began with loving spontaneity could end with disappointment and bitterness. He should have been more careful. He should have controlled himself.

''Time for bed,'' he murmured. She nodded vaguely.

As he helped her dry off, Dirk hoped that what had happened wouldn't damage their friendship. How could he have risked their closeness by yielding to impulse no matter how much gratification it gave him? Jeff needed them both, as parents, not as lovers in a volatile relationship.

After tucking Joni under the covers, he wrung out his clothes, wrapped himself in a towel and carried the wet garments to the utility room. Then he returned to the master bedroom.

It might be more prudent to spend the rest of the night in the sofa bed, but he couldn't bear to leave that much space between them. As he lay down beside Joni, her warmth flooded him, bringing back tingling memories.

Tomorrow, he would find a way to persuade her that they must go back to behaving as they had before. To being merely friends, for their son's sake.

BY THE TIME JONI AWAKENED on Wednesday morning, Dirk had left the room, but she could tell he'd slept there. The spare pillow retained a trace of his aftershave lotion, and there was an indentation where he'd lain. She wished he hadn't gone. But, for Jeff's sake, they needed to be discreet.

Not only for Jeff. What if the stalker realized they were sleeping together?

A chill crept down her spine. Could someone have been watching the house last night? She kept the blinds closed, but the stalker appeared to be both bold and intuitive.

If he suspected anything, she had no doubt there would be repercussions. Joni's throat clenched as she pictured someone attacking Dirk. He needed to be careful, and so did she.

She dressed and went out. Jeff was still asleep. In the utility room, she found Dirk removing his jeans from the dryer. He looked starchily remote in a business suit.

"Hello," she said.

When he glanced up, his face had an opaque tightness. "Good morning."

"I've been thinking," she said.

"So have I."

She pressed on. "It's about the killer. If he suspects what happened between us last night, he might act today."

Dirk straightened. He looked ill at ease in the cramped room. "There are a lot of reasons why we need to be cautious," he said quietly. "Last night—I don't want to call it a mistake, but we were careless."

"I don't think I'm pregnant," she said. "Wrong timing."

From his startled look, she gathered that hadn't been what he meant. "I never...well, that's fortunate. Because even though you mean a great deal to me, I don't want to raise false expectations.''

Expectations? Certainly she didn't expect Dirk to change his life to suit her, but she had hoped for something more than this studied coolness. ''Do you want to pretend it didn't happen?''

''We can hardly do that.'' Warmth flickered in his eyes. ''My first concern is for your safety, yours and Jeff's. MacDougall already believes I lack objectivity. We don't want to give him any further reason to discredit whatever clues we turn up. For that and other reasons, we need to back off.''

A tight band of disappointment squeezed her chest, but she supposed he was right. ''They're installing the alarm system this afternoon. You could move out if you think it's necessary.''

''There's no need to make a decision yet,'' he said. ''Right now, I want to get an early start at the office. I keep feeling there's some detail eluding me. Something I should be able to find in the computer or in Lowell's papers.''

Joni made a quick mental review of her plans for the day. She would be leaving her job early to let the workmen into the house and then she would pick up her son for soccer practice.

Kathryn had offered to take him since she got off early from her shift as a supermarket cashier. But Jeff needed as much support as possible right now, and Joni wanted to be with him.

''Jeff has soccer practice at four, in Del Mar Park,'' she said. ''You're welcome to join us.''

''I'll try.'' He gave her a distracted half smile. ''Don't ever think that last night didn't mean a great deal to me, because it did.''

"Me, too," she said, but when they tried to hug each other goodbye, they seemed to have too many arms and noses.

After Dirk left, Joni awakened her son and fixed breakfast. Unsettled emotions flickered through her, embryonic happiness dampened by an incipient sense of dread.

She was mature enough to understand that not every fierce attraction could grow into a long-lasting love. Dirk cared about her, but last night might remain forever a unique and isolated memory.

It had been worth it.

As usual, Dirk checked his car before getting in. There were no signs of tampering.

Criminals generally stuck to one method of dispatching their victims, and the stalker had shown a preference for knives. That didn't mean, however, that he might not be clever enough to employ whatever weapon suited his purpose.

Today, more than ever, Dirk ached to watch over Joni. But if danger threatened, it was more likely to target him. At least, he hoped so.

He checked the rearview mirror more often than usual in case he was being followed. Even the slightest anomaly, such as the rattle of a truck hitting a pothole or an odor that took a moment to identify as eau de skunk, set his adrenaline pumping.

Halloween witches and skeletons adorned the neighborhood windows along the way, some of them startlingly realistic. Beside the road, a figure swung from a tree. Dirk's grip tightened on the steering wheel until he registered the shape as a life-size scarecrow.

Still on edge, he turned into the parking lot of Peterson Printing. The copy shop in front wouldn't open for several hours, and he cut through an empty lot toward the main plant. Near a side entrance clustered a dozen cars belonging to night-shift workers. Beyond them, delivery trucks waited beside the closed loading dock.

Dirk's reserved space was located around back, next to the administrative offices. He would almost certainly be the first to arrive. He steered toward his space, then braked abruptly. Something dark lay crumpled in the middle of it.

It flashed into his mind that someone had dumped trash on the pavement. Then, as he stared at the shape, he remembered the scarecrow in the tree. But this sprawled, plastic-shrouded figure looked too solid to be stuffed with rags.

Dirk backed up and cut off the engine. The lot was secluded, with a small industrial park on one side and a warehouse on the other, although he could hear the swish of traffic from San Bernardo Road.

Holding his cellular phone in one hand, he got out and walked toward the parking space. He kept hoping his impression would prove wrong.

A few more steps, and he made out the contours of a human figure draped in a plastic sheet. Long dark hair pooled like blood around the head.

His gut clenching, Dirk dialed 911.

JONI HAD DROPPED JEFF at school and was en route to the hospital when she glimpsed flashing lights and police cars at the printing company.

Dirk. What if he'd been attacked?

Without hesitation, she spun into the lot. She couldn't bear to lose him, not this way, not now.

An ambulance jounced by her, going in the other direction. No lights, no siren. Either it was empty or the person inside must be dead.

A glaze came over her eyes. It took all Joni's presence of mind to steer through the maze of parked emergency vehicles toward the administrative office in back.

As she rounded the building, she recognized the lank form of Detective MacDougall, standing to one side, wearing what appeared to be the same rumpled jacket as always. He was talking to a tall man in a business suit who faced away from Joni.

She knew those broad shoulders, that short dark hair. Relief tingled through her, but her hands still felt slippery on the wheel.

Dirk was safe. What had happened, then, to bring out half the town's police force?

Leaving the car in the first available space, Joni hurried over. MacDougall spotted her first, and Dirk pivoted.

"What's going on?" To her surprise, she was nearly breathless. "I was going to work and I saw all the patrol cars."

"Come with me." The detective moved her away from Dirk and out of earshot. "Where were you last night?"

"At home." She regarded him quizzically.

"Where was Mr. Peterson?"

"At my house, too."

"All night?" When she nodded, the detective pressed, "Can you swear to that? Was he in the same room with you? Don't look at Mr. Peterson! I want your honest answer."

Joni sighed. There was no sense in denying it. "Yes, he was in the same room with me. Now what's happened?"

Apparently, she'd given the right answer, the one that matched Dirk's, because the detective's expression eased. "I'm afraid your brother-in-law has found the body of Mrs. DeLong."

"What?" This made no sense. Joni had believed the

stalker was after her or those close to her. "Why would anyone kill Kim?"

"Maybe they had reason to hold a grudge."

"You mean me?" Her hand flew to her throat. "You think *I* killed her?"

Dirk strode toward them. "Give her a break, Mac-Dougall. She had nothing to do with this."

The detective blocked his path. "I need to talk to Mrs. Peterson alone."

Above MacDougall's outstretched arm, deep blue eyes met hers. "You should have a lawyer present, Joni."

"I have nothing to hide." She knew she sounded naive. But waiting for a lawyer would only drag this matter out and reinforce the policeman's suspicion of her.

"This way, please." The detective gestured her toward the building.

In a private office, he questioned her for nearly an hour, taking particular note that both Celia and Dirk could attest to her whereabouts on Saturday night. She held nothing back, knowing he must have interrogated Dirk and that their answers would be compared.

When he was finished, he grudgingly answered a few questions of her own, probably because the information would soon be all over the media anyway. It appeared that Kim DeLong had been stabbed to death several days ago, possibly on Saturday night.

"The blood," Joni said, "on my patio. Could the killer have dumped it there?"

"Since it was washed off, we have no way of knowing who it belonged to." MacDougall's pouchy face looked gray, as if he were upset over the gruesome find, too.

"I'm sorry," she said. "Kim did some rotten things, but she didn't deserve this."

"I'm releasing you for now." The detective inhaled as

if intending to say more, then stood up and opened the door. "I may have more questions later."

"I understand," Joni said.

Outside, investigators were taking measurements and bagging evidence. Yellow tape encircled the rear of the building, and arriving employees had to use the side door.

Dirk stood near the secured area, watching the activity. When he caught sight of Joni, he started toward her, until the detective waved him away. Reluctantly, Joni got into her car. She wanted to stick this out, but she was late for work.

Although the alarm system would be installed at her home this afternoon, that prospect no longer reassured her. Kim's elegant Tudor mansion, adjacent to the country club, bore a sign proclaiming the name of her security service. What good had it done?

Trying to keep her thoughts trained on the day ahead, Joni drove to the hospital beneath low, ominous clouds.

THE DETECTIVE KEPT ASKING for the same information, trying to trip him up. After laboriously repeating his description of where he had been Saturday night and how he had found the body this morning, Dirk got annoyed.

"Look," he said, "Joni's in danger. Why are you more interested in trying to pin this on me than in protecting her?"

The detective tilted his jowly head. "What I'd like to know, Mr. Peterson, is why you aren't more concerned about your own safety. Do you have some inside information about where this guy's going to strike next?"

"I'm not the killer," Dirk said. "And I can take care of myself."

"Do you carry a gun?"

"Of course not." California had strict laws against concealed weapons. "Since you've already searched me and impounded my car, you're well aware that I don't."

He supposed it might be more forthright to admit that seeing Kim's body had left him with a chill deep in his gut. But it wouldn't do any good.

MacDougall must have serious doubts about whether Joni, newly released from the hospital, could have confronted Kim, murdered her and dragged the body away. So the detective was taking the easy way out by turning his sights on Dirk.

"We're aware that you don't have a gun on you," the detective conceded. "But then, the victim was stabbed."

If he were trying to get Dirk's goat, he was succeeding. "Let's put our cards on the table," Dirk snapped. "Why would I kill Kim DeLong? Because we had one argument at a soccer field?"

"According to witnesses, you were angry that she'd seduced your brother and embarrassed your family," the detective said mildly. Luring him, giving him an opening to spew out his fury.

Dirk sighed. "I had nothing to gain from her death and you know it. From my brother's, I got a job I didn't need."

"As well as half ownership of his property," the man prompted. "He was fairly wealthy, I gather."

MacDougall was clearly out of his depth. "This may come as a disappointment to you, but in this case, 'wealthy' is a relative term. First of all, in case you haven't already checked, my own net worth far exceeds my brother's. Furthermore, most of his capital is tied up in the printing company, which is still in debt from its expansion."

The detective rubbed his jaw. "The two of you didn't get along, did you?"

"You're fishing in the wrong creek," Dirk said. "Come

on, MacDougall. Don't tell me you haven't checked my whereabouts last Wednesday night. I wasn't even in Viento del Mar.''

He could see resistance in the man's face. The detective sure hated to give up an easy solution. ''Not as far as we can tell anyway.''

''Then I'm free to go?''

''I wouldn't say that.''

They'd been over the facts repeatedly. Moreover, they were wasting time. Somewhere nearby, a killer lurked. If MacDougall didn't intend to hunt down the clues, then someone else had to.

''Am I under arrest?'' Dirk demanded. ''If I am, I want a lawyer. If not, I've got work to do.''

The policeman's cheeks twitched as if he were chewing gum. Finally, he said, ''Don't leave town without notifying us.''

''I have no intention of leaving town until I'm sure Joni and my s—my nephew are safe.''

The other man's eyebrows rose. ''Your what, Mr. Peterson?''

He'd just slipped, Dirk realized. If the truth came out, it could look very bad indeed.

Chapter Thirteen

Your what, Mr. Peterson? The detective's words echoed in Dirk's ears.

"My son," he answered, since it was obvious that's what he'd started to say. "That's how I've come to think of him. I have no children of my own, as you should know."

"You wouldn't be planning to adopt your nephew, would you?" MacDougall pressed. "Say, once you and Mrs. Peterson get married?"

So that was what the man was implying. If Dirk had been secretly planning to marry Joni and wanted to adopt Jeff, it would give him a motive to get rid of Lowell.

"Until last week, I'd only met my sister-in-law at her wedding and my father's funeral, and I'd never met my nephew," Dirk said. "What's between Joni and me occurred *after* my brother's death. For your information, we haven't discussed marriage."

He stopped short of explaining that he wasn't the type to tie himself to one place. That was none of MacDougall's business.

"I suppose you wouldn't mind if we check Mrs. Peterson's phone records?" the detective said.

"You don't need my permission." Dirk had no doubt

the man would pursue that avenue if he hadn't already done so. "But you won't find any international calls to me. Also, my passport will show that I rarely visit this country."

The other man shrugged. "All right, Mr. Peterson." As Dirk withdrew, he added, "Hey!"

"Yes?"

"I'm real sorry about your printing plant being in debt. Inheriting it must have put a big strain on your finances." MacDougall kept his tone deadpan as he jingled the change in his pocket. "You need a small loan or anything?"

"I'll let you know," Dirk retorted, and headed for the side entrance.

ALL DAY, JONI JUMPED every time the phone rang. Her breath caught in her throat as she read through her e-mail, and she made a point of buying lunch.

No more surprises, please.

At least she didn't risk running into Mrs. Wright. Patients wouldn't normally undergo dialysis two days in a row.

The scene at the printing plant kept running through her mind: police cruisers and a fire truck parked helter-skelter; yellow tape blocking the crime scene; investigators poring over every pebble and fallen leaf.

Kim's body had already been removed, and Joni was glad she hadn't seen it. But a sense of horror remained, mixed with troubling questions. Why had the killer targeted Kim? Did he have the twisted notion that he was avenging her wrongs to Joni, or did he fear Kim might have information about Lowell's death? Or was there yet another, unsuspected motive?

She shivered at the possibility that Kim's blood had

been dumped on her patio after the murder. What about the pom-pom pin left at the house on Sunday? And the strands found in her lunch sack yesterday?

The killer was close to her. Much too close.

Did he really fantasize about winning Joni and then keeping her under his thumb? The very idea gave her the creeps.

Once she told Basil what had happened at Dirk's plant, he forgave her lateness, but he reminded her that the newsletter needed to go out. She set to work determined to make the best use of the few hours available.

Her boss helped by steering away a newspaper reporter who wanted to interview her. From the hallway, she could hear his gravelly voice explaining that Mrs. Peterson was too upset to talk.

The young woman apologized and left. Whether Herb had spoken to his friend, the publisher, or whether the reporter was simply respecting small-town sensibilities, Joni was grateful that she apparently wouldn't be harassed.

At one o'clock, as she drove home to meet the security service, the radio announcer was recounting the news of Kim's death.

"Police are withholding information about where Mrs. DeLong's body might have been hidden since Saturday," he intoned. "However, this station has learned that twigs and leaves were clinging to the plastic sheet found wrapped around her. This might indicate the hiding place was in a wooded area."

There were plenty of woods around Viento del Mar, Joni reminded herself. It didn't mean Kim's body had been kept near her house.

"There were no signs of forced entry at Mrs. DeLong's home," the man continued. "She was believed to have been alone Saturday night, and some observers speculate she might have opened the door to someone she knew.

"Mrs. DeLong was known to have argued earlier in the day with Joni Peterson, ex-wife of businessman, Lowell Peterson, and with Peterson's brother, Dirk. Lowell Peterson was stabbed to death one week ago—"

Joni switched off the radio. How dare the newscaster imply there was a connection between the argument and Kim's slaying?

It was also unreasonable for anyone to assume that a woman would only open the door to an acquaintance. Viento del Mar was a small town with a low crime rate. Lots of people opened their doors for salesmen, Mormon missionaries, and stranded motorists.

There was no mention of the police having found a murder weapon. She wondered whether the killer had used the same kind of knife and where it was now.

DIRK SPENT MUCH of the day reassuring employees about the murder, answering questions for the police and dodging a reporter and photographer who were hanging around the crime scene. He also had to arrange for another rental car, since his had been impounded pending a search.

In the little free time that remained, he checked the computer for anything in Kim's background that might provide a lead. Her ex-husband. Her financial situation. Her charitable activities.

If the information existed, it wasn't in her credit files or anywhere else that he could access. Although he wanted very much to interview the victim's friends, Dirk suspected MacDougall would arrest him for interfering with a police investigation if he tried.

At three-thirty, Joni called to say the alarm system had

been installed and she was going to collect Jeff for soccer practice. Dirk was relieved to hear her voice.

He wanted to talk about last night, about the need to maintain their friendship for Jeff's sake, but he preferred not to risk being overheard. Mostly he wanted to drive to her house and corner her in the bedroom, free her hair from its knot and remove both their clothes.

Exactly what he must not allow himself to do. Not now, and maybe never again.

"I'll try to make it to soccer practice," he told her, "but there's a news team outside. I don't want to risk having them follow me to the park and disrupt everything."

"I don't think they would, but we can't be sure," she said. "See you later, then."

After she hung up, Dirk sat at his desk, thinking about her. He missed the softness of her hair, the glow in her eyes and the silky vibrancy of her skin. He wanted an instant replay of last night.

But he could feel the past and the town itself closing around him like a vise. The expectations, speculations and intrusions left him no privacy. Now he couldn't even go for a walk without being pestered.

The world outside his hometown, Dirk had discovered long ago, was a wonderful place to hide. He loved the thrill of entering an unfamiliar country and meeting the unknown head-on.

After growing up in such a claustrophobic environment, he enjoyed the anonymity of strolling down a street where no one knew his name or expected anything from him. To be seen exclusively for oneself meant freedom.

Oddly, he didn't get the lift that usually accompanied his musings about travel. His mind kept returning to one small house, to one intriguing woman—

"Dirk?"

He looked up. His grandfather stood in the doorway. "Herb! Good to see you!"

The older man, as straight and confident as ever, returned the greeting. As he took a seat, however, Dirk could see the tension in his face. "I heard about Kim on the radio."

"I'm still in shock," Dirk admitted. "Even my experiences as a bodyguard didn't prepare me for finding the body of someone I've known for years."

"How's Joni taking it?"

"She had an alarm system installed and now she's on her way to soccer practice," he said. "She's trying to keep things normal for Jeff."

"I've been wondering if I should spend more time with them," Herb said. "Not that I'm much of a fighter. But this murderer, he might back off if she's with someone."

"Or it might make him angry," Dirk pointed out.

His grandfather cleared his throat and shifted on the hard chair. "You know, when I asked you to look into Lowell's death, I never meant to put you or anyone else in danger."

"You think my snooping contributed to Kim's getting killed?" Dirk couldn't see a connection, but Herb knew this town better than he did.

"I'm not sure." Thick silver hair stood up as the older man ran his fingers through it. "I've been mulling over this whole business all day, trying to come up with some useful approach."

It might not be Herb's job to solve crimes, but then, it wasn't Dirk's job, either, he mused. The Peterson men responded to life's blows by taking action or trying to, and his grandfather was no exception.

"I don't like them staying in the house where Lowell died," Herb went on. "Since Jeff owns half of the estate anyway, I think they should move there. I will, too. The boy needs masculine guidance.''

Dirk wondered how his grandfather would react if he learned the truth about Jeff's paternity, or that Dirk and Joni were having an affair. Most likely, it would only trouble him unnecessarily.

"I suggested they move back, but Joni vetoed it. In fact, I've listed it with a real-estate agent.'' Dirk glanced at the clock. It was after four; soccer practice should have started.

Herb frowned. "I don't like them living alone in that place after you leave. Alarm or not, I'm surprised Joni can stand it.''

"She thinks the stalker will follow her wherever she goes.'' Dirk hoped his grandfather's worrying wouldn't affect his heart condition. "I'll tell her you've offered to join her at the estate. Maybe that will make a difference. A couple of buyers want to see the property, but I don't expect it to sell right away.''

"Thanks.'' Herb stood and shook hands. "I appreciate everything you've done.''

After he left, the secretary buzzed Dirk. "You had a call while you were with Mr. Peterson. It didn't sound important, so I took a message.''

"What was it?'' Idly, Dirk jotted down a name and a phone number. Liz at the soccer league. Then he remembered that he'd requested information about the coach.

He returned the call immediately. Liz, a pleasant-sounding woman with a no-nonsense manner, told him it was Charlie's second year as a coach and that he worked for a plumbing contractor. He'd said that he'd never been convicted of a crime, but the league hadn't double-checked. If Dirk liked, she would fax over a copy of the application.

He would like it. Very much.

THE PARK'S SOCCER FIELD lacked bleachers, so Joni spread a blanket on the grass next to the Owenses. In the moisture-laden breeze, she could feel the curl evaporating from her hair and hoped she wasn't going to catch a chill through her light jacket.

The other parents kept their distance, but this time she was prepared to be cold-shouldered. Anyway, she preferred it to intrusive questions.

On the field, Charlie shouted encouragement as he put the boys through calisthenics. Although he wore jeans and a pullover, his close-cropped blond hair gave him a military air.

"I hope it's not going to rain tomorrow night," Kathryn said. "Not after all the work I put into those costumes."

"The kids could go to the Halloween party at church," Fred suggested. "That will be indoors."

"It's not the same as trick-or-treating, but I suppose they'd have to," his wife said. "What do you think, Joni?"

At the prompting, Joni gave voice to a nagging worry. "I've been concerned about letting Jeff go door-to-door this year, with a murderer loose in Viento del Mar. The church sounds like a good idea."

"I guess you're right," Kathryn said. "That was just horrible about Mrs. DeLong."

Her husband touched her arm warningly. "Maybe we should talk about something else."

"Oh! That reminds me," Kathryn told Joni. "I was going to suggest that Jeff come home with us tonight. That way, if you want to watch a newscast or if the police come by with questions, he won't have to see it. I know this whole situation's been tough on him."

The boy *would* enjoy staying overnight with Bobby.

More than that, it would give Joni a chance to talk privately with Dirk.

"That's a wonderful idea," she said. "I don't know what I'd do without you two."

"Don't thank us," said Fred. "Bobby's a lot less trouble when he has company. The two of them sit in front of the computer and we don't hear a peep out of them."

The boys began kicking the ball across the grass, each vying to get a whack at it. The Owenses' attention shifted away, and of their own accord, Joni's thoughts flew to Dirk.

She wished she knew how he felt about the change in their relationship last night. This morning, he'd seemed withdrawn.

Was he afraid she would try to cling to him? If so, she would soon disabuse him of that notion.

Joni had learned from her mother's experience that a woman needed to stand on her own two feet. All she wanted from Dirk was whatever part of himself he could give freely. If he wished, they could go back to being— what? Casual friends who shared only their affection for Jeff?

Anguish twisted inside her. She couldn't imagine never again enjoying the throbbing, tingling, steaming excitement they had discovered last night. She wanted to see those piercing blue eyes every morning, to meet him in the kitchen every evening and exchange impressions of the day.

Oh, Lord, what kind of mess had she made? She must accept that they could be nothing more than friends or she'd drive Dirk away completely.

A soccer ball whizzed by, grazing Joni. "Sorry," called a little boy who didn't look particularly sorry.

Fred scooped up the ball and flung it onto the field. As

Charlie caught it, his eyes met Joni's. His heavy lids and nearly invisible eyelashes gave his gaze a remote, inhuman quality. Then he tossed the ball into play, and a shouting mass of little boys battled for it. Had that been anger she saw on his face? she wondered. Or was she imagining it?

No one else appeared to have noticed anything amiss. Paranoia must be playing tricks on her.

DIRK PAGED THROUGH the data about Charlie Rogers. Age: 38. Marital status: Divorced. Military service in the navy. No children.

Two years ago, he'd moved from San Jose to Viento del Mar. He would have arrived just as Joni and Lowell were splitting up, so he could have read in the newspaper about her allegations that her husband was harassing her. Had he remembered the details and mimicked them later to discredit Lowell?

Through a service his business subscribed to, Dirk used Charlie's driver's license number to access his credit and police records. He found that the man hadn't told the whole truth about not having a criminal record.

There'd been one conviction for drunken driving and another for misdemeanor battery, no details provided. Then, three years ago, Charlie had been taken into custody for spousal abuse. As part of the sentencing, he'd had to complete an anger-management course. He'd also gotten a divorce.

The picture wasn't reassuring. Charlie Rogers had problems with alcohol and he'd beaten his wife.

Charlie had had an opportunity to throw paint at Dirk's car on Saturday. He would also have heard Kim's tirade against Joni. Plus, he presumably knew Del Mar Park well enough to have spied on Dirk and Joni on Sunday, then vanished when he was spotted.

On the other hand, the man hadn't exactly behaved like an ardent suitor, Dirk mused. He'd flirted with Joni previously and had brought flowers to the hospital. Still, aside from the way he'd glared at Dirk on Saturday, that didn't add up to much.

It was a long shot, but to be on the safe side, the police ought to check out his alibis for the times of the murders. And Joni should avoid being alone with him.

Dirk glanced at his watch; it was a minute past five. Nearly dark. She and Jeff would be leaving soccer practice soon. Although other people were likely to be around, he knew the killer was a master at manipulating people.

There was no way to contact her at the park short of going there himself. Dialing his cell phone as he walked, Dirk started for his car. He doubted a patrol officer would respond to his vague suspicions, so he put in a call directly to MacDougall. He got voice mail and left a terse message.

Outside, he couldn't spot his rental. It took several precious seconds to remember that he'd replaced it with a different model.

By the time he located it, the time on his watch clicked to 5:07.

THE SOCCER FAMILIES dispersed quickly into the cool night. Joni waited until Jeff retrieved his ball and started off with the Owenses before she headed in the other direction.

The rising ground blocked her view of the road. Only one streetlight marked her way and it cast more shadows than illumination. She hadn't realized the park could feel so isolated.

Off to her right, a figure moved into her range of vision. Her pulse pounding in her ears, Joni took another step and stumbled on a rough spot in the turf.

"You okay?" With two long strides, Charlie Rogers reached her. His hand closed over her arm with possessive tightness.

"Fine." Joni swallowed hard. She didn't want him to see how nervous she was.

"Where's Jeff?"

She wished she dared lie and say her son would be there any minute with Bobby's family in tow. But the field obviously stood deserted. "He went home with a friend."

"How's he taking all this?" The dim light gave the coach's square face a yellowish cast.

"All what?" Joni asked.

"A person can hardly help hearing what's on the news." He was so close she could smell peppermint gum on his breath.

With Charlie holding her arm, she couldn't move away unless she made a big production of it. Joni tried to shift backward unobtrusively, but he didn't release her. "He's taking it okay."

"And you?" he probed.

"Me?" She hated the way she kept responding with questions, but she couldn't concentrate on what he was asking.

A few minutes ago, they'd been surrounded. Now there was only dimness and silence. All she could think about was getting over the rise to the street, where there'd be houses facing them and, presumably, people arriving home from work.

"Look, I know you're under a lot of stress." His jaw worked. "It's none of my business anyway. But you know, Joni, I don't like hearing gossip about you."

"Gossip?" Oh, Lord, if he would only let go!

"People are talking about you and your brother-in-law.'' His forehead creased. "You're a classy lady. I've admired you for some time. Why are you doing this?''

She decided to take the direct approach. "Would you walk me to my car?''

"There might be other people hanging around," he said. "I don't think you want them to hear this conversation.''

"I don't care!" Joni tried to tug her arm free, but his grip tightened. The man had powerful hands; she remembered that he taught fitness classes. He probably worked out with weights, too.

"Why not? Because what they're saying is true?" He caught her other arm and swung her to face him. "Are you really that kind of woman, Joni?''

The movement pulled his sweater up enough for the dim light to glint off something thrust into his belt. Something hard and metallic.

A knife.

Chapter Fourteen

"Answer me!" He shook her. "I asked you a question!"

Where the fury came from, Joni didn't know. Welling up without warning, it galvanized her into action.

Her knee struck Charlie in the groin but not hard enough to hurt. It startled him, however, into releasing her arms, and she snatched at his ears, gripping them and digging in with her fingernails.

"What the—" Curses flew, but he couldn't jerk free without her nails ripping deeper into his ears.

Forcing his head down, Joni thrust upward with her knee and felt it connect with a crunch. With a curse, he shoved her back, and she stumbled to the ground. She scrambled for footing, but the darkness disoriented her and she staggered onto her knees. At any instant, she expected to feel the slash of a knife.

"I think you broke my damn nose!" Charlie gurgled from several feet away.

"Good!" Joni shouted.

On the street, a car door slammed. "Joni?" It was Dirk. "Joni, are you here?"

"Look out!" she yelled. "He's got a knife!"

"I—what?" Bent over, cradling his injured face, Charlie appeared to be trying to shake his head. "It's just a Swiss Army knife."

"Put your hands up!" Dirk came over the rise, hands clenched in front of him as if holding a service revolver. It was too dark to see if he was really armed.

"Aw, jeez, man!" Charlie dabbed at the air with his hands, then sank onto the grass. "Call an ambulance."

Lurching to her feet, Joni hurried to Dirk's side. She heard the harsh rush of his breathing, and when she touched him to steady herself, she felt the tightness in his muscles.

She could also see that what he held in his hands wasn't a gun but a phone.

While Charlie continued to sit on the ground complaining, Dirk punched a button and put the phone to his ear. "Joni Peterson was just attacked at Del Mar Park. We need the police and we need an ambulance."

"Hey!" Charlie gasped. "She attacked *me!*"

"You grabbed me and shook me!" Joni snapped. "What did you think you were doing?" The pent-up tension of the past week intensified her anger.

"I just wanted to talk," he muttered.

"Like you used to talk to your ex-wife?" Dirk challenged.

"What?" Joni brushed away the tears.

"He's a wife abuser," he said.

"Man, I've changed."

"I suspect the police have heard that line before," Dirk returned sharply.

The man was sniveling now. "Look, I wanted to ask her out, that's all."

He didn't sound to Joni like the monster she'd been fearing all week. But then, she reminded herself, no doubt he could act harmless when it suited him.

A few minutes later, sirens shrilled toward them. A patrolman and two paramedics ran into view, followed a short time later by Detective MacDougall. He grimaced as he watched the patrolman slap handcuffs on Charlie. ''Guess I was wrong about you two'' was the only comment he offered.

DIRK COULDN'T BELIEVE he'd let Joni get that close to danger. He should've foreseen it or done more to prevent it.

Something had changed between them last night. Joni had plugged into a long-buried need, connecting him to her and, in an inexplicable way, to himself. The prospect of harm coming to her was intolerable.

Heck, how much of an explanation did he require? She was the mother of his child, essential to Jeff's happiness. If for no other reason, Dirk would have gladly laid down his life to preserve hers.

Fortunately, she didn't appear to have suffered more than a few scrapes. And it was a lucky break that their son had gone home with the Owenses before the incident.

In Charlie's trunk, police found a nearly empty can of water-soluble red paint, left over from decorating booths at a soccer fund-raising carnival the previous spring. Charlie admitted having thrown the contents onto Dirk's car out of jealousy but denied any involvement with the murders. For the moment, he was being held for assault. The police were getting more warrants to search his apartment and health-club locker.

After a round of questioning, Dirk and Joni went home. It was hard to believe, as they unlocked the door and went inside, that they didn't have to be afraid anymore.

Unless, of course, the police screwed up and released

Charlie. "I'm staying tonight," Dirk said. "I'll sleep on the sofa bed."

Long lashes curtained Joni's eyes as she considered. He hoped she wasn't going to insist on staying alone because, in that case, he would sleep in his car outside.

She faced him across the den. "You don't have to stay on the sofa."

His body responded instantly, viscerally. After last night, he knew how warm her mouth would be and how quickly she would come to heat. But he didn't dare let down his guard again. In one day, he'd stumbled across Kim DeLong's body and nearly lost Joni to a man he should have suspected all along. What else had he overlooked?

"I'll be more alert if I stay by myself." He forced himself not to move toward her, not to touch.

"But Charlie's in custody."

"I'll feel better when the D.A.'s brought murder charges and a judge has denied bail," Dirk said. "Until then, he could get a lawyer to spring him."

She sighed. "I suppose you're right."

"By the way," he said, "Herb suggested you move back to the estate and offered to live there, too. If Mrs. Wright is a problem, I'll give her a pension or find her another job."

"This house does hold some terrible memories," Joni conceded. "But some wonderful ones, too." The look she gave him left no doubt what she was referring to.

"You'll think about Herb's offer?"

"Sure." Her expression softened. "Dirk, thank you. I'm so grateful you showed up tonight."

"You're the one who saved yourself."

"He made me mad. But…that was quite a trick with the phone. That took guts." She came closer, her palm reaching to cup his cheek. Slowly, her thumb traced his temple and jawline.

Dirk held himself motionless, and then the flood burst. Fiercely, he caught her against him and invaded her mouth with his tongue. Claiming her, stamping her.

His body hardened as she responded with silky sweetness. Beneath her clothes, he could feel her moving to a seductive beat. Inviting him to a private dance.

Then what? Dirk asked himself harshly. He couldn't promise her a future. Last night, he'd operated on pure instinct. Tonight, he had no such excuse. He had never felt as close to anyone as he did to Joni. All the more reason to avoid giving cause for bitterness. More than anything in the world, he needed to keep her as his friend.

When the kiss ended, he stepped regretfully away. "I don't want to make promises I can't keep. Let's leave it at that, Joni."

In her expressive face, he saw disappointment, but no anger. "What made you so gun-shy? Was it…that woman you mentioned?"

"Partly," Dirk said. "Her death made me face what kind of person I am and what kind of life I need. Sooner or later, I'd let you down, too. I don't want that to happen."

She released a long breath. "Once you're sure the police will hold Charlie, you'll be going away, won't you?"

Once, he'd loved the prospect of flying off to new places. Now he thought with displeasure of the dry air inside a jet, stiff plastic seat cushions and tough, flash-frozen food. Foreign airline terminals weren't romantic. They reeked of cigarette smoke, and the flight announcements echoed incomprehensibly.

Excitement. Adventure. Emptiness.

Yet beyond the tedium of air travel lay a wild unknown

that stirred Dirk's adrenaline and made him most truly himself. He needed the challenge. He needed the freedom.

"Yes," he said. "I'll only be a phone call away if you need me. I'm sorry I can't promise more."

Her lips curved into a weary smile. "My father never told us he was leaving. At least with you, I'll have a phone number. I guess that qualifies as an improvement."

When she said good-night and walked away, Dirk stood rooted to the spot. He wished she had slapped him. It would have hurt less.

BY THE TIME JONI GOT dressed on Thursday morning, she discovered Dirk was ready to go out. He had a long day ahead, he said. Two potential buyers wanted to see the Peterson estate, and he'd decided to keep the printing company in the family for Jeff's sake.

That meant whipping it into shape for someone else to step in, then finding that someone. He wanted to interview top employees as well as contact an executive search service.

At the door, he gave Joni one wistful glance and then he was gone. Not even a kiss.

Rationally, she knew he had a point. Lovers built up layers of emotion that could explode; friendship was steadier and more enduring. She didn't care. She wanted to enjoy every scrap of time together while they could. But there was no use beating her head against a brick wall.

After collecting the newspaper, Joni went inside to eat and read. The front page, as expected, was full of news about Kim DeLong's death and the arrest of Charlie Rogers. Apparently, he'd suffered a bloody nose but not a broken one, she learned.

Silence lengthened through the house as she finished her cereal and coffee. Suddenly, she ached to see her son.

She called Kathryn. "Did you hear about Charlie?" she asked right after saying hello.

"Yes!" Her friend sounded breathless. "I can't believe it. I mean, he was so nice to the kids. But I'm glad it's over."

"You two have been wonderful through this whole thing," Joni said. "Why don't I pick up the boys at day care, fix dinner and take them trick-or-treating? They can sleep over, too. You and Fred deserve a night to yourselves."

"We could use some time together," Kathryn agreed. "But aren't you and Dirk going to celebrate your birthday?"

Her birthday. Thirty years old. "I've been trying not to think about it," Joni admitted. Dirk hadn't said a word. She couldn't remember whether he even knew it was her birthday. "I'd like to celebrate with the kids, if that's okay with you. I'll take them both to school in the morning, too."

"That would be great." From the relief in Kathryn's voice, Joni realized she must have been feeling stressed.

At the back door came a light, rapid tapping. "That sounds like my neighbor," Joni said. "I'll see you later."

"Thanks again!" Her friend rang off.

Sure enough, it was Celia, her arms filled with small packages. "Happy birthday, Joni!"

"I can't believe you remembered!" Hoping that she wasn't going to be late for work but appreciative of her neighbor's kindness, Joni invited her inside. "What a delightful surprise!"

The older woman smiled, clearly enjoying herself as she presented each parcel in turn. "These are Chinese bean-curd pastries, not too sweet. I hope you like the flavor."

"I'm sure I will."

The next package, topped with clear cellophane, contained four round green fruits. "Asian pears," Celia explained. "You peel them and slice them. They taste like pears but they are crisp." Next, a box of pineapple-flavored cakes joined the gifts on the table.

Joni thanked her profusely, then said, "I wish I had more time to visit, but my boss must be getting impatient. Could you come over Saturday afternoon for coffee?"

"I look forward to it." Celia patted her on the arm. "I am so glad they arrested that man. Now you are safe." She glanced toward the den. "Is your brother-in-law still here?"

"He went to work." It didn't seem enough of an explanation, so Joni added, "He'll be leaving town soon. His business is overseas."

Her neighbor smiled. "Like my husband. But you are too smart to marry someone who is always gone. Well, I see you Saturday!"

After ushering her outside, Joni collected her purse. She still couldn't bring herself to take her own lunch, though.

How *had* Charlie managed to slip inside the hospital on Tuesday and put the fringe in her bag? she wondered. Perhaps he'd been making plumbing repairs.

On the way out, she remembered to set her new alarm system. Yesterday afternoon, she'd been in such a hurry to pick up Jeff for the soccer game that she'd forgotten. It might take a while to get used to this thing, which was ironic considering that her reason for installing it no longer existed.

Fog lay heavy on the ground, and Joni navigated her car with care. On San Bernardo Road, a scarecrow dangling from a tree startled her even though she'd seen it before. In light of the two recent murders, she wished whoever had chosen this ghoulish decoration would display better judgment.

At the hospital, a couple of people stopped her to ask if she'd been hurt yesterday and to express relief about the arrest. It helped the reality sink in that she no longer had to fear being stalked.

Joni's mood lightened further as she observed the costumes that many of the staff wore for the holiday. Although hospital policy discouraged anything that might interfere with patient care, workers indulged in face paints, shocking hair colors and offbeat sweatshirts.

Black and orange crepe paper festooned the public relations office, Joni noted as she arrived. When Basil padded from his office, she saw that he was chewing an unlit pipe and wearing a Sherlock Holmes cap and a tweed jacket with elbow patches.

"What do you think?" he asked.

"It suits you." She regarded his tall, gaunt frame. He *did* remind her somewhat of the legendary detective.

He cleared his throat, a sign that he was about to raise a more or less personal issue. "How are you holding up? The radio said you were assaulted."

"My knees are scraped, but you should see the other guy." Joni couldn't help chuckling. "Honest, I gave worse than I got."

"That's over, then." Her boss made a satisfied clucking noise. "In that case—"

"—you can expect me to get the newsletter out on time after all," she finished for him.

"Er, yes," he said.

Joni went to work at her computer. She lost track of time until the hospital florist appeared about ten o'clock with a large flower arrangement in black and orange. It was spectacular but, she reflected, a touch creepy.

"Is there a card?" she asked, giving him a tip.

"Right in there." He pointed to a small orange envelope. "Happy Halloween."

"Thanks."

Inside the envelope she found a white card. It read, "Glad they got the killer, but I hope you'll still consider living on the estate or buying a new house together so I can watch over you and Jeff. Happy birthday!" It was signed, "Herb."

Joni studied the note with mixed feelings. If money were no object, she'd be happy to consider moving to a different house, but the Peterson mansion retained too many memories of Lowell. She doubted she could ever feel comfortable there.

It was kind of Herb to offer to leave his condo development, where he enjoyed the games and classes sponsored by a senior citizens' club. And it *would* be nice for Jeff to have a father figure on the premises. She couldn't help reflecting that, in fact, he had a father, but one who wouldn't be around for long. The thought made her chest ache.

In some other lifetime, she and Dirk might have been destined to be together. But not in this one. The chasm between them was too great.

He bore the scars of a youth filled with his father's tyranny and rejection. Even the death of a woman he loved hadn't been enough to cure his restlessness.

Had he felt about this woman the way he felt about her? She supposed it was impossible to compare the two relationships at such different points in his life.

What she needed wasn't a man to lean on at every turn but an unshakable bond with someone she loved. Someone who would be there for her and Jeff when it counted, in the ways that mattered most.

Dirk seemed to think that was what he was offering. But he was holding back the essential part of himself. His love. His intimacy. His commitment.

She wondered how long it would take before she could regard him as someone whose absences didn't matter, and whose presence brought only mild pleasure. Would that ever be possible?

After setting the flowers on a side table, Joni returned to work. At lunchtime, she made a quick trip to the cafeteria and brought back a sandwich so she could continue editing.

In her distracted state, she had to rewrite more than usual and juggle the layout several times. By late afternoon, several hours of work remained, but at least she would be able to finish by midday Friday. Then she could drop the camera-ready art at Peterson Printing and pick it up on Monday. She would make her deadline. Barely.

By four o'clock, the part-time secretary had left for the day, so when the phone rang, Joni answered it herself. "Public relations."

"Mrs. Peterson? Detective MacDougall." Did she just imagine that his voice held an ominous note?

Her hands went cold. "Is something wrong?"

"We've released Charlie Rogers."

She couldn't believe it. "He made bail?"

"He's been released on his own recognizance," the detective said. "I'm afraid the only charges we can bring are simple assault and malicious mischief."

The receiver nearly slipped from her grasp. "What do you mean?"

"We can't link him to either of the murders." A trace of huskiness hinted at the detective's frustration. "Last Wednesday, at the time your husband was killed, Mr. Rogers was conducting an aerobics class. We have a dozen witnesses.''

Her mind searched frantically. ''What about Saturday?''

''He says he was home alone. That's not much of an alibi, but there's nothing to tie him to Mrs. DeLong,'' the policeman said. ''No witnesses, no evidence.''

''His knife?''

''We ran tests. It's clean.''

She yearned to feel safe a little while longer. ''Can't you hold him for a day or so?''

''He got out half an hour ago.'' MacDougall sighed. ''I was just informed and I thought you'd want to know.''

''Yes. Thank you.'' Numbly, Joni hung up. Into her mind flashed the scene from last night: the isolated soccer field, the eerie shadows from a distant streetlight.

Charlie had threatened her and grabbed her. How could they let him go?

But a man couldn't be in two places at once. If a dozen students confirmed that he'd been teaching aerobics, she didn't see how he could have murdered Lowell.

It was time to stop clutching at straws. Unwillingly, Joni forced herself to face the facts.

Charlie Rogers couldn't be the killer. That meant her stalker hadn't been arrested.

He was still out there.

Chapter Fifteen

The first of the two potential buyers, a tall, balding man with a handlebar mustache, arrived on schedule at the Peterson estate and proceeded to criticize everything from its winding driveway to the lack of a swimming pool. After a teeth-gritting hour and a half, both Dirk and the real-estate agent were relieved to see him go.

He'd encroached into the second prospect's time, but that didn't matter because she arrived late. Very late, towing her mother, her sister, her brother-in-law and two small children.

They loved the property, if only Dirk would agree to sell it for half price. And, in lieu of a down payment, to trade for a property they'd inherited in the Mojave Desert.

Leaving the agent to shoo them away, he drove to the printing plant in an edgy mood. Dirk wasn't sure what had set him off; the buyers were a pain, but he'd encountered their types before in his various business ventures: the nitpicker and the wheeler-dealer.

He cheered himself by reflecting back to his morning's review of the company books. Profits had risen steadily, costs had been kept at a reasonable level, and Lowell's publishing prospectus was exciting.

Best of all, Joni's stalker had been captured and put behind bars. She and Jeff were safe.

At least with you, I'll have a phone number. I guess that qualifies as an improvement.

The memory of her words seared Dirk. Joni hadn't intended to taunt him by comparing him to her runaway father, he felt sure. She'd merely been stating a fact, and that made it all the worse.

How could he reconcile his feelings for her, and for Jeff, with what he knew of his own nature? It would be worse to make a commitment and then break it than to make none at all. But it was also possible, Dirk knew, that he was simply afraid to risk everything on one roll of the dice.

Turning into the parking lot, he headed for his reserved space and nearly drove into the yellow police tape that roped it off. As he hit the brakes, his heart started to race with unexpected anxiety.

Taking a deep breath, he parked alongside the building. He hadn't given himself a chance to recover from finding Kim's body yesterday. No matter how tough a man imagined himself to be, a shock like that was bound to affect him.

What kind of a monster was Charlie Rogers anyway? Had he truly believed he would impress Joni by killing her one-time rival?

Mulling over that question, he exited the car and strode inside. When he entered the administrative wing, a stocky man in a tailored suit rose to greet him.

"Maynard!" Dirk shook hands enthusiastically. "What brings you here?"

Maynard Greenburg, a voluble man in his forties, headed a Los Angeles advertising and marketing firm that specialized in adapting promotions to local tastes anywhere in the world. He'd flown to out-of-the-way sites several times to meet Dirk and formulate strategies for boosting new businesses.

"Actually, I had an appointment with your brother," the man said. "He contacted me about writing a book for him. Your secretary just told me about his death. I'm very sorry."

"I regret that you had to get the news this way," Dirk said. "If I'd known about your appointment, I'd have called."

"It wasn't on my calendar," the secretary said apologetically. "Mr. Peterson must have forgotten to tell me."

"Now that you mention it, I remember recommending you to him," Dirk told Maynard. "I figured you'd be worth a couple of book ideas at least. Come on in. I apologize for keeping you waiting."

"No problem. I'm spending a few days in Santa Barbara with my daughter, so I didn't have to drive all that far."

"You have messages, Mr. Peterson!" the secretary called as they went into Dirk's private office.

"Thanks. I'll look at them later." He couldn't wait to go over ideas with Maynard. A writer this inventive and cutting edge would be perfect to help launch the publishing venture.

The discussion flowed. Dirk took copious notes, only wishing he would be on hand to see the project carried to fulfillment. On the other hand, it might take quite a while to find an executive to run the company and serve as publisher, and he would have to fill in until then. Dirk was surprised how much that prospect pleased him.

By the time Maynard departed, he discovered to his surprise that the daylight had gone. So had his secretary, since it was nearly six o'clock.

For the past few days, Dirk had always been aware on some level that he needed to keep tabs on Joni's safety.

Today, he'd cut himself some slack because that was no longer necessary.

Messages. Right.

He punched a command into his computer and the secretary's notes appeared. First, a major order was expected, and the foreman wanted his approval to reserve sufficient paper stock at the mill. Second, he needed to authorize the annual Christmas merit bonuses.

The third one was from Joni. "They've released Charlie Rogers. He has an alibi for last Wednesday."

Dirk pictured the short-haired man sitting on the grass last night, clutching his injured face and whining. He'd all but attacked Joni and he had a violent history.

Surely the police wouldn't have let him go unless the alibi was airtight. Their killer, however, might be clever enough to fake an alibi.

He put in a call to MacDougall and got his voice mail. The man had left for the day.

Where was Joni? Dirk tried her house, but the answering machine picked up. A call to the hospital public relations office brought the same result. She must be in transit. There was no reason to believe she faced any immediate danger, and yet…

He glanced out the window and remembered that it was Halloween. Rationally or not, Joni had believed matters would come to a head tonight.

It was also her thirtieth birthday. A turning point, a milestone in her life.

Any man who wanted to possess her badly enough to kill would surely intend to be part of this night. While Charlie's arrest made everyone complacent, the real killer could have been watching his chance and moving into position.

Joni was in danger; Dirk had no doubt of that. He grabbed his coat and headed for the door.

CARRYING THE OVERSIZE floral arrangement, Joni hurried down the hospital corridor. In her eagerness to finish screening photographs for the newsletter, she'd lost track of time, and the day-care center closed at six.

She hustled past the auditorium, where the Red Cross had chosen this rather ghoulish night to hold a blood donor clinic. It amused her, when she glanced inside, to see a man in a Dracula costume filling out his paperwork to give blood.

"Joni!"

She glanced up, startled. From the auditorium emerged a white-coated volunteer, none other than Herb.

"Oh, hi!" She smiled at Dirk's grandfather. "Thanks for the flowers!"

"Need some help with those?"

Joni was about to decline when she realized she really did need help. "Sure. Thanks."

Herb moved ahead of her to the heavy glass door and propped it open. "I just heard on the radio about them letting that coach go. I think it's terrible."

"Apparently he's innocent," she said. "Of murder anyway." A breeze misted her face, reminding her that showers were expected. The air felt ominously heavy, the way it had last Wednesday. The night Lowell was killed.

The older man relieved her of the flowers and walked beside her between rows of parked cars. "Do you have anything special planned tonight? I thought I might drop by later."

"That would be lovely." She stopped beside her sedan. "I'm taking Jeff and Bobby trick-or-treating, but we should be finished by eight. Probably earlier if this rain gets worse.''

''You mean that grandson of mine isn't planning a special celebration for your birthday?'' he asked.

Joni fished the key from her purse. Herb was perceptive enough to have noticed that she and Dirk were far from indifferent to each other, but she hoped he didn't guess how involved they'd become.

''Not that I know of.'' After setting the flowers in the passenger seat, she slid behind the wheel. Herb closed the door and leaned on it, watching her.

''Joni, I want to talk to you about the future,'' he said. ''Your plans, I mean.''

If she were more than ten minutes late to fetch the children, the center would bill her extra. A lot extra.

''I'm sorry but I've got to pick up the boys. Can we talk later? Please?'' She turned the key in the ignition.

Nothing happened. Not even a click.

Joni's stomach sank. She tried again. Still nothing.

Urgently, she considered her options. A jump-start? A cab?

''I'll give you a ride,'' Herb said.

''Aren't they depending on you at the blood drive?'' she asked.

''We can pick up the boys and I'll drop you off at home,'' he said. ''I'll be back before anyone notices I'm gone.''

She didn't feel right, taking him away from his volunteer duties. During the hospital's blood drives, the early evening hours were always the busiest.

Down the aisle cruised a white minivan with black and silver racing stripes. With a rush of relief, Joni recognized it, and the driver. ''That's Bobby's dad!''

"I've met him," Herb said stiffly. "What's he doing here?"

"Keeping his mother company, I presume. She has dialysis a couple of times a week." At Joni's wave, the van halted directly in front of her.

The window hummed down. "What's up?" Fred called across the passenger seat.

She told him.

"No problem. I'll jump-start your car and follow you to the garage. We don't want you getting stranded along the way." He lifted his cell phone to his ear. "I'll ask Kathryn to run by the day-care center and meet us at your house. We can pick up fast food for everybody."

Joni hated to impose, especially when she'd planned to give the Owenses a night off, but it was a sensible way to deal with the situation. "That should work out fine. Herb, thanks, but I know they need you inside."

The older man yielded. "As long as someone's looking after you." He strolled toward the building, not seeming to mind the rain pattering around him.

It had turned into a downpour by the time Fred got her car started. The motor sputtered alarmingly, and Joni was grateful that her garage was only a block away.

They arrived just as the mechanic was leaving. He let her put the car inside and promised to work on it first thing in the morning.

Fred's wipers arced across the windshield in a steady beat, welcoming Joni to the van. He smiled as he watched her put the flower arrangement in back.

"That's right, it's your thirtieth birthday, isn't it?" he said. "Such a special occasion. You know, I'm glad I have a chance to celebrate it with you."

Reaching across the seat, he patted her hand.

DIRK WAS CROSSING the outer office when the phone rang. On the verge of ignoring it, he realized that it might be Joni.

"Peterson Printing, Dirk speaking," he said into the mouthpiece.

"Thank goodness I reached you!" The woman's voice was sharp with tension. "This is Kathryn Owens, Bobby's mother. Do you know where Joni is?"

Fear coalesced inside him. "She's not answering the phone at home or at work. Why? What's happened?"

"She promised to pick up the boys, but the day-care director just called," Kathryn said. "She's late, which isn't like her."

He checked his watch. Ten past six. Even if he'd just missed Joni at the hospital, she should have reached the center by now.

"I'll run over to the hospital and retrace her route," he said. "You'll get the kids?"

"Of course," Kathryn said. "I'll take them to the Halloween party at the church." She gave him the phone number there. "And, Dirk..."

"Yes?"

"I didn't want to speak out of turn, and maybe this isn't relevant, but..."

What key piece of information had this woman been sitting on? Dirk's instincts screamed at him to reach across the phone line and shake her, but instead he said with tight control, "Tell me everything. Quickly."

"Fred and I have been having some problems." Strain made her tone high and thin. "He's Bobby's stepfather. My first husband died in a car crash. I didn't know much about Fred before we got married five years ago. He lived with his mother, and she's really nice. I met her at the supermarket where I work."

They didn't have time for Kathryn's life story. "Is there something you've learned about him? Something that makes you suspicious?"

"Nothing definite," she said. "I thought it was odd that his driver's license gives his name as Frederick Owens but on some of his papers it's Allen Frederick Owens. Also, I came across two social security cards with different numbers."

"Can you read them out to me?" Using a middle name as a first name might not be unusual, but honest people didn't carry two social security cards.

"Just a minute." Time dragged until she picked up the phone again. "Here they are." She gave him the numbers.

"Anything else?" Dirk asked.

Kathryn made a noise that was almost a sob. "He plays basketball a lot of nights, or that's what he says he's doing, but I don't know whom he plays with or where, and he gets angry when I ask. That's not all. I feel so stupid. I— I didn't want to make the connection, I didn't mention anything to Joni and now—"

"What else?" The words rapped out harshly. "What else, Kathryn?"

"Two of my kitchen knives are missing," she said. "The first one, I thought I'd just misplaced it, but I haven't been able to find the second one since I fixed dinner on Saturday."

Kim DeLong had been stabbed to death that same night. So far, the murder weapon hadn't turned up.

"Go get the boys." Dirk needed to make sure Jeff was taken care of. "I'll handle the rest. Is he driving your van?"

"Yes. Please hurry." She sounded scared.

He didn't even know for sure that Fred was anywhere

near Joni, Dirk reminded himself as he raced to his car. Nevertheless, he dialed the police as he took off for the hospital.

RAIN MUST HAVE BEEN falling heavily in the mountains inland, because Viento del Mar Creek was spilling over its banks. It had narrowed San Bernardo Road to one lane in each direction.

"What a mess," Fred said as they inched forward in a line of steaming cars.

"Maybe we should forget about stopping for food," Joni said. "I hate to make Kathryn wait. She doesn't even have a key to my house."

"She can use the one you hide," Fred said.

"It's not there anymore." Joni peered out into a blur of passing lights. "Anyway, I changed the locks."

"Smart move." He seemed remarkably jovial, considering that most men would be pounding their horns by this time. "We can't have you going hungry on such an important occasion."

"Oh, I can always find something in the fridge," she said. "But I suppose you're right. We don't want the boys to fill up on candy."

After the two eastbound lanes funneled into one, the traffic picked up. Through the rain, the oncoming headlights and neon signs formed a blurry glare.

As they crossed the bridge, it struck Joni that in the three years since Bobby and Jeff met at school, she'd never been alone with Fred before. Or if she had, the occasion hadn't stuck in her memory.

She glanced at him and found that, even now, it was hard to think of Fred apart from the roles of Kathryn's husband and Bobby's father. Everything about him, from his light brown hair and pleasantly rounded face to the spreading waistline, seemed designed to blend into a crowd.

All she knew about his background was that he'd once aspired to play professional baseball and that he remained strongly attached to his mother. Fred was, she guessed, in his early forties, and he and Kathryn must have been married at least nine years in order to have an eight-year-old son.

The van eased into the drive-through line of a fried-chicken restaurant. Around the building's eaves, Halloween decorations sagged in the rain.

"How's your mother?" Joni asked. When Fred continued staring at the taillights ahead of them, she added, "I know dialysis patients sometimes have a hard time accepting their dependence on a machine."

"Oh, she doesn't mind the machine as much as the dietary restrictions." Turning toward her, he studied Joni. "Say, why don't we skip this and I'll take you to the Chalet for a steak? That would be more festive."

"The Chalet?" The town's most expensive restaurant sat on a hill several miles out of town. "What about Kathryn and the kids?"

He laughed. "I almost forgot them! Must be something about you, Joni. You could make a man lose his head."

Gooseflesh prickled her arms. Obviously, Fred was joking, but didn't he realize how creepy it sounded?

They reached the order window, and she had to concentrate on which side dishes to select and how many drinks they needed. Then she and Fred fished out their wallets; she wanted to pay, but he wouldn't let her.

"It's my treat," he said. "Then let's stop at a bakery and I'll buy you a birthday cake. What do you say?"

"Thanks, but I'd rather get home." Joni was relieved when he didn't press the point.

The server handed him a cardboard bucket, several paper sacks and a cardboard tray of drinks. The smell of fried chicken filled the van.

Fred stuffed the food containers around her and placed the drink holder in her lap. She felt trapped, but she wasn't sure why.

As they turned onto the main road, Joni became increasingly nervous. The hazardous driving conditions must be affecting her appetite because she was no longer even hungry.

Something dark swung toward the windshield. With a thump, a hideous grinning face hit the glass. Joni shrieked. The drink tray slid toward the floor. She grabbed it, barely in time.

A scarecrow. The dangling figure must have torn loose from its ties and hit the car.

"There ought to be a law against that kind of thing," she grumbled. "We could've had an accident."

"I found it kind of exciting." Fred wore an expression that bordered on gloating. "Don't you enjoy the sense of danger?"

"Not particularly." Why was he talking this way? Usually he understood her feelings and offered helpful insights. Tonight, Fred seemed like a different person.

Joni's muscles tensed so hard her ribs ached. Alarm bells jangled in every nerve ending.

Painfully, she forced herself to examine the odd way Fred was behaving. Patting her hand, tucking the food around her, offering to take her to the Chalet. Most of all, wearing an air of triumph. He clearly enjoyed having her to himself and being in control of the situation.

The clues were all there; she just hadn't put them together, she realized with a jolt. Or was she getting carried away as she'd done with Charlie?

Fred had overheard Kim's tirade against her after the soccer game on Saturday. He also knew she kept a key hidden behind the house. He could have used it to get inside on Sunday.

Two days ago, Edith Owens had finished her dialysis session at lunchtime. If Fred had dropped by to visit during her session, he would have been in the hospital at the right time to tamper with Joni's lunch.

Fred? Could Fred be the killer?

She tried to get a grip on her fears. It wasn't a foolproof case, not by a long shot. Most likely, he had alibis for the times of the murders.

The van turned into Canyon Acres. Her panic abated.

They were only a few blocks from home. Kathryn and the boys would be waiting.

Chapter Sixteen

The dispatcher said Detective MacDougall was still in the field but offered to transfer Dirk to the watch commander. He thanked her and kept the phone pressed to his ear as he waited.

Although the printing plant lay only half a mile from the hospital, he'd been crawling through traffic for ten minutes. The way the rain was coming down, the situation could only get worse. He had to reach someone who could do something.

"Sergeant Cruz," a woman's voice announced in his ear.

"This is Dirk Peterson," he said. "Joni Peterson is missing and I've just learned that a family friend may be hiding a criminal history."

Since he hadn't stopped to check on Fred in the computer, Dirk was making a broad assumption. He didn't care. He would rather risk being wrong than lose Joni from an excess of caution.

"What is this individual's name?" the sergeant asked. She didn't ask who Joni was or what was going on; she must be well aware of the case.

"Frederick Owens. He also uses the name Allen Frederick Owens," Dirk said. "He has a couple of different social security numbers, and his wife is missing two knives from her kitchen.''

''Are you saying he's abducted Mrs. Peterson?''

''I don't know,'' he admitted. ''But she failed to pick up her son after work. Owens knew her schedule, and his wife can't locate him.''

''Do you have a description of his and Mrs. Peterson's vehicles?''

He provided them, along with the social security numbers. Computer keys clicked as she entered the information. ''Joni should've left her job at the hospital an hour ago,'' he added. ''I'm trying to get there, but the traffic's terrible.''

''We're working a lot of accidents and the creek's flooding,'' the sergeant said. ''I'll call Detective MacDougall in the field and put out an APB on both subject vehicles. Is there a number where I can reach you?''

Dirk gave it to her.

''Let us know if you find Mrs. Peterson,'' she said. ''I hope this is a false alarm.''

''You and me both,'' he said.

The conversation failed to reassure him. The storm had already spread the police too thin, and he doubted they would treat Joni's disappearance as an emergency. Lots of people might be temporarily missing tonight, thanks to the weather.

Minutes dragged by until, at last, he turned into the hospital. Whipping into a space marked for emergencies, Dirk yanked out the key and ran inside.

In the lobby, he stopped a candy striper. ''I need to find Joni Peterson. It's urgent. She works in the—''

''I know where she works,'' said the teenager, a pretty African-American girl with a serious expression. ''I'll take you there.'' She moved quickly ahead of him.

The public relations office was locked and dark. Dirk smacked his hand against the wall in frustration.

The candy striper considered for a moment. "There's a blood donor drive tonight. Maybe she stopped to donate."

Unlikely, but he might as well check. "Where is it?"

The teenager sprinted beside him along another corridor. Near the end, signs pointed donors toward an auditorium. After wishing him luck, the girl returned to her duties.

Dirk's gaze swept the large room. People waited on folding chairs; nurses in white tended the donors; volunteers took medical histories at a couple of tables. No sign of Joni.

At the aftercare table, Herb was pouring juice. Catching sight of Dirk, he set down the pitcher and whisked toward him. "You looking for Joni?" Herb asked. "She left half an hour ago."

Relief rushed through Dirk. "She's all right, then?"

"Sure, she's all right." His grandfather regarded him quizzically. "Something wrong?"

"Her friend Kathryn called. Joni didn't show up at the day-care center."

"Kathryn?" Herb's eyebrows rose in dismay. "Kathryn Owens?"

Dirk's anxiety returned, full force. "You sound surprised."

"Her husband said he was going to call and have her get the kids," the older man said.

"You talked to Fred?"

"Joni's car wouldn't start," Herb said. "Fred happened by and offered her a ride."

Fear tightened Dirk's throat. Fred hadn't called Kathryn. There could only be one reason why he would have lied.

"It's him," he said. "He's the killer."

THE HOUSE SAT ON THE HILL, barely discernible against the dark backdrop of trees. No lights shone at this end of the street, not even at Celia's place. To Joni, her home looked desolate and forlorn.

In the heavy rain, there was no sign of trick-or-treaters. None of the usual evening joggers and dog walkers would brave this kind of deluge, either. Right now, Joni wished the press *were* harassing her; at least there might be someone hanging around.

As the van turned into her driveway, she tried to spot Kathryn's station wagon. When they crested the rise, her last hope died. The turnaround was empty.

''They're not here yet,'' she said.

''No?'' Fred didn't sound surprised. ''Maybe they decided to go to the church party instead.''

He knew as well as she did that Kathryn wouldn't change plans without notifying them. Joni could hardly breathe.

Frantically, she tried to remember what Fred had said on his end of the phone conversation. But he'd placed the call from inside his van; she hadn't heard any of it.

He might not have called Kathryn at all.

Come to think of it, why had he been driving through the hospital parking lot at six o'clock? On Tuesday, Edith Owens had undergone dialysis in the morning. Why, two days later, would her son be visiting her in the evening?

Maybe he'd known Joni would be stranded and would need a ride. Maybe he'd disabled her car and driven around until she showed up.

Disbelief clouded her mind. She'd known this man for three years, trusted him with her son, become friends with his wife.

Fred switched off the engine. Rain sheeted against the roof and windows, isolating them.

When he turned toward Joni, she saw a face different from the one she knew. Subtle changes—a slackness of skin tone, a fixedness of the eyes, a looseness about the mouth—transformed Fred Owens into a stranger.

She swallowed hard. Instinctively, she tried not to let him see that she'd noticed anything. Maybe if she pretended everything was normal, he wouldn't take action.

"We need to call Kathryn," she said. "To make sure she's picked up the kids."

"Forget Kathryn," he said.

"Then we should go to the day-care center ourselves."

"This is our special time." His voice took on a wheedling quality, with a threat lingering below the surface. "Don't ruin it, Joni. Don't make me punish you again."

"Is that what you were doing?" It corresponded to what Dirk had surmised, yet she could still hardly comprehend it. "Framing me for murder? Breaking into my house, threatening me at work?"

"I knew they'd never charge you with murder," he said. "You needed to be taught a lesson. You're too independent, Joni. You need to let me take charge now."

"I don't understand." But she did, all too well. He wanted to control and dominate her. Dirk had been right.

"It's your birthday," Fred went on in that same hypnotic tone. "Turning thirty, that's important. It's when you put your mistakes behind you and start over."

"It is?" She wished she had a weapon. Or at least some way to bolt out of the van without having to extricate herself from all this food.

He leaned against his armrest, perfectly at ease. "When I turned thirty, Mom and I were living in Phoenix. The women I met there, well, they were low class. I decided to start over in a clean place. That's the special thing about this birthday, Joni. It's a chance to make a fresh start. With me.''

She didn't want a fresh start; she wanted to get away from him. How could he possibly fantasize a future together after he'd murdered two people?

She didn't want to antagonize him. The best thing would be to keep him talking, and maybe Celia would come home. Or Dirk.

An image formed in her mind, of Dirk's dark head bending over her, his blue eyes bright with concern. It steadied her.

"After we left Phoenix," Fred went on, "we tried L.A., but I didn't like it. Nothing but trash. I needed a small town where you can really get to know people. So we drove up the coast. Mom fell in love with this place and so did I.''

His fingers stroked her wrist. With all her strength, Joni resisted the urge to snatch her hand away.

"When I met Kathryn, I thought at first I'd found the right woman,'' he said. "She seemed like such a nice widow lady with a little boy.''

"Bobby isn't your son?'' Joni wasn't sure why that made a difference. But neither Fred nor Kathryn had mentioned the fact in the three years she'd known them, which meant he must have wanted it kept secret.

He liked to play roles, she realized. He liked to hide who he really was. It must give him a sense of superiority; it certainly had enabled him to fool people.

"At first, I had fun playing with the little boy, but now that he's getting older, he's annoying. Whiny, like his mother,'' Fred said. "Besides, Jeff's a better soccer player. He's more athletic. Like me.''

In your dreams!

"When I met you, I knew I'd found the right girl.'' Fred

leaned over, and his breath whispered across her neck. Joni gritted her teeth to keep from flinching. "More beautiful, more intelligent. You were married then, but I could see you weren't happy. It was just a question of time."

For three years he'd been stalking her, at least in his mind. Pretending to be her friend. Spending time with her son, giving her advice.

Lowell had come to her house, his last night on earth, to try to catch her stalker. Had he been able to see, in the moments before he died, that it was Fred? How terrible for him, not even to be able to warn her. She had to stop tormenting herself. She had to figure out what to do.

"Lowell was a selfish, low-class jerk," Fred said. "Aren't you glad I protected you from him after the way he treated you? And Kim DeLong. She deserved what she got."

He had killed Kim out of some misplaced sense of loyalty to Joni? She bit her lip in dismay. But she had to concentrate on keeping the man talking while she formulated a plan.

"Why didn't you leave your wife?" she asked. "Why didn't you simply tell me how you felt?"

He blinked as if the thought had never occurred to him. "What difference does it make? We're here now, aren't we? Just the two of us."

He seemed awfully certain that Dirk wouldn't show up. What if Fred had done something to him?

A vise clamped across Joni's chest. She had to find out even if it angered the man. "But you know my brother-in-law has been staying here."

"He left," Fred said. "I saw him go back to his old home. That was a wise decision, Joni. I'm glad you threw him out."

So Fred had been spying on Dirk today. He must have

seen him going to show the estate to buyers, she thought, and tried to hide her relief.

Dirk was safe. But he might be working late or stuck in traffic. For all she knew, he might still believe Charlie was in custody.

Fred's fingers crept up her cheek and brushed back some loose strands of hair. Fear and disgust made Joni start to shake.

"Are you cold, darling?" he whispered. "We should go inside."

She remembered the security system. The alarm was wired to the police station as well as rigged for earsplitting loudness. If she opened the door and punched in the wrong code, it would sound in—how long? A minute? Would people realize it wasn't a false alarm? How long would it take the police to get here?

As soon as it went off, Fred would know that she'd tricked him. Before it sounded, she would have to find some excuse to walk toward the utility room, then dash out the back door. But after that?

She couldn't think that far ahead. It was useless to worry; she just had to act.

"I guess I did get chilled," she said. "You're right. We should go in."

Fred grinned as if she'd given him the most wonderful present of his life. Or was about to.

DIRK WAS INCHING HIS CAR past the high school when his cell phone rang. He snatched it from his pocket. "Peterson here."

"MacDougall." Red taillights flashed ahead, and Dirk tapped the brakes. "The watch commander filled me in. You think she's with Owens?"

"I know she is." He relayed what he'd learned from Herb.

"Sergeant Cruz ran a check," the detective said. "Allen Frederick Owens has a dishonorable discharge from the marines and a couple of convictions in Arizona for assault and battery. He's also wanted for murder."

"A woman?"

"Ex-girlfriend. Or at least she was trying to leave." MacDougall uttered a curse. "He's had us chasing our tails all over town. I've been talking to some of Mrs. DeLong's friends and my car's stuck in the mud out near the country club. Any idea where he might take her?"

Dirk had instinctively driven toward Canyon Acres. "He seems to want to stake his claim, not kill her. If I'm right, he'll head for her house. Does your department have a helicopter?"

"Are you kidding?" MacDougall said. "Even if we did, it couldn't fly in this weather. I'll radio for a patrol car ASAP."

Unless there was one already in the vicinity, Dirk doubted it could get there ahead of him. "Do what you can."

"I will," the detective said. "Believe me."

As he clicked off, Dirk mulled over the discovery that Fred had killed his former girlfriend when they split up. It jibed with what police-science classes taught about spousal abusers.

He felt almost certain that Fred's intent was to claim Joni, not hurt her. The man wouldn't want to destroy the object of his obsession unless she rejected him.

But once she did, he would go after her with a vengeance.

FRED HELD AN UMBRELLA over Joni as they approached the front door. He had the bucket of chicken beneath the other arm.

She contemplated ditching the drinks and food sacks and making a run for it, but he was too close. The moment she tensed for action, he would notice.

Had everyone on the block already come home from work? Wasn't anyone giving a Halloween party? If only a car would turn onto the street, she could take the risk of running.

"You shouldn't have let Dirk stay with you," Fred said out of the blue. "That was wrong, Joni."

They reached the overhang. Setting the drinks on the porch, she fished out her key. "I didn't know who killed Lowell. I thought I needed protection."

"Did he touch you?" Fred closed the umbrella and set it aside. "Did you let him kiss you, Joni?"

Slimy, that was how this man made her feel. He ought to be crawling around in the garden with the rest of the slugs. Yet her life depended on placating him.

"Dirk's too much of a workaholic," she said. "I prefer a family man, like you."

Fred beamed. How could he be stupid enough to believe her? But he was hearing what he'd waited three years to hear.

"We belong together," he oozed. "Not here in this town. Too many gossips. We could go south. Mexico, maybe. Jeff would like that, don't you think?"

"Sure." She opened the door and went to the keypad. The code she'd chosen, a number she wasn't likely to forget but that didn't show up in her wallet, was Herb's birthday. Beneath Fred's gaze, she tapped in the date of Jeff's birthday.

Or was she mixed up? Maybe she'd intended to set Herb's birthday but instinctively used Jeff's. Suddenly Joni wasn't sure. She'd been so rattled about Kim's murder yesterday that she hadn't even set the alarm when she left for soccer practice, so she'd never had to deactivate it before. She could only hope now that she'd correctly punched in the wrong code.

Otherwise she'd be fleeing out the back with no alarm to summon help. Fred would have all the time in the world to hunt her down. He knew the woods better than she did. Obviously, he also felt comfortable scurrying around in the dark. But then, vermin usually did.

Behind her, he picked up the tray of drinks. Joni was about to cut through the den when it occurred to her that Dirk might have left some possessions in sight.

Instead, she went by the living room. Never mind that she was tracking mud onto the carpet. Nothing mattered except keeping a bright smile on her face while she dumped the food sacks onto the counter and moved toward the utility room.

"Where are you going?" Fred unloaded the drinks and the chicken.

"To get a sweater," she said as she went around the corner. "And change my shoes." Kicking off the heels with a thump, she stepped into her canvas slip-ons.

Then she threw open the back door and ran as if the hounds of hell were after her.

THIS WAS A NIGHTMARE come to life, Dirk thought as traffic stopped ahead of him. He couldn't be more than a quarter of a mile from the turnoff and yet he was idling in place.

He shouldn't have accepted Charlie's guilt so readily. He should have insisted on staying with Joni. But blaming himself was useless. A tubby, middle-aged soccer dad had played them all for fools. So what was he going to do about it?

Gripping the wheel, Dirk studied the terrain.

The road had no shoulder, only a streaming gutter that separated it from a medium-high curb. There were no pedestrians in sight and, in this weather, little danger of encountering any.

He gauged the height of the curb and was grateful that, out of habit, he'd chosen a heavy rental car. It ought to be able to handle a steep tilt without flipping.

Time for a little offensive driving.

OPERATING ON INSTINCT, Joni turned left and scrambled toward Celia's house. Somewhere down the block, somebody had to be home.

Rain streamed down her face, making it hard to see more than a few feet ahead. Her slip-ons squelched and sucked in the mud, and her skirt clung to her thighs.

Where was Fred? She couldn't hear him and she didn't dare turn around to look.

Behind her, the alarm went off with a shocking blare. She stumbled, grabbed at a post and felt splinters rip her palm. It stung but she scarcely minded. She wasn't cold anymore, either. Nothing existed except this blind need to keep going.

A slope dropped before her, not long but very slick, and she lost her balance on the rim. Out of control, Joni plunged into Celia's backyard. She jolted down onto her hands, scraping her knees and twisting one leg. When she tried to straighten, pain shot through her calf.

"Joni!" It was Fred, some distance away. "Come back here!"

He was still in her yard. Maybe he hadn't seen her tumble.

She forced herself to stand, despite the stabbing in her leg. It was a muscle cramp, she told herself. She just needed to work it out.

If only Celia kept a key hidden somewhere…but there wasn't time to look. Fred would be searching this way any minute.

Unable to move at more than a hobble, Joni pressed close to the trees that divided the two properties. If she edged uphill, maybe she could circle around in the near-zero visibility and get back into her own house.

It wasn't much of a plan. Even with an injured leg, it would be difficult to climb the slope, cut across it and work her way down. She was as likely to run into Fred as to escape him.

Still it was a chance. Once indoors, she could lock him out. She could find a weapon.

The clanging bell formed a steady throb in her mind. Joni prayed that someone would hear it and that the police wouldn't disregard the alarm at their end.

She couldn't trust her life to luck. Despite the throbbing in her leg, she started upward.

DIRK BRACED AS HE TOOK the curb, half-expecting the air bag to inflate at the shock. It stayed mercifully in place.

The car's suspension and tires might never be the same again, he reflected as he eased forward at a pronounced tilt, but the steering didn't appear to be affected. Repressing an impulse to hit the gas, he drove at a slowly accelerating pace past the clot of cars.

Someone honked, but he ignored it. If the police noticed, so much the better.

Gravity did its best to pull him sideways, and water spewed from beneath the left tire. Holding his body rigid, Dirk concentrated on watching for obstacles ahead. Even so, he didn't see the cross street in time to brake. The car overshot the curb, crunched downward, caught its chassis on the raised concrete and then scraped free with a bone-rattling thud.

Dirk veered right. The rain hid the street sign, but this should be the entrance to Joni's development. He hoped he was right. If not, he might have just taken a fatal wrong turn.

Chapter Seventeen

Joni crouched among the trees, afraid to venture onto the low brush of the slope. Despite the darkness and heavy rain, she felt as if Fred would surely spot her.

Water dripped from her hair and clothing, and her fingers were going numb. The fall into Celia's yard had jolted her ribs and set them aching again. She hadn't, she realized, fully healed from her encounter with this maniac a week ago.

Only a week? It felt as if a lifetime had gone by.

Below her, a thump and a string of curses, barely audible over the alarm bell, revealed that he, too, had slid into Celia's yard. That meant her patio was clear. Unless, of course, he decided to turn back.

She had to make a run for it. Now.

Fighting a gust of wind, Joni staggered onto the open slope. She felt exposed, even though there was no reason to believe Fred could see her through the downpour any more than she could see him.

Losing her footing, she grabbed a bush, then felt sharp leaves cut her already lacerated palm. Tears sprang to her eyes, but she ignored them and kept angling downward. If only her feet didn't nearly pull loose from the slip-ons at every step. If only she had something to hold on to. If only she knew where Fred was.

Again she skidded, this time landing hard on her backside. Her skirt pulled up, and burrs stuck to her thighs. With rain sluicing down her face, she could barely make out the pale orb of light that marked the rear door below.

With a suddenness like a blow, the alarm cut off. Rain swished across the hillside, sounding abnormally loud.

For a terrified moment, Joni thought Fred had gone inside and deactivated the security system. Then she remembered that the bell shut off automatically after five minutes. She missed the jangling. It had aided in covering her movements, although it also helped Fred sneak around undetected.

Had he gone down through Celia's yard to the next house, hoping to pick up her trail, or was he heading back? Did he have a knife, maybe the one that had killed Kim DeLong?

Was it going to be Joni's blood on the patio this time?

In her mind, Fred no longer bore any resemblance to the benign father figure she'd sometimes wished Lowell would emulate. The fact that he'd been able to win people's trust and affection made him seem even more of a monster now.

A new sound made her heart leap. A car, coming up the street. She tensed, praying for the familiar growl of an engine tackling the steepness of her driveway.

It stopped too soon, before Celia's house. Too far away for the driver to hear her if she screamed, and that would alert Fred to her whereabouts.

Mentally, Joni calculated the rest of her descent. Between her and the patio, nearly invisible in the deluge, lay a stone retaining wall, then a four-foot drop to the rose bed. If she fell over it, Fred would hear the crash. Worse, she might be badly injured.

She had to take that risk. Keeping low to the ground, Joni sidled down the hill. Sooner than expected, her foot touched the hard, flat top of the retaining wall. At least she'd found it without falling over.

At this point, she remained virtually invisible although she knew her safety was illusory. She needed to make a run for it. Why wouldn't her muscles obey? Once she jumped down, Joni knew she would be silhouetted against the porch light. She felt stiff, cold and sore. And terrified.

Last Wednesday night, on this patio, horror had come out of nowhere. She could hardly believe, even now, that it had been Fred who attacked and not some virulent, unknowable force.

If she moved, it might find her again.

Inside the house lay warmth. Civilization. Jeff's childish world of toys and games. The bed where she and Dirk had made love.

She had to reach it. She had to try.

Into the void, Joni leaped.

WHILE VEERING FROM one street to another, operating largely on instinct, Dirk became aware of an alarm sounding a few blocks away. He wondered if it could be Joni's and who had set it off. He gave the car more gas, felt it start to hydroplane and forced himself to ease out of the skid.

The noise stopped abruptly. Why?

Dirk cursed aloud as he swung onto her street and saw how dark it was. But not at her house; someone had turned on the interior lights. Also the one on the patio. Near the back edge of the house, a weak glow penetrated the pouring rain.

Could Fred be trying to re-create the scene of Lowell's murder?

Every fiber of his being shouted at Dirk to gun the motor and race to Joni's rescue. The impulse warred with his training, which demanded that he assess the situation and form a plan.

Well, he'd better do it in a damn hurry, he thought grimly. Because while he was sitting here deciding on a strategy, he might lose everything that mattered in this life.

JONI LANDED WITH A JOLT on the strip of grass between the rose bed and the concrete. The impact knocked her forward until the heels of her hands made raw contact with pavement. Her shoulders absorbed the blow with a wrenching throb. Her breath rasped, too loudly. For a moment, she couldn't move.

One of her shoes had flown off in the jump. No sense looking for it. She needed to get up, but the grass was slick. She staggered on all fours, regained her balance and straightened.

As she started moving, her head began to swim. It was like trying to run in a bad dream. She could see the back door but couldn't seem to reach it.

Then she noticed the silhouette near the garage. He'd come back. She could never reach the house before he did. But she had to do this, had to make it. For Jeff's sake. For Dirk's.

Joni flung herself forward.

As she stumbled across the hard surface, the cramp in her calf, nearly forgotten in the cold, shot white pain up through her leg. With a cry, she grabbed the glass table to keep from falling.

The man dived for her. She braced herself for the impact, but he didn't stop. As he went past, she made out the familiar beauty of broad shoulders and dark hair. Dirk!

She twisted, then saw why he'd bypassed her. Somehow Fred had gotten behind them. He must have circled around the front of the house to come at her from the opposite direction. Outfoxing her. Taking control.

He was shorter than Dirk but stockier, and he wielded a knife as smoothly as if it were an extension of himself. A superhuman madness glittered in his eyes.

She had to help. Maybe she could make it into the kitchen to fetch one of her own knives. No, the fire extinguisher would be better. Something with enough force to knock him over.

Joni took one step and her leg buckled. Her hands came down, ready to break her fall, but in midair the metal hose faucet caught her head with a mind-dimming whack.

DIRK HEARD JONI CRASH behind him. He knew she must be hurt, but he couldn't help her now.

He hadn't found so much as a jack in the rental car. Good sense had warned him to enter the house through the front and find a weapon, but he didn't want to take the time. Now only his martial-arts training could protect him against this madman.

Disarming a man with a blade wasn't usually difficult. Most people flailed wildly and struck from the outside, leaving their bodies vulnerable.

Not Allen Frederick Owens. Maybe he'd learned how to fight in the marines. Dirk suspected his fanaticism helped even more.

The man's lips curled with fiendish glee as he performed a back-and-forth dance on the concrete. "You're a loser just like Lowell," he said. "Now you'll die like him."

"Lowell wasn't prepared for your attack." Dirk

crouched, watching for an opening. *Let him lift his arms away from his body. Just for a second.* "It's easy killing helpless people, isn't it?"

Fred tossed the knife to his left hand, then back again, too quickly for Dirk to make his move. "You shouldn't be anywhere near Joni. You contaminate her, you piece of filth. But I'll make her clean again."

"Do you really think she could ever love you?" Dirk searched his opponent's face for a flicker of uncertainty, any sign that the man might be momentarily off guard. "We're lovers. Did she tell you that?"

"You're lying!" Rage bloated Fred's face, and he slashed fast and hard. The blade caught Dirk's jacket, inches from his stomach.

It hung there. In the split second before the knife was yanked free, Dirk lashed out with his foot, aiming to catch his opponent in the gut. But the man dodged away, re-claiming the knife as he went. With a roar, he lunged and slashed at Dirk's thigh, slicing the pants and drawing a stripe of blood.

Pain clawed up his leg. Dirk ignored it and resumed his fighting stance.

The two men faced each other, breathing hard. Fred bared his teeth and snarled like a wild animal. An animal possessed of feral cunning. And the scent of blood could only make it more dangerous.

JONI FOUGHT THE DARKNESS. Something was wrong. Lowell. Someone had attacked Lowell.

Her head hurt. She remembered someone grabbing her and slamming her skull against the hummingbird feeder. She recalled, just a moment ago, the sticky sugar water pouring over her neck and cheeks.

The men were still there, facing off on the patio. She

saw the knife in Fred's hand, just as it had been before. But the man with his back to her wasn't Lowell. She knew the compactness of his frame, the grace with which he moved. It was Dirk.

Lowell and Fred—that had been last week. The memory of that event must have lain buried in some deep recess of her mind. Now it was happening all over again. If she didn't find a way to stop it, this time it would be Dirk lying dead on the patio.

DIRK UNDERSTOOD that he had made the nearly fatal error of underestimating his opponent. He wouldn't do it again.

He shifted to keep Joni's crumpled form behind him. Fred would have to kill him to reach her.

On the hill, the downpour intensified, although a moment ago he wouldn't have thought that possible. Even here beneath the patio cover, rain was hitting sideways against Dirk's overheated skin.

The business suit cramped his movements. He wished he had Fred's ease of action in a sweatshirt and jeans. But Dirk had once disabled an armed robber even though his own gun jammed. He had also, in a burst of adrenaline, foiled a kidnap attempt by shoving an overweight businessman up half a dozen steps and through a doorway.

He wasn't going to let a minor annoyance like a suit jacket get in his way. Not when there was so much at stake.

At least this time he knew the other man's weakness. Jealousy. He must use it to goad Fred.

"You can't have her," Dirk panted. "She doesn't want you and she never will. Haven't you figured that out yet?"

The blade quivered. Dirk tensed, ready.

He was so focused on the knife that he almost didn't notice Fred's subtle change of position. As Dirk tried to jump away, a foot shot out and caught him on the side of the leg. If it had hit his knee, as intended, he would've been disabled. Instead, it knocked him off balance just enough to give Fred an opening.

The man darted in for the final thrust. A blast of water hit him directly in the face. Dirk dived and rolled under the stinging spray, toward his sputtering foe. Toward the knife Fred had just dropped.

Their hands met on the haft. The water stopped. Joni, hose in hand, couldn't hit one without hitting the other.

This was hand-to-hand fighting, no-holds-barred. Dirk knew all the dirty tricks. He knew where to kick and where to gouge. But Fred's sheer raging madness gave him an edge. It made him close his fingers over the blade itself, forcing Dirk's hand away. It enabled him to smash his forehead into Dirk's and keep going through the shock.

Toward Joni.

SHE SAW DIRK GO DOWN. She didn't know how badly he was hurt. Maybe another blast of water would protect him, but between the disorienting shadows and the thrumming in her head, she could scarcely tell one looming shape from the other.

By the time she saw Fred swooping toward her, he was too close. She couldn't swing the nozzle into position.

A booming sound filled her head, as if a great wind had hit the patio. Fred stopped, surprise rendering his evil face suddenly childlike.

Earthquake? she wondered dazedly. But earthquakes didn't strike precisely when you needed them. They also didn't make a man clutch the front of his sweatshirt and crumple to the ground.

Footsteps scuffed behind Joni. ''You can put the hose

down now, Mrs. Peterson.'' Someone reached around and removed the nozzle.

''It's about time you got here.'' Dirk sat up, rubbing his head. ''I don't suppose you put in a good word with the paramedics?''

''They're on their way,'' Detective MacDougall said, and caught Joni as her knees gave out.

''KATHRYN'S TAKING the boys to Herb's place,'' Dirk reported a short time later as they waited in the kitchen. Another detective was on his way to question them, since MacDougall had been involved in the shooting. ''Then she'll go to the police station to tell them what she knows.''

''She's a good person,'' Joni said. ''What happened is not her fault.''

''I hope she understands that. She'll have enough to deal with now.'' Dirk stopped. ''We're not supposed to discuss the case.''

''I know.'' MacDougall had allowed them to wait together only after they promised not to talk about what had happened. He wanted to make sure their testimony wasn't compromised.

Not that it would make any difference. This time, Joni had no fear of forgetting.

Once she grasped that Fred Owens was dead, relief had cleared her mind. She had even remembered to ask that a patrolman break the news gently to his mother. She hoped that Edith's closeness to Kathryn and Bobby would help her weather this blow.

Although the paramedics had offered to transport Dirk and Joni to the hospital, they had both declined. She had, however, allowed the men to bandage her right hand, and they'd checked but found no sign of concussion.

The crime-scene investigators had discovered suspicious hairs and bloodstains in the back of Fred's van. That, coupled with other evidence and Joni's restored memory of last Wednesday, was likely to close the books on Lowell's and Kim's deaths. There was no further reason for Dirk to hang around Viento del Mar.

Joni didn't want to come home from the hospital in a day or so and find him gone. She intended to stick around for what little time he remained in town.

"I'm going to sell the house," she said abruptly. "We can't stay here after this."

Dirk's eyes met hers across the table. A bruise purpled his forehead, and she knew his leg must be hurting, but warmth suffused his face. "It does have a few wonderful memories, though."

She glanced down at her scraped hands. "Also little pieces of me scattered all over it."

"Oh, by the way…" Dirk reached inside his jacket. "Happy birthday."

She didn't want to hear about birthdays, not another reminder after all Fred's prattling. But when she saw the velvet jeweler's box, she knew Dirk must have gone to a lot of trouble. He'd bought something for her to remember him by. As if she needed anything. As if his scent and his voice and his way of glancing at her sideways weren't seared into her heart.

"That was…very thoughtful." She let the case rest on her palm. What was inside hardly mattered because the only gift she wanted was sitting across from her, a smile teasing the corners of his mouth.

"Well?" he said. "Aren't you going to open it?"

Through the window, she could hear police officers calling to each other. It was beginning to be a familiar sound. Way too familiar.

"Sure." Joni pried at the tight lid. It took a couple of attempts to get the box open.

It was empty. Inside she saw nothing but a pink satin lining bearing the name of the town jewelry store.

"Is it supposed to be this way?" she asked.

Dirk chuckled. "I wasn't robbed, if that's what you mean."

"Well, it's lovely," Joni joked. "A girl can always use a few of these."

His hands closed over hers, enfolding them in warmth. "It's empty," he said, "because I didn't know what kind of wedding ring you wanted."

She couldn't believe she'd heard correctly. Maybe she wanted to hear the words so badly that she'd misinterpreted him.

"I'm not sure I understand," she said.

"I'm asking you to marry me." He leaned across the table until his head nearly touched hers. "Battered and bruised as I am, I promise I'll clean up and make a respectable husband."

It wasn't easy to resist the urge to shout, "Yes!" But Joni knew that happy endings only grew from sturdy roots.

"Your work is overseas," she said. "Isn't it?"

He sat back but didn't let go of her hands. "The answer's been growing on me all week. I've got a lot of companies already established and, with some adjustments, I can manage them from here most of the time."

"But don't you love a challenge? Starting something new?" she asked.

"I am starting something new, or at least launching something Lowell started," he said. "The publishing business. The more I get involved, the more I'm enjoying it. I suspect it will keep me occupied for a long time to come."

Joni had to get everything out in the open. There

couldn't be any doubts, for either of them. "I thought you didn't want to be tied down."

"Commitment felt like a ball and chain," he conceded. "I guess it took coming back to Viento del Mar, being around you and Jeff, to realize I was allowing myself to be haunted by my own childhood. I was afraid to relinquish control, to let myself be vulnerable."

"Now you're not?" she demanded.

"It happened anyway." Dirk gave her a rueful grin. "The two of you sneaked into my heart. Joni, you're not just the woman I love. You're my soul mate. You're part of me. Getting married is only a formality."

Laughter bubbled inside her. She didn't want this moment to end. She wanted to stretch it out and savor every nuance.

"So when did you change your mind?" she asked. "You didn't even give me a hint this morning."

He glanced down at the jeweler's box. "When I picked this up, my intention was to let you select whatever jewelry you wanted. But even then I think I was picturing a ring in here."

"So this is kind of a spur-of-the-moment thing?" she persisted.

His eyes flashed blue fire. "I've always known there was a piece missing inside me, but I didn't think it could be found. Tonight, when I nearly lost you, I realized that without you, my world isn't merely incomplete. It doesn't exist. I know I deserve to be tortured, but please put me out of my misery. Marry me, Joni."

She ran her thumb along his cheek and gazed into his bruised, fierce, loving face. "Try to stop me," she said.

Chapter Eighteen

If a blizzard hadn't hit Moscow, Dirk would have made it home in time for his first anniversary. As it was, it took two extra days to catch a plane out of Russia.

Then, if his connecting flight in London hadn't been canceled due to fog, at least he would have made it home before Thanksgiving. Instead, he got stuck for an extra day, spent nearly twenty hours in transit and arrived bleary-eyed in Los Angeles on the holiday with a two-hour drive ahead of him.

It was, he supposed, what he deserved for spending three weeks away from home. Travel held less and less appeal these days, except for the few times when Joni was able to travel with him.

As the publishing business got under way, she'd given up her public relations job and taken to editing with boundless excitement. Where Dirk enjoyed hunting down cutting-edge subject matter and authors, his wife had the patience for details and an instinct for identifying what wasn't working on the page.

They made a good team, he reflected as he drove north on the freeway toward Viento del Mar. After three weeks away from her, he didn't dare dwell on all the ways in which they fitted together or he might steer right off the road.

At least he'd be home in time for Thanksgiving dinner at their new house in a pleasant development north of downtown. By now, cooking aromas must be drifting from kitchen to den to cathedral-ceilinged living room, all the way upstairs to Jeff's room.

Selling the old Peterson estate hadn't been difficult once Mrs. Wright decided to accept a generous pension and move near her sister in Florida. Joni's old house had presented more difficulty because it had been the scene of a murder. Finally, Celia Lu had bought it as a rental. That way, she'd told them, she could always be sure of having neighbors whose company she enjoyed.

The investigation of Lowell's and Kim's murders had been formally closed. With the perpetrator dead, no further action was necessary.

Joni had dropped assault charges against Charlie Rogers after he agreed that he needed more counseling. He was no longer coaching soccer, but he still taught adult fitness and had had no further problems.

Although Edith Owens might never fully recover from her son's death, she'd admitted to the police that she knew he was capable of violence and had sometimes feared him herself. Moving in with Kathryn and Bobby gave her renewed purpose in life and helped all of them recover.

Both Herb and Jeff had been happy to learn the truth about Jeff's parentage. In fact, Herb had confided, he'd been intending to tell Joni not to let that fool Dirk get away because he would make a terrific father.

He was a father all right, Dirk reflected, warming at the memory of reading bedtime stories to Jeff. And accompanying him to ball games. And helping with his new hobby of building models of spaceships.

He wished he'd been part of Jeff's life earlier. Not that he would've wanted to deprive Lowell of the experience, but watching Joni as the baby grew inside her, witnessing the birth and seeing those first baby steps would've been a miracle beyond imagining.

Well, his cup was already overflowing. It was pure indulgence to wish for anything more.

Clouds hovered all the way to Santa Barbara and then the sun broke through. Dirk gave a sigh of satisfaction. He'd had enough bad weather on this trip to last him a long time.

Downtown Viento del Mar was shuttered except for the supermarket at the corner of San Bernardo Road. Dirk had called ahead and offered to pick up any items Joni needed, but she'd said that all she wanted was the sight of him, and the sooner the better.

He pushed back a hank of hair, askew from having been slept on crookedly aboard the plane. He should have gotten a cut last week but preferred to wait for his regular barber.

For a moment, when his hand brushed his forehead, Dirk flashed back to that Halloween night when he'd nearly lost Joni. The scars had faded in a year, but the trauma recurred now and again.

He could still see Fred's lunging shape and feel the slash of the knife on his leg. Could still hear Joni behind him, crashing against the faucet.

With time, though, the shock had softened. Now he could accept that night as a kind of crucible in which his old life had been melted down and transformed into a far better one.

A mile past downtown, Dirk turned left into the new development. The yards were small but brightened, even at this time of year, by well-tended flower beds. In front of several houses, people were getting out of cars, carrying covered dishes.

A surge of gratitude welled inside him that he was part of a family, too. That he was only a few blocks away from the sure and steady center of his universe.

He approached slowly, drinking in the sight of the two-story house with its windows aglow. In front, rosebushes burst forth with a final bloom, the scarlets and pinks so vivid that they stood out even in the twilight.

From the absence of a sports car parked in front, Dirk could see that his grandfather hadn't arrived yet. According to Joni, Herb would be bringing his new girlfriend, a lively widow.

At the touch of his finger on the remote control, the garage door slid open. Dirk pulled in next to Joni's car.

The interior door flew open and Jeff's head poked out. "Dad?" he called. Then, over his shoulder, "Dad's home! Can I tell him yet?"

Tell him what?

As he got out, delicious cooking smells flooded around Dirk, even better than he'd fantasized. He could detect turkey and stuffing and pumpkin pie.

Jeff came running out. There wasn't room to swing him around; besides, the boy was getting too big for such antics. But Dirk picked him up in a bear hug, all the same.

"Can I carry your suitcase?" his son asked as he was set down.

"It's a bit heavy, but you can handle my carry-on." Dirk lifted luggage from the trunk. "That's got the good stuff in it anyway."

"Good stuff?"

"Oh, presents. But you wouldn't be interested in anything like that."

The boy shot him a knowing look and reached for the bag. He marched proudly ahead of Dirk into the house.

Joni came from the kitchen to greet them. Her blond hair, cut in a chin-length pageboy, haloed her head as she wiped her hands on her apron.

It was such a domestic gesture that Dirk almost couldn't believe this same woman would, in a few days, rip through the new manuscripts he'd acquired and critique them within an inch of their lives.

He dropped his suitcase barely in time to catch her as she flew into his arms. She felt hot and alive against his cool body, which didn't stay cool for long.

He wished the cooking and the imminent arrival of guests and even their son's excitement could be suspended while he carried Joni upstairs. Three weeks ago, they'd said farewell after a lovemaking session that lasted most of the night. This time, he figured they'd need the entire four-day weekend.

"You feel wonderful," Joni murmured into his ear.

"He brought presents!" Jeff called. "Can I open the bag, Daddy?"

To his wife, Dirk whispered, "If you think I feel good now, just wait till later." To his son, he said, "If you're careful. There's a package with your name on it."

Reluctantly releasing Joni, he shrugged out of his overcoat and carried his large suitcase upstairs so it would be out of the way. Heading back down, he nearly collided with Jeff, who had opened his package to discover an intricate plastic model of a Russian spaceship, ready to be assembled. "I've never seen this one before! I can't wait to get started."

"It won't be on the market for another month. Need any help with that?"

Dirk was relieved when he received a resounding "No!

I can handle it.'' Much as he enjoyed building models with his son, he had other priorities right now.

When he reached the kitchen, Joni was removing a pan of stuffing from the oven. ''You look terrific, considering what you've been through the past few days. Airport lounges aren't exactly my idea of luxurious lodgings.''

Dirk regarded her longingly. ''I'm not going away again for a long, long time.'' Then he remembered his son's words earlier. ''What was it Jeff wanted to tell me?''

Joni removed the apron. Underneath, she wore a fuzzy pink sweater and tan slacks. ''Are you planning to go anywhere next July?''

''I don't think so,'' he said. ''Why? Is there some kind of publishing conference?''

''If there is, you'll have to cancel.'' Mischief danced in her eyes.

''Why?'' He knew she was up to something, but all he could think about was kissing her until they both got dizzy.

''Well, I assume you'll want to be in the delivery room,'' she said.

He stared at her, hardly daring to grasp the implication. ''We're—you're—pregnant?''

''I took a home test two days ago.'' She beamed at him. ''I didn't mean to tell Jeff, but he saw the kit in the bathroom and asked me what it meant.''

''It's all right.'' Gently, he gathered his wife against him. ''Maybe you should sit down. Are you sure that belt isn't too tight? Could it be cutting off the oxygen supply or something?''

She laughed. ''I'm not made out of porcelain. And I've had a baby before, remember?''

He had dozens of questions, most of which she probably couldn't answer yet. Whether it was a boy or a girl. What name they should choose. How soon they'd be able to see it on an ultrasound.

"I can't believe it," he admitted. "I was going to ask how you'd feel about having another child, but I wanted to give us all time to settle in."

"I'd say we're pretty settled." She stroked the hair back from his forehead. "You'll recall we forgot to take precautions before you left. Maybe that wasn't entirely a mistake."

"Maybe it wasn't a mistake at all," he conceded. "I figured you knew what you were doing. I certainly did."

"Now we've made a baby two different ways," she teased. "The results may be the same, but this method was more fun."

He wanted to say more, but the doorbell rang. "Would that be Herb?"

"And Mary Anne. She's quite a character. You'll like her." Joni winked. "Maybe by next Thanksgiving, we'll have a new member of the family." With a glance at her stomach, she amended, "Make that two new members."

"You're matchmaking!"

"Herb didn't need my help." She started for the door. "He found this lady himself."

Dirk lingered behind, treasuring the miraculous news she'd given him. It was impossible to absorb the implications all at once, but, he decided, he didn't need to. Half the fun of life was being surprised along the way.

With a prayer of thanksgiving humming through his mind, he straightened his tie and went to help his wife greet their guests.

A MAN OF SECRETS
Amanda Stevens

Chapter One

He was up to something. Natalie Silver twirled her glasses in one hand as she tracked her ex-husband's slow progress through her shop on San Antonio's famed Riverwalk. His presence seemed incongruous in the cheery warmth of Silver Bells, her potpourri-scented Christmas boutique.

Christmas music played softly in the background, and tiny white lights, trimming doorways and windows, glowed with subtle magic. But Anthony's presence reminded Natalie of darker times. Unpleasant times.

He picked up an Austrian-crystal snowflake and held it to the light, then laid it aside to admire a hand-carved wooden Christmas tree, meticulously detailed, done by a famous German craftsman. He left the tree and sauntered toward the Belgian angels.

"What exactly are you looking for?" Natalie finally asked.

Anthony looked up and gave her a cool smile. "I'll know it when I see it."

As he lifted his left hand to remove one of the angels from the shelf, the glint of sunlight flashing off his gold watch attracted Natalie's gaze. He wasn't wearing his wedding ring, she noted, feeling more wary by the moment. He'd been married to his current wife for six years—ever since he and Natalie had divorced—and the sudden absence of his wedding band seemed ominous to her somehow.

"Maybe if you told me who the gift is for, I could help you find something," she suggested. Not that she had any particular desire to be helpful to Anthony—or to any of the Bishops, for that matter—but the sooner he found what he was looking for, the sooner he would depart.

Of course, that notion wasn't exactly consoling since when he left, he would be taking her son with him for the evening. That alone was enough to fill Natalie with trepidation, but this new attitude of Anthony's…this new congeniality…

He was up to something, all right. Natalie hadn't yet figured out what, but she was very much afraid it had something to do with her son. In the six years since their divorce, Anthony had shown no interest whatsoever in Kyle, had done nothing more than have his secretary send the occasional birthday or Christmas card, along with an obligatory, impersonal check.

Even Irene, Kyle's grandmother, had kept her distance, and Natalie had begun to hope the Bishops were out of her life for good.

But a month ago, out of the blue, Anthony had called her to say he wanted to start spending time with Kyle on a regular basis. Since Anthony had legal visitation rights and he'd always paid his child support on time, there was nothing Natalie could do to prevent him from seeing her son—no matter how much she might wish to.

And besides, she knew Kyle was curious about Anthony. About all the Bishops. Because he *was* one.

"The gift is for the mother of one of my clients," Anthony explained. "She's very old and her son's been away for quite some time. I want to send her something that will help brighten her holidays.''

Natalie slipped on her glasses and scrutinized him again. He looked the same—impeccably dressed in a dark, double-breasted suit, black hair combed straight back from a high forehead winged with heavy eyebrows, green eyes fringed with thick lashes, and a wide, generous mouth that could look either sensuous or cruel, depending on his mood.

Natalie had had the misfortune to witness both those moods on occasion, but this new persona—showing fatherly interest, concern for a client's elderly mother—was a side of Anthony she hadn't seen since he had caught her on the rebound and swept her off her feet nearly seven years ago in a whirlwind courtship that had left her breathless; and almost immediately filled with regrets.

Her ex-husband was a master of deception. He could fool most of the people most of the time, but he would never again dupe Natalie. She'd been taken in once by his lies, by his impersonation of a caring man, but she would never believe him again. Natalie knew too well what Anthony Bishop was capable of.

She walked around the counter and faced him. ''Why don't you tell me what you really want?''

He gave her an innocent look. ''I don't know what you mean.''

''You know exactly what I mean. Why this sudden interest in Kyle?''

The dark eyebrows slowly rose. ''I'm his father. Or had you forgotten the details of his parentage?''

''I'm not likely to forget anything concerning my relationship with you,'' she said bitterly. ''But I can't help wondering why, after all these years, you suddenly want to be a part of my son's life.''

"He's a Bishop."

Natalie's lips tightened but she said nothing.

Sunlight silvered the gray at Anthony's temples as he turned to study her. "Like it or not, Natalie, the boy's my heir. I have certain legal and moral responsibilities toward him, which I intend to start exercising. You may as well get used to it. In fact, I'd like for him to spend the Christmas holidays with me at Fair Winds."

Over my dead body. Images of her first and only Christmas at the Bishop mansion raced through Natalie's mind. She'd been a new bride—shy, insecure, and still heartbroken from a love affair gone bad. Her marriage to Anthony, who was fifteen years older than she, had been an act of haste, an impulsive, desperate decision that she had, even then, begun to regret.

But after that week at Fair Winds, the full weight of what she had done hit her. Anthony's cruelty—no longer masked by a warm, caring facade—his mother's coldness and his sister's bitter resentment of Natalie had made the holiday season almost unbearable for her that year.

And through it all, the conspicuous absence of Anthony's younger brother, Spencer, the Bishop Natalie had come to hate the most, had been a constant reminder of how stupid she'd been. How gullible.

She rubbed her temples now, trying to rid herself of the dark visions dancing in her head. "There is no way I'll let Kyle spend Christmas at Fair Winds."

"Are you sure about that?" Anthony wasn't looking at her, but was gazing instead at the pine armoire in which she kept the more expensive antiques and rare collectibles. He glanced over his shoulder. "Supposing you don't have a choice in the matter?"

A dark premonition slipped over Natalie. She shivered

in spite of the seventy-degree weather San Antonio was enjoying. ''What do you mean?''

''I mean, why don't you let the boy decide? Ask him where he wants to spend Christmas. Or…are you afraid of his answer?''

Anthony's taunt sent a spasm of anger shooting through Natalie, but it wasn't quite enough to dispel the fear that had suddenly seized her. She'd been nineteen when she'd first seen the Bishop mansion. Her own impression had been one of starkness, of a cold, sterile mausoleum completely lacking in warmth or love. But Kyle was only six years old. He could easily be swayed by the ostentatious grandeur of Fair Winds; and even more persuasive was his own sense of adventure.

The thought of not having Kyle with her for Christmas filled Natalie with the kind of aching loneliness she hadn't known in years. Her son meant everything to her.

''Kyle will be with me for Christmas,'' she said firmly. ''And that's final. You may see him the day before or the day after, as per the custody agreement, but on Christmas Day, he *will* be with me.''

Anthony looked on the verge of arguing with her. Then, for some reason Natalie could only guess at, he merely smiled and inclined his head. ''Whatever you say, Natalie. In the meantime, I think I've found what I'm looking for.''

His green eyes swept her in a manner so proprietary, so intimate, Natalie felt herself blushing. Slowly, his gaze left her face to travel downward and linger where the neck of her dark red cotton sweater dipped demurely, and downward still, tracing the lines of her short pleated skirt and the black opaque stockings encasing her legs.

When his eyes moved back up to meet her defiant gaze, Natalie felt as if she'd just been undressed—against her will. It wasn't a pleasant sensation.

"I'd like to have a closer look."

The deep, seductive quality of his voice startled her. *"What?"*

He motioned toward a piece in the armoire, but his eyes told her he meant something else. "I'm interested in the music box. The one with Saint Nick on top."

Leave it to Anthony to zero in on the *pièce de résistance* of her collection, the one item Natalie had been hoping to keep for herself.

"It's an Étienne," she explained, brushing past him to remove the delicate porcelain music box from the shelf. "An exact replica of the ones made in Paris before the war and used by the underground during the occupation to smuggle messages back and forth." She touched a spring, cleverly concealed by the intricate design of the piece, and a hidden compartment popped out. She gave him an ironic glance. "I remember how much you love secrets."

He grinned. "And how much you hate them."

With good reason, she thought. During their short marriage, Anthony had kept a lot of things from her, but the worst had been his affair with Natalie's best friend, the woman who was now Mrs. Anthony Bishop.

Anthony removed the music box from Natalie's hands. "How much is it?"

She named a figure that was twice as much as she'd planned to ask, but she knew her ex-husband could afford it.

He whistled, studying the music box at length. "I had no idea you could command that kind of price for a Christmas ornament."

"Only from my most discriminating customers," Natalie said dryly.

Both dark eyebrows rose at that. "Well, that's a challenge I can hardly refuse, now, isn't it? I presume that price includes gift wrapping?''

''Of course.''

''And delivery?''

''Within the continental United States,'' Natalie said. ''Shall I wrap it up for you?''

''Why not?'' Anthony fished in the inside pocket of his coat and handed her a piece of paper. ''Here's the address I want you to send it to. It's here in San Antonio, so I'd like for you to make arrangements to have it delivered today.''

Natalie glanced up. ''That'll cost extra. I'll have to hire a special courier.''

Anthony shrugged. ''I'll leave the details to you. As long as my friend's mother has her present by tonight.''

''She will,'' Natalie assured him. ''Now, will this be cash?''

He handed her a platinum credit card. When Natalie tried to take the music box from him, he nodded toward the door, where two women had just walked in. ''Looks like you're a little shorthanded today. Why don't you go ahead and wait on your customers? I'm in no hurry.''

Natalie could hardly believe her ears. In the old days, Anthony would have insisted on being served first. He would have thought it his due as a Bishop. Now he seemed content to browse while Natalie took care of her other customers. She didn't quite know what to make of this new attitude.

Something about him had changed, but then, some things never did. By the frank perusal he'd given her earlier, Natalie suspected her ex-husband still had a roving eye. She wished she could take pleasure in the knowledge that he and Melinda's marriage seemed to have gone sour, but none of that mattered in the least to her anymore. If it wasn't for Kyle, she would never want to see another Bishop as long as she lived.

By the time she finished with the barrage of customers who had suddenly descended on Silver Bells, Anthony was pacing the shop impatiently. He handed her the music box and glanced at his watch.

"I'm late for a meeting," he said. "I won't be able to wait for Kyle after all."

"But you were supposed to take him to the Spurs game tonight," Natalie protested. Not that she wanted Anthony anywhere near her son, but she didn't want Kyle to be disappointed, either. She didn't want Anthony turning up in her son's life only at *his* convenience.

"I'm afraid something's come up." He glanced over his shoulder, toward the front of the shop. Outside, a man in a loud print shirt had stopped to study the animated Santa's workshop scene in the display window.

Anthony turned back to the counter. "Can you speed this up?"

"I thought you weren't in any hurry."

"Well, I am now."

So the old Anthony *was* still lurking nearby. In a way Natalie was relieved.

Carefully, she placed the music box inside a silver carton embossed with her shop's logo—a pair of beribboned bells—and taped the delivery address to the counter so it wouldn't get misplaced.

"You're sure it'll go out today?" Anthony asked anxiously.

"I'll call the courier immediately," Natalie assured him, shoving her wire-rimmed glasses up her nose.

"Okay." He tapped the counter with one fist as he glanced over his shoulder again, and Natalie automatically followed his gaze. The man at the display window had moved on.

She said, "You don't have to worry. I'll take care of everything."

"I'm counting on that," said Anthony.

As soon as Natalie had a free minute, she called the courier, then picked up the silver carton containing the music box and carried it back to her workroom. Placing it carefully on her desk, she got out several sheets of bubble wrap and removed a shipping label from her desk drawer. But before she finished, the bells outside chimed again.

This time, the Bishop who walked through her door was one Natalie was delighted to see. Her six-year-old son came rushing in, pulling Blanche Jones behind him. Both of them were windblown and laughing.

Blanche, one of Natalie's closest friends, owned Blanche DuBois's, a vintage clothing shop on the third level of the same building that housed Silver Bells. An Italian restaurant, owned by a man named Frank Delmontico, occupied the ground level.

Blanche and Natalie had hit it off immediately, five years ago when Natalie first opened her shop, but Frank Delmontico still remained somewhat of a mystery man.

The two women often lunched in his restaurant and speculated about his past. Natalie thought he looked like a hit man for the Mafia, but Blanche insisted his tough, swarthy looks belonged to someone who had once sailed the high seas, a merchant marine perhaps, or even a treasure hunter.

Neither of them had ever asked him about his background, though, because Blanche, always the romantic, had said it was much more fun to create one for him. Think how disappointed they would be, she had pointed out, if he turned out to be an accountant.

Natalie thought Blanche one of the most interesting women she'd ever met, in both personality and appearance. She was not just pretty, but intriguing. Today she wore a crocheted sweater paired with a long lace skirt in winter white, beneath which peeked old-fashioned, lace-up boots.

Her thick dark hair was pulled back and held in place by an antique ivory comb her grandmother had given to her, and an exquisite cameo, tied with a satin ribbon, adorned her throat. Natalie thought that her own cotton sweater and plaid skirt must look positively drab by comparison.

"Well, you two sure look happy," she commented. Their laughter was contagious. The dark cloud that had been hanging over Natalie's head since Anthony's departure began to dispel.

Kyle grinned from ear to ear, displaying the gap where his two adult front teeth hadn't yet grown in. "I came in first, Mom!" he shouted, lisping a little on the word "first." "I won the Reindeer Run! I did what you told me. I closed my eyes and pretended I really *was* a reindeer. And it worked! It really worked! You should have been there!"

His excited tone contained not even a hint of censure, but Natalie felt a pang of guilt just the same. She *should* have been there. Being a single parent was hard enough, but owning and operating a small business spread her even thinner.

She'd wanted to take the afternoon off to watch Kyle run, but unfortunately, she'd had two deliveries arriving that day, coupled with the fact that one of her part-time clerks had been out sick all week. Michelle, who came in after school and worked until closing, wouldn't be in until later. This was Natalie's busiest time of year. There was no way she could close up shop, even for an hour or so. Kyle, bless him, seemed to understand. At least as much as a six-year-old could.

He tore off his windbreaker and puffed out his chest, proudly displaying the T-shirt he'd won.

"See? It says First Place, Reindeer Run." He pointed to the words, then looked up, beaming.

"All right!" Natalie walked over and gave him a high five. Then she bent down and hugged him. "I knew you could do it. You're fast as the wind!"

"The fastest kid in first grade, anyway," Blanche said.

Kyle squinted up at Natalie. "Are you proud of me, Mom?"

"I'm always proud of you, sweetie." And it was true. Kyle could be a handful at times, and like his father, he had a secretive quality that could drive Natalie crazy. But most of the time, he brought her nothing but joy. Most of the time, she managed to forget that he was a Bishop.

"Did you get Miss Riley's present ready?" he asked in an anxious tone that reminded her of Anthony's.

"It's in the silver box sitting on the bench in my workroom. Why don't you go get it and when Wendy comes to pick you up, you can take it home, and we'll wrap it together tonight."

"Can I do the bow?"

"Of course."

He dashed off now to the workroom, and Natalie turned to Blanche. "Thanks for going to pick him up. And for this morning." Blanche had come over to Natalie's house and stayed with Kyle until the school bus arrived, while Natalie had raced to the store to meet the first of the deliveries.

Blanche waved Natalie's gratitude aside. "No problem.

I enjoy being with Kyle. Besides, my shop isn't as busy as yours this time of year, and I've got good help. I can afford to take a few hours off.''

Natalie secretly envied Blanche her full-time clerk. Natalie wished she could afford more help, but some months it was hard enough to make the rent in the pricey Riverwalk location. Blanche never seemed to have that problem.

Sometimes Natalie wondered if the man Blanche was involved with helped her out financially. From some of the presents he'd given her, Natalie assumed he was well-to-do, and from the secretive way Blanche acted—never mentioning his name, never introducing him to her friends— Natalie suspected he was married.

She hoped that wasn't true. Blanche was a good friend, and Natalie didn't want to see her get hurt.

''You saved my life and I owe you, big time. I didn't get a chance to ask you before, but did everything go all right this morning?'' Natalie asked.

''Well, actually, we did have to play hide-and-seek with his backpack before the bus came. He hid it last night so robbers couldn't steal it—his words, not mine—then this morning he couldn't remember where he'd put it.''

''Where did you finally find it?''

''Kyle's the one who found it, and he wouldn't tell me where because he said it must be a really awesome hiding place if even *he* couldn't find it.''

Natalie just shook her head. If there was anything she would change about her son, it was his penchant for hiding things, then forgetting where he'd put them.

Just last week, when Anthony had taken Kyle to his law office one afternoon, Kyle had brought back a state-of-the-art, fancy tape recorder that evidently had fascinated him so much, Anthony had impulsively given it to him. The gift was extravagant and meaningless and much too expensive for a six-year-old, but when Natalie had suggested Kyle should give it back, he'd sworn he couldn't find it. Anywhere.

Natalie sighed. "If I had five bucks for everything that kid has hidden and lost in his short lifetime, I'd be a rich woman."

Blanche laughed, then said in a low voice, "You already were a rich woman. You were married to a Bishop and you gave it all up."

Natalie grimaced. "Don't remind me. Speaking of the devil, he was here today."

Blanche's dark eyebrows rose. "Anthony was here? When?"

"A little while ago. You just missed him. I know you said you were dying to meet him."

"Yes, I am," Blanche said, smiling a little. "What did he want?"

Natalie shrugged. "He said he came to shop for a present for a client's mother."

"That's all he wanted, just to shop?"

Natalie frowned, removing her glasses to polish the lenses with the hem of her sweater. "He did buy something—a music box. Quite an expensive one. But I don't think that's really why he was here. He's up to something, Blanche. I just know it."

"What do you mean?" Blanche rested her forearms on the counter, her dark brown gaze intent.

"He says he wants to do his fatherly duty by Kyle, but I don't buy that. Why now, after all these years?"

Blanche shrugged. "Maybe he feels guilty for his past neglect and wants to make up for it."

Natalie glared at her friend. "You're talking as though he's human. He's not."

Something flashed in Blanche's eyes—something that

Natalie couldn't quite discern. "If he's really that bad, why in the world did you ever marry him?"

"You don't know how many times I've asked myself that same question."

"And?"

Natalie hesitated. What was she supposed to say? What excuse could she possibly offer? That she'd been nineteen when she met Anthony? That she'd been working part-time in his law office to help pay her way through college? That her parents were out of the country that year, and she'd been on her own for the first time in her life?

Was she supposed to explain how lonely she'd been? How vulnerable and naive and stupid she'd been? How she'd fallen madly in love with one man and married another? How, by the time she'd turned twenty, she'd been pregnant, miserable, and contemplating divorce?

It was an old story, and a tawdry one. One that didn't bear repeating.

"At least I learned from my mistakes," she finally said. "I'll never trust Anthony Bishop again as long as I live."

"Well," Blanche said carefully. "I guess if the animosity is still that strong between you two, there is another possible reason for Anthony's sudden interest in Kyle."

"What?"

Blanche paused, then shook her dark head and glanced away. "Nothing. It's a crazy idea."

"Nothing concerning Anthony is beyond the realm of possibility," Natalie insisted. "Tell me what you're thinking."

Blanche bit her lip worriedly. "Well, I just wondered.... I mean...he and his current wife don't have any children, do they?"

"No." A fact that still surprised Natalie. She would have thought Melinda would have tied herself to Anthony in any way she could, but the marriage thus far had remained childless.

"Supposing they can't have children? Supposing Anthony means to go after custody of Kyle?"

Blanche's words hit Natalie like bits of hot shrapnel. Fear exploded inside her. He couldn't. He wouldn't.

But what if—

Suddenly, Anthony's earlier words took on a more sinister meaning.

"He's a Bishop.

Like it or not, Natalie, the boy's my heir.

I'd like him to spend the Christmas holidays with me at Fair Winds.

Supposing you don't have a choice in the matter?"

Anthony had threatened to take Kyle away from her once before, until Natalie had desperately agreed to his terms. She'd held up her end of the bargain all these years, and she'd expected Anthony to do the same.

But maybe that was expecting too much.

She put her hands to the sides of her face. "What if you're right, Blanche? What if he does want custody? He's an attorney. He'd know what to do, who to bribe. The Bishops are so powerful in this city. How would I be able to fight him?" Natalie's tone had risen with each word, until her voice sounded shrill and panicky, even to her own ears.

"Shush. You don't want Kyle to hear you." Blanche reached across the counter and grabbed Natalie's hands, giving them a little shake. "I shouldn't have said anything. It's purely speculation. I had no idea it would upset you this much."

Natalie pulled her hands free from Blanche's and wrapped her arms around her middle. "But it's just like something Anthony would do. He's never forgiven me for leaving like I did. For not taking his guilt money or keeping his name. He thinks I publicly humiliated him. Even after all this time, if he thought he could get back at me by taking Kyle away from me, he'd do it. I know he'd do it.''

Anger flickered in Blanche's eyes ''But he must really care about his own son—''

''Care? Anthony doesn't know the meaning of the word. None of the Bishops do.''

Blanche straightened from her position at the counter, but her gaze was still on Natalie. ''I'm sorry. I didn't mean to get you so worked up. I just thought it might be something you ought to consider. You know, forewarned is forearmed.''

Natalie began to pace—short, agitated steps that took her to the end of the counter and back. ''I won't lose Kyle, Blanche. I can't.''

''You're not going to lose Kyle.''

''The thought of Anthony raising my son makes my skin crawl.''

''It'll never happen,'' Blanche assured her.

''Damn right, it won't,'' Natalie said through clenched teeth. ''I'll see Anthony Bishop in hell first.''

Blanche looked at her in shock. ''I've never heard you talk like this.''

''You've never seen me threatened.'' Natalie placed her palms flat on the counter. ''I mean it, Blanche. There is no way I would ever let Anthony take Kyle away from me. I don't care what I have to do to stop him.''

She was not without a defense, Natalie thought. There was a way to stop Anthony, but before she played that card, she knew she had to be ready to deal with the consequences. Lives would be changed, perhaps forever, and she wasn't at all sure that was a scenario she was ready to face.

Kyle came out of her workroom carrying the silver box that contained the present for his teacher—his light brown, baby-fine hair so like hers and his green eyes so like his father's—and Natalie's throat knotted with emotion. She loved Kyle more than anything, so much so that at times it was a little frightening. If she ever lost him…

You're being ridiculous, she told herself sternly. She was not going to lose Kyle. Not to Anthony or to anyone else.

She and her son were going to have a wonderful Christmas with her parents, who were back in San Antonio now after having lived abroad off and on for the past seven years. And even if the weather was darn near balmy outside, nothing would keep them from getting into the spirit of the season. Christmas had always been Natalie's favorite holiday, and this year would be no exception.

But even as she gave herself a mental pep talk, a sense of unease lingered as she watched her son leave the store with Wendy, his baby-sitter, who had come to pick him up.

What if Blanche was right? What if Anthony was planning to take Kyle away from her?

Chapter Two

Anthony Bishop stood at the floor-to-ceiling windows in his law office and stared out at the ever-changing skyline of the Alamo city. San Antonio, now the ninth-largest city in the country, was growing by leaps and bounds, and it excited Anthony no end to know that he was as much a part of the city's future as his father, grandfather and great-grandfather had been of its past.

Single-handedly, Anthony had guided Bishop, Bishop, and Winslow—once a small, but extremely prestigious law practice—toward the twenty-first century, expanding and diversifying until the firm now boasted more than fifty partners and associates. And he had been able to do so in the amazingly short period of time since his father had died because Anthony wasn't afraid of taking a few chances. He wasn't afraid to gamble now and then. What was life without risk?

Truth be told, he liked living on the edge. He liked flirting with disaster, and he always, *always* loved to win.

Anthony thought about his latest coup as his gaze scanned the horizon. Darkness had fallen and he could see the lights twinkling on the Tower of the Americas, built for the 1968 World's Fair, and farther east, the newer, but no less impressive architectural wonder called the Alamodome.

Partially obscured by towering office buildings, a ribbon of light festooned the heart of downtown known as the Riverwalk—a shimmering collage of restaurants and specialty shops built along the banks of the San Antonio River.

Anthony stared at the spot where Natalie's store was located. Who would have thought that little venture—a Christmas specialty shop open the year around—would have turned out so successfully?

Certainly not him, Anthony had to admit. That was one gamble that hadn't paid off. When Natalie had opened Silver Bells five years ago, a year after the divorce, he'd been sure she would fall flat on her face and come crying back to him, begging for a second chance.

But Natalie Silver never begged for anything. She was too proud. Too stubborn. She hadn't asked for a cent of his money when they'd split up, and had only grudgingly accepted the child support Anthony had instructed his attorney to offer. She hadn't taken anything but Kyle when she'd moved out. Hadn't even kept the Bishop name, damn her. Damn her all to hell.

But in the next instant he was telling himself, *It's not too late. You can win her back if you want her.*

He'd won her once from his own brother. He could do so again, if he chose to. After all, everyone had a price. Even Natalie.

"Mr. Bishop?"

He whirled at the sound of his secretary's voice. "What is it?"

"Your wife called earlier while you were out. I told her you were in a meeting and couldn't be disturbed. Was that all right?"

"Exactly right." The last person he wanted to talk to tonight was that shrew who passed herself off as his loving wife.

He walked over and sat down at his desk, running his finger down the neat list of the next day's appointments.

"Did you get the McGruder meeting rescheduled?" he asked abruptly.

"Yes. He's coming in next week." The secretary wavered in the doorway.

Anthony glanced up, scowling. "Well?"

"Will you be needing anything else tonight?" she asked hesitantly, as if dreading to hear his answer.

Anthony glanced at his Rolex. It was after eight. He supposed the woman was anxious to get home to her family—did she even have a family?—or perhaps meet a boyfriend for drinks or some Christmas shopping. Later, they would probably go back to her place or to his and...

Anthony's thoughts trailed off as he let his eyes linger on the woman's legs. She really was very attractive. Why hadn't he noticed her before?

She cleared her throat, blushing prettily as she became aware of his attention. "If there's nothing else..."

Anthony sighed with regret. Another night, perhaps. He had too many things on his mind right now to pursue the subtle art of seduction, and besides, he already had too many entanglements, both personal and professional, from which he needed to extricate himself. Speaking of which—"Is my sister still here?"

"She's in her office. Shall I get her for you?"

"No, no." Absently he waved the secretary away. If his wife was the last person he wanted to see tonight, his sister was a close second. Anthea was getting just a little too ambitious for her own good. And a little too clever. She'd been asking him a lot of questions about the Russo case, as if she suspected something. As if she *knew* something.

In spite of the bond Anthony shared with his twin sister, he knew the time was fast approaching when he would have to do something about her. But like Melinda, his current wife, she would have to be handled carefully. Neither of them would go quietly.

And, of course, there was the matter of his mistress to contend with; a woman of unparalleled talents and tastes, to be sure, but lately she'd become possessive, clinging. Desperate. And she'd been making threats. Nothing to be concerned about, of course, but still, after their interlude here a little while ago, she'd left in tears, begging him not to send her away. Begging him for more than he was willing to give. Anthony had known then that something would have to be done, and soon.

A clean break from all of them was exactly what he needed right now. Maybe then…

He stared at the picture of Kyle on the corner of his desk. It was time for the boy to come home. Preferably with his mother, but if that wasn't possible—

The phone on Anthony's desk rang, and he noticed it was his private line. Only a handful of people had access to that number, his wife not among them. Warily, he picked up the phone and said hello.

A gruff voice he recognized instantly said, "It's me. Is the line clear?"

"It's clear." Anthony routinely had his office and phone lines swept for electronic bugs, but since Jack Russo had gotten out of prison a few days ago, Anthony had to be twice as careful. He knew the feds were watching him closely, and he couldn't afford to let his guard down even for a second.

Of course, there were ways around the surveillance, he

thought, smiling. Ways of slipping in and out of his office without anyone—even his secretary—being the wiser.

From the other end came a long hesitation, then Russo said, "I received your package."

"And?"

"And? *And?*" Russo screamed. "There was nothing inside that box but a goddamned ceramic Santa Claus thing."

"What? That's impossible—"

"What the hell's going on here, Bishop? Where the hell are my diamonds?"

Anthony swallowed, tasting bile. What the hell *was* going on? "Look, Jack, just calm down. The diamonds have to be in that package. All of them, except for my cut. I put them inside the music box. There's a catch on the back that opens a secret compartment—"

"I've smashed it to bits and I'm telling you, those diamonds are not here. Now you better come clean with me, Bishop. I didn't rot in no stinking federal pen for two and a half years to be double-crossed by my own attorney."

Anthony felt as if a noose were slowly tightening around his neck. He reached up and loosened his tie. "I'm telling you, I put them in there myself. Someone on your end—"

"There's no one here but me and my mother," Russo growled. "And I sure as hell didn't give myself the shaft. If you're implying that my mother—"

"No, no. I didn't mean that," Anthony said quickly, remembering the devotion Russo felt for his elderly mother.

"Well, then. That just leaves you now, don't it?"

Anthony's mind raced. What the hell had happened? Was it possible? Could Natalie have found the diamonds and removed them? He might expect a double cross like that from Melinda, but Natalie?

"Those diamonds are the only thing tying me to that murder, Bishop. If I go down, you go down."

"No one's going down," Anthony said hastily, running his fingers through his hair. "This is some kind of mistake."

"Damn right, it's a mistake. *Your* mistake, buddy, and you better, by God, fix it. You've got twenty-four hours before my boys come calling."

Anthony closed his eyes briefly as an image of Russo's thugs sprang to mind. "Trust me," he said. "Haven't I always taken care of you? Didn't I get the murder charges thrown out for lack of evidence?"

"Yeah, but if those sparklers turn up in the wrong hands—"

"They won't," Anthony assured him. The diamonds had to be still in Natalie's store. Somehow the wrong music box must have been sent. Whether deliberately or by mistake, Anthony had no idea, but he was damned well going to find out. "I'll go over to my ex-wife's shop tonight after she closes. I'll search every inch of that damned store until I find those diamonds."

"You better hope to hell she didn't rat you out," Russo said ominously. "It'll be your hide I come looking for."

Anthony got the message loud and clear. He stared at the silent phone for a moment, then hung up the receiver with trembling hands.

Outside his office, a soft rustling sound startled him. Silently, he got up and strode across the carpeted floor to his door. He pulled it open and gazed around his secretary's office.

No one was about. The desk was tidied for the night, the computer turned off, the files all locked away. But the door that led into the hallway was slightly ajar, and from outside the office came the unmistakable hum of the elevator, as someone made an exit.

"DAMN, DAMN, DOUBLE DAMN," Natalie muttered as she gazed at the glowing red light on her security system in Silver Bells. She'd been in such a hurry to close up shop and get home, that she must have forgotten to turn on the alarm.

She sighed wearily. It was after eleven and she was exhausted. Normally she closed the shop at six, but during the Christmas season, she stayed open until nine. Tonight she hadn't gotten rid of the last customer until almost ten, and then she'd had to close out the register and tidy the shop before locking up.

She'd made it almost all the way home before remembering that she hadn't put her bank bag in the safe before leaving. She'd tried to convince herself that the bag would be perfectly safe in her desk drawer until morning. She'd never had a break-in, and the Riverwalk was well patrolled, especially this time of year. But a little voice in the back of her mind kept warning: *There's always a first time for everything.*

Natalie had known that niggling little voice wouldn't give her a moment's peace until she drove back to the shop and locked the bank bag in her safe. And now, as she gazed at the mocking red light, she decided it was a good thing she had.

The overhead lights were off, but the Christmas lights were still on, illuminating the interior of Silver Bells with a soft, sterling glow. Natalie stopped, her breath catching slightly at the beauty, at the magic of the moment.

She had done this, she thought, gazing around in wonder. She had done this all on her own. She'd made a success of her shop, made her dream come true, and although she didn't expect to ever be rich, at least she and Kyle would be comfortable.

That was important to her; being able to provide for her son without any help from the Bishops. Because if Natalie had learned anything during her short marriage to Anthony, it was that the Bishops never gave anything without demanding something in return.

Without turning on the overhead lights, Natalie made her way around the counter and headed for the workroom when suddenly she came to a full stop. The door to the workroom was open, and Natalie always kept it closed. Something—a subtle sound, a current of displaced air, a scent?—warned her that she wasn't alone. Someone was inside the darkened workroom, listening to the silence just as she was.

How had the intruder gotten in? The front door had been locked. There was no sign of a forced entry, but the alarm had been turned off. Maybe she hadn't forgotten to turn it on after all. Maybe the intruder had managed to pick the lock neatly and disarm her security system, which meant she was dealing with a professional. Someone as dangerous as he was experienced.

Natalie's heart hammered in her chest. What should she do? Turn and make a run for it? Find a weapon? What? *What?*

For a split second, fear paralyzed her and she stood rooted to the spot, listening to the sound of her own blood pounding in her ears. Then, before she had time to regain her senses, the intruder stepped out of the workroom to confront her in the cool glow of Christmas lights.

"Where are they?" he demanded.

Natalie stared at Anthony in shock. "What are you doing here?" she finally managed to gasp. "How did you get in?"

He grabbed her arm and pulled her roughly into the workroom. For the first time in her life, Natalie was actually frightened of her ex-husband. She'd never seen him look so dangerous. So out of control.

She gazed around at the wreckage that was her workroom. Drawers were pulled out of her desk, the contents dumped on the floor. The shelves against the wall had been ruthlessly cleared, and even the garbage can had been overturned.

Anger warred with fear. Natalie jerked her arm from his grasp and whirled to face him. "What the hell do you think you're doing?"

His green gaze, usually so cool, flashed with fire. "Where are they, Natalie?"

"I don't know what you're talking about, but I'm calling the police. Even you can't get away with this, Anthony." She started toward the phone on her desk, but he reached it first, grabbed it, and ripped it from the jack.

"You found them, didn't you?" He threw the phone against the wall, shattering the plastic housing. "You thought you could pull a fast one on me, didn't you? You've always been just a little too clever for your own good, Natalie. But not this time. Now hand them over before I do something we might both regret—"

The door to the shop was behind Natalie, and Anthony's gaze moved over her right shoulder. His eyes widened in surprise. "What are you doing he—"

Before Natalie could turn, something hit her on the back of the head, sending sharp, shooting pains through her skull. Stunned, she felt her knees buckle and she collapsed to the floor.

Chapter Three

Anthony Bishop had been dead for hours, and his brother still found it hard to believe. As Spence stared at the police report, the words blurred before his eyes. It didn't matter. He'd read it so many times since Anthony's body had been found that he knew the words by heart, anyway.

Anthony had been stabbed in the back with a long, serrated knife that Natalie Silver kept in her workroom to open shipping cartons. When the police had answered a disturbance call at her shop just after midnight last night, they'd found Natalie kneeling over Anthony, clutching the bloody weapon in her hand.

But perhaps the most compelling evidence of all was Anthony's own words, spoken just seconds before he died. "Natalie…not you…"

It had been nearly twelve hours since Spence had learned of his brother's murder. He'd only left police headquarters once, very briefly, to break the news to his mother and sister, who hadn't even known Spence was in town.

His return to San Antonio had been masked in secrecy, cloaked in subterfuge, and now it had all blown up in his face.

He rubbed his eyes, wondering how the hell it had come to this. His assignment had been to bring down Jack Russo by finding the diamonds that would tie the mobster to a brutal murder in Dallas three years ago—before Russo had been sent to prison on racketeering charges.

Spence had known all along that in bringing down Russo there was a good chance Anthony would be implicated; that his brother might have to face criminal charges if the FBI's suspicions about him proved true.

But that fact hadn't deterred Spence. He'd been willing to do whatever it took to get Jack Russo—even sacrifice his own brother—because he'd convinced himself over the years that the end justified the means.

Now Anthony was dead and Natalie Silver was accused of his murder. Spence wished he could appreciate the irony of the situation, but he couldn't. He felt empty inside. Hollow in the place where his grief should have been. No matter what Anthony had done, he hadn't deserved this.

And Natalie?

Did she deserve the hell she was being put through?

Spence closed his eyes, telling himself that if she had done this to his brother, he wouldn't lift one finger to help her.

But he would.

He knew he would, because his gut instinct told him that she was as much a part of his assignment as Anthony had been. She held the key, and if he wanted to win, if he wanted to crack this case, Spence would have to keep his eye—a close eye—on Natalie Silver.

Jack Russo was a cold-blooded murderer, and Spence knew he would do whatever it took to bring him to justice. Even if it meant helping a woman who had once betrayed him.

Or bringing her down.

THIS WAS A NIGHTMARE, Natalie thought, as she gazed at the stony-eyed detectives intent on interrogating her again.

She'd answered so many questions, told her story so many times since last night, she felt numb with exhaustion. She could almost understand how a suspect could be coerced into a confession. Just say yes, and maybe they would leave you alone; give you a moment's peace.

But Natalie had a feeling that for her, peace would be a long time in coming.

The worst part was she hadn't been able to see Kyle. She hadn't been the one to tell him Anthony was dead. Instead, after her desperate phone call from police headquarters last night, Natalie's parents had rushed over to her house, relieved the baby-sitter—who had been frantic with worry by that time—and when Kyle had awakened this morning, they'd told him what had happened as gently as possible, leaving out the gruesome aspects of Anthony's death and the fact that Natalie had been arrested for his murder.

Oh, God, if only she could remember, Natalie thought desperately. If only she could recall what had happened before she'd blacked out. Someone had come in, hit her on the head, then killed Anthony while she was still unconscious. But who? Who would do such a terrible thing and leave her to take the blame?

"If you didn't stab him, why were you holding the murder weapon when the officers arrived on the scene?" one of the detectives, a Sergeant Phillips, asked her.

Natalie stared at him, bleary-eyed. "I told you. I didn't even realize I was holding it. I don't even know how the knife got in my hand. When I regained consciousness, I saw Anthony on the floor. There was so much blood...I knelt over him to see if he was still alive, and that's when the police came storming in."

"How do you explain that cut on your right hand?" the other detective asked.

"I...I can't explain it," Natalie said, moistening her dry lips. She hadn't even realized she was cut until the officers who arrived on the scene wrapped a bandage around it to stop the bleeding.

Sergeant Phillips propped one foot on a chair and folded his arms across his bent knee. "Your divorce from Anthony Bishop was pretty nasty, wasn't it? Accusations all around. Rumors and innuendos flying. You didn't get a settlement from that divorce, did you?"

"No."

"You must have thought you were entitled to one."

"I didn't want one. I didn't want anything from Anthony except my freedom. And my son."

Sergeant Phillips arched an eyebrow at that. He and the other detective exchanged glances. Then Phillips said, "Anthony Bishop married his current wife just three weeks after his divorce from you became final, isn't that so?"

Natalie nodded.

"Her name was Seagrass before she became a Bishop. Melinda Seagrass. The two of you were once close. You went to school together. In fact, she was your best friend, wasn't she?"

"Yes."

"Married her just three weeks after he divorced you." Sergeant Phillips stared at her. "It's a pretty safe bet the two of them were seeing each other before the divorce. Wouldn't you say so?"

Natalie sighed. "I know what you're getting at. But I didn't carry a grudge against Anthony because of his affair with Melinda. That happened years ago. I didn't kill him for revenge, if that's what you're thinking."

"Then why did you kill him?"

"I didn't!" Dear God, she had to make them believe her. Why wouldn't they listen to her? She pushed back her hair with both hands. "I told you, I walked in on Anthony at the shop last night. I have no idea what he was doing there, but evidently he was looking for something. He thought I had something of his. But before he could tell me what it was, someone else came in and hit me from behind. I lost consciousness. When I woke up, I saw Anthony lying on the floor…covered in blood…" She closed her eyes, trying to maintain her composure. "I swear that's all I know," she said through trembling lips.

"If he was already inside the shop when you got there, how did he get in? There was no sign of a forced entry, and the security system had been turned off. How do you explain that?"

"I…don't know. I might have forgotten to turn the alarm on when I left earlier."

"Did you also forget to lock the front door?"

"No…"

Sergeant Phillips got up from the chair and walked around the table to sit directly across from Natalie. His dark eyes bored into hers so intently that she even began to feel guilty. She clasped her hands in her lap to try and control the shaking. "Did you know that your ex-husband was about to haul you into court and sue you for sole custody of your son?"

Natalie gasped. "No—"

"The papers were already drawn up. Are you telling me you had no idea of his intentions? Not even an inkling?"

Natalie hesitated, remembering her conversation yesterday with Blanche. They'd talked about the possibility then, and Natalie had said something like— Dear God—she'd said if Anthony were to try to take away her son, she would do whatever it took to stop him. But she hadn't meant it! She hadn't meant she would kill him!

"You did know, didn't you?"

Natalie shook her head. "No. I mean…I wondered why he'd suddenly come back into our lives, why he wanted to start seeing Kyle again. But I didn't know he planned to sue for custody. He never said anything."

"He never threatened you?"

"No."

"You didn't call him down to your shop last night to confront him with your suspicions?"

"No."

"He didn't taunt you with how easy it would be for a high-powered attorney like him, a *Bishop,* to win in court? To take your son away from you?"

"No."

"The two of you didn't fight? He didn't get physical? Shove you around? You didn't take that knife out of your desk, catch him off guard, and stab him in the back?"

"No! No!" Natalie screamed, jumping to her feet. "I was knocked unconscious, just like I've told you a million times. I have a bump on my head to prove it."

"Sit down," Sergeant Phillips instructed calmly. When she complied, he said, "You could have gotten that during the struggle."

"I didn't," Natalie cried. "And I didn't kill Anthony!" She dropped her head in her hands. "Oh, God, why won't you believe me?"

"I'm not unsympathetic to your predicament," Sergeant Phillips said in a deceptively soft voice. Natalie looked up, wanting to believe that note of kindness, that hint of empathy in his dark eyes. "You love your son very much, don't you?"

Natalie swallowed and nodded.

"A boy needs his mother."

Tears flooded Natalie's eyes as she thought about Kyle. How had he taken the news of Anthony's death? Was he sad, grieving? Until a few weeks ago, Kyle hadn't seen Anthony since he was a baby. He didn't know him. But still, Natalie knew her son had thought about him over the years, wondered about him. Kyle must be so upset, so confused. And she wasn't there for him.

"You would do anything to protect him, wouldn't you?"

Natalie looked up through teary eyes but she said nothing.

"He needs you now more than ever. And you need to be with him. Cooperate with me, Natalie, and I'll see that you and your son are together again very soon."

"What do I have to do?" she asked weakly.

"Just tell me the truth." Sergeant Phillips leaned forward, gazing earnestly into her eyes. "You see, I think you killed Anthony Bishop in self-defense. I think what we have here is a case of justifiable homicide. Just admit it, and the chances are, you'll walk out of here a free woman."

SILENCE FELL LIKE A heavy cloak over the interrogation room. Everyone seemed to be waiting with bated breath for Natalie's answer. She sat stone still, gazing at the sergeant with the most haunted-looking eyes Spence had ever seen.

He found himself leaning toward the two-way mirror, his gaze searching her face for the truth. But he hadn't seen Natalie Silver in seven years. He wasn't sure he would recognize the truth in her eyes if he saw it.

Seven years, he thought. Seven years since he had returned to San Antonio following his first big undercover assignment, only to find that she had married his brother while he'd been gone. She'd wasted no time in discovering who had the money in his family. Who had the power.

Natalie Silver had fooled him once with her sweet smile and innocent eyes, but Spence didn't think she was capable of doing so again. He wasn't a rookie anymore. During the years he'd been an agent, he'd dealt with plenty of liars. And murderers.

He studied her features now, looking for the telltale clues that would give her away, surprised to find that his memories of her were amazingly accurate. Her light brown hair was longer now, shoulder length and cut in layers that fell softly around her face. She wore a dark red sweater and a short plaid skirt that made her seem very young, almost schoolgirlish. And vulnerable. Still vulnerable.

She wasn't wearing her glasses, and Spence wanted to believe that was why her blue eyes looked so lost. So haunted.

Or maybe it was because of what she'd done, he told himself grimly.

As if she sensed his anger, Natalie's gaze shifted from Sergeant Phillips and for one split second, she seemed to be gazing at the blind side of the mirror, staring through the glass directly into Spence's soul. The sensation startled him, and before he realized what he was doing, he took a step back, as if protecting himself from her.

Then her gaze refocused on Phillips and she said in a soft, quivering voice, "I want to see my son. More than anything."

"Of course, you do. We want that, too." The two detectives exchanged triumphant looks. They were working her well. Had her right where they wanted her. Exhaustion and fear had worn her down, stripped away her defenses, and now they were playing on her emotions. Making her think they had only her best interests at heart before they zeroed in for the kill.

In their place, Spence would have done exactly the same thing.

"Tell us what really happened, Natalie," Sergeant Phillips urged softly. "We only want to help you."

Natalie closed her eyes for a moment, as if gathering her courage. Spence felt the muscles in the back of his neck tighten in anticipation. He found himself straining toward the speaker.

When she opened her eyes, they seemed even bluer than before. And clearer somehow. "I...can't lie to get out of here. I can't tell you something that isn't true. I didn't kill Anthony. Not in self-defense or for any other reason."

Anger flashed across Sergeant Phillips's usually stoic features. "The evidence says otherwise."

"I didn't do it," Natalie repeated.

"Then my best advice to you," Phillips said, rising, "is to get your lawyer down here, pronto. You're in a lot of trouble, lady."

NATALIE SAT AT THE wooden table, staring down at her bandaged hand. Funny, she couldn't feel the cut beneath the gauze. Not even so much as a sting, and yet she knew the cut was fairly deep. Before bringing her to police headquarters last night, the officers had taken her to the emergency room at one of the local hospitals for stitches.

Natalie had no idea how she'd gotten that cut. Or if the dark stains across the front of her skirt and sweater were her blood or...Anthony's.

The detectives—Sergeant Phillips and the other one— had left her alone several minutes ago, probably to let her contemplate her predicament before they came back in for another round of questions. She was sure this was one of their tactics. Attack and retreat, attack and retreat, so that the waiting between rounds became unbearable.

Natalie wasn't sure how much more she could take. Her father had advised her this morning to say nothing until he could find her a good attorney, but Natalie had been so sure that once she told her story to the police, everything would be okay; she would be released. All she had to do was tell the truth, and she would be set free.

But that hadn't been the case at all. No one believed her. Everyone seemed convinced of her guilt. Dear God, what was she going to do?

She rested her head in her hands, tempted to give in to despair. But she had to think about Kyle. She had to be strong for him. She had to get out of here so she could take care of her son.

Even though she had been expecting it, when the door opened a few minutes later, Natalie jumped. She swung her gaze around, determined to face the next round of interrogation bravely, but the moment she saw the man in the doorway, her courage all but deserted her.

For the space of a heartbeat, she thought she might be seeing things. Thought he might be a mirage. Spencer Bishop was the last person on earth she'd expected to see.

Or wanted to see.

Their gazes held for the longest moment, then Spence slowly closed the door behind him. Natalie had never felt so defenseless. She sat huddled at the table, shivering beneath the piercing glare of his cold, green eyes.

Bishop eyes.

"What are you doing here?" she finally managed.

The expression on his face never wavered. He walked to the table and stood over her, tall, dark, and dangerously handsome. "I would have thought that obvious."

She gazed up at him, the very sight of him—the memories of him—making her tremble. "I didn't do it," she whispered. "I didn't kill Anthony."

He didn't say anything, merely studied her for a moment longer, then said, "I should advise you that you don't have to talk to me. You don't have to talk to any of us without an attorney present. They told you that, didn't they? They advised you of your rights?"

"Yes. But I don't have an attorney."

"Then you'd better get one."

"But I'm innocent!"

Spence shrugged. "It's in your best interests to have someone here advising you. Anything you say can and will be used against you."

"Then you're here in an official capacity?" she asked.

His gazed darkened on her. "I'm here because my brother is dead."

"And you think I killed him, just like the police do." The irony of the situation was devastating. Natalie didn't know which was worse—facing a steely-eyed FBI agent or the accusing eyes of the man she had once loved.

Spence sat down at the table across from her. Natalie tried not to look up, but his gaze was too penetrating, his presence too compelling. She glanced up, searching his face for a sign of the man she'd once loved.

But then, that man hadn't really existed, had he? Just like Anthony, he'd made her believe what she'd wanted to believe. Until he'd gotten what he wanted.

Natalie's faced burned with humiliation. Even after seven years, the thought that she had been little more than a one-night stand to Spencer Bishop still shamed her. How could she have been so stupid, falling for a man she'd known less than a week? The dashing young FBI agent, so dark and intense…

He hadn't changed that much, she thought weakly. A

little older, maybe. A little harder. He was wearing jeans, snug and riding low on his lean frame, and a dark shirt, dark tie, and sports coat. Natalie wondered where his gun was.

His green eyes narrowed on her, as if reading her thoughts. He reached up and drew his fingers through his dark hair, making Natalie remember yet another intimacy.

"The evidence is pretty damning," Spence said. "Especially Anthony's last words. What do you think he meant if he wasn't pointing the finger at you? 'Natalie…not you…' Those were his exact words, I believe."

"I know. I was there." Her eyes filled with tears as she remembered those last few moments of Anthony's life, when she had awakened to see him lying on the floor, so still and covered with blood. She'd knelt over him, unaware of picking up the murder weapon, intent only on finding out if he was still alive, if she could help him.

And then the police had burst through the front door. The lights had come on, and Natalie had looked up to find the officers' guns drawn on her. "Move away from the body. Now!" And another one shouting, "Drop your weapon!"

Dazed, Natalie had complied. While one of the officers had stood guard over her, the other had rushed to Anthony's side to try and stanch the flow of blood. But it had been too late. Too late for anything other than Anthony's last dying words.

Natalie…not you…

Natalie had no idea why her ex-husband had said what he'd said, but the thought had crossed her mind that perhaps he had deliberately tried to implicate her. But why, unless he hadn't known he was mortally wounded? Unless he'd thought, even on his deathbed, that he could somehow use his attack against her? If he hadn't known he was dying, he might still have been thinking of his custody suit. What better way to get Kyle than by sending his mother to prison?

But Anthony had died, and Natalie was accused of his murder. Where did that leave Kyle now? Surely Irene wouldn't go after custody. She'd never shown the slightest interest in her grandson. But what if…

Another possibility occurred to her, and a cold chill swept through her as she stared at Spence. Things had changed since Anthony's death. Natalie was not only fighting for her own life, she was fighting for her son's life, as well.

Spence was still looking at her, as if he could read her every thought. Shaken, Natalie glanced away. "I won't say another word," she said, "until I get an attorney."

"Suit yourself." He got up, but leaned toward her over the table, invading her space. She could smell the subtle scent of his cologne, see the faint shadow of his beard. The effect was powerful. Natalie's pulse hammered in her throat. She had to fight the urge to back away from him, to protect herself from the memories his presence stirred to life.

Then he straightened and strode across the room to the door, glancing back over his shoulder. "Believe it or not, I'm not after you, Natalie. I'm after the truth."

"I wish I could believe that," she whispered as the door closed between them.

Chapter Four

Daylight had come and gone, and twilight fell softly on the city as Natalie prepared to spend her first full night in jail. She gazed around her dismal surroundings—the grim tile floor, the cinder-block walls, the sink and toilet, and the two cots, one of them occupied by her only cell mate, a woman named Jessie who had slept almost the whole time since Natalie had been back from the bail-review hearing.

She wished the woman would wake up and talk to her, and then again, she didn't. She'd seen movies about innocent people being locked up with hardened criminals, and she had no idea what Jessie was in for.

And then the shocking thought occurred to Natalie that perhaps the woman was only pretending to sleep. Maybe she was the one who was scared. Scared to be incarcerated with a murderer.

Natalie sat down on the other cot and shivered. She'd already been branded a killer. It didn't matter that she was innocent. The police thought she was guilty, and so would everyone else when they heard the evidence. Maybe even the jury.

Natalie wrapped her arms around herself as her shivering grew worse. What if she was convicted? What if she was sent to prison for the rest of her life? What if the only time she got to see Kyle or her parents was on visitors' day, and even then through a sheet of bulletproof glass?

She squeezed her eyes closed as she rocked back and forth, not wanting to cry. Not wanting to give in to the despair, because if she did, she knew she would be lost.

But it was difficult to hold on to her courage when everything seemed so hopeless. With the police so convinced of her guilt, they wouldn't be looking for any other suspects. And bail had been set so high—a quarter of a million dollars—that Natalie wouldn't be able to get out of here to search for the real killer herself.

That had been the Bishops' doing, Natalie thought bitterly. Having bail set so high that she couldn't possibly make it, not even if she sold her house, her shop, and cleaned out her savings account. Irene Bishop had obviously called in her markers, and Natalie would have to remain in jail, possibly until the trial, which could be weeks or even months away. The loss of Christmas sales would force her out of business. She would lose everything.

But worst of all, she wouldn't be able to be with Kyle, to protect him and shelter him from the nightmare their lives had suddenly become.

"Natalie Silver?"

She looked up to find a female police officer opening the cell door.

"Ye-yes." Natalie rose.

"Come with me," the officer said. "Your bail's been posted. You're free to go."

Natalie stared at the woman in shock. "But how? Who?"

The officer shrugged. "He's downstairs now, filling out

the paperwork. Come on. You want to get out of here, don't you?''

Natalie had never wanted anything so badly in her life. She didn't know how her father had managed to come up with the money in so short a time, but she was thankful that he had.

As she walked through the cell door, she glanced back. Her cell mate had rolled over and was staring at her with the most haunted eyes Natalie had ever seen, and it occurred to her that looking at Jessie was like looking into a mirror.

''OPEN IT UP,'' the officer instructed as she shoved a manila envelope toward Natalie. ''Make sure everything's there.''

Natalie did as she was told, but if anything was missing, she wouldn't know it. She couldn't remember what personal effects had been taken from her last night.

''Where's my father?'' she asked, signing for the articles.

The officer shrugged. ''How should I know?''

Natalie glanced up. ''He's the one who posted bail for me, isn't he?''

She pointed past Natalie's right shoulder. ''That's him over there.''

Natalie turned around, clutching the manila envelope to her breast. Spencer Bishop stood in the doorway of an office, talking to someone. He hadn't seen her yet, and Natalie started to back away. But then he turned, and his gaze, like the touch of a chill wind, fell on her.

Slowly he left the doorway and walked toward her. Natalie's heart beat like a tom-tom as he stopped in front of her and stared down into her upturned face.

In the years since she'd seen him, Natalie had managed

to forget—or at least she told herself she had—how tall he was, how broad his shoulders were. How masculine he could seem with the five o'clock shadow that never quite went away. His green eyes looked darker and deeper than she remembered, almost sinister as he held her gaze without wavering.

"Why?" she whispered, not trusting herself to say much else.

He merely stared at her for a moment longer, then shrugged. "I figured you were ready to get out of that place. Was I wrong?"

Natalie shook her head. God, no, he wasn't wrong. If there was one thing she'd discovered during this whole ordeal, it was that a jail cell was the loneliest place in the world. The thought of spending the night in there—of spending a *lifetime* of nights in there—sent a shiver of dread coursing through Natalie.

"You're not wrong," she said softly. "But I don't understand why you did it. Your family—"

"Let's leave my family out of it, shall we?"

"I just don't understand why you would do this for me."

"Unless I want something in return?" he asked, his voice edged with sarcasm.

Natalie glanced away. That was exactly what she was thinking.

"Well, you're right," he said. "I do want something from you."

"What?" she asked, although she was almost afraid to hear his answer. He was a Bishop, after all.

"I want to find out the truth," he said. "I want to know why Anthony was murdered. You're the only one who can help me find the answers I need."

She took a deep breath, staring up at him, not trusting him. "Does this mean you think I'm innocent?"

"In the eyes of the law, you're innocent until proven guilty."

"That doesn't really answer my question," she said.

"It's the best I can give you right now."

"Then I guess it'll have to do," she said quietly. Lifting her chin, Natalie met his gaze evenly, until, this time, it was Spence who glanced away. "Thank you for getting me out of here," she said, even though she still didn't understand why he had. She didn't know anything. If Spence was looking for answers from her, he was going to be sadly disappointed.

"I didn't do it for thanks," he said. "Like I said, I want to find out the truth. And having you free makes that a whole lot easier for me."

"How?"

He hesitated, as if contemplating how much to tell her. "We can work together. You must want those answers as badly as I do."

"But I don't know anything," she said. "I've told the police everything. What more can I do?"

"Something may come back to you," he said. "And if it does, I want to be the first to know."

"By bailing me out of jail, you think you've bought my cooperation. Is that it?" she asked bitterly.

He shrugged. "Maybe. Like it or not, Natalie, I'm all you've got right now." His eyes grew even darker, deeper, until Natalie felt as though she were drowning in those green depths. As if suddenly, unexpectedly, she was once again over her head in dangerous waters.

She shivered, wishing she could trust Spence's motives. But he'd lied to her before. Deceived her just as cruelly as Anthony had. Natalie didn't trust any of the Bishops and she knew she never would.

"If you'll excuse me, I need to call a cab," she said, turning away.

"I'll drive you home."

That stopped her. She turned back, staring at him suspiciously. "Why? So you can grill me on the way?"

"I was just leaving, and this time of night, cabs are hard to come by. No ulterior motive," he said, holding up his hands.

And what did it matter if he did have an ulterior motive? Natalie decided. She wasn't going to tell him anything, and besides, ulterior motives could work both ways. Maybe she could do a little grilling of her own, find out the real reason he'd posted her bail. Because she knew, intuitively, that he wasn't telling her the whole truth.

"In that case, I accept," she said, praying she didn't live to regret this night. "Thank you, again."

"No problem."

It took them twenty minutes to get to Natalie's parents' house in Alamo Heights. Twenty excruciatingly silent minutes, during which time both of them seemed equally determined not to tell the other one anything. When Spence pulled into the driveway, Natalie's eyes filled with sudden tears.

Christmas lights outlined the curves and gables of the roof and every window and doorway of the modest-but-comfortable house. A wreath hung on the front door and a big red bow adorned the mailbox.

Had there ever been a more welcome sight? Natalie thought fleetingly.

But as Spence got out of the car and followed her up the drive, she hesitated. They stood at the bottom of the porch steps, suspended in the warm glow of Christmas lights, as she gazed with trepidation at the front door.

"What's the matter?" he asked. "I thought you would be anxious to get home."

"I am." Natalie took a deep breath. The whole thing was just too much, she thought. She'd been accused of murdering her ex-husband, while here she stood with his brother in her parents' front yard. Could her life get any more bizarre?

"It's just… What if I look into their eyes and see that they don't believe me? What if my own son thinks I'm a murderer?"

In the glow of the Christmas lights, she saw a shadow crossing his features, and Natalie had a sudden premonition of what he was thinking. If the situation were reversed, it wouldn't matter much whether his family believed in his innocence or not. They would condemn him for dragging the Bishop name through the mud.

"Well, there's only one way to find out," he said, his voice hard.

Natalie nodded, but before she could say anything, the front door swung open and a deep voice said excitedly, "Natalie! I thought that was you! Come here, sweetheart!"

And suddenly Natalie knew everything was going to be all right. The tears that she'd managed to hold at bay for so long came flooding out at the sight of her father's outstretched arms. She flew up the steps and into that waiting comfort.

"Daddy," she whispered, squeezing her eyes tightly shut against the rush of emotions brought on by the warmth and security of Paul Silver's embrace. The scent of Old Spice had always reminded her of her father, but never had it smelled more wonderful, conjured more memories, than it did at that moment.

"I know," he said, holding her tightly. "I know, sweetheart, but everything's going to be okay now. You'll see."

He whispered to her and soothed her just as he had when she was a little girl, when she'd come to him with nothing more traumatic than a skinned knee or a broken doll. He was not a big man—only five foot seven or so—and he was still recovering from a heart attack he'd suffered two months ago. But Natalie thought his arms had never felt stronger.

Presently they both became aware of Spence, standing at the bottom of the steps, and her father cleared his throat gruffly. "Why don't you both come in and tell me how you got out. I've had our lawyer and accountant working non-stop since the hearing this afternoon, but I didn't have any hope of getting anything done until morning."

Natalie hesitated, realizing her father had just invited Spencer Bishop into his home, and neither she nor Spence seemed to know what to do about the request.

"I can't stay," he said.

At the same time, she said, "It's okay. Please come in."

Spence hesitated, as if staying here was the last thing in the world he wanted to do at that moment. But then he shrugged, and climbed the porch steps to follow them inside.

The interior of the house was even more welcoming. Boughs of fresh fir and holly, draping the banister and mantel, perfumed the air, and a cheery fire crackled in the fireplace. A huge Christmas tree, decorated with colored lights and a myriad of ornaments in every conceivable shape and size, dominated one whole corner of the living room.

The fire must have been her mother's idea, Natalie thought. Joy Silver always said there was nothing quite so comforting as a fire on a winter evening—even if, in San

Antonio, it often meant running the air conditioner at the same time.

Her father kept his left arm around Natalie's shoulders as he turned to Spence. For the first time, Natalie realized there was more gray than brown in her father's hair, more lines around his eyes and mouth than she remembered. A pang of guilt darted through her.

"I don't believe we've met," he said to Spence, "even though you do look familiar to me."

"This is Spencer Bishop, Dad. Anthony's brother."

Natalie felt more than saw her father's slight hesitation before he extended his hand to Spence. The two men shook hands, then her dad said, "Come on into the living room. Your mother's out in the kitchen. I'd better go get her or she'll have my hide."

Natalie said, "Where's Kyle?"

"He's out back feeding your mother's dog. I'll get him, too." Her mother's dog was a ten-year-old keeshond that had been a part of the Silver family since the day he was born. But her father never referred to him as anything but "your mother's dog," even though he was just as crazy about Major as the rest of them were.

Just then, the kitchen door swung open and Natalie's mother came through. "Paul, I thought I heard voices—" She saw Natalie and her eyes lit up with happiness. "Natalie!"

Mother and daughter met halfway across the room and flung their arms around each other. Natalie had to lean down to embrace her mother. Trim, petite, a bundle of energy, Joy Silver looked at least ten years younger than her fifty-two years. Her hair was darker than Natalie's, her eyes a different shade of blue, but there was still a strong resemblance between them.

"Oh, my God," her mother cried. "I didn't think we

would be able to get you out until tomorrow. It broke my heart, thinking about you spending the night in that horrible place. But I should have known your father would come up with some way to get you out. Why didn't you tell me?'' she asked, craning her head around Natalie to stare accusingly at her husband.

''Because I didn't know,'' her father said. ''I'm not the one who posted her bail.''

''Then who did?'' her mother demanded.

''Actually…it was Spence who posted the bail.''

''Spence?''

Natalie looped her arm through her mother's and pulled her forward. ''This is Spencer Bishop, Mom. Anthony's brother.''

Her mother's hand fluttered to her heart. ''Oh, my,'' she murmured. Her gaze flew to her husband's, and Natalie saw her father's shoulders lift in a slight shrug as if to say, *I'm as confused by all this as you are.*

As if sensing the undercurrents, Spence said, ''I should be shoving off. I'm sure the three of you must have a lot to talk about.''

''You don't want to do that,'' her father said.

''I beg your pardon?''

''You don't want to leave before you have a chance to see your nephew.''

Spence looked at Natalie, who quickly glanced away.

''Some other time, perhaps—'' he started.

''We don't want to hold you up any longer—'' Natalie began.

''Mom! You're back!''

Before either of them could say another word, Kyle, dressed in a San Antonio Spurs sweatshirt, blue jeans, and sneakers, sprang through the kitchen door and launched himself at Natalie. She caught him in her arms, twirling him around and around until both of them collapsed on the plaid sofa, dizzy and laughing.

"I missed you so much," she said, kissing his cheek, but he was already pushing her slightly away as he turned to stare at Spence.

Green eyes met green eyes.

They measured each other for a long moment before Kyle wiggled off Natalie's lap and sat on the couch beside her. "You look like my father," he said.

Natalie's gaze flew to Spence's. He was studying Kyle just as intently as Kyle was studying him. From where Natalie sat, their profiles looked identical. But then, all the Bishops looked alike.

"I'm your uncle," Spence said. "Your father's brother. It's nice to finally meet you."

"You're not here to take my mother away again, are you?" Kyle demanded, his eyes narrowing on Spence.

Spence looked slightly startled, then said, "No. I brought her home, so you could take care of her."

Kyle pondered this, then nodded, seemingly satisfied with the answer. "Good," he said. "That's good."

"Would you like something to drink, Spence?" her mother asked, having gotten over her initial shock. "Hot chocolate or wassail, perhaps?"

Spence turned to her. "No, thanks. I really do have to be going."

"Let me walk you out." Her father put his hand on Spence's shoulder. The two of them turned toward the front door, and Natalie could hear her father speaking in a low voice as they stood in the foyer before Spence departed. She couldn't help wondering what her father was saying to him. And what Spence was saying in return.

As if drawn by her intense scrutiny, Spence turned at the door. His gaze captured Natalie's and her breath caught in her throat. She asked herself again, what he was doing here? Why he had bailed her out?

Dear God, she thought, what was he up to?

SPENCE PAUSED ON THE porch, unsettled by his brief encounter with the Silvers. The night suddenly seemed cold and bleak compared to the warmth he'd just left behind. For a moment, he had the strongest urge to turn around and go back, to join them in their cozy little domain, but there was no place for him inside that house. No place for him anywhere.

He'd always told himself that, in his line of work, it was better not to have ties. Better not to have a family—people who depended on you coming home every night.

He told himself that same thing now, but he couldn't seem to shake the disquiet that being with Natalie's family had awakened in him.

Starting across the yard toward his car, he glanced back, unable to resist. Through the large front window, he could see clearly into the house. He felt like a voyeur, but he couldn't seem to tear his gaze away.

The Silvers had all grouped themselves around the fireplace. Paul was seated in an overstuffed chair, while his wife perched on the arm. Joy. What an apt name, he thought, seeing the woman's smile flash down at her husband.

Spence thought that looking at Joy Silver was probably like getting a glimpse of what Natalie would look like in twenty years. They had the same bone structure, were both very thin and petite, and they both had the same soul-melting smile.

Natalie was seated on the floor in front of her father's chair with Kyle on her lap, her arms wrapped tightly around him, as if she would never let him go. But she was gazing up at her father, obviously clinging to every word Paul spoke.

In the split second that Spence stood gazing inside that window, it seemed to him that Paul Silver must be the luckiest man in the world.

"NATALIE? YOU STILL UP?"

Natalie turned from the window in her parents' guest room as her father poked his head inside the door. "Come in, Daddy."

Paul, dressed in dark blue pajamas and robe, crossed the room to stand at the window beside her. They stood silently for a few minutes, gazing at the Christmas lights on the house across the street.

Finally her father said, "What do you know about this Spencer Bishop?"

"Not much," Natalie hedged.

"I can't help worrying about his motives. If he's anything like Anthony, I can't see him doing anything out of the goodness of his heart."

"I know," Natalie said. "That worries me, too."

"Then you don't trust him?"

She shrugged. "I can't afford to. I can't afford to trust anyone right now, except you and Mom and Kyle." She turned to her father, gazing up at him earnestly. "I'm so sorry about…all this. All the trouble I've caused."

"Now, you listen to me," he said sternly. "This is not your fault. Any of it."

"I know, but if I'd never married Anthony—"

"You wouldn't have that great little guy in the next room. Think about that."

Natalie turned back to stare out the window. She'd thought of little else but Kyle since this whole ordeal had begun.

Paul put his arm around her and drew her close. "This family's been through a lot over the years, and we've always come through just fine. We'll get through this just like we've gotten through everything else—by sticking together. You hear me?"

Natalie smiled at the gruffness in his tone. "I hear you."

"Okay." He squeezed her arm. "Try to get a good night's sleep. Things always seem brighter in the morning."

At the door, he turned back suddenly.

"Natalie, about the bail…"

"What about it?"

He paused, then said, "You know I would have sold my soul to get you out of that place, don't you?"

Her eyes filled with tears. "I know that."

He nodded. "'Night."

"Good night, Daddy."

Chapter Five

Sunlight streamed in through the tall windows in the morning room, highlighting the silver streaks in Irene Bishop's perfectly coifed blond hair. She sat on the very edge of a tapestried armchair, her posture stick straight, her bearing regal, her air one of aloofness. She resembled her surroundings, Spence thought, not for the first time. Beautiful, elegant, and completely untouchable.

"Thank you for coming by so early this morning, Spencer," she said formally.

"How are you feeling?"

"How would you expect me to feel? My son has been brutally murdered." But whatever grief she might have been experiencing was carefully masked behind the perfect makeup, the perfect hairdo, the perfect black dress.

"I'm sorry," he said inadequately. "I know how difficult this must be for you."

"You have no idea," she replied, still without so much as a quiver of emotion in her voice or expression. Although he did notice that the hand holding the fragile ivory demitasse trembled as she lifted it to her lips. She took a delicate sip, then set the cup down on a marble-topped table. "The funeral is set for tomorrow. All the arrangements have been made. Only close friends and family and, of course, a few of Anthony's most trusted associates will be invited.''

Who, in their right mind, had trusted Anthony? Spence wondered, then immediately felt guilty. His brother had been dead for little more than twenty-four hours. Couldn't he find it in himself to show even an ounce of compassion, one measure of regret?

Spence turned away from his mother, his gaze going automatically to the portrait of his father and brother that hung over the marble fireplace. Anthony, Sr., was seated, while his favorite son stood slightly behind him, one hand resting on his father's shoulder. They stared down from their lofty position with the same handsome face, the same arrogant expression, the same cool green eyes.

The same eyes Spence saw when he looked at himself in the mirror.

But the similarities between him and Anthony—or with any of the other Bishops—ended there. Or at least Spence had always told himself so. He'd always told himself he was different, and that was the reason he was treated like an outsider in his own family. That was the reason there wasn't a single Bishop he'd ever been close to. Not his mother, not his sister, and especially not his brother.

He and Anthony had never gotten along, even as children. But seven years ago, when Spence had learned of Anthony's treachery and Natalie's betrayal, he'd known then that there would never be a reconciliation between his brother and him. Their differences were too great. The paths they'd each chosen for themselves, too divergent.

And now it was too late.

He rubbed his face with both hands as he turned back to Irene. ''Is that why you wanted to see me this morning? To tell me about the arrangements?''

"You're her son," Anthea said from the doorway. "Does she need a reason other than that?"

She always has before, Spence thought bitterly, glancing up to find his sister glaring at him from the doorway.

She walked into the room, tall and thin, head held high, striving to attain the Bishop air, but somehow not quite managing to pull it off.

Perhaps it was the almost-imperceptible slump of her shoulders, Spence thought. Or perhaps the way her suit— no doubt expensive—hung on her lanky frame like a bag. Her dark hair was cut in a short, boyish style that did nothing to soften her angular features. But, even given all that, she might still have been mildly attractive if not for the permanent scowl that darkened her face.

Anthea Bishop possessed not one ounce of her mother's sense of style or elegance, and Irene never seemed to let her forget it. Her critical gaze measured her daughter's progress across the room, but she said nothing. She didn't have to. Her silent disapproval echoed like a scream.

Spence could almost feel sorry for his sister. He'd been on the receiving end of Irene's cold disapproval far more times than he cared to remember. Only when she had looked at Anthony had her eyes lit with an inner glow. Only then had Spence ever glimpsed an emotion that remotely resembled maternal pride.

But instead of their lowly positions in the family drawing them closer together, Spence and Anthea were hardly more than strangers to each other. While Spence had compensated for the lack of parental affection by becoming wild and rebellious in his teenage years, then later pulling away from the family altogether, Anthea had become cold and sullen, steadfastly clinging to her heritage as a Bishop. She was forty-one years old and still living at home with her mother.

His sister's cool, assessing eyes seemed to challenge him now, although Spence had no idea what she might be thinking. He'd never been able to read Anthea.

"The reason I wanted to see you this morning," Irene was saying, "is because I'd like for you to come home, Spencer."

He gazed down at her in surprise. "What do you mean, come home?"

"I'd like for you to move back into this house, with Anthea and me."

His surprise turned to astonishment, and he found himself at a complete loss for words. He wondered fleetingly what his mother would think if she knew the real reason he'd come back to San Antonio; if she found out that his assignment had been to get Jack Russo at any cost, even if it meant implicating his own brother in a crime so dark and vile, the Bishop name would never again be the same.

Spence didn't think she would be inviting him to move back home, that was for sure.

"I told you yesterday I'm only here for the holidays. I live in Washington."

"I'm aware of that." Rising, Irene walked to the window and parted the heavy brocade curtains to gaze out at the sunlit courtyard.

She's still so beautiful, Spence thought, watching her. He'd once thought her the most beautiful woman in the world. Her figure was still straight and slender, her hair still thick and lush. The only thing that gave away her age was the blue-veined hand that trembled on the curtain.

He remembered how unblemished and elegant her hands had once been. How, as a child, he had admired the way her diamond rings sparkled against their ivory smoothness. How he had longed to have those hands smooth back his hair, soothe away his tears...

Irene let the curtain fall back into place and turned to him. "It may surprise you to learn that I've kept abreast of your career, Spencer. I know you've done quite well for yourself with the FBI. I'm told you're a very good agent."

Spence lifted an eyebrow at her placating tone, automatically suspicious of his mother's motives. Across the room, Anthea watched him carefully, her expression grim.

"Of course, it certainly isn't the profession your father or I would have chosen for you," Irene continued. "But you always were headstrong. You always did have your own way of doing things. You never wanted to listen to your father or to me about anything."

Maybe because you never listened to me. But that was old ground and Spence had no intention of covering it again. "I made the decision that was right for me," he said. "I was never cut out to be a lawyer."

A spark of something that might have been anger flashed in Irene's light blue eyes. As if to hide the betraying emotion, she turned back to the window. "Ironically, it's because of your job, Spencer, because of who you are and what you do, that makes me ask this of you now. I want you to move back into this house until after the trial. I want you to promise me that you will do everything you can to bring Natalie Silver to justice."

Spence stared at his mother's back, telling himself he was a fool to feel disappointed. What had he thought? That she'd wanted him to move back home so she could take some measure of comfort or solace from his presence? That in losing one son, she'd realized she still had another?

He should have known better.

"I don't trust the local authorities," she said. "Neither your father nor your brother had the slightest bit of confidence in the police department. There has always been too much corruption, too many officers willing to take a bribe—or have their heads turned by a pretty face. I won't allow that to happen in this case.''

It was pointless to argue with her, so all Spence said was, ''And where do I come in?''

She faced him. ''You have experience dealing with this sort of thing. In your line of work, you've conducted investigations not unlike the one involving Anthony's murder.''

He waited, saying nothing. He could feel Anthea's eyes, boring into his back, and he wondered what she thought. Had she known Irene's intentions? Or was all this as much a surprise to her as it was to Spence?

He glanced at her, but her expression gave away nothing.

Suddenly Irene's composure snapped. She took a step toward him, her eyes blazing with rage. ''I want you to follow this investigation yourself, Spencer. I want you to use your contacts in the police department to find out everything you can about this case. I want you to make sure *that woman* doesn't get off on some kind of trumped-up technicality.''

Irene lifted her wrinkled hand, as if to touch him, and the emerald-cut diamond on her finger emitted a cold, white light. Once he would have been mesmerized by the movement of her hand reaching out to him, but now Spence saw no beauty in the gesture at all, just a grotesque reminder of what might have been.

As if realizing the same thing, Irene let her hand fall back to her side.

''I want that woman put away for life,'' she said. ''I want her confined to a cold, dark cell with no hope of salvation. I want her to spend every waking hour remembering what she did to my son. What she did to this family.

I want her to suffer, Spencer. I want to take her son from her just like she took mine.''

Spence glared down at her. ''What are you saying?''

''The boy. Kyle. I want to take him away from her. I want that woman to know what it's like to lose her only son.''

''Anthony wasn't your only son, Mother,'' Spence replied, his voice taut with anger.

''Of course not,'' Irene said, having the grace at least to look slightly ruffled at her slip, but she almost immediately regained her composure. ''You are my son, too, Spencer. My only son now, and I'm counting on you to help me. Natalie Silver will rot in prison for the rest of her life. And, just like me, she will never see her son again.''

''WHAT A DILEMMA this must be for you.''

Spence turned from the window where he'd been standing since his mother had left a few minutes ago to go upstairs and rest. Anthea had gone, too, but now she was back, and by the sound of the sarcasm in her voice, she was spoiling for a fight.

''What do you mean?''

She smiled smugly, reminding him of Anthony. ''I mean, considering how you felt about 'that woman.' I remember when you first met her. I saw the way you looked at her that day, the way you couldn't take your eyes off her. Still can't, for all we know.''

Spence remembered the day he'd met Natalie, too. She'd been nineteen, a student working her way through Trinity University with a part-time job at his family's law firm. And Spence had been twenty-three, fresh out of Quantico, a rookie agent out to make a name for himself on his first big case.

He was on assignment in San Antonio, and word had reached his father that he was in town. Anthony, Sr., had summoned Spence to his law office, and he'd reluctantly gone.

Natalie had been working with his father's assistant in the outer office, and from the moment Spence had laid eyes on her, he'd known there was something very special about Natalie Silver, something so appealing about the way her soft, brown hair framed her lovely face and the way her blue eyes shimmered behind the wire-rimmed glasses she wore. And her smile. That shy, sweet smile that stole his breath away.

The chemistry between them had been immediate and explosive, leading to the inevitable. But their brief affair might have become, after all these years, nothing more than a bittersweet memory…if Natalie hadn't gone and done the unforgivable.

If she hadn't betrayed him with his own brother.

His voice took on a bitter edge when he said, ''You've got this all wrong, Anthea. Natalie Silver means nothing to me. She never did.''

''Oh, really? Then why did you bail her out of jail? Oh, yes, I know all about that.'' Anthea gloated, her green eyes gleaming with satisfaction. ''You're not the only one with connections at the police department, you know.''

''Why didn't you tell Mother?'' Spence demanded, studying his sister carefully. Something had changed about Anthea, but he couldn't quite put his finger on it.

''Oh, I plan to,'' she said. ''When it suits me. *If* it suits me.'' She smiled again, and suddenly Spence knew what it was that was different about his sister. Her defiance. Her confidence. Her whole demeanor. Anthea was no longer the meek, mild sister who had lived all her life in her brother's shadow. She was no longer a pale, faded copy of her twin but was now the only original.

And she liked it, Spence realized. She liked it very much.

"Just think about it," Anthea told him. "For the first time in your life, you have a chance to win our dear mother's undying gratitude and admiration. And all you have to do is put away for life a woman you were once in love with. All you have to do is take away Natalie Silver's son."

She laughed, lifting her hands to study them intently. "Now, granted, that would have been a piece of cake for Anthony, but what about you, Spencer? Can you keep an open mind about this case? Or will you let your feelings for 'that woman' undermine your loyalty to your family?"

Her voice had turned into a taunt, grating on Spence's nerves. He gave her a cool, cynical appraisal that did justice to his last name. "You don't have to worry about me, Anthea. No one could ever make me change the way I feel about my family."

THE DAY OF ANTHONY'S funeral dawned warm and sunny with the high expected to be around eighty. It didn't seem at all like Christmas to Natalie, but she knew her flagging spirits had very little to do with the soaring temperature, and everything to do with the fact that she'd been charged with her ex-husband's murder.

She was truly sorry Anthony was dead. At times, she'd hated him during their short marriage. She'd despised his coldness and the cruel streak he kept so cleverly hidden. Later, she'd detested his careless disregard for her son's feelings. But no matter what Anthony had done, no matter how bitterly they had disagreed on just about everything, she had never wanted him dead.

The house seemed so silent this morning, Natalie thought, wrapping her arms around herself as she stared out the window. She saw her neighbor pass by, walking her dog, and gaze toward Natalie's house. But instead of waving when she saw Natalie at the window, the woman turned and hurried down the street.

She thinks I did it, Natalie thought numbly. *She's known me for almost five years, and now, suddenly, she thinks I'm a cold-blooded killer.*

Her neighbor wasn't the only one who thought so. Yesterday, when Natalie and Kyle had moved back to their own house, the phone had rung nonstop. Some of the callers were well-wishers—friends and family who still had faith in her—but most of the calls had been from reporters wanting a sensational story, or from crackpots who wanted the perverse thrill of talking to someone they thought was a murderer.

Natalie shuddered. She'd called the phone company to get an unlisted number to try and halt the barrage. Only her parents and her attorney knew her new number, and so far, the morning had been blessedly quiet.

Almost too quiet. She wished she could go back to work, but her shop was still considered a crime scene. No one except authorized police personnel were allowed in or out, while Silver Bells's Christmas sales slowly went down the drain.

The period between Thanksgiving and Christmas comprised a good thirty-five percent of Natalie's annual sales. The last week of November and the first two weeks of December had been so promising this year, and she'd hoped to show her biggest profit ever.

But even when she was allowed to reopen the store, what then? Would the customers come back? Or had the publicity surrounding Anthony's murder and her arrest driven them all away?

Don't think about that now, Natalie advised herself sternly as she heard Kyle walk into the room. There was nothing she could do about it, so why waste time worrying? Especially when she had so many other things to worry about.

She forced herself to smile as Kyle came to stand in front of her for inspection. She bent to adjust his tie.

"It's choking me," he complained, pulling on the tie the moment Natalie finished straightening it.

"Leave it alone, Kyle," she said in exasperation. "Pulling on it just makes it tighter." She gave it another adjustment, then stood back and studied him. "You look very handsome."

Kyle screwed up his freshly scrubbed face. The freckles on his nose stood out like tiny copper coins. "I look like a dork."

"No, you don't. And quit messing with your hair. It took me ten minutes to get all the cowlicks to lie down."

"Well, what *can* I do?" he asked in frustration. "I can't ride my bike. I can't go skating. I can't even go to school."

"You can sit there and wait for your grandmother's car to come pick you up," Natalie said, trying to keep the heaviness out of her voice.

When Irene Bishop had called yesterday, before Natalie's number was changed, to say that she wanted Kyle to accompany the family to the funeral today, Natalie's first instinct had been to refuse. But then, she knew that wouldn't be right. Later, Kyle might have wondered why she had kept him from Anthony's funeral. He might have one day regretted it, and Natalie didn't want that. Letting Kyle go to the funeral was the decent thing to do, and so she'd finally agreed.

Irene told her that Anthea would accompany their driver to pick Kyle up this morning, and they would deliver him home again after the service. Then she had hung up without another word.

As if sensing his mother's dread, Kyle said, "I don't want to go."

"I know, but we talked about this last night, remember? It's the right thing to do." Natalie took his hand and held it between hers. "Your grandmother needs you. Your being there today will help her a lot."

"Why can't you go with me?"

"Because…that wouldn't be the right thing to do."

"Because you and my dad were divorced?"

"That's…part of it."

"Because you don't like Grandmother Bishop?"

Natalie looked at him in shock. "I never said that."

He shrugged. "It's okay. I don't like her, neither."

"Kyle!"

"Well, I don't," he said defiantly. "And she can't make me like her."

"Oh, Kyle." Natalie didn't know what to say to her son; how to explain to him the difficulties she had with the Bishops. She'd told him very little of the ordeal she'd been through since Anthony's death, only that the police had wanted to ask her some questions because they were trying to figure out exactly what had happened to Anthony.

But children were a lot smarter and more perceptive than adults gave them credit for, and Kyle was no exception. Natalie had a feeling he knew a good deal more about what was going on than he was letting on, and she thought that he was probably a lot more upset than he seemed. But he was a Bishop. He didn't like to show emotion.

"Kyle—" She wasn't sure what she'd been about to say to him, but just then she heard a car outside. She got up and went to the window. A black limo pulled up to the curb and the driver got out to open the back door.

Natalie turned back to Kyle. "Your aunt's here to pick you up." She knelt to straighten his tie once again. "Now, I want you to be a good boy, okay?"

He nodded. Suddenly, his green eyes looked suspiciously bright. "Why can't you come with me?" he asked again.

"It'll be okay," she promised. "I'll be here waiting for you when you get back."

She stood then and went to answer the doorbell. When she drew back the door, her hand flew to her heart in surprise. "Oh! It's…you. I was expecting Anthea."

"Something came up," Spence said. "Anthea couldn't make it."

Natalie wondered uneasily if something had really come up, or if Spence had engineered this whole thing himself, just to be with Kyle. But then, why would he? He didn't even know her son.

She chided herself for her suspicions, but like it or not, she didn't trust Spencer Bishop. He'd bailed her out of jail, and Natalie still couldn't help wondering why.

Reluctantly, she let her gaze travel over him. He was dressed in a dark suit, a white shirt, and a somber silk tie. Like Kyle, his dark hair looked freshly dampened and combed, as tamed as it probably ever would be. He wore it a little shorter than she remembered, but it was still thick, without a trace of gray, and she wondered suddenly if he remembered the way she had once run her fingers through those dark, unruly strands. If he remembered the way—

She stopped, gazing up at him. Her pulse hammered in her throat, for she suddenly remembered something else about Spence—that he had always been able to read her thoughts.

"No one told me about this change of plans," she said coldly.

"Is there a problem?" Spence asked. "What difference does it make who takes him to the church?"

"It makes a difference to me. I should have been told."

"Why? Don't you trust me with your son?"

Before she could answer, Natalie felt Kyle lean against her leg, and she reached down automatically to put her arm around his shoulders—to draw him close, to protect him.

"Hi," he said.

"Hi," Spence said.

"Do I get to ride in that big car out there?"

"You sure do. That is, if your mother says it's okay." Spence's gaze challenged hers.

"Does it have a TV?" Kyle asked.

"Yeah, it does."

"Wow," Kyle said, taking a step or two away from Natalie to stare out the door at the big black limo waiting at the curb.

Resentment flooded through her. It was so easy to turn a young boy's head with a fancy car. She wondered if Spence had deliberately tried to do just that.

She lifted her chin and met Spence's gaze. "I want him home as soon as the service is over."

Something flashed in Spence's eyes. Something that made Natalie want to snatch her son back inside, and never let him go. Then Spence said, "You don't have to worry about Kyle. I'll take good care of him."

Leaning down, she gave her son a quick hug. "I'll see you in a little while," she whispered.

"Okay." He hugged her back, then, without another word, followed Spence outside.

Natalie stood at the door and watched the two of them walk away. Spence and her son.

It'll only be for an hour or two, she told herself. What could happen in such a short time? Kyle would go to Anthony's funeral, and then her son would come back home to her and the two of them would get on with their lives and never have to deal with the Bishops again.

But as she watched Spence and Kyle disappear inside the car, Natalie was suddenly overcome by a premonition, a dark feeling that her son was in danger...and there was nothing she could do about it.

THE MOMENT THEY JOINED the rest of the family at the church, Spence sensed Kyle's panic. Everyone kept staring at him, shaking their heads and whispering behind gloved hands. No wonder the little guy looked a little green around the gills, Spence thought. The Bishops and their entourage were a bit much for anyone to take.

He bent down and said in Kyle's ear, "Let's get some air."

Kyle nodded, obviously relieved. He followed Spence outside into a walled courtyard. Spence sat down on a stone bench near a fountain and Kyle did the same. For several moments they said nothing, just sat there staring into the water.

Finally, Spence said, "It's all right if you're feeling a little scared about all this."

Kyle turned his green eyes on him but said nothing.

"It's even okay," Spence added quietly, "if you feel like crying. It's perfectly natural in this situation."

"But I don't," Kyle replied. His gaze dropped to his shoes. He studied them intently. "That's the problem," he muttered.

"What is?"

"I don't feel like crying. I don't feel sad or anything."

So that was it. Spence thought it was probably appropriate that Kyle was talking to him about all this. If anyone in the world could understand the boy's confusion, his conflicting emotions about his father, it was Spence. Anthony's brother.

"I think I see what you mean," he said. "You didn't know your father very well, did you?"

Kyle shook his head, his eyes still on his shoes.

"That wasn't your fault, you know. It was his. He chose not to be a part of your life for a very long time. There's no reason for you to feel guilty. About anything. Do you understand what I'm saying?"

"I think so." Kyle fell silent for a moment, then turned suddenly to Spence, squinting in the dappled sunlight. "Do *you* feel sad?"

"In some ways," he said honestly. Anthony hadn't been an easy man to know or to love, but he'd still been Spence's brother and, like it or not, there had still been a bond between them.

A bond that Spence had been perfectly willing to break, all in the name of justice.

"My mom's sad," Kyle was saying. "I heard her crying last night when she thought I was asleep."

Spence didn't like to picture Natalie crying. He didn't like to think about her alone and frightened, vulnerable.

Better to remember the woman who had betrayed him. The woman who had chosen his brother over him.

"Mom doesn't like for me to see her cry," Kyle said solemnly. "She doesn't want me to worry about her."

"Well, that's the way mothers are," Spence said. He grinned, trying to lighten the moment. "It's kind of a 'mother thing,' you know?"

Kyle grinned back, displaying the gap created by his

two missing front teeth. "Yeah," he said. "It's kind of a 'mother thing.'" He started to say something else, then his eyes widened and he pointed over Spence's shoulder. "Hey! There's a guy hiding in the bushes over there! Look!"

Spence whirled in time to see a man spring out of a clump of oleander and sprint toward the stone wall, a camera and an equipment bag slung over his shoulder.

Without thinking, Spence took off after him. He caught the man before he could make his getaway.

Spence whirled the man around, grabbing a fistful of his shirt. "What the hell are you doing here?"

"Just taking a few pictures," he gasped. "I work for the *Scimitar*. I didn't mean any harm—just trying to get a story. That kid over there's Anthony Bishop's son, isn't he?"

"That kid over there is my nephew, and I don't like scum like you sneaking around taking his picture." Spence's blood boiled at the thought of a stranger, a reporter bent only on getting a story, eavesdropping on his and Kyle's private conversation. A conversation that had meant a lot to him, although he couldn't say why, exactly.

"Is it true the kid's mother whacked Bishop?"

The guy never even saw it coming. Spence's fist shot out and connected with the reporter's face. He fell sprawling to the ground. "My nose! You broke my nose, you son of a bitch!"

Spence reached down and grabbed the camera.

"Hey! What do you think you're doing?"

Calmly, Spence opened the back of the camera and removed the film, exposing it to light.

Outraged, the reporter leaped to his feet. "You can't do that!" he screamed, holding his nose.

"I just did. Now you get the hell out of here and don't ever let me catch you hanging around my nephew again."

"I'll sue you for every penny you've got. Not even a Bishop can get away with this. You haven't heard the last of me!" The man spouted a string of obscenities as he took his camera and ruined film and climbed over the wall with as much dignity as he could muster. Which wasn't much, in Spence's opinion.

He walked back over to Kyle, who sat gazing up at him in awe. "Did that guy really take a picture of me? Is that really why you hit him?"

Spence grinned and shrugged. "Yeah. I guess you could say it was kind of an 'uncle thing' to do."

"Awesome," Kyle said. "I sure hope I get to be an uncle someday."

KYLE HAD BEEN GONE little more than an hour when the phone rang. Thinking it was probably her mother or possibly her attorney, Natalie picked up without hesitation.

"Hello?"

There was a pause, then a male voice said gruffly, "You've got something of mine, lady."

"I beg your pardon?"

"You know what I'm talking about. You've got something of mine, and I want them back."

A finger of dread crawled up Natalie's spine. "How did you get this number?"

"Let's just say, I've got friends in high places."

"Who are you?"

"You don't need to know who I am. It's enough that I know who you are. I know all about you, Natalie, because I've been watching you. I know where you live, I know where you work, and I know where your kid is at this very moment."

Natalie gasped. "Who are you?" she cried. "What do you want?"

"You know what I want. I want what's mine. Cooperate, and nobody else has to get hurt."

The phone clicked, then went dead in her ear.

Natalie sat holding the receiver for a long moment, her hand shaking in fear. She wanted to believe it was just another crank call, but she didn't dare. Not when her son had just been threatened.

Natalie started to panic. How could she have let Kyle out of her sight for even a minute? What had she been thinking? What if someone came up to him at the funeral, threatened him somehow? There would be no one around to protect him. Certainly not Irene or Anthea—two colder women Natalie had never had the misfortune of knowing. And Spence? He was a Bishop, wasn't he? She couldn't exactly rely on him.

She thought about calling the police, but what if they didn't believe her? What if they thought she'd made the whole thing up, just to try and throw suspicion off herself? They didn't even believe Anthony had ransacked her workroom that night. Sergeant Phillips had suggested she'd done it herself, just to throw them off track.

No, she couldn't call the police. She wasn't even sure there was cause for alarm, but before she had time to talk herself out of what she was contemplating, Natalie grabbed her purse and car keys and headed for the garage. Within minutes she was driving out of her neighborhood, fighting the heavy Christmas-shopping traffic on the freeway.

She glanced at her watch. The church service would be over, and the mourners would be on their way to the cemetery by now. But as she pulled into the parking area at Oak Lawn Cemetery, where the Bishops had an enormous mausoleum, she saw that the funeral procession had already arrived.

Natalie got out of her car and walked toward the gates. She had no intention of interrupting the service. She only wanted to see Kyle from a distance, make sure he was okay. She could remain where she was and watch over him, and no one would ever have to know.

But as she stood there in the cool shade of a water oak, a chill crept over her. She turned and saw that she was the one who was being watched.

For a moment, he looked so much like Anthony that Natalie's breath rushed out of her in a painful gasp. Then she realized it was Spence, and her heartbeat slowed. But only temporarily. The moment he started toward her, her blood began to pound again.

He looked so menacing, she thought. So…dangerous. His green eyes flashed with anger, and his heavy eyebrows were drawn together in a scowl. Although it was early, she could see the faint trace of beard that shadowed his face, making him seem even darker. More threatening. Never had his presence affected her more powerfully than it did at that moment. Natalie stared up at him, as if mesmerized.

But when he spoke, his voice, as threatening as his thunderous appearance, broke the spell. "What the hell are you doing here?"

"I…came to see Kyle," she said. "I wanted to make sure he was all right."

"Why wouldn't he be all right?"

"Reporters have been hounding us since I got out of jail. We've been getting a lot of prank calls. I didn't want him to get upset if…someone said something to him. About what happened."

Spence glared at her. "I don't have to tell you how upset

my family would be if they saw you here. This wasn't a good idea, Natalie.''

''Maybe not,'' she retorted. ''But I've done a lot of things in my life that weren't such hot ideas. That's never stopped me before.''

He lifted his eyebrows in a challenge. ''Like killing my brother?''

Her face colored with anger. ''Like *marrying* him,'' she countered. ''Like getting involved with *you*.'' The moment the words were out, she regretted them. Regretted the power they gave him over her. Because now he knew she hadn't forgotten him or the brief relationship they'd once shared. Now he knew that he had once hurt her deeply, and that she had never gotten over it.

''Involved?'' He laughed. ''Your memories are kinder than mine. I thought we had an affair. A one-night stand.''

Before she thought, Natalie's hand lifted to slap him, but he caught her wrist in mid-swing and stood staring down at her, his green eyes blazing with anger. ''Do you think our *involvement* meant anything to me? Do you think I've wasted one minute thinking about you? Thinking about the way you married my brother the minute my back was turned? You and Anthony deserved each other. You were perfect for each other. You both knew exactly what you wanted and how to get it, and you didn't care who you stepped on in the process.''

His words would have been like nails hammered into her heart, except for one thing—except for the glimmer of hurt in the depths of his eyes, belying his bitter words.

Natalie saw that hurt and recognized it for what it was, because she'd seen it in her own eyes. More times than she cared to remember.

''You're the one who left,'' she whispered.

''Not that it matters,'' he said, ''but I left because I had an assignment. I was called back to Washington. I told you that. I told you I wouldn't be able to see you for a while—''

''Because you were working *under cover?*''

He frowned at her sarcastic emphasis. ''Yes.''

She laughed bitterly. ''It may surprise you to learn that I knew all about that little undercover assignment of yours. I even saw pictures.''

He gazed down at her in astonishment. ''What the hell are you talking about?''

''Anthony told me all about it. He said—''

Although Spence had been gazing at her intently, his attention suddenly shifted to somewhere over her right shoulder. A commotion sounded behind her—fierce whispers, the rustle of silk—and Natalie whirled, coming face-to-face with the three Bishop women leaving the cemetery.

They were all dressed in black, all wore veils, and as she gazed at them, a line from *Macbeth* flashed through Natalie's mind: ''By the pricking of my thumbs,/ Something wicked this way comes.''

Enter three witches.

Irene, the undisputed leader of the coven, stopped dead in her tracks when she saw Natalie. She lifted her veil to rake her former daughter-in-law with icy contempt. The black dress she wore was stark, except for the pearl choker, trimmed with diamonds, that glittered at her throat.

Beside Irene, clad in a short black dress that displayed a shocking amount of black-stockinged leg, Melinda Bishop, the grieving widow, clutched Irene's arm with one gloved hand. Her red curls were piled under a wide-brimmed black hat, and dark glasses shielded her eyes. Natalie couldn't tell if Melinda was looking at her or not.

On the other side of Irene stood Anthea, also dressed in black, but her face and her bearing held none of her mother's regal elegance. Instead, Anthea looked like a pale copy of Anthony.

Once Natalie had gotten to know the Bishops, she'd learned quickly that Anthony was the only offspring who meant anything to Irene. She'd adored her eldest son while merely tolerating Anthea who, in spite of her brilliance, was obviously a huge disappointment.

Spence, Anthony had once told Natalie, had been disowned by the time he was eighteen because of his failure to conform to Bishop standards.

And yet, here he was today, the very picture of solidarity as he walked over to his mother. For some reason she couldn't fathom, Natalie felt oddly betrayed.

When Kyle saw Natalie, he rushed toward her. "Mommy!"

Natalie met him, bending to wrap her arms around him. He clung to her for a moment, then gazed up at her. "Can we go home now? Please?"

She smoothed back his hair. "Yes."

Melinda took off her dark glasses, her gaze scouring Natalie with scorn. "How dare you come here like this? Have you no shame?"

Natalie stood, clutching Kyle's hand. "I might ask you the same thing." She met Melinda's gaze evenly, until the grieving widow had to look away. Natalie thought she detected a hint of a blush on Melinda's face beneath the veil, but that was probably assuming too much. That was assuming Melinda Bishop had a conscience, and obviously she never had. How else could she have let her best friend pour out her heart and soul, while all the time having an affair with that same best friend's husband?

In some ways, Melinda's betrayal had hurt worse than Anthony's, because Natalie hadn't seen it coming. Right up to the bitter end, Melinda had pretended to care about Natalie, until she'd finally gotten what she wanted.

Natalie turned to Irene. "I'm sorry. I didn't mean to intrude. I only wanted to make sure my son was okay."

Kyle tugged frantically on Natalie's hand. "I want to go home, Mommy."

"We are, sweetheart." She turned to leave.

"One moment," Irene said.

Although the words were spoken softly, something in her tone stopped Natalie. She glanced back. Melinda was climbing into the back of the waiting limo, but Anthea remained at her mother's side, still as a statue. Her eyes— those Bishop eyes—bored into Natalie with open hostility.

For a moment, they all seemed frozen in time. Then Irene said, "I have something to say to you."

Spence was still standing beside Irene, but now he stepped forward, placing himself between her and Natalie. "This is not the time or place," he said harshly.

Irene spared him a brief glance. "It is exactly the time and place."

"Don't do this," Spence warned.

His voice sent shivers of alarm up Natalie's spine. Kyle pulled harder on her arm, as if he, too, sensed something was about to happen. "Mommy!"

Natalie put her arm around him, drawing him close. "It's okay, Kyle. Go wait for me in the car."

"But—"

"I'll be there in one minute. I promise."

Reluctantly, he did as he was told. Natalie could see her car from where she stood, and she watched as Kyle opened the door and climbed inside. Then she turned back to Irene.

"You were wise to wait and hear me out," Irene said. "I wouldn't have been pleased to have had to track you down to say what I have to say to you."

''Then say it,'' Natalie returned, bracing herself for another assault.

''Have you any idea what I'm feeling at this moment?'' Irene asked, her cold blue eyes fixed on Natalie.

''I can only imagine,'' Natalie replied. ''But I am truly sorry for your loss.''

''Are you?''

''I didn't kill Anthony, Mrs. Bishop.''

''Your innocence—or guilt—will be decided in a court of law. But even if a jury were to convict you, even if you were to spend the rest of your life behind bars, you still wouldn't know what I'm feeling. The kind of pain I've had to endure. The torment I've been put through. There's only one way that could happen.''

Natalie's throat closed in fear. ''What do you mean?''

Irene smiled slightly. ''If you were to lose your child, your son, you would know then what I'm feeling at this moment.''

Dear God, what was she saying? What was she threatening? Natalie's heart raced wildly. ''You wouldn't hurt Kyle. He's just a baby—''

''You're right,'' Irene agreed, but there was something in her voice that chilled Natalie's blood. ''I wouldn't hurt Kyle. He's my only grandson, my only link to Anthony. I wouldn't harm a single hair on his head, nor would I allow anyone else to.''

Natalie wanted to feel relief, but the icy blue eyes had narrowed to menacing slits. The blue-veined hands at Irene's sides balled into fists as her aristocratic face flashed with fury.

''I won't harm your son,'' she said softly. ''But I will take him away from you. Only then will you know the pain and torment I've been put through. Only then will you have some inkling of the hell I'm going through now—and all because of you.''

Chapter Six

"Natalie!"

"Stay away from me!" she warned as she hurried across the parking lot to her car.

Spence caught up with her. "Wait a minute."

She spun to face him. "What for? So you can attack me again? So you and your mother can team up against me? You two make quite a pair."

"Look," he said, running his fingers through his dark hair. "Can we go somewhere and talk about this?"

"Why?"

"Because I can see you're upset."

"Upset?" She gazed at him in astonishment. "You think that's all I am? Your mother just threatened to take my son away from me. I'm a little more than upset."

He glanced away.

"You knew about this, didn't you?" Natalie demanded. "You knew what she was planning to do."

Spence rubbed the side of his face with his hand. He suddenly looked indescribably weary. "She mentioned it to me earlier."

"In front of Kyle?"

"No. The night after Anthony died."

A red veil of anger descended over Natalie as she glared

up at him. "If you knew when you came to get Kyle what your mother was planning, why didn't you tell me? Didn't you think I had a right to know?"

"Yes. But I also didn't think you'd let him come if you knew."

"You were right about that," she answered coldly. "It's amazing how all you Bishops stick together. Blood certainly does tell, doesn't it?"

"I know how this must make you feel," Spence said carefully. "But try to look at this from her perspective. Her son is dead, and she thinks you killed him. Can you blame her for not wanting the woman she thinks is a murderess to raise her only grandson?"

"Don't you dare!" Natalie lashed out. "Don't you dare defend your mother to me. She doesn't care about Kyle. She only wants revenge against me. Well, let me tell you something. She will never get her hands on my son. She will never turn him into the kind of man Anthony was." *The kind of man you are,* she thought. "I'll do whatever it takes to stop her."

Spence's gaze hardened on her. "Is that how you felt when you found out Anthony was planning to sue you for custody of Kyle? Were you willing to do whatever it took to stop him?"

Natalie felt as if he had just punched her, very hard, in the stomach. Her breath left her in a painful rush. "I didn't kill Anthony," she said. "And I'm getting tired of having to tell you that. Why don't you just get out of my way and leave me alone?"

She tried to brush past him, but he caught her arm. "I can't do that."

"Why not? You obviously think I'm a murderer. Why waste your time with the likes of me?"

His green gaze darkened. "Because I told you before. I

want answers, and you're the only one who can help me find them.''

"Answers to *what?*" she cried in frustration. "I don't know anything. I was knocked unconscious while Anthony was being murdered. I didn't see or hear anything. I don't know anything, so just leave me and my son alone!''

She jerked her arm free of him and walked to the car door. Before she could open it, Spence said, "I'm not the one trying to take Kyle away from you, Natalie. I'm not your enemy.''

Her gaze challenged his. "You're a Bishop, aren't you?''

"Yes," he said quietly. "But so is your son.''

"DID SHE MEAN IT, MOM? Can she really take me away from you?''

Natalie looked down at Kyle in alarm. "Oh, honey, you heard all that?''

He shrugged sheepishly, but his eyes still looked frightened. "I rolled down my window.''

"Kyle—''

"I know. I'm not supposed to eavesdrop. Are you mad at me?''

She smiled. "No, I'm not mad at you. I'm just sorry you had to hear all that. Your Grandmother Bishop is…very upset right now. She said a lot of things she didn't really mean.'' Or at least, Natalie prayed Irene hadn't meant them.

"She thinks you killed my dad, doesn't she?'' The solemn little eyes, so innocent and trusting, gazed up at her.

Natalie bit back her tears and nodded.

The tips of Kyle's ears turned bright pink with anger. "I'd like to go punch her right in the nose.''

Natalie put her fingertips to her lips, smiling. "That's

the nicest thing anyone's said to me in a long time. Thank you, Kyle.''

''You're welcome,'' he said earnestly. ''I'd like to punch Anthea, too. But not Spence. I like him.''

''You…do?''

''Yeah. He's way cool. He's not like the others. He talks to you and stuff. He doesn't just look at you. And he has a really neat car.''

''The limo?''

''Naw, his real car. It's black and shiny and looks like a race car or something. It's fast as anything. He let me ride to the church with him in it, so I wouldn't have to go with the others. I hate the way they all stare at me, Mom. Especially *her*.''

''Which her?'' Natalie started the car and drove out of the parking area.

''Melinda. I don't like her. And you know what?''

''What?''

''She doesn't like me.''

Natalie glanced at her son. ''I'm sure that's not true. She's upset now, too—''

He shook his head emphatically. ''She didn't like me even before. I heard her say so to my dad once, when he took me to their house.''

''You were in Melinda's house?''

Kyle nodded. ''He told me not to tell you. He said it would be our secret.''

That sounded like Anthony. Natalie's grip tightened on the steering wheel. ''Did you and he have other secrets?''

Kyle turned to look out the side window. He said nothing.

''Well, did you?'' Natalie persisted, feeling alarmed by her son's silence.

"Do you want to know what I heard her tell my dad or not?"

Natalie sighed. Like his father, Kyle had a neat way of changing the subject when it suited him. "What did she say?"

Kyle screwed up his face in concentration. "She said, 'How dare you bring that little brat into my home, flaunting him in my face when you know I can never have a baby of my own?'"

Natalie looked at him in shock. He'd mimicked Melinda's whining tone perfectly. "How do... How do you remember that conversation so well, honey?"

"I recorded it," he said proudly. "And I listened to it over and over. I thought it was funny."

"You recorded it? On that tape recorder your dad gave you?"

He nodded.

"I thought you said you lost it," Natalie reminded him. "You told me you couldn't find it anywhere."

Kyle looked stricken for a moment, as if realizing he'd given himself away, then said, "Well, that was before I lost it."

Natalie let that one pass for the moment. She braked for a light, automatically glancing in her rearview mirror. A black sports car pulled up behind her, but behind the tinted windshield, Natalie couldn't make out the driver.

"What did your dad say to Melinda?" she asked Kyle.

"He said he wanted a divorce."

"He did?"

"He told Melinda he wanted a divorce and he wasn't giving her any money. Or something like that."

"Kyle, are you sure about this?"

"I told you. I listened to it over and over. Melinda's got a really dumb voice, doesn't she, Mom?"

Natalie nodded absently. So Anthony had been ready to divorce Melinda, and she'd known it. Natalie wondered if the police had dug up that tidbit when they'd unearthed the fact that Anthony was going after custody of Kyle. Wouldn't that make Melinda an equal suspect?

Except, of course, for the fact that Melinda hadn't been found at the crime scene, holding the bloody murder weapon.

It all came back to that. Natalie had the feeling that the answer to all her troubles was hidden somewhere in the back of her mind, only there was no way she could get to it. No way she could find it. Because while Anthony was being murdered, she'd been out cold—

"Mom, look out!"

The light had turned green and she'd automatically entered the intersection. When she glanced over at Kyle's yell, she saw a car heading straight toward them.

It was too late to brake. The car would plow right into them on Kyle's side. Natalie did the only other thing she could do. She stepped on the gas and the car shot forward. But not before the other car had rammed the right rear fender of Natalie's car.

There was a terrible crunching sound, an awful bone-jarring impact and for a second, the steering wheel in Natalie's hand spun out of control. As if in a daze, she heard the distant sound of horns honking and tires squealing. Finally she managed to get the car stopped, and she sat for a moment, her head spinning.

Then she looked at Kyle. Even though he was wearing his seat belt, his head must have hit the side window on impact, because the window was shattered, and a stream of blood coursed down his face.

"Kyle! Oh, dear God." She fumbled with her seat belt, trying to free herself so she could reach for him.

"I'm hurt, Mommy!"

"I know, baby. Let me see how badly. Kyle, move your hand out of the way."

He brought his hand down from his face and gazed at it. "I'm bleeding!" he wailed. "I'm gonna die!"

Traffic was stopped all around them. They had been knocked out of the intersection, but the rear of the car still blocked one lane. "You're not going to die," Natalie told him, although her own heart was beating so hard she thought she might have a heart attack. "I have to get you out of the car. We can't just sit here. We might get hit again."

She unfastened his seat belt and reached across to open his door. It was stuck. She opened her own door and started to get out to go around, when Kyle's door was suddenly yanked open and Spence leaned down to gaze inside.

Natalie was almost glad to see him. Almost.

"I was right behind you," he said. "I saw the crash."

"I'm bleeding," Kyle said unnecessarily.

"So I see." Spence slipped his arms around the little boy and easily lifted him from the seat. "Looks like you're going to have quite a shiner there, too. Let's get you out of there, buddy, and have a look."

Natalie climbed out of the car and joined them at the side of the road. Spence had knelt and was cradling Kyle across his lap. "It's not that bad, but he probably needs stitches," he told Natalie. "We'd better get him to a hospital."

"What about the car? Should I just leave it?"

A couple of passersby had stopped to help. One of them said, "The other guy's long gone. He just hightailed it out of here after he hit you. Probably a DWI."

"Call the police," Spence said. "When they get here,

tell them they can find us at the hospital. Meanwhile, maybe a couple of you could push the car out of the street.''

''Sure. But isn't it against the law to leave the scene of an accident?''

Spence stood, still holding Kyle in his arms. ''You let me worry about that.''

''WE WANT A PLASTIC surgeon,'' Spence said. Natalie just gazed at him in surprise. They were seated in an emergency-room cubicle, watching while a nurse and the resident on duty examined Kyle. Natalie had been so relieved to get him to the hospital that it had never even occurred to her to request a plastic surgeon.

The nurse glanced up. ''I saw Dr. Redmond in the hallway a few minutes ago. He may still be here.''

''Page him,'' Dr. Whitting said, obviously unfazed by Spence's request.

Within minutes the plastic surgeon had been summoned, and while he worked on Kyle, Spence and Natalie stood outside in the waiting room.

''What happened?'' Spence asked, after Natalie had declined his offer of a cup of coffee.

''Didn't you see? Whoever hit us ran a red light,'' Natalie said. ''I had a green light, and I was already in the intersection when the other car just came blazing through. I couldn't get out of the way in time.''

Natalie shivered, thinking about the accident. Suddenly, the strange phone call she'd gotten earlier came rushing back to her. The gruff voice warning her, *''You know what I want. I want what's mine. Cooperate, and nobody else has to get hurt.''*

And Anthony in a rage the night he'd been murdered: *''You thought you could pull a fast one on me, didn't you?*

You've always been just a little too clever for your own good, Natalie. But not this time. Now hand them over before I do something we might both regret.''

Natalie's heart thudded against her chest. What was going on here? Anthony had accused her of finding something that belonged to him. The voice on the phone accused her of having something that belonged to *him*. But what? What were they looking for? What had she inadvertently gotten herself involved in?

And what did it have to do with Anthony's murder?

''Natalie?'' She jumped when Spence's hand touched her arm. He was gazing down at her strangely. ''What's wrong?''

''I'm…not sure.'' She was on the verge of telling him about the phone call earlier when she stopped suddenly, realizing who he was. He was a Bishop. He believed she'd murdered his brother. How could she confide in him? How could she trust him?

But a little voice in the back of her mind reminded her that he was a seasoned professional, an FBI agent. If anyone would know what to do about the voice on the phone, about the accident, it was Spence.

Still, something held her back. An image of Irene at the cemetery threatening to take away her son. And Spence had known about it. He'd known about it and he hadn't warned her. How could she trust him now? Supposing she confided in him and he ran straight to Irene? She could use this as ammunition in a custody fight. If she could prove Natalie couldn't take care of Kyle, or that Kyle was in danger because of her…

Another thought occurred to Natalie. What if the Bishops were behind all this? What if they had paid someone to call her earlier, and then hired that same someone to ram her car? She wouldn't put it past Irene or Anthea to do something that underhanded, and she knew exactly what Melinda was capable of. But what about Spence? How far would he be willing to go to prove his loyalty to his family? And why had he been following her from the cemetery? That seemed just a little too convenient to Natalie.

She opened her mouth to ask him about that, but just then the cubicle door opened and Dr. Redmond stepped out. He smiled at them both. "Mr. and Mrs. Bishop?"

Natalie started to correct him, but Spence spoke first. "How's Kyle?"

"He'll be fine. I'm recommending you keep him here overnight, though, just as a precaution. I've talked to Dr. Whitting and he agrees."

Fear knotted Natalie's stomach. "But I thought you said he was going to be fine."

The doctor turned to her. "He is. But he took a nasty bump on the head, and at his age, his condition should be closely monitored for the next several hours. I've already called upstairs and arranged a room."

"Can I see him?" Natalie asked, unable to keep the quiver of emotion out of her voice.

"Sure. Go on in. I've explained the situation to him, but I'm sure he'd like to hear it from you." Dr. Redmond placed a reassuring hand on Spence's shoulder. "Don't worry. We patched him up just fine. That's a real good-looking kid you got there."

"Thanks," Spence mumbled.

Natalie said nothing. She didn't dare.

Chapter Seven

"Mom, you didn't have to do that. He's only going to be in here overnight."

"I don't care," her mother said, placing the tiny Christmas tree on the nightstand beside Kyle's hospital bed and plugging in the lights. "When he wakes up, the first thing he'll see is his Christmas tree. That's bound to cheer him up."

Natalie stared down at her sleeping son. It was still early, but after Kyle had eaten his dinner, he'd fallen promptly asleep. She had been sitting by his bedside, watching him closely even though a nurse came in regularly to check on him.

"How's Dad?" she asked anxiously.

"Now don't you go worrying about him," her mother said, fussing with Kyle's bedcovers. "He's fine. He said to tell you he'll be by in the morning to pick us all up."

"But you don't have to spend the night," Natalie protested. Her mother had spent countless hours in the hospital when her father had his heart attack. Another night in a hospital room was probably the last place she wanted to be.

But she waved off Natalie's protest. "Do you honestly think I'm going to let my only grandson stay overnight in the hospital without me here to keep an eye on him? I'm staying, and that's final.''

Natalie smiled, relieved in spite of herself. ''Thanks, Mom. To tell you the truth, I could use the company right now. I've been sitting here thinking about how badly he could have been hurt….''

''But he wasn't. Concentrate on the positive,'' her mother told her. ''Isn't that what I always taught you?''

Natalie nodded, trying to do as her mother instructed. She was right. The accident could have been a lot worse. Natalie had a lot to be grateful for, and she would do well to remember that in the trying times ahead.

But still…

She couldn't help thinking. She couldn't help worrying.

Her gaze returned to her son. The lights in the room had been dimmed, and the soft flash of the tiny Christmas-tree lights cast little dancing shadows across Kyle's sleeping face. ''He really is beautiful, isn't he?'' she said quietly, thinking that of all her blessings, he was her most precious.

''He's almost as beautiful as my own child.'' Her mother came around the bed and wrapped her arms around Natalie.

Natalie rested her head on her mother's shoulder. ''I'm so scared,'' she whispered.

''I know. But everything's going to be okay. You'll see.''

''You really believe that, don't you?''

''With all my heart.''

Restless, Natalie walked over to the window to stare out at the parking lot. It was a clear night with a full moon and a light breeze that skimmed through the oasis of magnolia trees and azalea bushes planted in the center of the lot. The bushes were trimmed with little green lights that winked like fireflies in the darkness.

Natalie focused on one of the lights, thinking about the fullness of her life, about everything she had to be grateful for, and yet, like Gatsby staring at that green light across the water, she yearned for something that could never be.

"What is it, Natalie?"

She continued to stare at the light. "I'm just feeling a little down tonight and I can't seem to shake it."

"Is it something you want to talk about?"

Natalie hesitated, then shrugged. "I know you and Dad would never ask, but I want you to know something. I want you to hear it from me." She turned and faced her mother. "I didn't kill Anthony."

Her mother walked over and took Natalie's hands in hers. "Do you remember that time when you were nine, maybe ten years old and you found a squirrel on the side of the street that had been hit by a car? The poor little thing was still alive, but just barely. Without hesitation you took off your brand-new sweater and wrapped it around the squirrel's little body, then picked it up and carried it ten blocks to the vet. The squirrel died in your arms while you were sitting in the waiting room, and you cried all the way home. You told me later that you knew the exact moment when the poor little thing's heart stopped beating, and it was as if a part of you had died, too. Do you remember that?"

Natalie nodded.

Her mother put her hands up to the sides of Natalie's face. "Do you think for one moment, for even one second, that I could ever believe that same sweet, sensitive girl could ever take another life? Why, I'd sooner believe it about myself."

A tear spilled over and ran down Natalie's cheek.

SPENCE STOOD IN THE HALL, listening to that quiet, melodious voice comforting Natalie. He closed his eyes for a moment, wondering what it would be like to have that kind of unconditional love and support, the kind of blind faith Joy Silver had in her daughter.

He thought back to his conversation yesterday with his own mother. After more than ten years of estrangement, Irene had finally asked him to come home. But not because she wanted his comfort or support. Not because she loved him or needed him, but because she wanted him to help her exact her revenge. Irene wanted him to help her punish the woman who had taken away her other son, the only son she had ever cared about.

Spence told himself it didn't matter anymore. He'd come to terms with all that years ago. He didn't need anyone. In fact, in his line of work, it was better to be able to pick up and leave at a moment's notice, leaving no one or nothing of importance behind. In his line of work, a family made you vulnerable. Made you care too much.

Or so he'd always told himself.

But looking at Natalie and her mother now was like staring into a looking glass and glimpsing a whole new world. A foreign world. A world in which people actually cared whether you lived or died, and suddenly Spence wondered what his own life might have been like if he'd had that same kind of love and devotion. That same kind of blind faith.

Would he have been a kinder man? A happier man? Would he still have chosen the same profession? A profession that often led him into the darkest, seediest corners of humanity. A profession that sometimes demanded the cruelest of sacrifices. A profession that had irrevocably changed him over the years, turned him into the steely-eyed stranger that stared back at him from the mirror every morning and every night; a man who had been willing to betray his own brother in the name of justice, because fighting for justice was the only thing that gave his life meaning.

He gazed around the hospital room, his eyes resting on the tiny Christmas tree, a scrawny affair with branches barely able to support a single string of colored lights, and yet, at that moment, it seemed to symbolize so much that had always been missing from his life. Love, hope, joy. And peace. He couldn't remember a time when he'd known any peace in his life, except maybe for seven years ago, very briefly, when he'd met Natalie. When he had fallen in love with her.

But that was before he'd gone away.

That was before she'd married Anthony and had a child with him.

Of all the things that Anthony had been given in his lifetime, of all the riches he'd possessed, there had only been one thing that Spence had ever really coveted. He'd taken some measure of satisfaction in that knowledge. But as he gazed at Anthony's sleeping son, he suddenly realized with a pang of guilt that now there were two.

You're getting maudlin, he told himself grimly. *As bad as an old woman.*

The spirit of the season was obviously getting to him in a way it never had before, and that wouldn't do. He was here in San Antonio to do a job, and it was time to get on with it.

He looked down at the stuffed bear he'd picked up in the hospital gift shop. Purely an impulse purchase, because the Santa Claus hat perched on the bear's pudgy head had caught his eye. But Kyle was probably too old for stuffed animals.

Showed how much he knew about kids, Spence thought.

Better stick to the things he did know about. Like looking for lost diamonds. And putting murderers away for life.

He turned away, looking for a trash can.

NATALIE STOOD IN THE hallway and gazed at the man walking toward the nurse's station. She thought she'd glimpsed Spence in the doorway of Kyle's room a second ago, but before she could say anything, he'd turned and walked away.

Surely it wasn't him. Why would he have come back? After Kyle had been moved upstairs earlier, it had seemed to Natalie that Spence couldn't wait to get away from them.

She'd told herself that was fine by her. He'd bailed her out of jail and she was grateful to him for that, although she still suspected he had an ulterior motive. She was also grateful that he'd helped her with Kyle this afternoon after the accident and had run interference for her with the police. She appreciated everything he'd done, but anything beyond gratitude was treading on dangerous ground. Anything remotely resembling attraction was asking for trouble.

The kind of trouble Natalie didn't want or need.

Unfortunately, it was the kind of trouble one rarely had control over. She'd known it the moment she'd seen him standing in the doorway of the interrogation room, his eyes dark with suspicion and accusation and maybe even hate. She'd known then, as she knew now, that what she had once felt for Spencer Bishop had never really died.

God, help me, she thought. *How can I be so stupid? So weak? He's a Bishop, for God's sake. Anthony's brother. A man you had little more than a one-night stand with. There is nothing there. There never was. You were young and stupid and impressionable. And Spence was…*

She closed her eyes, remembering.

Spence had been young, too. And handsome. A dark and brooding FBI agent with an inner intensity that had frightened her at first. And then thrilled her.

It had been raining the day they first met, and Natalie was feeling bluer than usual. Her parents had been gone several months by that time, and she was having trouble adjusting to a new college.

Spence had seemed to sense her loneliness, and at first, she'd thought it was because he was lonely, too. Later, of course, she realized that he was simply an expert at reading people. It was all a part of his job.

But that first day, when he'd walked over to her, leaned across her desk, and whispered to her that it was his birthday and he didn't want to spend it alone, Natalie didn't have it in her heart to resist. No one should spend a birthday alone.

So they made arrangements for him to pick her up after work, and then went to dinner at a quaint, candlelit restaurant off the beaten track. They talked some, but not a lot because both of them were introverts and a little uneasy about the developing attraction between them.

Afterward, they strolled along the Riverwalk, and Spence kissed her in a secluded corner beneath a bridge, with mariachi music playing in the background and a fountain splashing nearby. Then he asked her to come back to his hotel room with him, but Natalie shyly refused. That night.

The following week they were together constantly. He picked her up daily from work and they went out to dinner or to a movie or sometimes for a walk. They kissed and touched—their attraction was simmering by this time—but always Natalie managed to keep her senses under control. Until that last night, when Spence told her he'd been called back to Washington and they wouldn't be able to see each other for a while.

That night Natalie invited him back to her apartment, and he stayed until the wee hours of the morning. They had one glorious, passion-filled night, and then he was gone.

He didn't come back to San Antonio for almost two months, during which time Natalie had no phone calls and no letters from him. During which time, doubts and fear besieged her.

During which time, Anthony began to pursue her.

Smooth, suave, aristocratic Anthony, who told Natalie all about his little brother—how Spence made a habit of using women, then throwing them away like so much garbage. How Spence had never cared about anyone but himself. How he already had a fiancée in Washington, and that was why he'd rushed back at a moment's notice.

Anthony even showed Natalie pictures taken in Washington of Spence and a gorgeous, sophisticated-looking woman who obviously adored him, and Natalie had burned with anger and humiliation. How had she allowed herself to succumb so easily to his seduction? Why had she believed him when he'd told her that he'd never felt this way about another woman?

It was the oldest line in the book, and Natalie had fallen for it so easily, when, in reality, she had been nothing more to Spencer Bishop than a new conquest—someone he wanted to sleep with, but certainly not the kind of woman he wanted to marry.

And through it all, Anthony had been there to hold her hand, to tell her that she *was* special, and that his brother was a fool. Any man would be proud to have a woman like Natalie for his wife. Any man would want to take care of her, have a family with her.

If Natalie would just trust him, he would help her out of a desperate situation. He would love, honor, and cherish her in a way his brother never could.

By the time Spence returned to San Antonio, Natalie and Anthony were married. And even in that short period of time, she'd already realized what a horrible mistake she'd made, what kind of man her husband really was. Which had made her wonder if he'd lied to her about Spence, but by then, it was too late. She'd already struck a bargain with Anthony, and there was no going back.

As all those memories rushed through her, Natalie hesitated in the hallway, wondering if she should call out to Spence. Or if she should let him go.

But he seemed to have sensed her intense scrutiny. He stopped and turned to glance over his shoulder. When he saw her, something flashed in his green eyes—a look Natalie couldn't quite define. For a moment, she wondered if he had been thinking about the past, too. About the night that had seemed so right…so inevitable.

The night that had changed her life forever.

He turned slowly and started walking back toward her. Natalie's pulse raced as she stared up at him, taking in in a heartbeat the dark expression on his face, the glimpse of secrets in his eyes…so dangerous and yet so irresistible.

How had her life come back to this? she wondered with a sinking feeling in her stomach. How had she managed to come full circle in seven years? Anthony Bishop was still controlling her life, even from his grave, and Spence… Spence was still making her want what she knew she couldn't have.

In seven years she'd learned nothing.

In seven years, she was still weak and vulnerable where Spencer Bishop was concerned.

But now she had her son to think about, she told herself firmly. Now she had Kyle to protect.

"How is he?" Spence asked, as if reading her thoughts. He stopped directly in front of her, so that she had to look up at him. How like a Bishop, she reflected.

She stepped back and crossed her arms as she leaned against the wall, taking away some of his advantage. "He's fine. I didn't expect to see you again tonight." Her gaze dropped to the stuffed bear he held in one hand, and for some insane reason, she felt her throat knot.

What was the matter with her, for God's sake? She hadn't broken down when she'd been arrested for Anthony's murder, and she hadn't fallen apart after the car accident and Kyle's session with the plastic surgeon. So why did the sight of Spencer Bishop clutching a teddy bear he'd bought for Kyle make her want to weep uncontrollably?

Seeing the direction of her stare, Spence held up the bear and looked at it for a moment as though he hadn't a clue how he came to be holding it. Then he shrugged. "I bought this for Kyle…saw it in the gift shop…. But I guess…he's probably too old for stuffed toys."

"No, he's not," Natalie said quietly. "He'll love it."

With another shrug, Spence held it out to her. She raised her eyebrows. "Don't you want to give it to him yourself?"

"I thought he was sleeping."

"He is, but the nurses come to check on him every so often. They have to wake him to make sure he's…okay."

"He is, isn't he?"

Natalie smiled. "Yes. He's tough. Takes more than a bump on the head to slow him down."

Spence laughed softly, and Natalie realized with a start

that she'd never heard him laugh before. Not once. And that fact struck her as being incredibly sad.

Don't, she warned herself. *Don't feel sorry for Spencer Bishop.*

If he lived in a world without laughter, it was because he chose to. Chose to retreat into his own cold, dark, unreachable place. A place of lies and deceit. A world that had once sucked Natalie in, and then almost destroyed her.

She pushed her hair back with one hand as she gazed up at him, her sadness and sympathy gone. Her eyes, she knew, mirrored the suspicion and distrust she saw in his. "Why did you really come back here, Spence? I don't think it was to see Kyle."

He hesitated for a moment, then said, "You're right. I wanted to talk to you."

"About?"

"Everything."

"That's a broad topic," she said, straightening away from the wall. She glanced around, wondering what people might think if they saw them together and recognized them—the woman accused of murdering Anthony Bishop, and Anthony Bishop's brother, the man who had bailed her out of jail. The man who had once been her lover, one night long ago.

"I want to ask you some questions about the night Anthony died," Spence said.

"Why?"

"Because there are a few things I'd like to clear up."

"It's all in the police report."

"Maybe. But I'd rather hear it from you."

Natalie removed her glasses and rubbed her eyes. "I've been through it so many times. It's a nightmare. I can't bear to repeat it again. Not now. Not with my son lying in there hurt because…"

"Because?" Spence's eyes darkened. "What were you about to say, Natalie?"

"Nothing," she mumbled, still unable to bring herself to trust him. She slipped her glasses back on, as if they somehow gave her courage. "Only that…I had so much on my mind today, I might not have been paying enough attention to my driving. I might have avoided that accident."

"I don't think so. You were already in the intersection when the other car ran the red light. There was nothing you could have done."

"Maybe not." But she still wasn't convinced. The voice on the telephone earlier had implied a threat when he'd told her he knew where her son was. What if that car had deliberately hit them, because someone wanted something Natalie had? Except she had no idea what it was.

Tell him, she ordered herself. *Tell him and demand police protection for Kyle.* While another voice whispered through her mind, *Anything you say can and will be used against you in a court of law.*

But it wasn't the murder trial she was worried about now. It was the custody battle with Irene that made her turn away from Spence in order to hide the fear in her eyes.

"There's nothing more I can tell you," she said. "About anything."

"Oh, I think there is."

Natalie started to protest, but just then her mother popped her head around the door. "Natalie? Kyle's awake. He's asking for you, honey."

"I'll be right there." She turned back to Spence, hoping to end the conversation then and there, but to her chagrin, she heard her mother say, "Why, hello again. It's Spence, isn't it?"

"Mrs. Silver. Nice to see you again."

"Joy, please. I'm not one to stand on ceremony." Her eyes lit on the bear in Spence's hand. "Oh, how adorable! Did you bring it for Kyle? Well, then, you have to come in, so he can thank you."

Natalie went quickly to her son's bedside, and bent to kiss him on each cheek and then lightly on his bandaged forehead. "How are you feeling, sweetie?"

"Good," he said. "I'm thirsty."

Natalie poured him a glass of water from the pitcher on the nightstand. Kyle's eyes widened when he saw the tree for the first time. "Awesome! Where did that come from?"

"From Santa, who else?" his grandmother piped in. She was standing on the other side of the bed and she winked at Kyle, then patted his little arm. "He couldn't let you stay in here without a Christmas tree, now could he? That wouldn't seem like Christmas at all. And speaking of Christmas, look who's brought you a present."

As if on cue, Kyle's gaze turned to the foot of his bed, where Spence had just stepped into the room. "Hi," Kyle said.

"Hey, there." Spence looked decidedly uncomfortable, as if he didn't quite know what to do or say. Then he held the bear out to Kyle and said apologetically, "I hope this is okay. I guess I don't know much about what six-year-old boys are into these days."

"Wow! You bought this for me? Thanks!" Kyle exclaimed, as if a stuffed bear wearing a Santa Claus hat was the one present he'd been waiting his whole life for. Natalie could have kissed him, especially when she saw the spark of pleasure in Spence's eyes.

"You're welcome," he said, smiling at Kyle in a way

Natalie had never seen him smile before. That smile made her heart do funny things inside her chest.

"I see I was right," Spence said. "You've got yourself quite a shiner."

"Really?" Kyle perked right up at the thought of a black eye. "Can I see?"

Shaking her head, Natalie handed him a mirror.

"Whoa, dude," Kyle exclaimed, obviously quite impressed with his bruised and battered reflection. "I never had a black eye before."

"Yes, you have," Natalie corrected him. "When you were only a year old. You fell off the dining-room table. How you managed to get up there, I never quite figured out."

Her mother laughed. "I remember you writing to me about that. And then there was the time when he was three, and your father and I were home that one summer. Dad took him to a company softball game. Poor little thing got hit right in the eye with a foul ball. Dad felt terrible."

"How come I don't remember any of this?" Kyle demanded.

"Because you were too small," Natalie said.

"So why didn't you tell me?"

"I didn't know it was something you'd want to know. Silly me, I didn't realize black eyes were so important."

"Sure, they are," Spence said. "Just like bikes without training wheels and real baseball bats, not plastic ones, and really gross skinned knees. Right?"

Kyle nodded, terribly pleased that someone understood him, and that that someone was a man. Male bonding was a concept Natalie tried not to think about too much. She was a single mother raising her son the best way she knew how. Surely she couldn't be faulted for that.

But Kyle missed having a man in his life. Natalie had

always known that, but there wasn't much she could do about it. Anthony hadn't been in the picture until a few weeks before he died, and even then, only at his own convenience. Natalie's father had been out of the country off and on for the last seven years or so, and there hadn't been any other men in her life to speak of. No wonder Kyle seemed so taken with Spence.

Or at least, that was what Natalie told herself. She couldn't let herself believe it was anything more—that Kyle and Spence shared any kind of bond, other than a last name and a somewhat vague physical resemblance. They both had the Bishop eyes. But then, so had Anthony.

Natalie glanced down at her son, who was contentedly playing with his bear. Spence and her mother had moved away from the bed and were talking in low tones. Natalie heard her mother say, ''…needs to get out of here for a while. Would you mind taking her out to dinner?''

Natalie was horrified. Her mother was arranging for her to spend time with a Bishop. Spencer Bishop. She was actually asking him to take her poor, pitiful daughter out to dinner.

Heat crept up her neck and spread across her face. What was her mother thinking? But, of course, she knew nothing of Spence and Natalie's background, their brief interlude. She only knew that he was Anthony's brother and that he had bailed her daughter out of jail. Because of the latter, Joy seemed perfectly willing to overlook the former.

But Natalie wasn't.

She said, ''I'm fine, Mom. I don't want to leave right now.''

But her mother had that look on her face—the one that clearly said, *I'm your mother. I know best, so don't argue.*

''You've been cooped up in this hospital room all afternoon and evening, and this morning you were cooped

up at home. Before that you were in that awful place—''
She stopped herself, staring down at Kyle's wide green
eyes, bright and alert and taking in her every word. ''All
I'm saying is that a little fresh air and a hot meal would
do you a world of good.''

Before Natalie could offer another protest, Spence said,
''She's right. It would do you good to get out for a while.''

Natalie had no desire to spend the evening with Spencer
Bishop, but unfortunately, everyone seemed to be conspir-
ing against her. Even her own son. ''I don't mind, Mom.
Honest. Gram can tell me a story while you're gone.''

''Ah, yes,'' his grandmother said, coming to stand beside Kyle's bed. ''I believe we did leave our starship captain stranded on that dismal little planet in the Chymmy-
rian galaxy, didn't we?''

Kyle nodded eagerly. ''He lost his phaser.''

''And his communicator,'' his grandmother said. ''Well,
things did, indeed, look dire for Captain Killian.…''

Out in the hall, Natalie hesitated, gazing up at Spence.
''Look…you really don't have to be railroaded into doing
this. I can just go down to the cafeteria and grab a bite to
eat.''

''I'd really like to take you to dinner.''

''Why? So you can grill me some more?'' She had no
delusions about his intentions.

His eyes darkened for a moment at her deliberate prov-
ocation. Then he shrugged and said, ''No. So we can talk.
That's something you and I have never done much of, is
it, Natalie?''

Chapter Eight

Natalie's trepidation steadily mounted as Spence headed downtown, found a public parking area, and pulled his car into a space. He cut the engine and turned to her, his arm resting lightly along the back of her seat. Natalie didn't know why, but she was acutely aware of his hand so close to her hair, of having his face mere inches from hers in the small confines of the car.

In the light from the street, she could see his eyes—dark and shadowy—studying her intently and she grew even more nervous. He said something, and the movement of his lips drew her gaze like a moth to flame, irresistibly attracted to danger.

"So you don't mind?" he was saying.

"Mind?" Reluctantly she lifted her gaze to meet his questioning eyes.

"That I brought you here."

She shrugged. "Why should I mind? I love the River-walk. My shop's located here."

"I know."

"But how—"

"I was there the night Anthony was murdered," he said and got out of the car.

Natalie had no choice but to follow. She joined him at

the top of the steps, and together they descended to the river level. It was still fairly early and the stores were buzzing with shoppers, the restaurants and bistros spilling over with music and laughter.

Luminarias glowed softly along the sidewalks, while thousands and thousands of colored lights hung in streamers from the huge trees lining the river. Against the dark green surface of the water, the glistening lights sparkled like jewels.

It was a fairyland, a place of enchantment, and Natalie suddenly felt as though she had stepped through a wardrobe into a world where everything might not be as it seemed. Where danger and darkness might well be disguised by the beauty and magic of the moment.

Spence took her elbow and guided her through the maze of tables hugging the banks of the river, and the throng of tourists and revelers strolling along the sidewalk. Finally he stopped in front of her own building, and Natalie's eyes were drawn upward.

On the top level, light shone from Blanche's windows proclaiming her shop open for business, while on the bottom level, Delmontico's drew a brisk dinner crowd. But in between, on the second level, the windows of Silver Bells remained ominously dark, and although she couldn't see it, Natalie knew the yellow police tape stamped "Crime Scene" would still be barricading her door. She turned away, saddened by the sight and the memories.

"I've heard good things about this restaurant," Spence said. "But if you don't want to stay, we can go somewhere else."

"No, it's fine." Natalie gazed around, looking everywhere but at the second story. She couldn't avoid it forever, though. This moment was bound to happen, and she might as well get it over with.

Sooner or later, she would have to come back here and reopen her shop. She would have to find a way to deal with the memories of that night and move on, because she still had a business to run, she still had a child to support, and she still had a life to live. She couldn't hide in Narnia forever.

Frank Delmontico saw them and wove his way through the tables. He was not a tall man—five seven or so, only a couple of inches taller than Natalie. But he was toughly built, his arms and shoulders powerful looking beneath the loose white shirt he wore. His black hair was slicked straight back, highlighting his dark, fathomless eyes and his swarthy complexion.

When Natalie introduced him to Spence, something flashed in those dark eyes, a wariness that vanished almost instantly. Then he turned on his heel and led them to a candlelit table near the river.

It was a warm night, but the breeze off the water was chilly. Natalie wrapped her light jacket around her shoulders and shivered as they sat down.

"Would you rather eat inside?" Spence asked.

"No, I like it out here. I love looking at all the lights. It's so beautiful. I never get tired of this place. Every season brings its own magic."

"I've missed San Antonio," Spence said unexpectedly, after a waiter had come by to take their drink order. "When I left Washington, it was bitterly cold and pouring rain. Very depressing."

"No snow?"

"Not yet, but there were predictions for Christmas."

Natalie's gaze scanned the water, fastened on a barge outlined in lights carrying a group of loud tourists downriver. "As much as I love this warm weather, sometimes

I think it would be nice to have snow for the holidays. I've never had a white Christmas.''

''In San Antonio that would take a miracle.''

''I'm not sure I believe in miracles anymore,'' Natalie said softly, her voice full of regret.

''I don't think I ever did. Miracles are for fairy tales and dreams. In the real world, if you want something badly enough, you have to make it happen. You can't just sit around waiting for it to snow.''

She glanced up sharply. His eyes, dark and seductive, stared back at her, and Natalie felt something tremble inside her. ''But some things are beyond our control.''

''And some things aren't.'' He leaned toward her across the table. Candlelight flashed in his eyes. ''Do you want to find out what really happened to Anthony?''

She looked at him in shock. ''Of course, I do. But I thought you were convinced...of my guilt.''

''Do you really think I would have bailed you out of jail if I thought you killed my brother?''

The breeze picked up and the candle flickered wildly between them. His eyes deepened mysteriously. What was he really saying? Natalie wondered. Did he really believe in her innocence? Or, as before, years ago, was he merely telling her what he knew she wanted to hear? Was he playing on her emotions to get what he wanted?

The question was, what exactly did he want this time?

''What did you have in mind?'' Natalie asked suspiciously.

''I'd like to help you get to the bottom of this mystery. I'd like to help you find the real killer.''

''I never said I was looking for the killer,'' she said quickly, her heart bouncing off the wall of her chest. She wasn't a detective, for God's sake.

Spence sat back in his chair and studied the candle

flame. "I've had some experience in dealing with local law enforcement. Once they have their suspect in custody, their investigation is pretty much over."

"Are you saying that since they believe I'm guilty, they won't even look for anyone else?"

"That's what I'm saying, Natalie."

"Then I could go to jail," she whispered in horror. "I could be convicted of a crime I didn't commit."

"It's possible. A lot of innocent people are in prison. More than you imagine."

Images flashed through her mind. Dark, dreary cells. Endless hours crawling by. And the loneliness, the sheer helplessness...

Natalie suddenly felt sick at her stomach. "Why would you want to help me?"

Spence lifted the drink the waiter put in front of him. "Anthony was my brother. We had our differences, but he was still my brother. My own flesh and blood. And somewhere out there, his killer roams free. Anthony may not be his last victim."

Cooperate, and no one else has to get hurt.

"How do you know it's a man?" Natalie asked. "Anthony had a lot of enemies. Many of them were probably women." She was thinking of one in particular. He'd been about to divorce Melinda and not give her a cent. Texas was a community-property state, but Natalie knew her ex-husband had been expert in finding ways around the law when it suited him.

"Who, specifically, are you talking about?"

"Kyle overheard Anthony telling Melinda he wanted a divorce. He was going to cut her off without a penny."

Spence's brows rose. "Kyle said this?"

Natalie nodded. "In fact, he recorded their conversation."

This seemed to interest Spence a great deal. He leaned forward again. "Does he still have the tape?"

"I don't know. He claims to have lost the recorder."

"Claims?"

Natalie toyed with her own drink, a glass of red wine. "Kyle has a habit of hiding things—for safekeeping, he says—then forgetting where he put them."

"I'd like to talk to him," Spence said.

"Not now. He's been through too much. Maybe in a few days—"

"In a few days, the trail will only grow colder. We have to move fast."

He *was* moving fast. Too fast to suit Natalie. She hadn't agreed to work with him. She still wasn't sure she even trusted him.

"Kyle doesn't know anything about the murder," she said angrily. "He's just a little boy."

"I would never say or do anything to hurt him."

Their eyes met over the candle flame. Natalie wanted to deny the quiver in her stomach, the shiver of nerves along her spine, but she couldn't. Not with the way he was suddenly looking at her.

She forced her gaze away. "I thought we came here to eat," she said. "So let's order. I need to get back to the hospital."

For the next several minutes, after they'd placed their orders and waited for their food to arrive, they turned their talk from murder. Natalie asked him about his work in Washington, and he asked her about her shop.

"A Christmas store," he said. "That suits you."

Natalie laughed softly. "You might even say it was inevitable, since I was born on Christmas Eve."

"I didn't know that."

There were a lot of things about her he didn't know. It

was ironic, she thought. He'd been her lover, and yet he didn't even know the date of her birth. He hadn't even asked. Hadn't cared enough, she realized now.

"My birthday's in November," he commented, making small talk.

"November 16th," she said, before thinking.

"So you remembered." His gaze met hers.

She tried to laugh lightly. "I remember that you're a Scorpio. Dark, brooding, intense. And secretive," she couldn't resist adding. "Anthony was a Gemini. Dual personalities."

"So what are you?"

"Capricorn. Impulsive. Easily fooled."

"And Kyle?"

Natalie studied her wineglass. "A Leo. Powerful, commanding, kinglike. He loves that one."

"When is his birthday?"

Natalie glanced up. "You…don't know?"

"I never asked."

Never cared enough to, she thought again. The knowledge hurt her, although she knew it shouldn't. Spence hadn't married his fiancée, the woman Anthony had shown her in the picture, and Natalie had never asked why. She liked to think it was because she hadn't cared enough, either.

"I didn't keep in touch with my family back then," Spence was saying. "In fact, two days ago, when I went over to tell my mother that Anthony was dead, was the first time I'd talked to her in years."

Just then, the waiter brought their dinners, and Natalie was saved from having to respond. She thought about Spence's estrangement from his family. In the year that Anthony and Natalie had been married, she hadn't been around Irene Bishop that much. The older woman's open disapproval was like the thrust of a knife blade. Natalie had avoided her whenever possible, but even during the few brief audiences Irene had granted to her, Natalie had discerned very quickly that Anthony was the favorite, and that the worth of Irene's other children was measured by their devotion to him.

In spite of herself, Natalie felt a stab of sympathy for Spence. Her own parents had adored her from the moment she was born, and they'd let her know every day of her life how wonderful she was, what a precious gift she was to them.

Having been surrounded by their love, Natalie couldn't imagine what it must have been like for Spence, growing up in that cold mausoleum of a home with an even colder mother, a father who ignored him, and a sister and brother who despised him.

Unlike her own magical youth, Spence's childhood had been a cold, barren wasteland—a place where it was always winter but never Christmas.

They finished eating in silence. While Spence settled the check, Natalie got up and walked to the water's edge, staring at the dazzling reflection of lights. Sensing a presence behind her, she turned to find Frank Delmontico watching her.

Even though she and Blanche had eaten here often, Frank had always kept his distance, treating them as he would any other customers, always careful to foster nothing more than a nodding acquaintance. His intense scrutiny now made her uneasy. She wondered if he, like everyone else, was now looking at her in a new light, thinking that all these years he'd been located downstairs from a cold-blooded killer.

Rather than turning away when he saw that she'd caught

him staring, he walked over to her. The full sleeves of his white shirt billowed softly in the breeze.

He came right to the point. "That man with you. He's a cop, right?"

"FBI," Natalie said, glancing back at their table.

Frank's eyes darkened. "Why is a federal agent working on a simple murder case?"

Natalie had no idea why Frank Delmontico had taken such a sudden interest in her, but she saw no harm in answering him. She shrugged and said, "He's not officially on the case. Anthony Bishop was his brother."

Frank showed not the slightest hint of surprise. He turned and his gaze followed Natalie's to their table, where Spence waited for his credit card to be returned. He looked up and his gaze met Natalie's briefly before narrowing on Frank.

"I can see the resemblance," Frank muttered. He shook his head, turning away. "Anthony Bishop's brother an FBI agent. Who would have thought that?"

Natalie stared at him in surprise. "You *knew* Anthony?"

"Only by reputation," Frank was quick to amend. "We had a mutual acquaintance."

Before she could ask him who that acquaintance might be, Frank leaned toward her. His voice lowered ominously. "Your ex-husband was into some dirty business, Natalie. I'd hate to see you get drawn into something you can't handle."

"What kind of dirty business?" she asked quickly.

"Dealings with the underworld," Frank said. "Anthony Bishop had his fingers in a lot of pies."

"Do you know something about his murder?"

"I don't know anything," Frank replied. "But I hear things. And the word on the street is, you could be in a lot of trouble."

"With whom?"

He shrugged, obviously having said all he intended to.

"I've been accused of Anthony's murder," she said desperately. "If you know something that could help clear my name, please tell me."

"Just be careful," Frank said. "Be careful who you trust."

He stared over her shoulder, and Natalie glanced behind to see that Spence had left their table and was walking toward them.

She turned back to Frank, but he had already melted into the shadows near the restaurant.

"WHAT DID HE WANT?" Spence asked.

"I'm not sure. He...warned me."

"About what?"

"About you, I think." She looked up to find Spence staring down at her, his gaze hard, suspicious.

"And what did you say?"

"I didn't say anything, but I can take care of myself. I know better than to trust the wrong people."

"Do you?" They walked in silence for a moment, then he asked suddenly, "How long have you known Frank Delmontico?"

"Five years. He was already in the building when I opened my store. Why?"

Spence shrugged. "He looks familiar to me."

"You said you were here before...right after Anthony's...death. Maybe you saw him then."

Spence shook his head. "It was too early in the morning for the restaurants and shops to be open. I know I've seen him somewhere before, though. Sooner or later, it'll come to me." He paused for a moment, as if in deep concentration, then asked, "Who owns the store on the top level?"

"Blanche Jones. She's a good friend of mine."

"We might want to come back and talk to both of them. Find out if either of them saw or heard anything unusual the night of the murder."

"The police have already questioned them both," Natalie said. "I talked to Blanche the day after it happened." Blanche had been very distraught to learn that Natalie had been arrested for Anthony's murder. She'd been so upset, in fact, that she could hardly talk at first. Finally, she'd settled down and told Natalie that the police had been around, asking a lot of questions. Unfortunately, Blanche had closed early that night and had been home at the time of the murder. She hadn't seen or heard anything that could help Natalie. As for Frank, Blanche couldn't say.

"The police might not have asked the right questions," Spence said. "Tomorrow, I think we should come back and talk to them."

Natalie didn't point out that she hadn't agreed to work with him. But he'd frightened her with what he'd told her earlier about the investigation coming to a halt because the police had their suspect. If they weren't looking for the real killer, then who would?

At least Spence was a professional, an FBI agent. Who better to have helping her?

Someone you can trust, a little voice reminded her.

Unfortunately, no one filled that bill at the moment.

She sighed wearily. "All right. I guess it won't hurt to talk to them."

Another uneasy silence fell between them. They strolled along the Riverwalk, and Natalie tried very hard not to remember the last time they'd walked here together. But Spence's presence was making it difficult. He wasn't touching her, but she couldn't help remembering when he once had. He wasn't looking at her, but she couldn't stop thinking about the way he used to.

At the bottom of the steps that would take them to the street level and the parking lot where they'd left his car, Spence stopped and gazed down at her. Behind them the music and laughter faded away. The Christmas lights seemed to dim, and the only thing Natalie was aware of was the way his eyes deepened, and the way his lips opened, and the way her heart pounded inside her.

For a split second—an eternity—no one said anything. Then, very softly, Spence said, "Why did you marry him?"

He was still gazing down at her, and Natalie's breath caught in her throat. It was seven years too late to be having this conversation. Too late to change anything. But she found herself answering him anyway. "I married him because he was here and you weren't."

"As simple as that?" His voice turned bitter.

"No." She glanced away from those probing eyes. "There wasn't anything simple about it."

"Did you love him?"

"No."

Her blunt answer seemed to surprise him. "Then I repeat, why did you marry him?"

To get back at you, Natalie thought. *To prove to you that I was better than a one-night stand and to prove to myself that someone else wanted me, even if you didn't.*

And because she'd been nineteen, and pregnant, with nowhere else to turn.

Natalie had always wondered how differently things might have worked out if her parents hadn't been out of the country back then—if she'd had their love and wisdom to rely on. But as it was, she'd had no one. And the shame and embarrassment of what she'd done had made her unable to confide in her mother by letter or over the telephone. She knew her parents would have been devastated, and her father would have turned down an important promotion—an opportunity he'd worked for all his life—just to come home and be with her.

And Anthony had been there—an older man guiding her, protecting her, providing her with a solution that seemed to be the best for everyone. At that time, Natalie had no idea that he had his own hidden agenda, his own secret reasons for wanting to marry her.

"Why, Natalie?"

She sighed, trying to diminish the painful memories. "What difference does it make? It was all a long time ago. Anthony's dead and—"

"You and I are still here."

"So?"

The breeze loosened her hair, and automatically he reached up to smooth back the stray lock, then trailed the back of his hand down the side of her face.

And everything stilled within her.

"You still feel it, don't you?"

"No!"

He smiled slightly. "So emphatic. You didn't even have to ask what I was talking about. You know why? Because you do still feel it. It's still there."

"I don't know what you're talking about," she insisted, her nerve endings dancing along her spine.

"Then let me explain."

Before Natalie had time to turn away, before she even had time to catch her breath, he reached out to remove her glasses. His mouth lowered to hers.

And seven years vanished.

The moment his lips touched hers, she was once again that lonely, vulnerable nineteen-year-old and he was...

Spence. A brooding, complex man who stirred powerful emotions inside her. A man who had always made her tremble at his nearness. A man who made her want nothing more than to be the one to turn on the light in his cold, dark, dismal world.

The kiss was surprisingly gentle. No demands, no recriminations, and for the moment, no regrets. Just a soft melting of souls as his fingers wove through her hair and his lips moved against hers.

A thousand emotions raced through Natalie. She'd forgotten this side of him. The tender, warm, caring side that, with just one kiss, could somehow bring her to her knees.

She wanted to slip her arms around his waist and hold him close. She wanted to tell him how many times over the years she'd dreamed of this moment. She wanted to share with him her most precious of secrets.

But she did none of that. Because even with his lips pressing against hers, even with his heart hammering beneath her splayed hand on his chest, she knew that all of this was a lie. Spencer Bishop was a lie. A chameleon as talented and ruthless as his brother. A man who was not what he seemed. A man of secrets...

She pulled away and he let her go. Her fingertips trembled against her lips as she gazed up at him. "Why did you do that?" she whispered.

"To prove a point."

"As simple as that?" she asked, using his own bitter words. She almost expected him to come back with hers. *Nothing about it was simple.* The kiss had undoubtedly complicated their already complex lives.

But Spence simply shrugged, his shoulders lifting slightly beneath the black leather jacket he wore. "As simple as that." His eyes never wavered from hers. "At least now we know what we're dealing with."

He said it so matter-of-factly, he might have been talking about a case instead of a kiss. Natalie didn't know why his tone suddenly angered her. "And what is that?"

"For a smart woman, you can certainly act dense when it suits you."

Her anger blossomed, mercifully dimming the other emotions storming through her. "I've made too many stupid mistakes in my life to ever claim to be smart. Letting you kiss me just now was one of them."

"Why?"

"Because—" Because it had stirred to life emotions that were best left dead. Because it had made her feel weak and vulnerable when she needed to be strong and invincible.

He'd trapped her and he knew it. His green eyes gleamed in the moonlight. "Because you know I'm right," he said softly. "The attraction is still there."

"Yes, it's still there," she acknowledged, lifting her chin in a tiny act of defiance. "But I don't want it to be."

He reached out and slipped her glasses back on her. The act was oddly gentle, belying the darkness in his eyes. "We don't always get what we want, Natalie. Haven't you learned that by now?"

Since they'd been gone longer than Natalie had meant to be, she called the hospital from Spence's cellular phone. Her mother answered and assured her Kyle was fine. Natalie could hear murmuring in the background, then her mother said, "There is just one tiny problem." Kyle's voice rose in distress, but Natalie couldn't make out what he was saying. "He wants to talk to you."

When Kyle got on the phone, Natalie asked quickly, "What's wrong, honey?"

"It's Fred."

"Fred? What about him?"

"I forgot to feed him before I left, and now Grandma says I can't go home till morning. He'll starve to death."

"No, he won't. He'll be fine until we get home. Turtles don't need much food."

"Fred does. And besides, you always say I'll get sick if I don't eat right. I don't want Fred to get sick. You have to go feed him, Mom. You just have to."

"Honey, Fred will be fine—"

"Please, Mom. If he gets sick…"

Natalie winced. If Fred got sick, Kyle would never forgive her. He thought the world of that turtle, ever since he'd rescued it from a drainage ditch after a rainstorm one day.

She sighed. "All right, I'll go feed Fred, if it'll make you feel better. But you have to promise me you'll try to get some sleep. That's the deal."

"I promise," Kyle said, smothering a yawn. It seemed she'd said the magic words.

She hung up and glanced at Spence. "Do you mind? Kyle insists that I go home and feed his turtle before coming back to the hospital. I know he won't get a bit of rest if I don't."

Spence shrugged. "It's no problem for me."

Natalie gave him directions to her bungalow-style house in Alamo Heights, a few blocks from her parents' home. Spence pulled into the driveway, and Natalie reached for the door handle. His arm shot out to stop her.

"Better let me check it out first," he said. "Where's your key?"

Natalie glanced at him in the dark. "I'm sure everything's fine." Why wouldn't it be? Unless he suspected something. *Knew* something…

Natalie couldn't help wondering what Irene's next move might be. And if Spence was in on it.

"Blame it on my training," he said, accepting the key she handed him. He got out of the car, then bent down to ask, "Do you have an alarm?"

She shook her head. The crime rate in her area was low. She'd never felt the need for a home-security system, but as she thought about the phone call she'd received earlier, the threatening tone in the man's voice, she shivered, suddenly glad that Spence was with her.

She watched him disappear inside her house, and then waited for the lights to come on, expecting him to reappear at any moment to give her the all-clear sign. But the house remained dark and he didn't come back.

Minutes passed.

Natalie began to get really nervous. What in the world was keeping him? She hated to think the worst about him, but what if he was in her house, searching through her things, looking for evidence that would convict her of Anthony's murder? He and Anthony had never gotten along, but Spence had said himself tonight at dinner that Anthony had still been his brother, and blood, more often than not, was thicker than water.

And that disconcerting thought brought her back to Irene. Just how far would Spence be willing to go to help his mother? To perhaps get in her good graces for the first time in his life.

Natalie got out of the car and stood for a moment, staring at the darkened house. Something was wrong inside. She didn't know how she knew, but she knew. Something was definitely wrong.

She walked to the front door, pushed it open, and stepped inside. Her hand automatically sought the light switch, and when the light came on, she gasped in terror at the destruction that lay before her.

The room had been thoroughly ransacked. Books had been flung from the shelves, chair and sofa cushions slashed, paintings ripped from the walls. Every vase, jar and glass box had been smashed into a million pieces and every drawer had been jerked free of her desk, the contents dumped on the hardwood floor.

But the cruelest destruction of all was the presents under the Christmas tree. Their colorful paper and ribbons were shredded and crumpled, the boxes plundered.

And Spence was nowhere to be seen.

Natalie stood for a moment, taking in the devastation as her heart hammered inside her. Her fear subsided and anger plunged through her at the violation. These were her things. Her personal belongings. She'd worked long and hard for every last one of them, and now someone had come in here and ruthlessly destroyed her possessions. Her home. Her sanctuary.

Thank God, Kyle wasn't here to see this, she thought. Thank God, he was safe in the hospital with her mother to watch over him. For a split second, Natalie was almost grateful to the driver who had rammed into their car earlier. Otherwise, she and Kyle might both have been at home tonight.

As Natalie gazed around her ruined living room, she realized that whoever had done this would not have let a woman and a small boy stand in his or her way. Whoever had done this had been in a rage, although, for the life of her, Natalie didn't know why.

Then another thought occurred to her. What if whoever had done this was also responsible for the accident earlier? What if it had all been coolly calculated?

Natalie wasn't sure which scenario scared her the most.

She started across the floor, her feet crunching on bits of broken glass as she made her way toward the dining room and the kitchen beyond.

She called Spence's name but he didn't answer. A shiver of alarm scurried up her spine. Supposing whoever did this was still here? Supposing Spence had walked in and surprised him? Supposing—

By this time, Natalie's heart and imagination were both working overtime. She tried to calm herself by glancing around, looking for the phone. But a noise from the kitchen startled her again. Someone was in there! She started to turn and run for the front door, but something stopped her; some instinct that told her Spence might be in trouble and need her help.

Without thinking, Natalie crossed the dining room and pushed open the kitchen door. Moonlight poured in through the double windows over the sink, but it still took a moment for her eyes to adjust to the dimness. She reached for the light switch just as her gaze dropped to the figure lying on the floor.

Natalie's heart slammed into her chest. She started forward. A movement just inside the door caught her attention and she whirled, but not in time to save herself. Without warning, something flew out of the darkness to strike her left temple.

White-hot pain pierced through her head, and then mercifully everything went black.

Chapter Nine

Natalie opened her eyes. It took her a moment to get her bearings as she lay there, trying to focus. Trying to remember.

Then it all came back to her. The destruction to her home. The hand flying out of the darkness to strike her. And the body lying on the floor.

Spence!

Natalie tried to get up, but pain shot through her skull and a wave of dizziness washed over her. She tentatively probed her temple with her fingertips, and felt the knot where she had been struck. But when she brought her fingers down, they were dry. No blood, thank God.

Then...what were those stains on her clothes? Natalie sat up and stared down at the front of her white blouse. In the moonlight, she could see the dark drips across her chest and for a moment, she wondered if she'd sustained another injury. But other than her head, she felt no pain.

Gingerly she touched the spots on her blouse and found they were still wet. When she lifted her fingertips to her nose, her stomach rolled sickeningly at the unmistakable metallic scent.

Dear God, she thought. It was just like the night Anthony had been murdered. She'd been knocked unconscious, and when she'd awakened, her clothes had been stained with blood. Anthony's blood.

Not again, she thought dizzily. *Please, not again.*

Not Spence.

She struggled to get up, gazing around to find the figure she'd glimpsed on the floor. The moonlight was brilliant enough for her to see blood on her own clothing, but not bright enough for her to locate a body on the floor. There was something wrong with that picture, but Natalie didn't take the time to sort it out. Using the door frame for support, she pulled herself up and felt for the light switch.

Light flooded the room, illuminating every nook and crevice. There was more blood on the floor, along with her glasses, but nothing else. No body. No Spence.

Natalie leaned weakly against the wall, closing her eyes, trying to ignore the pounding in her head. What was happening here? What was happening to her life? How had it suddenly gotten so out of control? She had never felt so helpless, not even when she'd found out she was pregnant. Not even when Anthony had threatened to take away her son if she didn't agree to his terms.

Where, in God's name, was Spence? It seemed he was always disappearing when Natalie needed him the most.

The door beside her opened, and she gasped, jumping back, looking around wildly for something with which to defend herself. But as if summoned by her silent plea, Spence walked through the door.

His presence was hardly comforting. Blood trickled down the side of his face, and his own shirt was splotched with big red circles. His eyes seemed to have a hard time focusing on her.

"Natalie," he said, sounding relieved. "Are you all right?"

"I think so," she said hesitantly. "Are you?"

''At the moment, that's debatable.''

He came into the room and Natalie realized for the first time that he was carrying something in each hand—his cell phone in one, and her first-aid kit in the other. He sat down wearily at the kitchen table.

''I've called 911,'' he said. ''The police and an ambulance should be here soon, but maybe you'd better let me have a look at that bump anyway. You were out cold for a couple of minutes.''

''What about you?'' she asked, bending to retrieve her glasses before coming to sit down beside him. ''I saw you on the floor— At least, I thought it was you. Then someone hit me. Next thing I knew, I was waking up and you were nowhere to be found. What happened?''

He grimaced, putting his hand to the cut on his head. ''I'm losing my touch, that's what happened. Bastard jumped me from behind. I never even saw it coming.''

''Maybe you'd better let me have a look at you,'' Natalie said. ''Judging by all that blood, I'd say you're in worse shape than I am.''

''It's nothing,'' he mumbled, but winced when her fingers explored the cut on his head. ''Sorry about your blouse.''

''So this *is* your blood.'' Natalie wondered why that notion didn't particularly relieve her.

''I bent over you to see if you were okay. When I couldn't get you to come around, I decided I'd better get an ambulance over here.''

The image of him, hurt and bleeding, disregarding his own wound to tend to her filled Natalie with an emotion she didn't understand. Then again, maybe she did. Maybe that was why her heart was pounding away inside her as she stood over him to tend to his.

"It's not that deep," she told him. "But you may need a few stitches."

"They'll have to wait." He took her arm and pulled her down in the chair beside him. "Before the police get here, there's something you and I need to talk about."

"Like what?"

"Like what happened here tonight."

"But I don't know what happened. I don't know any more than you do."

His green eyes seemed to have no trouble focusing on her now. Cool and relentless, they searched her face. "I think you do know. I think you know a lot more than you've been telling me."

"About what?"

Those same green eyes hardened on her. His every feature seemed to tighten into a mask of cold, dark suspicion. "About Anthony's murder. About the diamonds."

"Diamonds? I don't know—"

"Game's over, Natalie. Where are they? Hand them over before someone else ends up dead."

"What are you talking about? What diamonds?"

Spence watched her, looking for the telltale signs of guilt—dry mouth, darting eyes, trembling fingers.

Natalie displayed none of those as she glared at him. If she was lying, she was a damned good actress.

But hadn't he known that she was? Hadn't he been taken in by her before?

"Where are they?" he repeated.

"I have no idea what you're talking about. I don't know anything about any diamonds."

She looked so bewildered, Spence could almost feel sorry for her, but he wouldn't let himself. He wouldn't let anything dim his assessment of her reaction to what he was telling her. Not even the kiss they'd shared earlier.

Not even the memories that kiss had awakened, nor the emotions it had aroused.

He studied her now, wondering if he was doing the right thing by laying his cards on the table. It wasn't in his nature to be so forthcoming, but he needed Natalie's help. And he needed to know if he could trust her.

"The diamonds Anthony was looking for in your store the night he was murdered."

Her eyes widened. "Why on earth was he looking for diamonds in Silver Bells?"

"He came in earlier that day and bought something that he wanted you to deliver, right?"

Her eyes grew even rounder behind her glasses and their blue deepened. "Yes! How did you know that?"

"We had him under surveillance."

"Surveillance? But why?" Suddenly, a light seemed to dawn for her. "Why didn't you tell me this before, when I was trying to convince the police Anthony was looking for something that night? They didn't believe me. Why didn't you come forward and tell them the truth?"

"I had my reasons."

Her eyes flashed with fire, but not the deep, sultry warmth he'd glimpsed earlier when he kissed her. The heat he saw in those blue depths now was pure, unadulterated anger. And in some strange way, it was no less stirring.

"What possible reason could you have to justify withholding information like that from the police? Information that might clear *me*." Then she said slowly, "Wait a minute. If you followed Anthony to Silver Bells that day, what about that night, when he was murdered? Were you following him then? Do you know who killed him? *Do you?*"

Behind her wire-rimmed glasses, Natalie's eyes shot daggers at him. Spence thought that he had never seen anyone look so angry, and with good reason, he had to admit. He had withheld things from Natalie and from the police, and now he was going to have to ask her to do the same.

"After Anthony left your shop that day, he went back to his office, where he stayed the rest of the afternoon and evening," Spence told her. "Sometime later, he gave us the slip. We still haven't figured out exactly how he managed to leave the building without our seeing him. But we figure he must have come straight to Silver Bells, somehow got in and turned off the alarm, and was looking for the diamonds when you walked in on him."

She crossed her arms and glared at him. "You still haven't told me why Anthony was looking for diamonds in my shop in the first place."

"We think he meant to send them in the package he had you deliver, only something went wrong. When the package was delivered to the drop, the diamonds were missing."

"But how did you know where the package was being delivered?" she asked incredulously.

"We had an agent in the store while Anthony was there. She got the address off the counter while you were busy with another customer."

"Real cloak-and-dagger-type stuff." Natalie shook her head, unable to believe everything she was hearing.

"More like life-and-death," Spence replied, not wishing to scare her any more than she already was, but knowing he had to impress upon her the seriousness of the situation. "Someone has already been murdered because of those diamonds, Natalie. I don't want to see anybody else get hurt."

She put trembling fingertips to her temple as she gazed at Spence with troubled eyes. The bluest eyes he'd ever looked into, and he had the sudden, almost-irresistible urge to pull her into his arms, to shield her from the dirt that both he and Anthony had wittingly drawn her into.

But now was not the time, and this was certainly not the place. Besides, once he told her the rest of his story, his arms would be the last place she would want to seek shelter, he thought with a stab of bitter remorse.

"Who is it that wants those diamonds?" she asked. "Besides you, I mean."

"Have you ever heard of a man named Jack Russo?"

Something flickered across her features. A glimmer of recognition. Then she shook her head. "Who is he?"

"A crime boss who was arrested three years ago for murdering a diamond dealer in Dallas. The man was killed during a robbery, but the only witness who came forward to testify against Russo was later found dead. There was nothing tying Russo to the murder except the fortune in diamonds that was stolen from the dealer. Anthony was Russo's attorney. He got the murder charges thrown out for insufficient evidence. Russo was later sent to a federal penitentiary on racketeering charges, but he's out now. And the diamonds were never recovered. We think Anthony was holding them for Russo until he got out of prison."

"You mean Anthony deliberately hid evidence from the police that would have sent Russo to prison for murder? Why?"

"Why would he agree to defend a man like Russo in the first place? Anthony isn't here to tell us, but I'm guessing it was greed. Russo probably agreed to give him a cut."

"But Anthony was rich. He was a Bishop."

"Anthony was not rich," Spence said. "At least, not in the sense you mean. He had money—plenty, by most people's standards. But Anthony wasn't most people. He lived an extravagant life-style, and he had an image to uphold.''

"What do you mean?" Natalie asked.

Spence got up and walked to the window, staring out into the darkness. "The Bishop family has money, including the law firm and several real-estate holdings worth millions. But my father's will left everything in trust. Everyone gets an allowance—Mother, Anthony, and Anthea—but the bulk of the estate was to be held in trust for the first Bishop grandson.''

He turned from the window in time to see the color drain from Natalie's face. She looked beyond shocked. She looked devastated, and Spence's first thought was one of relief. She hadn't known. Anthony hadn't told her about the money.

Her hand fluttered to her heart. "Are you saying—"

"Kyle is the sole Bishop heir."

"Why didn't anyone ever tell me?" she asked in a stunned whisper.

"The terms of my father's will were not something my family wanted to make public. Besides the law firm, the family has always dealt heavily in real estate. If word had gotten out that the Bishop fortune was out of the picture, important deals could have fallen through. Besides the fact that the Bishop reputation had to be maintained. Appearances had to be considered. Mother and Anthony, and even Anthea to a lesser degree, would have been publicly humiliated if it were known they no longer had the Bishop fortune backing them.''

"How long have you known about this?" Natalie asked weakly.

"Since before my father died ten years ago. He wanted to make certain I understood certain aspects of the will, so that I wouldn't contest it.''

"What aspects?"

"That he had cut me out completely." He said it flatly, with no emotion whatsoever, but Spence could still remember the pain that had knifed through him at his father's arrogant dismissal of him.

"You've refused to do as I say. You've cut yourself off from this family, and now I have no recourse but to do the same to you. You will never get your hands on one cent of Bishop money. Your flagrant disregard for my wishes and this reckless, rebellious behavior you seem to take so much pleasure in flaunting before my face leads me to conclude that any money given to you would not only be ill-spent, but also ill-advised...."

There had been more, but Spence cut off the memories and returned them to where they belonged—in the deepest, darkest recesses of his mind. He focused once again on Natalie and what this information had done to her. Her face was still white and drawn, her whole demeanor so fragile she looked as if she might pass out at any second.

Not exactly the reaction you would expect from someone who had just learned her son would someday inherit a fortune worth millions.

"The trust," she said, still looking dazed. "You said...it was to be held for the first Bishop grandson. Did you mean...Anthony's son?"

"He's the only Bishop grandson."

"I know...but..." She trailed off, as if uncertain how to voice her next question. She took a deep breath, but her eyes refused to meet his. "What if...you had a son first. Would...the money still have gone to Anthony's first son, since you were cut out of the will?"

"That's the strange part." Spence came back over and sat down beside her at the table. "The will stipulated first grandson, not necessarily Anthony's, and I wondered about that, too. But I think I figured out why my father did what he did. He wanted Anthony to marry and have children. At the time of my father's death, Anthony was thirty-one years old, and showed no sign of settling down. That was the only bone of contention between the two of them that I ever knew about. The old man wanted to make sure the Bishop line was carried on, and he knew the one sure way to make Anthony comply with his wishes was to hold the money over his head."

"H-how could he have been so sure Anthony would have the first grandson? What if you had met someone…fallen in love…had children…?" Natalie left the question dangling as she searched his face for some clue, some hint of what he might be feeling. But his face was like a mask, wiped clean of every last emotion.

Was this the same man who had kissed her earlier? The same man who had brought her to her emotional knees with the intense feelings he'd unleashed inside her?

Natalie tried to put the memories of that kiss aside as she concentrated on what he was saying. Because everything he'd told her had hit her with terrific force. Suddenly, so many things became clear, and the past took on a new and more ominous meaning for her. She understood Anthony better than she ever had before. No wonder he'd been so desperate to marry her—and to get custody of Kyle.

"My father knew he could count on Anthony to make sure I stayed out of the picture," Spence was saying. "And I'm equally certain that Anthony was prepared for such a contingency. He knew I'd never cared about the money, so there was no reason for him to think I'd rush out and father a child simply to try and get my hands on the inheritance. But if I'd become serious about someone— fallen in love, as you said…" His words faded away as their gazes held for the briefest of moments. "I'm sure he would have found a willing accomplice and rushed her to the altar in record time."

Like he did me, Natalie thought. Anthony had always taken great pleasure in thwarting his brother at every turn. This must have been the ultimate coup.

"What about Anthea?" Natalie asked.

"My father was a chauvinist of the worst kind. In his eyes, Anthea's children wouldn't have been Bishops. He made that clear in the will, and besides, he knew she would never go against his wishes. Anthea wasn't a threat, but I was, so he pitted Anthony against me in order to force Anthony to carry out his wishes."

And in the meantime, driving Spence and Anthony even further apart, Natalie thought. To make matters worse, she had entered both brothers' lives, and had unwittingly become a part of the drama. And the tragedy...

"I can't believe no one ever told me about this," she said. "Why did your family keep it from me?"

"Probably because they were afraid you would try to get your hands on the money. Everyone else has," Spence said dryly.

"So that's why Anthony was going after custody of Kyle," Natalie said. "He wanted the money."

"Maybe. The trust is protected until Kyle turns twenty-one, but Anthony might have thought it was time he began feathering his nest, so to speak. Getting in Kyle's good graces."

For a moment, neither of them said anything. They didn't have to. Both of them knew what kind of man Anthony had been—greedy, ruthless, and arrogant. And now, it seemed, he'd also been a criminal.

Natalie glanced up, wary. "All of this explains why Anthony would have gotten involved with a man like Russo, and why he would have hidden the diamonds that could have been used for evidence. But what you haven't told me is what happened to those diamonds.''

''I was hoping you could tell me.''

She'd been in the process of getting up, but that stopped her cold. She looked at him in shock. ''You can't still think *I* have them.''

''We're almost certain Anthony planted those diamonds in the package he had you deliver. The diamonds were missing when the package arrived a few hours later. We know for a fact the courier went straight from your shop to the delivery address. Unless he somehow managed to unwrap the package, find the diamonds and remove them, then rewrap the box while he was driving, we can pretty much rule him out. That leaves a very small window of opportunity. The diamonds had to have been taken while they were still in your possession.''

Their gazes held for the longest moment, and Natalie's heart sank at the suspicion she saw glittering in his eyes. How could he? How could he think she took those diamonds? How could he think her capable of something that devious?

And yet, just a few days ago, hadn't he thought her capable of murder? Put in that context, he probably thought stealing a few diamonds was child's play for her.

Obviously, he'd never known the first thing about her. To think she'd once let him make love to her. To think she'd let him kiss her only a few hours ago. And that, just a few minutes ago, she was wishing he would do it again.

''How could you think that about *me?*'' she whispered, feeling the sting of tears threaten behind her lids.

Something flashed in his eyes, a brief emotion that Natalie wanted to believe was regret, but then his gaze hardened in resolve before he glanced away. ''I don't know what happened to those diamonds, Natalie, but it's my job to find out. I can't afford to overlook any possibility, dismiss any scenario just because it might be something I don't want to believe. Too much is at stake to let personal feelings get in the way.''

''You're right,'' she said, lifting her chin. She got up and moved away from the table, putting distance between them. ''Too much *is* at stake, and I have to look out for myself. So I'm sure you'll understand when I tell you to get out of my house. And don't come back.''

''Natalie—'' Spence stood, too. The two of them faced each other, and suddenly Natalie's fragile self-control deserted her.

''How dare you?'' she cried. ''How dare you pretend to help me when all you wanted was to find out where those stupid diamonds are? That's why you bailed me out of jail, isn't it? *Isn't* it?''

''I bailed you out of jail because you didn't belong in there.''

''Why?'' she demanded. ''Because behind bars, I wouldn't be of any use to you? Because I couldn't lead you to the diamonds? Oh, I can't believe I ever trusted you, for even one second.'' She tore her hands through her hair as she spun away from him. ''I should have known better! You're a Bishop. You're all just alike. You don't care who you use. All you care about is getting what you want!'' She jerked around to face him again, only to find that his own eyes were blazing back at her.

''Are you finished?''

''No. I've got one more thing to say to you. Get out!''

He grabbed her arms and held her, although Natalie didn't try to run. ''I can't do that. The police will be here any minute, and they'll want an explanation for all this. Are you prepared to give them one?''

"I'll simply tell them the truth."

"And look where that got you last time," he reminded her. "Like it or not, you need me. I'm the only one who can help you out of this mess."

"*Help* me? You almost got me *killed.* If you bailed me out of jail so that I could lead you to the diamonds, don't you think Russo thought the same thing? I'm sure that's why I got that threat today."

"What threat?" Spence glared down at her. His hands tightened on her arms.

"Someone called me and said that I had something of his, and he wanted them back. He said he knew where I lived and worked, and where my son was at that moment. He told me to cooperate and no one else had to get hurt."

"Why didn't you tell me about this?"

"Because I had a few other things on my mind," Natalie retorted. "Like your mother threatening to take my son away from me. And then after the accident, after I started thinking about Irene's threat, I didn't think I could trust you...because you were on her side."

"I never said I was on her side," Spence said quietly.

Something in his tone made Natalie's heart start to hammer all over again, but not in fear this time, not in anger.

He'd always had that ability, she thought weakly. Even from the first, when she hadn't known him very well and then later, when she had, he'd always been able to make her want to believe in him.

"You have to trust me, Natalie."

"How can I trust you? You think I'm a thief and a murderer."

"No, I don't."

"But you just said—"

"I said I can't afford to overlook any possibility, regardless of what I might be feeling...for you." His gaze intensified, and Natalie's breath clogged her throat. "You have to trust me. You don't have a choice. You have to let me help you."

"Help yourself, don't you mean?" But her voice had lost some of its resistance. "How can this be happening to me?" she whispered. To her horror, Natalie felt a tear spill over and course down her cheek. She didn't want to cry in front of Spence. She didn't want him to see her weakness; to know that no matter what kind of front she put up, deep down, she was still that same lonely, vulnerable girl he'd once made fall in love with him. And he still had the power to hurt her.

His hands slid up her arms to cradle her face. He thumbed away her tear as he stared deeply into her eyes, and Natalie's heart went wild, despite her mind's objection.

For a moment, time seemed to stop, as they gazed into each other's eyes. Natalie's emotions were at war with her sanity. What sort of hold did this man have over her?

"The police will be here any minute," he whispered, as he rested his forehead against hers.

Dimly, Natalie heard the sirens, still in the distance. But the beating of her heart, the pounding of her blood was so much louder, so much more urgent. She closed her eyes, reveling in the feel of Spence's body so close to hers. Never had she felt so near the edge, and yet, oddly, so protected.

Spence's hand feathered through her hair as his chest lifted in a deep sigh. Natalie thought she knew exactly what he was thinking. What he was feeling. It was strange, in a way. She had once been madly in love with him. He was the first man who'd ever made love to her. And yet now, after all the bitter tears and angry accusations, all the hopeless mistakes and shattered dreams, she had never felt closer to him than she did at this moment.

She drew away and stared up at him, not trusting herself to speak.

"Natalie—" The sirens screamed just outside the house. "Damn." His hands grasped her forearms as he said urgently, "Listen. We have to get our stories straight before they get in here."

"Stories...straight?" Still dazed, Natalie could only look at him in confusion. "What do you mean?"

"The police don't know anything about the diamonds."

"But...we have to tell them. Those diamonds give someone else a motive for Anthony's murder. Like Jack Russo."

He let his hands drop from her arms. "I know, but we can't pin anything on Russo. Without those diamonds, he'll walk again."

"So...you're willing to sacrifice me to catch him?" Natalie couldn't believe what she was hearing. Couldn't believe that just moments ago, she'd been almost ready to start trusting him. "You can't expect me to go along with that."

"Natalie, listen to me." He reached for her again, but she jerked away from him. "In the eyes of the police, this won't change anything. You're still their number-one suspect. Until those diamonds are recovered—"

"Until those diamonds are recovered, you're perfectly willing to have everyone believe I killed Anthony."

"We don't even know for sure Russo killed Anthony."

"But you think he did."

"I think there's an excellent chance of that, yes."

"Then why not tell the police?"

"Because if Russo knows we're on to him, he'll disappear, without the diamonds. And a cold-blooded murderer will go free. Is that what you want, Natalie?''

''And what do *you* want?'' she demanded. ''Your man, at any cost? What if Kyle and I had been home tonight, Spence? What would have happened to us? Have you thought about that?''

Spence had been thinking of little else ever since he'd walked into Natalie's house and seen the destruction. But when he'd bailed her out of jail, he'd been so sure he could protect her. He hadn't thought Russo would make a move so soon, not until the heat died down over Anthony's murder. But obviously he'd been wrong, and he couldn't afford to make another mistake like that. Not where Natalie and Kyle were concerned.

He wanted to tell her not to worry. That she could trust him; that he would never do anything to harm her or her son. But why should she believe him? Anthony had done a real number on her, and now their mother was threatening to take Kyle away. No wonder Natalie didn't trust any of the Bishops. Spence couldn't blame her, because he didn't trust his family, either.

They stood in the middle of the kitchen floor, eyeing each other warily as car doors slammed outside and the police swarmed into the house.

''Without those diamonds, we don't have anything on Russo,'' Spence whispered. ''If he gets wind of our surveillance, he'll run. But the police will still need someone to pin Anthony's murder on.''

''And that someone is me, isn't it?'' Natalie whispered back, feeling the crushing weight of defeat bearing down on her shoulders.

Spence didn't answer, but his eyes—those Bishop eyes—said it all.

Chapter Ten

The first thing Natalie did when she got back to the hospital was go straight to Kyle's bedside and stare down at him, sending up a prayer of thanks that he was all right.

Her mother was dozing in the chair by the window, and Natalie was careful not to wake her. For once, even her mother's presence couldn't soothe the churning emotions inside her.

First, Spence had kissed her tonight. Then she had gone home to find her house all but destroyed; learned that her son was the sole heir to the Bishop fortune, and that Spencer Bishop had used her once again. Used her to get what he wanted.

He had deliberately put her and her son in danger in an attempt to recover stolen diamonds. For that, Natalie didn't think she could ever forgive him. Especially after she had begun to have a glimmer of hope that she could trust him.

In some ways, Natalie had never felt so betrayed. She hadn't even wanted him to drive her back to the hospital, but after the police had left her house, she'd had little choice, other than call a cab, and she was too anxious to get back to Kyle to wait around for that. So she'd allowed Spence to drive her back here, but the moment he'd walked her to Kyle's room, she'd sent him away.

He'd wanted to come in. Natalie had known that, but by then she'd had enough for one night. Even the argument she'd overheard between him and Sergeant Phillips, who had already been irate for having been called out in the middle of the night, had done nothing to restore her faith in Spence.

If anything, it had only made her feel worse—because he'd been right. The break-in hadn't changed anything. Sergeant Phillips still didn't believe her. He'd looked around at the devastation to her home, then looked at her as if to say, *this doesn't prove anything*.

The phone beside the bed rang, and Natalie reached out to jerk it up before the second ring. Kyle stirred in his sleep, and her mother shifted position in the chair, but neither of them awakened.

It was so late, Natalie couldn't imagine who would be calling. She brought the receiver to her ear and said very softly, "Hello?"

"You got real lucky tonight, lady."

Natalie recognized the gruff voice instantly. It was the same man who had called her at home earlier. The man she now suspected was Jack Russo. Her heart slammed into her chest. "Who is this?"

"I told you before, it doesn't matter who I am. What matters is that you still have what's mine."

"I—I don't know what you're talking about."

"You know exactly what I'm talking about."

Natalie's hand shook so hard she could barely grip the telephone. She remembered what Spence had said earlier, that if Russo knew he was being watched, he would skip town. Somehow she managed to process this information and keep her voice relatively steady as she said, "I don't know who you are or what you want. Why don't you just leave me alone?"

There was a long silence. In a deceptively soft voice, the man said, "How's the boy?"

And then the significance of Russo—if that's who he was—calling Kyle's hospital room hit her. He'd known Kyle was here, just as he'd somehow managed to get her unlisted number. He knew everything about them.

The power of the moment was paralyzing. Natalie had never dealt with anyone like him before. A cold-blooded murderer who had killed once for those diamonds. Who was to say he wouldn't do so again?

"Sorry the kid had to get hurt," the man said, "but I get a little irritated when somebody has something of mine and won't give it back."

"Please," she whispered. "I don't have what you want."

"Then you better find them." The affable note in his voice had vanished, was replaced by an edge as keen as a knife blade. "Because a few scrapes and bruises are nothing compared to what could happen to that kid if you refuse to cooperate. You understand what I'm saying?"

"Yes," she whispered, gripping the phone.

"Good. I'll be in touch and arrange for the drop. I don't think I need to remind you that this little business is just between you and me. The police wouldn't believe you anyway, but they could become a nuisance and then I might really get pissed off."

The line clicked, then went dead. With shaking hands, Natalie hung up the phone. She gazed down at Kyle as her heart hammered in her throat. Dear God, what was she going to do?

She ran the back of her index finger down the side of Kyle's soft cheek. He looked so sweet, lying there. So very defenseless. And her blood froze at the thought of his being in danger. She had to find a way to protect him.

Against Russo, against Irene, and maybe even against Spence.

She couldn't let anything else happen to Kyle. Somehow, she had to remove him from harm's way.

No matter what happened to her, she had to find a way to protect her son at any cost.

At *any* cost.

BY THE TIME SPENCE pulled into the circular drive of his family's mansion, the clock on his dash read four minutes past midnight, but he knew his mother would still be up. She always kept late hours, and he didn't want to wait until morning to say what he had to say to her.

If Irene thought that he would back her in a custody suit against Natalie, she'd better think again. He might not be able to do much about the Russo situation just yet, but he sure as hell could alleviate Natalie's fears where his mother was concerned.

The boy belonged with Natalie. That point had been brought home earlier at the hospital, when he'd watched the two of them together. There was no doubt in Spence's mind how much Natalie loved her son, and it gave him cold chills to think about Kyle being taken away from that love and put in this cold, dreary, lifeless house, to be raised by a cold, dreary, lifeless woman who didn't know the first thing about love.

Oh, Irene had adored Anthony. He'd been her idea of the perfect son—handsome, popular, charismatic. But love? No. Not even Anthony had won Irene's love, because she simply wasn't capable of giving it.

Using the key his mother had given him two days ago when she'd asked him to move back home, Spence let himself in. Almost immediately the butler appeared in the foyer, apparently undaunted by Spence's appearance so late at night.

"Hello, Williams. Is Mother still up?"

"She's retired for the evening, sir."

"How about Anthea?"

"I believe she's still at the office."

"This late?"

"Yes, sir."

"Mind if I wait for her?"

"As you wish. May I get you something to drink?"

"No, thanks. I'll help myself."

Williams nodded curtly, then turned on his heel and disappeared down the hallway. Spence walked into the library and headed for the bar. The night was mild, but the breeze blowing in through the open French doors was distinctly chilly. He crossed the room to close the doors when a sound from outside stopped him.

The French doors opened onto a wide terrace with stone steps that led down to the swimming pool. The pool lights were off, but the moon glimmered in silvery ripples across the surface. The sound came to him again—soft, feminine laughter.

He stepped through the doors onto the terrace. The breeze carried the murmur of voices and the lapping of water against the sides of the pool as he stood there listening to the darkness. Someone was obviously out for a late-night swim.

More whispers, more soft laughter, then silence.

Spence started to go back inside, when a man's voice— low and urgent—said, "When can I see you again?"

He couldn't hear the woman's response, but the man's voice rose angrily. "Don't play games with me! Not after everything I've done for you."

Silence reigned again, during which time Spence assumed the man's anger was somehow being appeased. Then a male figure, tall and muscular, hitched himself from the pool, grabbed a towel from one of the lounges, and took off toward the back of the house.

Spence frowned, not liking the idea of a stranger roaming the grounds. He started to follow the man, but a movement in the pool caught his attention, and for a moment, he watched the slender figure in the moonlight as she cut gracefully through the water. When she turned and came back, Spence was standing at the pool's edge.

Melinda's gaze darted to each side, no doubt wondering if her companion had made a clean getaway. Obviously deciding that he had, she turned back to Spence with a coy smile.

"Well, well," she said. "What brings you calling this time of night?"

"I couldn't sleep."

Her elegant eyebrows rose. "Maybe you're too tense, Spencer. A midnight swim could do wonders for you." She laughed again as she slicked back her red hair with one slim hand. The action lifted her bare breasts out of the water, but she either didn't notice or didn't care. Judging by her demure smile, Spence decided it was probably the latter.

"Come on in," she invited. "The water's great."

"It's the middle of winter, in case you hadn't noticed."

"It's a warm night, in case *you* hadn't noticed, and besides, the pool's heated."

"I'm not in the mood for a swim."

Her voice lowered seductively. "What *are* you in the mood for?"

"I want to talk to you."

Melinda shrugged her shapely shoulders. "Well, if you

won't come in, then I guess I'll just have to come out, won't I?''

She stood, and in the moonlight, water ran off her smooth, bare skin like liquid glass. Her long red hair clung to her shoulders in damp clusters, and she slung her head so that the dark tresses hung in ringlets down her back.

Walking deliberately past Spence, she picked up another towel from the lounge and took her time as she blotted herself dry. Then she wrapped the towel around her body and knotted it just above her full breasts as she turned to find Spence watching her.

She smiled knowingly as she picked up a glass from the table beside the lounge and lifted it to her lips. Moonlight sparked off the cut crystal like sunlight on diamonds.

''Who was he?'' Spence asked.

''Ah. So you did see.'' She took a deep drink from the glass. ''It was nothing,'' she said, coming to stand very close to him. ''A harmless little dalliance. But I suppose you're going to run straight to Mommy Dearest, aren't you?''

Spence could smell Scotch on her breath. ''I don't like the idea of strange men roaming around this house at all hours. You should know better than to bring somebody here.''

She reached out and traced a scarlet nail down the front of his jacket. ''I didn't bring him here. He lives on the grounds. He's the gardener's son.''

''Johnny?''

''He likes to be called John now.''

Spence had a vague recollection of a scrawny little boy with a gap-toothed smile helping his father weed the flower beds. A mercenary kid, all too willing to desert his post for more lucrative endeavors, like washing Spence's car.

Hardly the image of the muscular man who had climbed out of the pool—and Melinda's arms—a few minutes ago.

"Your grief is touching," Spence said in disgust.

The smile vanished from Melinda's face. She lifted her chin so that he could see the sudden shimmer of tears in her eyes. "I am grieving," she whispered. "But we all have different ways of coping."

"So I heard a few minutes ago."

She at least had the grace to look embarrassed, but only momentarily. Turning, she walked back to the lounge and sat down, crossing her legs in a way that left very little to the imagination. But then, Spence didn't have to imagine. He'd already seen, and the view hadn't moved him. Melinda was a beautiful woman, but she wasn't his type.

She wasn't Natalie.

"No matter what you think about me," Melinda said, her lips quivering in distress, "I loved Anthony. He was my whole world."

"Then you must have been devastated when he told you he wanted a divorce."

Her mouth literally dropped open. A dozen emotions flashed across her face until, after several painful seconds, she seemed to get them all under control. She gave him an outraged glance. "Where in the world did you get an idea like that?"

"Is it true?"

"Of course not! Anthony loved me. We were planning a family together. He wanted children with me. A son by *me*."

"You were married for six years," Spence observed. "Why wait so long?"

"We saw no hurry. After all, we thought we had years and years ahead of us. How could we have known—" She broke off, and with some effort, squeezed a tear from one eye. With a flourish, she wiped it away with the back of her hand. "How could we have known that woman would destroy everything? She was always so jealous of me. She couldn't stand it that Anthony wanted *me,* that he chose *me* over her. She killed him because she couldn't have him."

With an effort, Spence kept his expression even. "Natalie and Anthony have been divorced for years," he said.

"That didn't matter to her! Anthony told me that she was always coming on to him, begging him to take her back. Her and her…son." She made the last word sound like an unpleasantness that was beyond bearable.

An image of Kyle came to Spence now—the dark, unruly hair, the deep green eyes, and the quick smile that always seemed to have a hint of mischief lurking at the corners.

How could Anthony have ignored Kyle for so long, and then decided, for whatever reason Spence could only guess, that it was time he had custody regardless of how his actions would affect the boy?

Because Anthony had been a ruthless, greedy man. A Bishop. And after tonight, Spence had to wonder if he was really any better. He'd deliberately set out to use Natalie for his own agenda, and regardless of what he'd tried to tell himself over the years, the end did not always justify the means. He'd put her and Kyle's lives in danger, and Spence knew he would have a hard time ever justifying that.

And so would Natalie.

"I don't believe she killed Anthony," he said quietly.

Melinda gasped. "What? Of course, she killed him! Look at the evidence."

"There were no eyewitnesses."

"But she was found kneeling over the body with the murder weapon in her hand. His blood was all over her."

"She was knocked unconscious. When she came to, she tried to see about Anthony, not even realizing the knife had been placed in her hand."

"Oh, please. That's what *she* says."

"I'm inclined to believe her. How else do you explain her workroom being ransacked?"

"She and Anthony struggled. Or, more likely, she did it herself after she killed him, to make herself look like the victim."

"That's what the police seem to think," Spence admitted. "But it all seems just a little too perfect to me. Like someone planned it all out."

"Someone did. *She* did." Melinda's full lips drew together in a practiced pout as she stared up at him. "What is the matter with you, Spencer? Where's your loyalty to this family?"

That was rich, coming from her. But Spence let it pass, saying instead, "My loyalty belongs with the truth, and I'm beginning to think there might have been someone else who stood to gain more from Anthony's death than Natalie Silver."

Someone who was about to be divorced and cut off without a penny.

Spence didn't say the words, but they hung in the air between them. Melinda's gaze faltered and she turned away, but not before he saw the outrage in her eyes turn to fear. He'd gotten what he came for, Spence thought, turning and walking back toward the house. He didn't need to wait for Anthea after all.

"I CAN'T BELIEVE YOU'RE coming back to work today," Blanche said, reaching over to squeeze Natalie's hand.

They were having a morning cup of coffee at one of the riverside tables at Delmontico's. "It hasn't been the same without you. Every time I saw that police tape—" She broke off, closing her eyes briefly.

Natalie nodded. "I know. Believe me, I'm not looking forward to going back in there, but the police have given their okay, and I can't delay any longer. I've lost too much business, as it is. I've been afraid to even try to calculate the damage." She'd been afraid of so many things lately, especially the threat she'd gotten from Russo last night. He'd said he would be in touch to arrange the drop, but what would he do when she couldn't produce the diamonds?

Natalie shuddered, thinking about Kyle. He was safe, she told herself, tucked away in her parents' house. Her father had recently installed a state-of-the-art security system, and the neighborhood was regularly patrolled by the police.

He was safe for now, but in the meantime, she'd already begun to make arrangements for her parents and son to leave town. Just in case.

For a moment, Natalie toyed with the idea of confessing all to Blanche. She needed someone to talk to, and for some reason that she couldn't—or didn't want to—understand, she'd done as Spence had asked. She hadn't told the police about Russo and the diamonds, mainly because she didn't think they would believe her—not without Spence backing her up. And he'd made it clear his main objective was nailing Russo.

She sighed deeply, feeling the weight of the world on her shoulders this morning.

"Well," Blanche was saying, "you know I'll help you in any way I can."

Natalie smiled. "You've been a good friend."

Such a good friend that Natalie knew when something was wrong. As wrapped up as she was in her own problems, she could still tell that Blanche wasn't herself. Her complexion looked pale and sickly, and her brown eyes— usually so vibrant—were dull and listless. She looked as if she hadn't slept in days. Even her attire—always a point of pride with Blanche—was drab and unflattering, the baggy, dark green sweater she wore making the shadows beneath her eyes even more pronounced.

"Blanche, is something wrong?" Natalie asked carefully.

"I've been worried sick about you," Blanche said over the rim of her coffee cup.

"I know, but…is there something else? You look so… You don't look yourself."

Blanche smiled ruefully. "I look like hell. Be honest."

"What's wrong?" Natalie asked in concern.

"It's nothing, really. Not compared to your problems." Blanche set down her cup and stared at the dark brew swirling inside.

"It's him, isn't it?"

Blanche looked up, startled. "Him?"

"That man you've being seeing. He's married, isn't he?"

Blanche looked as if she was about to deny it, then she shrugged. "It doesn't matter now, anyway."

"Why? He didn't…leave you, did he?"

Blanche's gaze darted away. "You might say that."

"Oh, Blanche. I was afraid something like this would happen. And right before Christmas. I'm so sorry."

"No sorrier than I am."

Natalie leaned toward her and patted the back of Blanche's hand. "He isn't worth it, you know. He isn't worth letting it get to you like this."

Blanche took a deep breath, her eyes on a blackbird that had come to feed on bread crumbs at the river's edge. "I know he wasn't worth it. I've told myself that a hundred times. But it still hurts."

"What are you going to do?" Natalie asked.

"What can I do? Life goes on, doesn't it?" She paused, then said, "What are you going to do?"

"What do you mean?"

"What's the latest word on your case?"

Natalie sat back in her chair and stared glumly at the river. "I talked to my lawyer this morning. The police aren't dropping the charges against me." She'd had some hope that they might after last night, but her attorney had said the D.A. was adamant. A grand jury would have to decide whether or not the evidence against her was sufficient to warrant a trial.

"Meanwhile, like you, I have to get on with my life. And that means reopening the shop."

"How's Kyle taking all this?"

"He's…incredible." Natalie forced a smile and told Blanche about her son threatening to punch Irene Bishop in the nose for thinking his mother was guilty.

For the first time that morning, Blanche laughed. Her mood seemed to lighten a little as they talked about Kyle, but then sobered again when she said, "You don't really think Irene means to take Kyle away from you, do you?"

Natalie shivered in the bright sunlight, thinking about Irene Bishop and her threats, and the revelations Spence had made last night. Just where did Kyle's inheritance fit into Irene's plans?

There was no way Natalie would ever let Irene get her hands on Kyle. Even if it meant making a few revelations of her own. But would that help? Or would it create even more problems? A whole different set of concerns. And threats.

"If she tries," Natalie said, "I'll fight her. There's no way I'll ever let her take Kyle. No matter what I have to do to stop her."

Blanche's eyes looked worried as she gazed at Natalie in distress. "I remember you saying almost exactly the same thing about Anthony. And a few hours later, he turned up dead."

"SHE DIDN'T DO IT."

"The evidence says she did," Sergeant Phillips growled as he shoved a file into his drawer and slammed it shut. "Besides, it's out of my hands. The D.A. thinks there's sufficient evidence to prosecute."

"You could still intervene and you know it," Spence insisted.

Sergeant Phillips shook his head. "That isn't the way it works, and *you* know it. What is it about this broad that has you so worked up, anyway? For an ex-sister-in-law, she certainly seems to have made an impression on you."

Spence ran an annoyed hand through his hair. "Look, I've told you the facts of the case as I know them. I've told you more than I should have."

"Yeah, well, you're a day late and a dollar short as far as I'm concerned. I really don't appreciate the feds waltzing in here and laying claim to one of my cases."

"I'm not doing that. I'm giving you what I know in order to help in your investigation."

Phillips's pale eyes studied him suspiciously. "And what do you want in return? Because if you want the charges dropped against Natalie Silver—"

Spence shook his head. He'd given up on that. "I want

you to keep an open mind. I want you to investigate the leads I've given you.''

Sergeant Phillips looked down at the paper on his desk. "Interesting list. What about Russo?''

"He's mine.''

"Figures.'' Phillips glanced up. His pale eyes met Spence's and he shook his head. "You are one crazy son of a bitch, you know that? I'd bet my pension that woman's guilty.''

"I'm sure you would.'' Spence rose and planted his hands on the sergeant's desk. "And that's exactly the kind of mind-set that worries me.''

BEFORE SPENCE LEFT the area, he went by the local FBI office to pick up a fax he'd received from headquarters. He opened the folder and studied the dossier inside.

The man in the grainy but recognizable photo had gotten out of Joliet Federal Penitentiary six years ago, after having served ten years for manslaughter. Before that, he had been sent up on federal racketeering charges, and before that, for grand larceny. He had been in and out of prison for the better part of his adult life, and had known ties to the mob, in both Dallas and San Antonio.

Spence studied the picture of Frank Delmontico and smiled in satisfaction. He never forgot a face.

"Gotcha,'' he muttered.

NATALIE UNLOCKED THE front door of Silver Bells and started to step inside, but someone called her name, and she turned to see Frank Delmontico climbing the stairs to the second-story landing.

He was dressed all in black today—black tailored pants and a black silk shirt open at the neck. Two young men—

presumably busboys, since they wore stained white aprons over their clothes—followed him up the stairs.

Natalie paused, not understanding why Frank had taken such a sudden interest in her. Since the murder, almost everyone else couldn't distance themselves fast enough from her, but Frank Delmontico chose this particular time to befriend her. Strange, to say the least.

"You're opening your shop today." It was a statement not a question, as if he'd already known she would be here.

Natalie nodded. "The police have given their okay. I guess they've done everything they need to do."

Frank paused for a moment, then said, "Have you been inside since the murder?"

He didn't stumble or look away when he said "murder." In a way, his bluntness was something of a relief. Natalie shook her head. "No. This is the first time."

"Then no one's been in to clean up."

At first Natalie thought he was talking about the broken glass and debris in her office, but then she realized he meant the blood. Her stomach took a sickening jolt at the crimson memory of that night.

"That isn't something a woman should have to do," Frank said.

Natalie's mind was only half on what he was saying. "What isn't?"

"The cleanup. My boys will do it for you." With a jerk of his wrist, he summoned the two young men and they stepped forward, eager to take charge.

Natalie was touched, but at the same time, she didn't quite know what to think. "Why…why would you do this for me? You don't even really know me."

Frank shrugged. "It isn't something a woman should have to do," he repeated, as if that were explanation enough. "My boys are trustworthy. You don't have to worry about that."

"I'm not." But Natalie realized that on the fringes of her mind, she had been. Perhaps everything she'd been through had jaded her, made her too ready to distrust someone's motives. She didn't like that about herself. It was too...Bishop-like.

She forced herself to smile gratefully. "Okay. I accept your offer. Thank you."

Frank smiled, too. "Don't you worry. My boys will take care of everything."

AND THEY DID. Two hours later Natalie stood in her office and gazed around. The glass and debris had been swept away, the books and packaging returned to the shelves, and the contents of her desk drawers neatly stacked on her desk. The only thing to remind her of that awful night was the dark water stain on the carpet where they had scrubbed away the blood.

As she stared at the stain, the horror of that night came rushing back to her. She'd tried to forget, but there was no way she ever would. The moment she'd opened her eyes and turned her head to see Anthony lying on the floor beside her, his blood covering them both...

She put her hands to her eyes, trying to block the images. Her cheeks were wet with tears, and she rubbed her fingertips across them.

"So it's true," someone said behind her. "The murderer always returns to the scene of the crime."

Natalie spun at that voice. Anthea stood in the doorway, clad in a dark pin-striped suit with a double-breasted jacket and man-tailored slacks. She wore loafers, carried a briefcase, and her short, dark hair was heavily gelled and combed straight back from her unmade-up face.

Caught off guard, Natalie stared at her for a moment, realizing she'd forgotten how tall Anthea was. Almost as tall as Anthony had been. In fact, she looked very much like her twin brother today. The resemblance was... startling.

Seemingly unaware of the effect her appearance had on Natalie, Anthea walked into the office, then stopped short, her gaze dropping to the water stain on the floor. As if in fascination, she studied it for a long moment before lifting her green eyes to meet Natalie's. "Do you really think a little water will wash away what you've done?"

"What do you want, Anthea?" Natalie asked wearily, in no mood to proclaim her innocence yet again.

Anthea's gaze darted to the floor, then lifted. "I'm here to offer you a deal."

Natalie was immediately suspicious. "What kind of deal?"

Anthea plopped her briefcase on the desk and snapped open the locks. She lifted the lid to reveal neat stacks of twenty-dollar bills.

"Two hundred and fifty thousand dollars. A quarter of a million. How long would it take you to make that kind of money here?"

Considering what the publicity surrounding Anthony's murder and her arrest would do to her business, Natalie didn't even want to speculate.

"It's yours," Anthea said. "All you have to do is strike a bargain with me."

Natalie had a feeling that would be like bargaining with the devil, and that the ultimate price might very well be her soul. "I don't make bargains," she said, remembering the one she had struck with Anthony and what it had cost her.

"I think you might want to change your mind." Anthea's gaze was as hard as concrete. "I want you to take this money and get out of town. Leave the country. Take your son and don't either one of you ever come back."

"Why?" Natalie demanded. "If you think I'm guilty, why help me leave town?"

Anthea shrugged. "Because it would be easier that way. You would be out of our lives for good, and Mother wouldn't have to go through the torment of a trial, hearing the gruesome details of Anthony's death, facing reporters and their endless questions day in and day out. I don't want her to go through that."

"If I run, I'll look guilty," Natalie said.

"And if you don't, I'll make your life a living hell. I'll personally see to it that you're put away for life. And Mother will get Kyle. Anthony's precious son."

Something in her tone sent a cold chill up Natalie's spine. The way she looked when she talked about Kyle. The flash of hate that filled her eyes. The barest hint of rage that colored her voice.

For a moment, Natalie stared at the money. A quarter of a million dollars would solve a lot of her problems. She and Kyle could simply disappear, get away from the danger that faced them here. They could go someplace where Russo—and the Bishops—would never be able to find them.

But running never solved anything, and Natalie knew that by taking Anthea's money, she would only be making her situation worse. She would never be free of the Bishops, no matter how far and how fast she ran. Because every time she looked into her son's eyes, they would be there, mocking her from those green depths.

Her hands were shaking as she reached over and slammed the briefcase shut. "Take your filthy money and get out of here, Anthea. And don't *ever* let me catch you near my son. Do you understand me?''

One thick eyebrow rose in mock disdain. ''Oh, I understand you, Natalie. Better than you think.'' She snapped closed the locks on the briefcase. ''You're making a big mistake. This is the only Bishop money you or your son will ever get your hands on.''

''I don't want your money. Any of it. I just want your family to leave Kyle and me alone.''

The eyebrow arched again. ''Does that include Spencer?'' When Natalie refused to answer, Anthea smiled coolly. ''I thought not.''

She jerked up the briefcase and turned toward the door, very deliberately striding across the dark stain in the middle of the floor.

Chapter Eleven

Christmas music played softly from overhead speakers, and the tiny white lights on the Christmas tree glowed in the gloom of late afternoon. Natalie busied herself checking stock. There was a lot to do, and she tried to tell herself it was a good thing she'd had so few customers that afternoon.

But who was she trying to kid? The holiday season was a complete disaster, and with only a few more days until Christmas, there wasn't much hope of salvaging it. The shop should have been a hub of frenzied activity, but only two people—an elderly couple shopping for their granddaughter—had stopped in.

It was just after six and the three hours until closing loomed before Natalie like miles and miles of bad road. In the deep silence of the store, with only the recorded Christmas carols to buoy her spirits, she found it difficult not to dwell on her problems. Suddenly, it all seemed too much. Natalie dropped her head in her hands, not wanting to give in to the despair, but somehow no longer feeling able to fight it.

When the bells over the door pealed, she hastily wiped her face with the back of her hand, and plastered on a smile as she walked around the counter to greet her customer. The smile slid from her face as she saw who stood inside her doorway.

"This must be my lucky day," she said, hoping the telltale traces of tears had been wiped clean from her face. She lifted her chin and glared at Spence. "First Anthea, and now you."

But in spite of her bravado, she couldn't help the tiny thrill of nerves that coursed down her spine at the sight of him. He wore jeans, faded and snug, and a dark collarless shirt that did interesting things to his eyes. His face was shadowed with just the barest hint of beard, making him look a little too dangerous in the deserted confines of her shop.

He looked at her in surprise. "Anthea was here? What did she want?"

"She offered me a bribe to leave town. A quarter of a million dollars."

"Damn," Spence muttered. "What the hell is she up to?"

"I don't know and I don't care," Natalie said. "I just want her—and the rest of your family—to leave me alone. And that includes you."

Something flashed in his eyes. Something dark and... deadly. "I can't do that, Natalie. Like it or not, we're in this together and we need to talk." Slowly he walked toward her.

She had to fight the urge to retreat, not because she thought he would physically harm her, but because she didn't quite trust herself in his presence. The memory of his kiss—and what it had done to her—was still too fresh.

"About what?" She forced her tone to remain wary. "Didn't you say enough last night? I did what you asked me. I didn't tell the police about Russo, and now, because of that, I may have to send my son into hiding."

"What do you mean?"

"I mean Russo is still threatening me. He called me at the hospital last night after you dropped me off. At least, I'm assuming it was Russo. Naturally, he didn't identify himself. He implied the car accident yesterday was a warning, and that if I didn't cooperate, something worse would happen. He said he would be in touch to arrange the drop, and that if I went to the police—" She broke off, shuddering at the memory of Russo's threat.

"What else did he say?" Spence asked, his voice hard.

"Nothing. But what happens when he calls to arrange the drop?" Natalie asked desperately. "What happens when I can't produce the diamonds? Because no matter what you or anyone else thinks, I don't have them."

Spence came to stand directly in front of her, staring down at her. "I know you don't. But I had to make sure."

"If that's supposed to make me feel better, it doesn't." She turned away, fiddling with a price tag on a blue and silver wreath as she tried to pretend his nearness had no effect on her. There could be any number of reasons for her shortness of breath, the hammering of her heart.

"I'm sorry you had to get dragged into all this."

Natalie could feel his warm breath on the back of her neck, and she was afraid to move an inch, afraid to turn her head and discover just how close he was.

"I never meant for you and Kyle to be put in any danger."

She did turn then, slowly, her gaze lifting to his. "Kyle is my whole world. If anything happens to him, I will never forgive you."

The bleakness in her eyes took Spence's breath away. She stood only to his shoulder. She seemed so small and fragile at that moment—so very vulnerable. And yet he sensed an inner strength, a steely determination to protect her son at any cost.

His mother didn't know it yet, but she was up against a formidable opponent, he thought, not without some pride.

Natalie's straight brown hair fell softly against the sides of her face, and with an effort, he restrained himself from reaching out to tuck a loose strand behind her ear. She wore a short gray skirt that showed off her slender legs, and a dark blue sweater that deepened the blue of her eyes behind her glasses. In spite of the obvious weariness in her face, Spence thought that she had never looked more beautiful. More desirable.

Memories of the kiss they had shared last night flashed through him, and he found himself wanting to kiss her again. And again.

With an effort, he shook off those forbidden urges. Now was not the time, and besides, he had the distinct impression Natalie just might slap his face if he tried to kiss her today. After last night, he could hardly blame her.

"I want to talk about that window of opportunity we discussed last night. If we can find those diamonds, all our problems will be solved." He deliberately moved away from her. He wanted to think the flicker of emotion in her eyes was disappointment, but he knew better. He'd seen Natalie's anger too many times in the past few days to mistake it for anything else.

"Who else had access to that package before the courier picked it up that day?" he asked.

"No one. I boxed it up myself."

"Are you sure? Think hard. A lot's happened since then. Something may have slipped your mind."

Natalie sighed, wanting to object to his demands on

principle, but knowing her cooperation was too important. Her life depended on it, and so might Kyle's.

She began to pace back and forth as she thought out loud. "Anthony came in around four o'clock. He was supposed to take Kyle to a Spurs game that night, so I thought that was why he was here, even though Kyle wasn't home from school yet. He was late because he was in a race after school that day. Anyway, Anthony said he wanted to do some shopping for the mother of one of his clients. He said…his client had been away for a long time."

"Yeah, in Joliet," Spence said dryly.

"He looked around for a long time. Finally, he asked to see a music box. It was an Étienne—" she started to explain, then waved her hand impatiently. "It had a secret compartment that seemed to particularly appeal to him."

"I'll bet. Go on."

Natalie shrugged. "That's it. He bought the music box."

"Did you ring it up for him immediately?"

Natalie frowned in concentration. "No. Some customers came in and he told me to wait on them first. I thought it was an unusual request for Anthony, but he insisted he wasn't in any hurry. But after the customers left, he acted as if he couldn't wait to get out of here. He didn't even wait for Kyle."

"Can you remember anything special about any of the customers? Did anyone act suspicious, overly nervous, anything like that?"

Natalie shook her head. "I remember it was extremely busy that day." She glanced around her empty shop, thinking ironically how she had lamented being shorthanded that day. If only that was her problem now. "I don't remember anything special about any of them. Nobody caught my attention, not even the FBI agent you sent in," she added with an edge of sarcasm.

Spence refused to rise to the bait. "What did you do with the music box after Anthony left?"

"I took it back to my workroom and put it on my desk. I remember getting down packaging material and a label, and then I called the delivery service to pick it up."

"Did you leave the box in your workroom?"

"I'm pretty sure I did. Kyle came in then, and after that, things got even more hectic. When Michelle—she's the high-school student who works...worked for me part-time during the Christmas season—came in, I asked her to make out the shipping label and get the package ready for the courier."

"So you didn't actually see the music box again?"

Natalie shook her head. "I guess I didn't."

"And then the courier picked it up just before six," Spence said.

"You said last night he didn't have enough time to open the package, find the diamonds, then repack the box before he delivered it. So that just leaves me, doesn't it?" Natalie asked, the despair overcoming her again.

"And this Michelle, you mentioned."

"But she's just a kid," Natalie protested. "I've known her and her parents for ages."

"I still want to talk to her."

Dear God, Natalie thought. When would it end? How many more innocent people had to be dragged into this dirty business before it was resolved? Who else would have to get hurt?

She put her hands to her face. "This is a nightmare," she whispered.

Gently, Spence removed her hands. He held them in his own hands as he gazed down at her. "Just hang on a little while longer," he said. "We'll get to the bottom of all this. I promise you that."

"If it was just me," Natalie said, "I could take it. But Kyle… I can't stand to think of him being in danger. What am I going to do?"

Spence's hands slid up her arms, and before Natalie quite knew how it happened, she was in his embrace. He held her close, and for the first time in a long time, Natalie felt completely safe. She knew it was only an illusion, but that didn't seem to matter at the moment. She laid her head against his shoulder and sighed.

"I won't let anything happen to you or Kyle." His voice was a low rumble in his chest. She could feel his heart beating beneath her hand, and its steady cadence gave her a measure of comfort.

Natalie closed her eyes, wanting to believe him. "You may not be able to stop it. Spence…" Her voice trailed off in a quiver. "I'm so afraid for Kyle. He's staying with my parents because I thought he would be safer away from me. But if Russo found us at the hospital—"

"Kyle's safe, Natalie."

"How can you be so sure?"

"The house is being watched."

She drew back and gazed up at him. "By whom?"

"Some friends of mine."

"Agents?"

Spence nodded. "You can trust them. They're the best in the business. There's no way anyone can get to Kyle."

"But…how did you know he was with my parents?"

"I called the hospital early this morning. Your mother told me you were taking him to their house."

"She wasn't supposed to tell anyone," Natalie said worriedly.

"Maybe she thinks I'm not just anyone."

Their eyes met, and Natalie sensed that something important was happening between them. Something inevitable.

He *wasn't* just anyone, and they both knew it.

She drew a deep, shuddering breath as their gazes held. "Thank you for protecting my son," she whispered.

He touched his fingertips to her face—a butterfly caress that Natalie felt all the way to her soul.

SINCE BUSINESS WAS SLOW—nonexistent, in fact—Natalie closed shop early, and she and Spence drove to her house to have another look around.

"What exactly are we looking for?" she asked, as she let them in and flipped the light switch. Although she knew what to expect, the way her living room had been torn apart still shocked her. She gazed around, trying to suppress her tears.

"I'm not sure," Spence admitted. "I just want to have another look. Something doesn't fit—"

"Like what?"

As if he were a diviner looking for water, Spence slowly walked around the room. "What is it?" he muttered. "What am I missing?"

Watching him, Natalie was struck by the realization of just how far they'd come since he'd walked into that interrogation room a few days ago. Until then, she hadn't seen him in seven years, and she had been filled with distrust, anger, and not a small amount of fear.

Now they were working together to protect her son and clear her of a murder charge. Natalie wasn't sure when she had decided to trust him. She'd had no one else to turn to and he had volunteered for the job. But it was more than that, and she knew it.

What she was feeling for Spencer Bishop was more than gratitude, and she would be a fool not to acknowledge it, to pretend it wasn't there, or that it would somehow go away.

Because it wouldn't. Not in seven years had her feelings for him disappeared. Oh, there was still a residual anger inside her for what he had done to her. For having misled her. For having made love to her when he had been engaged to another woman. For having left her desperate enough to believe in Anthony.

But there were other emotions that remained. The attraction, of course, but that was the least of it. When she thought about the way he had been raised, how he had been shunned by his family—his own mother—Natalie wanted to reach out and draw him into her world. When she glimpsed the bleakness in his eyes, the loneliness in his soul, she wanted to wrap her arms around him and show him what it meant to be loved.

That thought startled her. That she was even contemplating giving her love to Spencer Bishop again was a frightening prospect. He'd hurt her terribly once, and because of that pain, she'd done something that had changed her life forever. Spence's, too, although he didn't know it. What if he found out? What if he somehow learned that—

"Kyle?"

"What? I—I'm sorry," she stammered. "I wasn't listening."

Spence looked at her strangely. "You said Kyle came into the shop that afternoon. Was anyone with him?"

"Oh, that. Blanche picked him up after school and brought him to the shop. Then a little while later, Wendy, his baby-sitter, came by and got him."

"Did any of them have access to the package?"

Natalie frowned. "No. Blanche stayed and talked for a while, but she never went back to the workroom. Neither did Wendy."

"What about Kyle?"

Natalie glanced at him in surprise. "What about him?"

"Was he in the workroom at any time?"

In spite of her previous thoughts, Natalie's hackles rose. "He's just a little boy! You're not suggesting—" Her hand flew to her mouth. She looked up at Spence. "My God," she whispered. "He went back to the workroom to get a present I'd boxed for his teacher."

"In the same kind of box Anthony's music box was in?"

She nodded.

"Same size?"

She swallowed and nodded again.

"What happened to the box he brought home?"

"I assumed he put it under the tree." They both turned and stared at the ravaged presents under her tree. In unison, they crossed the floor and began to scavenge through the opened boxes and ripped paper.

After a few moments, Natalie sat back. "It isn't here."

"What do you think he could have done with it?"

"I have no idea."

"You said it was a present for his teacher. Is there a possibility he already gave it to her?"

Natalie shook her head. "He hasn't been back to school since that day. And besides, he wouldn't have taken it until the Christmas party, which is tomorrow."

"Then there's only one thing to do," Spence said.

They both turned and headed for the front door.

KYLE SAT ON THE SOFA, one knee drawn up as he picked at a scab on the top of his foot. It was late, and Natalie had awakened him from a deep sleep. He wore Wolverine pajamas, his dark hair was tousled—cowlicks sticking out in all directions—and the look on his face was anything but that of a happy camper.

"What'd I do?" he asked, his gaze bouncing back and forth from Natalie to Spence.

"Maybe nothing," Natalie said, trying to ignore the wide, innocent eyes he turned on her. "We just need to ask you a few questions."

"Have you ever heard of the FBI?" Spence asked, taking out his badge and showing it to Kyle.

Kyle's green eyes widened. "Am I under arrest?"

Natalie saw Spence smother a quick grin as he sat down in the chair across from them. "No, you're not under arrest. I need your help with one of my investigations."

Kyle sat up straighter, suddenly looking wide-awake. "No kidding? Really?" When Spence nodded, Kyle asked, "Do I get a gun?"

"Absolutely not," Natalie said.

Kyle turned back to Spence. "Do you have a gun? Can I see it?"

"Maybe later," Spence replied, flashing Natalie an apologetic glance. "What I want to do now is ask you a few questions."

"Oh." Kyle looked thoroughly disappointed. "But I don't think I should talk to you."

Again, Natalie caught the surprise in Spence's eyes. Obviously he hadn't been around six-year-old boys very much if he thought interrogating one would be easy. Kyle was always one step ahead of her, and she suspected he would be no different with Spence, FBI agent or not.

"Why not?" Spence asked.

"I heard my dad tell someone on the phone that you should never talk to the cops unless you have your attorney with you."

"I hear you," Spence said. "But your mother can represent you. You trust her, don't you?"

Kyle rubbed his nose and considered. "Okay."

For the next several minutes, Spence questioned Kyle gently about the day Anthony was killed. When he came to the subject of the teacher's present, Kyle suddenly became fascinated once again with the scab on his foot.

"Kyle," Natalie said. "What did you do with Miss Riley's present? It's not under the tree."

"I hid it," Kyle said. "Because I didn't want robbers stealing it."

The irony of his words was not something Natalie could appreciate at the moment.

"Where did you hide it?" she asked.

"I forget."

Natalie held her breath, waiting for Spence's temper to erupt or, at the very least, for his patience to wear thin, but he merely said softly, "Think real hard, Kyle. This is important. Remember, I need your help."

Kyle seemed to take this under advisement. He scratched his head, then turned to stare up at Natalie. "What do you think I should do, Mom?"

"If you know where the present is, I think you should tell him, Kyle. He's right. This is very important."

"Will it help you?"

"It might."

He nodded, then turned back to Spence without hesitation. "It's in my tree house."

Spence and Natalie exchanged glances. Spence stood and offered Kyle his hand. "You've been a big help," he said solemnly. "If I crack this case, I'll put your name in for a citation."

"Okay," Kyle said, shaking Spence's hand. "But I'd rather have a Super Nintendo."

Chapter Twelve

In the moonlight, the diamonds winked at them. Perched in Kyle's tree house, Natalie stared in fascination at the flash and sparkle of the gemstones. The half dozen or so—a mere sampling of what they had found in the music box—nestled in Spence's palm were each several karats in weight and more brilliant than wildfire at midnight.

Natalie caught her breath. To think that lives had been lost because of those diamonds. To think that she and Kyle were still in mortal peril because of those bits of cold stone glittering against Spence's palm.

They had found the music box, along with an odd assortment of action figures, broken pencils and crayons, and a few items Natalie had yet to identify, inside the old metal army locker her father had given to Kyle. The two of them had hauled it up to Kyle's tree house one afternoon, and Kyle called it his treasure chest—an apt description, considering.

Using the flashlight they'd brought along, Natalie rummaged inside the locker, wondering what else Kyle might have squirreled away up here and forgotten about. She examined and discarded several items, then, toward the bottom, saw something that looked familiar to her.

"What is it?" Spence asked, still cradling the diamonds in his fist.

"It's an antique ivory comb," Natalie said, holding it out to him.

Spence took the comb and studied it briefly before handing it back. "Looks expensive."

"It is. It belongs to Blanche. I can't imagine how Kyle got it."

Spence glanced up. "You don't think he stole it, do you?"

Natalie winced at his bluntness. "No. He wouldn't do that. He may hide things and forget where he puts them, but he would never intentionally take something that didn't belong to him." Natalie frowned as she slipped the comb into her pocket. Blanche must be worried sick about it. The comb had belonged to her grandmother, and was one of Blanche's most prized possessions.

Tomorrow, Natalie would have to find out how her son got that comb, and then she would make sure it was returned to Blanche, safe and sound. But for now, there was still the matter of the diamonds and Jack Russo to worry about.

Spence opened the velvet pouch, and Natalie caught the flash of fire as he let the stones slide back inside.

She looked up and met his gaze. "What do we do now?"

"We have our bait," he said, stuffing the diamonds into his jacket pocket. "Now we set our trap."

"What happens if Russo doesn't call?"

"He'll call," Spence said. "Those diamonds can buy him a new life."

"But what if he finds out who you are? What if he

thinks I've gone to the FBI? He specifically warned me not to go to the police,'' Natalie reminded him.

''Even if Anthony told him I'm with the Bureau, there's still no reason for Russo to be overly suspicious of my presence. As Anthony's brother, I have a legitimate reason for being in San Antonio. And for being around you,'' he added, gazing down at her.

Natalie shivered. They were standing on the balcony of Spence's hotel room overlooking the Riverwalk. After finding the diamonds, they'd both agreed that it wasn't a good idea for her to go back to her parents' house. She was the one Russo was after, and the farther she stayed away from Kyle, the better.

But gazing up at Spence now, seeing the reflection of moonlight in his eyes, she wasn't so sure this was such a good idea, either. The danger and drama of the last few days had drawn them closer together, rekindled an old flame Natalie had hoped was long dead.

She'd tried to deny it—to herself and to Spence—but now she couldn't, and for the first time in a long time, she allowed herself to wish for the impossible. She wished they could go back seven years and start all over.

For a while, neither of them said anything. A breeze gusted across the balcony and Natalie wrapped her arms around herself as she stared down at the Christmas lights reflected on the river.

A thousand regrets washed over her. She'd made so many mistakes. Trusted the wrong people. And now she'd come full circle. Spencer Bishop was back in her life, and she was feeling things she had no business feeling; wishing for things that could never be.

Finally, unable to bear the silence any longer, she asked, ''Why did you never marry, Spence?''

She wasn't looking at him, but she sensed his surprise

at the question. Sensed his shrug. "In my line of work, it's easier not to be tied down."

He said it so flatly, with no trace of emotion, that the line sounded practiced, as if he'd been telling himself that same thing for a long, long time. She gave him a sidelong glance. "Is that why you didn't marry…her? Because of your job?"

He frowned in the moonlight. "Her? I don't know who you're talking about."

Natalie turned to face him. "I'm talking about *her*. The woman you were engaged to while you were…seeing me," she said, more bitterly than she'd intended.

Spence looked genuinely perplexed. "I repeat, I don't know who or what you're talking about, Natalie. Why do you think I was engaged?"

"I…was told you were."

"By whom?"

"Anthony."

She saw him stiffen. Saw his eyes darken with anger and something else she couldn't quite define. "Then he lied to you. I wasn't seeing anyone but you. There was never anyone else."

Natalie's breath backed up in her throat. She didn't dare believe what he was telling her could be true. "But he showed me pictures—"

"You mentioned something about pictures that day at his funeral," Spence interrupted. "What kind of pictures?"

Natalie's hand was shaking as she lifted it to push back her windblown hair. "Pictures of you…and a woman. A beautiful woman. Anthony said she was your fiancée."

A muscle in Spence's jaw tightened. "When did all this happen?" His voice was edged with an emotion that almost frightened Natalie, and his eyes deepened with an intensity that took her breath away.

"It was a few weeks after you'd left," she said. "He came to me at work one day and said he needed to talk to me. He took me to lunch and told me very gently that you weren't the man I thought you were. When he saw how upset I was, he got angry at you and he said I shouldn't blame myself, because you had a history of using women—pretending to care about them until you got what you wanted—and then just leaving them. He said the reason you left San Antonio so abruptly wasn't because you had an assignment back in Washington, but because you had a fiancée. He showed me pictures of you and her together and then he said…he said she was the reason why I couldn't call you. And why you never called me."

"I did call you," Spence said. "At work one day. Anthony answered the phone. I gave him a number to give to you. He said he would."

"He didn't."

"I wondered why you didn't call," Spence said. "So I called you another time, at your apartment. Anthony answered again."

"It must have been one of the days he took me home from work. I was sick.…" Natalie trailed off, not wanting to explain further, then asked, "What did he tell you?"

Spence's voice was like ice. "He said he'd given you the number and you'd thrown it away. He said you didn't want to talk to me, because the two of you…the two of you were together."

Natalie gasped. "No! We weren't. Not then…not until…"

"Until when?" If possible, his eyes grew even icier.

Natalie said in a rush, "He never gave me your phone number. I didn't know how to get in touch with you, and the longer you were gone, the more everything he said made sense. I started to believe that you had lied to me, that you had used me, and I felt so humiliated. So ashamed.''

Spence's hands balled into fists at his sides. He said very quietly, ''If Anthony wasn't already dead, I believe I could kill him. My own brother.''

Natalie's heart started pounding painfully inside her. Anthony was the one who had lied to her. He was the one who had used her. Not Spence.

She should have known. Somehow she should have known, but even after she'd learned what kind of man Anthony really was, even when she'd questioned whether what he'd told her about Spence was true, she'd done nothing about it, because by that time, she hadn't trusted any of the Bishops. She'd been hurt too deeply, and by that time, there had been too much at stake to allow her feelings to cloud her judgment.

Dear God, she thought. *How could I have been so wrong?*

She closed her eyes against the wave of emotion rolling over her. ''Why?'' she whispered. ''Why did he go to all that trouble to keep us apart?''

''For the money,'' Spence said flatly. ''He saw that you and I were getting close, that what we had…was something special, and he was probably worried that when I came back, we might eventually marry. He must have thought that he not only had to get a wife of his own, but that he had to somehow keep you and me apart.'' He had been pacing the balcony, but now he spun to face her. His green eyes flashed with unexpected fire. ''And you made it easy for him, didn't you? What did you think, Natalie? That if you couldn't have one brother, you'd take the other? The richer, more powerful Bishop?''

His words stung her to the quick. "No! It wasn't like that. I thought I'd lost you. I thought you'd lied to me, used me—"

"And so you fell into Anthony's arms the moment my back was turned."

"It wasn't like that," Natalie repeated, trying to calm her racing heart, trying to stem the rising tide of her own anger. "I married Anthony for all the wrong reasons. I admit that. I was hurt and ashamed and…on the rebound from you. But from the very first, I knew what a horrible mistake I'd made. I paid dearly for what I did." Her eyes flooded with tears and she turned away quickly, before Spence could see how deeply his words had wounded her.

There was a long silence, then Spence asked, "If the marriage was such a mistake, why didn't you leave him? Why didn't you get an annulment?"

"I tried to, but you don't just walk out on a Bishop," Natalie said bitterly. "There were…complications."

"Kyle?"

She nodded, still not daring to look at him. "He threatened to take the baby away from me if I didn't agree to stay with him, at least until after Kyle was born. He said he would prove in court I was an unfit mother. He said evidence could be created and judges could be bought, and I believed him. I knew he could do it, because by that time, I'd found out what kind of man he really was. I'd seen just what he was capable of." Impatiently, she wiped the back of her hand across her wet cheek.

"If you knew what kind of man he was, you never thought to doubt what he'd told you about me?" The question compelled her to face him. His eyes burned into hers, and Natalie wanted to look away again. To run away before his accusations turned into something darker.

But she couldn't, because she knew if she left now, there

would be no coming back. No second chances. And even though something told her that might be for the best, she couldn't bring herself to leave him. Not like this. Not with the ugliness Anthony had created still wedged between them.

She took a deep breath. "I might have doubted what he told me...if it hadn't been for Anthea."

"What did she have to do with it?"

"She told me virtually the same thing Anthony had. That you were about to be married, and that your...fling with me wasn't your first and probably wouldn't be your last."

"So he got her to lie for him," Spence said, his voice more resigned now than angry. He turned and rested his forearms against the balcony railing, gazing down at the water. "Anthea always did whatever Anthony asked of her. Her devotion to him—and her contempt for me—was the only thing that ever endeared her to our mother, and Anthea knew it. She knew how to play the game. I never learned."

"I'm sorry," Natalie said, not knowing what else to say. She ached to touch him, to comfort him, but he seemed so remote. So...cold.

"It doesn't matter anymore."

But Natalie sensed that it did still matter to him. A great deal. Not for the first time, she tried to imagine what it had been like for him, growing up in that cold, dismal household, knowing there was no one he could turn to, no one who cared about him. He had never been taught how to love, and Natalie thought that was the saddest legacy of all.

She stared at his silent profile, wondering what he would do if she wrapped her arms around him and laid her head against his shoulder. Would he push her away? Somehow she didn't think he would, but it was a chance she wasn't yet willing to take.

After a few moments, he started talking again, but he didn't look at her. Instead he continued to stare out into the darkness. "When I came back and found out that you had married Anthony, I could have strangled you both with my bare hands." She saw his knuckles whiten on the railing. "But even then, as angry as I was, I was still so crazy about you I wanted to come to you and ask you to leave him, to give us a second chance."

Natalie's heart skipped a beat. Her breath tightened in her throat. "Why didn't you?" she whispered. Her hand touched his sleeve before she could stop herself, and he turned suddenly to stare down at her.

"Because Anthony got to me first. He told me you were the one who came on to him, the moment I'd left town. He said the marriage was your idea."

Natalie shook her head. "It wasn't. I swear—"

"I know that now," Spence said grimly. "But back then, even knowing what Anthony was capable of, I thought the proof was pretty damning. You were married to him, after all, and I'd only been gone a short while."

Although nothing should have surprised her by now, Natalie stood speechless, reeling from his words as if each one of them had been a physical blow. "That's why you looked at me with such contempt that day. Such hatred. I might have come to you, too, told you…everything, if it hadn't been for that look in your eyes. I've never forgotten it."

Without Anthony's lies coloring her perception, Natalie suddenly had a clear vision of what Spence's homecoming must have been like for him. For the first time in his life, he thought he had someone waiting for him who loved him—and then to find out that she had married his brother behind his back...

"I'm so sorry," she whispered. "I'm sorry for everything you had to go through."

He stared down at her, his features stark in the moonlight. "Anthony lied to us, Natalie. He tricked us both. He deliberately set out to keep us apart."

"Because we let him," she said sadly. "Because we didn't trust each other enough."

"Maybe. But we hadn't known each other that long, and it's hard to trust when someone like Anthony is feeding on your insecurities. He won. He got what he wanted. He broke us apart and kept us that way for seven long years." He paused, his hand reaching out to whisper against her hair. "The question now is, are we going to let him keep winning?"

Natalie's heart stopped at the look in his eyes. She shivered as he drew the back of his hand down her cheek. Her eyes drifted closed. Oh, how she relished his touch! Craved it with all her heart and soul. How she wanted him as she had never wanted anyone else.

"Spence—"

His fingertip trailed across her lips, silencing her. Gently he removed her glasses and set them aside. Then he pulled her to him, cupping her face with his hands as he feathered kisses along her jawline, drawing a deep shudder from her.

"There's still so much you don't know," she murmured, trying to steel her resolve, but failing. "I have to tell you something. Before it's too late."

Spence drew back and gazed into her eyes. "Does it have to do with Anthony?"

"Yes—"

"Then I don't want to hear it," he said.

"But you have to know—"

''The past is over, Natalie. At least for now. This moment belongs to us.''

''But—''

This time he silenced her with his mouth. Natalie's lips opened instantly for him, and their tongues touched and mingled as thrill after thrill pulsed through her.

She squeezed her eyes closed, wrapping her arms around him and holding him close, knowing that at any moment, what she was feeling could be torn away from her. She'd learned the hard way that nothing lasts forever, and if she could have even one moment of happiness, one moment of the exquisite desire Spence unleashed inside her, she would be a fool not to take it.

He kissed her, whispered to her, touched her everywhere until her whole body ignited with passion. When he would have pulled away, she drew him back for another kiss, whispering to him, caressing him until she could feel his heart hammering beneath her hand on his chest—until she knew he wanted her as much as she wanted him.

Lips still meshed, fingers busy with their clothing, they began a slow dance toward the bedroom. Moonlight cascaded through the window, shadowing Spence's face as he stared down at her. Natalie shivered at the dark intensity in his eyes, knowing what was about to happen, yearning for it, and yet wishing, somehow, that this moment could be preserved forever.

''You're the only man I've ever wanted,'' she told him shyly. ''I want you to know that.''

His eyes softened, and he smiled at her so tenderly Natalie wanted to weep. He sat down on the bed and held out his hand. Without hesitation, she took it, allowing herself to be drawn once again into the thrilling warmth of his arms.

Chapter Thirteen

"Do you think anyone can tell?"

It was the next morning, and they were seated at a table near the river, having breakfast before Natalie went to work. She looked around at the half-dozen or so other diners scattered about the terrace, certain that every one of them would be able to tell by looking at her face what she and Spence had been up to last night. And this morning.

She glanced at him and smiled shyly, her gaze adoring his every feature.

Spence leaned across the table toward her, his eyes deepening to the color of the river. "If you keep looking at me like that, everyone will know, because I won't be able to keep my hands off you."

He touched her leg beneath the table, and a thrill raced up Natalie's spine. Images of last night danced in her head, drawing a blush to her cheeks. Their lovemaking had been so amazingly...*intimate*. She'd never dreamed that the touch of his lips behind her knee or the sound of his whisper in her ear could elicit such erotic sensations.

She'd never dreamed that she could be so uninhibited, so...*wanton*.

As Natalie sipped her coffee, she tried not to think about the consequences last night could bring. She tried not to think about the future at all, but it was there, looming before her, casting a dark shadow on the ray of happiness being with Spence had brought her.

As if sensing her unease, he said softly, "Try to relax, Natalie. It'll all be over soon."

She sighed. "I hope you're right. But what if Russo doesn't call? What if he gives up on the diamonds? You said yourself if he skipped town, the police would still need someone to pin Anthony's murder on."

"Russo isn't going to skip town." Slowly he picked up his coffee cup while he scanned the surroundings. His expression was one of casual interest, but Natalie knew that, like herself, he was anything but relaxed. He wanted to make sure everything was going according to plan, that all the agents were in place and every contingency had been covered.

The green eyes swept back to her. "He needs those diamonds. He'll call and set up the drop. When he does, we'll have him."

And this nightmare will finally be over, Natalie thought. But there were no guarantees and she knew it. Any number of things could go wrong. Russo might get cold feet and flee the country. He might get wind of the FBI's surveillance. And even if he were caught with the diamonds, the police might still refuse to drop their charges against her.

And Spence…might find out the truth.

After he had fallen asleep last night, Natalie had remained awake until the wee hours of the morning, thinking about all the lies that Anthony had told to keep them apart. And there was yet another lie between them. A lie that might tear asunder the fragile bond they had only just begun to mend last night.

Natalie closed her eyes briefly, wishing that she could tell Spence everything, but she'd kept the secret too well hidden for too many years. She'd protected her son for so long, the instinct was deeply ingrained in her being.

The truth was, she was afraid to tell him. Afraid of what he might do. She couldn't bear it if he aligned himself against her with Irene.

Natalie knew that if she didn't tell him, he would go back to Washington when all this was over. He would get on with his life, and she would get on with hers. The years loomed before her, bleak and lonely, but safe.

If she told Spence the truth, he might remain in San Antonio, but he might also demand more than Natalie was willing to give.

Suddenly, she didn't know which prospect was more frightening—a life with him or a life without him.

"Natalie?"

She glanced up.

"Are you all right?" His eyes burned into hers, and Natalie wondered suddenly what he would say if he knew what she was thinking. What he would do.

It was that question that had tormented her as Spence had lain sleeping beside her this morning. What would he do if he found out the truth?

"I'm fine," she said, but she could tell by the look in his eyes that he didn't believe her.

His hand slipped over hers. "You're thinking about Kyle, aren't you?"

She nodded, not trusting herself to speak.

"I won't let anything happen to him. You have my word."

"What about your mother?" she whispered. "Can you keep her from taking him away from me?"

Spence glanced away, running his hand through his dark hair. "I can only imagine how her threat must make you feel. If Kyle were my son…"

Her heart stopped as her eyes met his.

His gaze hardened. "If Kyle were my son, I'd do the same thing you are. I'd fight anyone who tried to take him away from me."

NATALIE WORKED IN HER shop all day, waiting on the few customers who drifted in, but she was ever mindful of the clock, the silent telephone, and Spence, waiting out of sight in her workroom.

The workroom door was open and Natalie could hear Spence and the female agent, who had already been inside the shop when they'd arrived that morning, talking in low voices. When the bells over the door chimed, signaling a customer, the sounds from the back room immediately ceased, only to start up again the moment the customer left.

Natalie wondered what they were talking about, but neither of them seemed inclined to draw her into their confidence. Even though they were in her shop, she was the outsider, and Natalie didn't much like it.

Agent Dianne Skelley was one of those women who had been born to intimidate other women. She was about the same height as Natalie, same fair skin, same light brown hair, but the resemblance ended there. Where Natalie was slender, almost reed-thin, Dianne Skelley was full-breasted and long-legged, with big, brown eyes and lush, full lips. *Ripe* was the word that came to mind. She carried herself with an air of supreme self-confidence that Natalie could only admire. The very air around her seemed charged with electricity.

And to make matters worse, she was a toucher, at least as far as Spence was concerned. She was constantly taking his arm, touching his hand, finding a million-and-one ways to come into physical contact with him. They were on a first-name basis, and judging by the familiar way they worked together, Natalie couldn't help wondering if they'd once been something more.

She frowned, not liking the direction of her thoughts. She didn't like feeling jealous, but there it was. Spence had barely glanced at her since they'd arrived at the shop to find Agent Skelley waiting for them, and Natalie couldn't help but resent the way the agent now had his undivided attention, or the way she seemed to have completely taken over Natalie's workroom, turning it into a temporary surveillance-and-monitoring headquarters without so much as a word.

From her position by the counter, Natalie still couldn't make out what the two of them were saying back there, but she'd glanced inside the workroom a time or two, only to quickly retreat. The sophisticated-looking equipment was daunting enough, but the sight of those two heads bent together in cozy conspiracy was a little more than she could take.

Natalie told herself she should be glad Spence had such a compelling distraction at the moment. Because if he didn't, he might start to wonder about her reaction earlier at the restaurant, when he'd told her that if Kyle were his son, he would fight anyone who tried to take him away. He might start to wonder why she had looked so stunned by his revelation when his words had undoubtedly been uttered in sympathy.

He might start to wonder about a lot of things, and Natalie wasn't at all sure she was ready for explanations.

Needing to touch base with her son, she picked up the phone, hoping that talking to Kyle might alleviate some of her worries.

When she got him on the line, they chatted for several minutes about his day, about the cookies he'd made with his grandmother that morning and the game of Chinese checkers he'd played with his grandfather that afternoon.

Toward the end of the conversation, Natalie brought up the subject of the ivory comb she'd found in his treasure chest the night before, and how it had come to be in his possession.

"I didn't steal it, Mom, honest," he rushed to assure her. "I found it."

"Found it where?"

Kyle hesitated for a long moment, then said, "In my dad's office."

"*What?*" How had Blanche's antique comb ended up in Anthony's office? "Kyle, are you sure about that?"

"I promise," he said. "I was looking for my silver dollar Grandpa gave me, and I found it under a cushion on Dad's couch. He said it was just a piece of trash and he threw it away."

"If he threw it away, how did you come to have it?"

There was another long silence, then, "When he wasn't looking, I dug it out of the trash can," Kyle admitted. "But that's not the same thing as stealing, is it? He threw it away. He didn't want it."

Natalie didn't want to get into a discussion with a six-year-old about the ethics of going through someone else's trash can. She was still too shocked by what he'd told her. "What did you want with that comb, anyway, Kyle?"

"I thought it was pretty," he said in a quiet voice, sensing Natalie's displeasure with him. "I wanted to give it to you for Christmas. Are you mad at me, Mom? Did I do something bad?"

Natalie took a deep breath. "I'm not mad at you, honey. We'll talk about this later, okay?"

"Okay. When are you coming to get me? When can we go home?"

"Aren't you having a good time with Grandma and Grandpa?"

"Yeah, but…I wanna be with you."

"I want to be with you, too, sweetheart. And we will be. Very, very soon."

After a few more soothing words, Natalie hung up, then turned to find Spence standing in the workroom doorway, staring at her.

"What's wrong?" he asked.

"You remember the antique ivory comb I found in Kyle's tree house last night?" When he nodded, she said, "I told you it belonged to Blanche. Well, I just asked Kyle where he got it, and he said he found it in Anthony's office. But how could it have gotten there?"

"The answer seems pretty obvious. Blanche must have been there at one time or another."

"But she didn't even know Anthony," Natalie said.

"Are you sure about that?"

"Of course, I'm sure."

But as Natalie stood there relating her conversation with Kyle to Spence, her last meeting with Blanche came rushing back to her. The way Blanche had looked—as if she were deeply troubled about something. And then she'd admitted that the man she'd been seeing—the married man—had left her.

Naturally, Natalie had assumed her friend had meant that the man had dumped her. But, supposing Blanche had meant he'd left her *literally*? That he had died? And that the man had been Anthony?

Anthony and Blanche.

Natalie's heart flip-flopped inside her. Was it possible? And if so, why hadn't Blanche confided in her? Because she knew Natalie wouldn't approve? Or was it something else—something Natalie was afraid to even think about?

Had another friend betrayed her?

Although Natalie hadn't said anything for several seconds, Spence's thoughts must have been following hers exactly. He finally said, "Does Blanche have a key to this shop, Natalie?"

She looked up at him and nodded. "She offered to open up for me a few weeks ago when I had to take Kyle to the doctor. She has full-time help and I don't, so she said it was no big deal."

"She must have known the alarm code as well, then."

Again Natalie nodded.

"It's always puzzled me how Anthony was able to get in here the night he died without setting off the alarm. There was no sign of a forced entry. The police assumed that you had let him in, but—"

"I didn't," Natalie said. "So someone else must have."

"Exactly."

Blanche and Anthony. The names were like a litany inside Natalie's head. Had Blanche given Anthony the key to Natalie's store? Did Blanche know about the diamonds? Was she the one who had come in behind Natalie and—

She cut off her thoughts, reluctant to take them to the next step, not wanting to believe that Blanche had betrayed her, just as Melinda had once done.

But what if she had? What if Blanche knew something about the murder, but had deliberately withheld it from the police to implicate Natalie?

But why? What could she hope to gain—except perhaps her own freedom—if she were the one who had killed Anthony?

Spence turned to explain the situation to Agent Skelley, who lurked just behind him in the workroom. "Get someone up there to talk to Blanche Jones," he said. "I want to know where she was the night my brother was killed."

"We're not investigating Anthony's murder," Skelley objected. "That's the local P.D.'s jurisdiction."

"I'm making it mine," Spence said.

Skelley's elegant eyebrows drew together in a deep scowl. "Friend of yours or not, Sergeant Phillips will have a conniption if he finds out we've been interrogating suspects behind his back, not to mention withholding evidence."

Spence muttered something Natalie didn't quite catch, but by the look on Agent Skelley's face, it wasn't something she would want him to repeat.

"What about Washington?" Skelley challenged. "We have our assignment."

"And I'm broadening the parameters," Spence retorted. "Any problem with that?"

Their gazes clashed for the longest moment, and Natalie caught her breath at the look on Spence's face. Never had she seen him look so determined. Or so dangerous.

Finally, Agent Skelley shrugged, backing down. She reached for the phone, and Natalie was left facing Spence, shivering at the dark look of triumph in his eyes.

A chilling thought rocked through her. She would hate to have him for an enemy. Spence wasn't afraid to break a few rules when it suited him.

Like all the other Bishops, he did whatever was necessary to win.

THE CALL FROM RUSSO—or at least the man they believed to be Russo—came just as Natalie was closing up shop that night. She glanced at Spence who nodded as he picked up the extension in the workroom. Natalie knew the call was being traced, just as every call that had come in that day had been.

Her fingers were shaking as she gripped the phone, recognizing Russo's gruff voice immediately. He got right to the point.

"For your sake, I hope you've decided to cooperate," he said.

"You left me little choice," Natalie said, hoping her statement didn't sound as practiced to Russo as it did to her. If he guessed that she had been coached, the natural assumption would be that she had gone to the police, and Natalie shuddered to think what Russo would do in that case. "If I give you the diamonds, what assurance do I have that you'll leave my son and me alone?"

There was a pause, then Russo laughed softly, a sound that sent deep chills up Natalie's spine. "If you give me the diamonds, what reason would I have to kill you? Pleasure?"

Yes, Natalie thought, shuddering. A man like Russo would probably take a great deal of pleasure in killing. Maybe that was why he'd killed Anthony.

"At least give me your word," Natalie said, trying to hold him on the phone for as long as she could.

Another laugh. "All right," he said. "You have my word. But if you double-cross me, if I see a cop within a mile of you, your son's as good as dead. Understand?"

Natalie gripped the phone even tighter. "I understand," she whispered.

"There's a pay phone at the corner of Houston and Alamo," Russo said. "You have fifteen minutes to get there."

The phone clicked and the line went dead. On shaky legs, Natalie went to the doorway of the workroom. Spence was talking softly on the phone, but his gaze was on her.

"Did you get a trace?"

"A pay phone," Agent Skelley said. "On Commerce."

"Get the area staked out," Spence said, checking the clip on his weapon.

Both of them looked keyed up, wired, ready to move, but Natalie's words stopped them.

"I think I should be the one to go," she said.

Identical expressions of exasperation crossed Skelley's and Spence's features. Spence said, "We've been through this, Natalie. It's too dangerous."

"But why should she have to take my place?" Natalie demanded, glancing at Skelley who had changed into a sweater and skirt identical to hers. The agent had even combed the curls out of her light brown hair in imitation of Natalie's more casual style.

Spence said, "Agent Skelley's been through rigorous training. She knows the risks."

Skelley shrugged, as if the danger she was about to face was inconsequential.

The easy thing would be to sit back and let her do it, Natalie thought. She had no wish to play heroine, but she would do whatever was necessary to protect her son. If Russo suspected a trap, he might go straight for Kyle.

She said as much to Spence. He glanced at Skelley. "Wait for me outside. I'll just be a minute."

Skelley rolled her eyes as she walked by, giving him a look that clearly said, *Where did you get* her?

Spence closed the door behind Skelley, then turned and placed his hands on Natalie's arms. "You have to trust me. I know what I'm doing. We all do."

"But if it doesn't work… If he suspects a trap…"

"He won't," Spence said. "Agent Skelley's an expert at this, believe me. She could fool her own mother if she had to, and as far as we know, Russo has never seen you up close. It'll work."

"And if it doesn't?" Natalie challenged.

"It will." He bent and kissed her quickly. "Keep the door locked and stay out of sight. I'll let you know as soon as there's news."

TIME CRAWLED. Natalie lost count of how many times she'd glanced at her watch. She couldn't help worrying that something had gone wrong. Her imagination went wild, thinking up the worst possible scenarios. What if the plan hadn't worked? What if Russo smelled a trap and opened fire? What if Spence had gotten hurt or...worse?

Stop it! she ordered herself. *Don't borrow trouble.*

Finally, just to occupy her mind, Natalie got up and started straightening her workroom. Frank's ''boys,'' as he'd called the young men who had cleaned up the room, hadn't known what to do with some of the boxes and packing material she'd had stored on the shelves, so they'd stacked them all in a corner. Natalie began to put all the materials away.

Finishing that, she dusted her hands and glanced around, wondering what she could do now. Her eyes fell on the asparagus fern hanging in the small window behind her desk, and she realized she couldn't remember the last time she'd watered it. Filling a pitcher from the bathroom, Natalie pulled a stepladder over to the window and climbed up, feeling the soil with her fingers to determine dryness.

Suddenly her hand touched something solid, and her first instinct was to recoil at the unknown. Then her curiosity got the better of her, and she lifted the item from the pot, staring down at the little black tape recorder she held in her hand.

Natalie recognized it immediately. It was the one Anthony had given to Kyle, the one she'd asked her son to return, only he'd said he couldn't find it. A small fabrication, to say the least. Natalie remembered the day Kyle had come back to the workroom to get his teacher's present. Later, she'd noticed the stepladder had been pulled over to the fern, but she'd assumed Michelle had used it to water the plant. Now Natalie realized that Kyle must have climbed up on the ladder and hidden the recorder in the fern, so Natalie wouldn't make him give it back to his father.

She studied the controls for a moment. The recorder was voice activated, and the tape was all the way to the end. Natalie rewound, then pushed the Play button. Her own voice startled her in the deep quiet of the shop. The beginning was chopped off, while the recorder activated itself, then her voice came in loud and clear. She was talking to Michelle, issuing a string of instructions before rushing out on an errand. The next sound, again chopped at the very beginning, came from Michelle. She was talking on the telephone, obviously to her boyfriend.

So much for following instructions, Natalie thought dryly.

She reached down and fast-forwarded the tape. Again she heard her own voice, this time talking on the phone to a supplier, then to a courier, making arrangements for a package to be picked up and delivered.

Natalie was about to fast-forward again, when the significance of the last conversation hit her, slamming her heart against her chest. She had been making arrangements for *Anthony's* package to be picked up. The tape recorder had been turned on the day of Anthony's murder. Kyle had hidden it late that afternoon. And if it had been recording that day…what about that night?

Her hands shaking, Natalie sat down at her desk and listened to another phone conversation, then another before fast-forwarding once again. Suddenly, her breath suspended in her throat as she heard the voice she'd been searching for. She rewound for just an instant, then pressed Play.

"...are they?" Anthony's voice demanded.

Her own voice, sounding shocked, asked, "What are you doing here? How did you get in?"

Natalie heard herself gasp on the tape as Anthony grabbed her arm. Memories of that night came crashing in on her. She remembered how surprised she'd been to see Anthony in her shop, then afraid because of the way he was acting. She'd never seen him look so desperate, so out of control. Now Natalie understood why. The diamonds were missing and he must have known Russo would come after him.

"What the hell do you think you're doing?" her voice demanded on the tape.

"Where are they, Natalie?"

"I don't know what you're talking about, but I'm calling the police. Even you can't get away with this, Anthony."

There was a hesitation, as Anthony pulled the phone jack out of the wall, then, "You found them, didn't you?" A crash, as he threw the phone against the wall. "You thought you could pull a fast one on me, didn't you? You've always been just a little too clever for your own good, Natalie. But not this time. Now hand them over before I do something we might both regret—"

Natalie remembered how he had glanced over her shoulder as someone came up behind her. "What are you doing he—"

She gasped as the sound of her body crashing to the floor came over the tape. Her whole being tensed as she leaned forward, staring at the little black box on her desk. Whose voice would she hear next? The murderer's?

"What the hell did you do that for?" Anthony demanded on the tape. Another silence, then, "She's still breathing. You're damned lucky you didn't kill her."

A second or two went by, during which the only sounds Natalie heard were background noises as someone moved about the workroom. Then Anthony's voice, taunting, said, "What were you doing, following me? Did you think I'd come here for an assignation with my ex-wife?" He laughed—a mean, nasty sound that chilled Natalie to the bone. "Were you hoping to watch?"

The response was a low, garbled sound, like someone in pain. Then Anthony laughed again and said, "Look at her. Even unconscious, she's twice the woman you are. Did you really think you could take her place? You're nothing more than a high-priced call girl."

There was another sound of protest, then almost in a whisper the woman spoke for the first time, and Natalie's heart stopped for a painful second as she recognized the voice on the tape. The voice of Anthony's killer.

"Do you know how much I hate you?" Melinda whispered. "How much I hate *her?*"

"I have some idea," Anthony answered, unconcerned. "How did you get in here, anyway?"

"The same way you did," Melinda replied. "With a key. For someone who thinks he's so smart, you can be awfully stupid, Anthony, leaving your keys lying around for your wife to find and duplicate. I have keys to your car, to your office, to your private files, and to that cozy little apartment you share with your mistress. You didn't know I knew about her, did you? Sleeping with Natalie's best friend. Couldn't you be a little more original, darling?"

She must have gotten his attention with that, because Anthony's voice lost its mocking edge. He said grimly,

"You never answered my question, Melinda. What are you doing here?"

"I've come to kill you," she said. It was Melinda's turn to laugh, and she did so, with gusto, obviously relishing having the upper hand for once. "You didn't really think I'd let you walk out on me, did you? Not after everything I've done for you, you bastard."

"Where did you get that gun?" Anthony asked. His voice sounded strained, unnatural, as if he were striving for a calmness he was far from feeling.

"From your office." The mirth had disappeared from Melinda's voice, and she sounded grim now, completely resolved. "It's registered to Natalie. You bought it for her right after the two of you were married, remember? She told me all about it, how she despised guns and wouldn't have it in the house so you took it away. Everyone forgot all about it, but I didn't. I knew you still had it, and now, when I kill you, everyone will think Natalie did it. She'll go to prison for your murder. It's too perfect."

"It *is* too perfect," Anthony agreed. "Too clever by far for you to have dreamed up all by yourself."

"I'm a lot smarter than you ever gave me credit for," Melinda retorted angrily.

"No, you're not," Anthony said. "You're just a stupid little nobody who would stab her own mother in the back if the price was right—"

Suddenly, Melinda screamed as something crashed to the floor, followed by definite sounds of a struggle. Then Anthony, breathing hard, said, "You stupid little fool. Did you really think you could pull that trigger? You haven't got the guts or the gumption—" His voice cut off sharply on a gasp, as if he'd been taken by surprise.

Then another voice—a voice Natalie thought she recognized—said, "She may not have the guts or the gumption to kill you, but I do."

Anthea? Natalie thought in disbelief.

Anthony gasped again and groaned—a low, animal sound that sent chill after chill pulsing through Natalie. A loud thud followed, presumably his body falling to the floor, and Natalie's hand flew to her mouth as she realized she'd just heard the sounds of Anthony's murder on tape. Her heart flailed against her chest as she closed her eyes tightly, trying to fight the nausea rising inside her.

Then Melinda screamed, drawing Natalie's attention back to the tape. Anthea said harshly, "Shut up, you idiot. We've got work to do. You very nearly cost us everything."

Definitely Anthea, Natalie thought.

"It wasn't my fault," Melinda whined. "He jumped me and took the gun away from me—"

"Shut up," Anthea ordered. "And help me move Natalie over here, near the body. Put the knife in her hand."

Natalie was shocked to hear herself groan in protest on the tape.

"Hurry!" Anthea urged. "She's coming around. We'll call 911 from the pay phone downstairs—"

There were more sounds of frenzied activity and then in the background, a door closed softly. Then everything was silent.

Natalie, her heart pounding, stared at the tape, thinking that it was all over. She'd heard everything, but then the recorder had been activated again, and Anthony, gasping, struggling for breath, said, "Natalie...not...the one. Natalie...not you...not you..."

It was the same thing he'd been whispering when the police had arrived to find Natalie, murder weapon in hand, kneeling over him. "Natalie...not you..."

The police, of course, had interpreted that as a dying man's accusation, pointing the finger at his murderer, when in actuality, Anthony had been trying to clear her.

Natalie sat stunned by the revelations she'd heard on that tape. When she looked up, there was a shadow in the doorway—tall, thin, with short black hair slicked back...

Chapter Fourteen

For a moment, Natalie thought it was Anthony who stared across the room at her, and then, with a painful plunging of her heart, she realized it was Anthea. Anthea, dressed in black trousers and a black turtleneck, the masculine clothing adding to the ghostly illusion. Anthea, holding a gun leveled at Natalie.

In spite of the weapon, she looked as stunned as Natalie felt. Her eyes were glued to the tape recorder, which was still running. Loud voices sprang from the tape—police officers ordering Natalie to drop the knife and move away from the body, Natalie's stuttered responses to their questions, and then Anthony whispering into the hushed silence one last time, "Natalie…not you…"

Slowly, taking care to make no sudden moves, Natalie lifted her finger and pushed the Stop button. Anthea was still standing in the doorway, but now the stunned look had left her face to be replaced by one of anger. She advanced toward Natalie and held out her hand.

"I'll take that tape."

When Natalie hesitated, Anthea said, "After listening to that, do you doubt I would pull this trigger?"

Natalie shook her head, her eyes on Anthea, but her

mind was casting about frantically for a weapon or a means of escape. Unfortunately, she seemed to be trapped.

She placed the recorder in Anthea's hand. Quickly, Anthea ejected the tape, slipped it in her pocket, then placed the recorder on Natalie's desk. For the first time, Natalie realized Anthea was wearing gloves, and that—perhaps even more than the gun—brought home the woman's sinister intent.

Anthea motioned with the gun. "Get your car keys," she ordered. "Nice and slow. We're going for a little drive."

"Why should I go with you?" Natalie asked, her heart pounding like a piston inside her. "You obviously intend to kill me. Why should I make it easier for you?"

"Because if you don't," Anthea said matter-of-factly, "I'll shoot you dead where you stand. Now, get the keys."

Natalie knew Anthea meant what she said. In either case, her chances didn't look good, but at least, if she went with Anthea, she would be buying herself a little more time.

Natalie removed her purse from her desk drawer and fished for her keys. She held them up, and Anthea grabbed them out of her hand.

"Let's go."

As Natalie walked ahead of Anthea into the shop, her gaze went automatically to the front door, praying that Spence would walk through at that moment…and praying that he wouldn't. Anthea had already killed one brother. There was no reason to believe she wouldn't kill another.

As if reading her mind, Anthea said, "Spence won't be coming to save you, if that's what you're hoping. In fact, he may not be coming back at all."

Natalie glanced over her shoulder. "What do you mean?"

"He's walking into an ambush," Anthea said and smiled. "A setup. Russo knows the feds are on to him, and he's laid a little trap of his own."

Natalie gasped, her heart tripping in fear. "You told him?"

"Just like I tipped the FBI to the fact that Anthony was holding the diamonds. Men are so stupid," Anthea added in disgust. "None of them have a clue."

"But you do," Natalie said, forcing an admiring note into her voice. "I always thought you were the clever Bishop. Smarter by far than Anthony."

"Stuff it," Anthea retorted, jabbing the gun into Natalie's ribs. "You're not going to get anywhere by trying to keep me talking."

They were outside now, going down the steps. Anthea was right beside Natalie, holding her arm. Natalie could feel the gun poking against her side as they descended the steps together.

"Where are we going?" Natalie asked, her gaze scanning the surroundings.

"Just keep walking."

It was late and a weeknight, so the Riverwalk was deserted, the restaurants and shops having long since closed. Natalie wondered if she should try to break away and make a run for it, but, as if sensing her intention, Anthea tightened her grip—as strong as any man's—on Natalie's arm.

They ascended the concrete steps to the parking area, where Natalie's car was parked. The right rear fender was still smashed in, where she and Kyle had been rammed the day of Anthony's funeral. She wondered now if Anthea had had something to do with that, as well.

Anthea released Natalie's arm long enough to unlock the passenger door, and then, after some difficulty, opened it. She made Natalie slide in first and get behind the wheel, then Anthea climbed in and slammed the door. She handed Natalie the keys. "Let's go."

"Where to?" Natalie inserted the key into the ignition. She prayed the car wouldn't start, but the engine turned over on the first crank.

"You'll find out soon enough." Anthea motioned with the gun for Natalie to head out of the parking lot.

They drove for fifteen or twenty minutes, taking Broadway away from downtown. They passed the zoo and the Japanese Tea Garden with its sky tram and took a back street to a remote area of the park. And all the while Natalie's thoughts were on Kyle. She had to find a way to protect him, to save him from Russo.

And Spence. *Dear God, please let him be all right,* she prayed. What if she lost both Kyle and Spence? What if she never got the chance to tell them the truth?

At Anthea's direction, Natalie pulled the car to the side of the road and parked. They both got out, and Anthea took Natalie's arm and steered her through the dense forest of cypress trees and water oaks toward the river.

"Just tell me one thing," Natalie said, as they neared the water. "If you had all this planned, why did you try to bribe me to leave town that day?"

"Because I would have followed you," Anthea said, as if she couldn't believe Natalie hadn't figured it out for herself. "It would have been so much easier to get rid of you and the kid away from here, away from all the suspicions. You would have just disappeared, and no one would ever have known. But you wouldn't go and so now I'll just have to be patient."

"What do you mean?" Natalie stumbled over a dead branch, and Anthea grabbed her arm roughly.

"Anthony's dead, Spence is walking into an ambush,

and you're about to commit suicide. That leaves just one person standing in my way.''

''Kyle,'' Natalie breathed.

''The kid will have to wait awhile,'' Anthea said. ''Though, after you're gone, Mother will undoubtedly get custody. That'll make an…unfortunate accident so much easier to arrange.''

Natalie's heart pounded in terror. She had to find a way out of here. She had to protect Kyle.

But how could she get away? Anthea had a death grip on her arm.

Melinda was waiting for them by the river. She stood shivering in the moonlight, her arms wrapped around her middle as she watched them approach.

Natalie turned to Anthea. ''Why did you bring me here?''

''I told you,'' Anthea said. ''You're about to commit suicide.''

''Poor thing,'' Melinda cooed. ''You've been so distraught. Overcome with guilt for what you did. The idea of facing a trial and then life in prison is too much for you. You simply can't go on.''

''No one will believe that,'' Natalie argued, her heart racing as fast as her mind. She had to get out of here. Now. Before it was too late. She had to make sure Kyle was safe, and she had to somehow get to Spence—if he was still alive.

''The police will believe it. After all, they already think you're a murderer.'' Anthea waved the gun at their surroundings. ''It's pretty isolated out here. It may take a couple of days for them to find your body. By that time, the D.A. will have received your suicide note in the mail.''

Moonlight gleamed in Anthea's eyes, but what Natalie

saw wasn't madness. It was greed. It was hate. And it was triumph.

Melinda glanced around uneasily. "Let's get on with it," she said. "It's creepy out here."

"You'll never get away with it," Natalie said, desperate now to stall the inevitable.

"We already have gotten away with it," Anthea said. "I've been planning this for a long, long time, every last detail. I even planted the custody papers in Anthony's office, so the police would think you had a motive to kill him. I've thought of everything. Nothing can go wrong now."

"What about the tape?" Natalie said quickly. "You didn't plan on that, did you?"

Momentary doubt flashed in Anthea's eyes. Melinda said, "What tape?"

When Anthea didn't answer, Natalie did, "There was a tape recorder in my office the night Anthony was killed. The murder...everything was captured on tape."

Melinda gasped. "Is that true, Anthea?"

Anthea shrugged. "I have the tape now, so what difference does it make?"

"I made a copy," Natalie said.

Melinda swore viciously, but Anthea just shook her head. "She's lying. I saw her face. She was as surprised by that tape as I was. There's no copy. Is there?" She sneered at Natalie, daring her to try and make a run for it.

"The point is," Natalie said, striving to keep the fear and desperation out of her voice, "you didn't plan for that tape. What else might you have missed? What else is out there that will give you two away?"

"You said nothing could go wrong," Melinda whined. "You said everything would go according to plan. You said if we stuck together, we'd get it all. With Anthony and Spence gone and Natalie dead or in prison, the only person standing in our way would be Kyle. You said you'd take care of him, when the time was right. You said—''

''Shut up!'' Anthea whirled around, turning the gun on Melinda. ''Shut up, you whining bitch!''

Melinda's eyes widened in the moonlight. Natalie could see the fear on her face as she said urgently, ''If you shoot me, what happens to your alibi for the night Anthony was murdered? Or tonight, for that matter? We're in this together, Anthea. You need me just as much as I need you.''

As Natalie listened to the conspirators argue, she edged back, one tiny step at a time, toward the woods. Then, taking a deep breath, she whirled to run, diving headlong for cover. Melinda screamed a warning. Anthea turned and fired just as Natalie's foot caught a tree root and she fell sprawling to the ground. The bullet whizzed over her head and slammed into a tree trunk, the sound reverberating across the river.

Half crawling, half running, Natalie scrambled toward the woods, but Anthea was right behind her. ''Stop right there,'' she said in a voice filled with deadly intent, ''or I'll shoot you in the back.''

Natalie hesitated, then turned.

''Face it, Natalie. There's no way out for you.''

''You won't get away with this,'' Natalie whispered again.

Anthea shrugged. ''I'm a Bishop. I can get away with anything. And once this tape is destroyed—'' she pulled the tape from her pocket and held it up in the moonlight ''—no one will ever know who killed Anthony. Or you. I'll have everything I ever wanted. Money, power, and—''

''Mother's undying devotion,'' said a voice from the darkness. ''That's really why you did it, isn't it, Anthea?''

In unison, Natalie and Anthea swung toward the sound.

Spence came out of the woods and faced his sister. "It's over, Anthea. Give me the tape."

Natalie stared at his dark profile, relief flooding through her. He was all right!

While sister and brother stared at each other, Melinda tried to make a run for it, but someone else emerged from the woods and caught her, holding her fast. Melinda struggled for a moment, then dropped to her knees, sobbing hysterically.

"She made me do it!" she screamed. "It was all her idea!"

"Shut up!" Anthea whirled toward Melinda. "Keep your mouth shut, you idiot!"

In a flash, Spence grabbed Anthea's arm and wrenched away the gun. The tape went flying through the air. For one breathless moment Natalie thought it would fall into the water, and the evidence that would clear her would be forever lost. But the tape landed on the bank, mere inches from the river. She walked over and picked it up. Her hand trembling, she clutched it to her breast.

Spence turned back to Anthea. "That's why you killed him, isn't it? You wanted Mother's love. With Anthony gone, you thought she would turn to you."

Anthea said nothing, but Melinda couldn't seem to keep her mouth shut. It was as if a dam had burst wide open. "Yes! *She* killed him! And she threatened to kill me if I didn't go along with her. Look at her! Look at the way she's dressed. She's a flaming psychopath. Half the time, she thinks she *is* Anthony. That's why she killed him, so she could take his place!"

The whole bizarre circle now focused on Melinda. As if aware that this could well be the performance of a lifetime, she dissolved into tears once again. "You have to believe me, Spence," she sobbed. "It was all her idea, and she frightened me into helping her. I didn't want to do it. I loved Anthony!'' Melinda would have collapsed to the ground again if not for the man who was holding her up, the man Natalie now recognized as Frank Delmontico.

''You're lying,'' Anthea said, defending herself at last. ''You wanted him dead as much as I did.''

''No! I loved him—''

''You wanted him dead because he wanted a divorce. He despised you. He still loved Natalie and you knew it.''

''He never loved her—''

Once her own flood started, Anthea couldn't seem to stem it. The words gushed from her mouth, frothing with venom. ''The only reason he married you was to spite her. He hated you from the very first. He told me he couldn't stand to look at you, touch you. That the only way he could…perform in bed was to pretend you were her.''

Natalie's skin crawled as she listened to the two of them fight. She could only imagine what Spence must be feeling. She glanced at his face, but all she saw was darkness and shadow.

Dimly, Natalie became aware of other people moving in from the woods, police officers surrounding the clearing. But Melinda and Anthea seemed not to notice. They were too intent on blaming the other, too bent on destroying each other.

''You hated him because he loved her,'' Anthea taunted again.

Then, suddenly, Melinda seemed to snap. She screamed as if mortally wounded, and tore her hands through her hair. ''Yes, I hated him! I hated him for what he did to me! I wanted him dead. All these years he let me think I was the one who couldn't have children. He called me barren, empty, half a woman when all the time *he* was the one. He was sterile, and he didn't tell me. He let the whole world think it was me!''

Her words fell like bombs in the stillness of the night. Natalie gasped as their meaning struck her. She felt Spence's eyes on her in the darkness, but she didn't turn and look at him. She couldn't.

''What about Kyle?'' Spence asked, although Natalie had no idea to whom he was addressing the question.

''Take a wild guess,'' Melinda replied. ''He can't be Anthony's.''

''Is this true?''

Natalie glanced up. Although she couldn't see his face in the darkness, she could feel the power of his eyes on her. Those Bishop eyes. Eyes so like his son's.

''Is it true?'' he asked again.

But before Natalie could speak, Spence turned and walked away.

Chapter Fifteen

Natalie watched numbly as Melinda and Anthea were handcuffed and led away by the officers. Frank Delmontico came over to her and handed her his jacket.

"It's cold out here," he said.

"Thanks," she mumbled, accepting the jacket and spreading it over her shoulders. It was colder than he could ever imagine, Natalie thought, fighting back tears.

"Are you ready to go?"

She looked up at him. "Go where?"

He shrugged. "The police station. I suspect we're all in for a long night."

For the first time, Frank's part in the night's events hit Natalie. She stared at him in the darkness. "What are you doing here, anyway?"

He shrugged again. "I still have a lot of friends on the street, and I heard what was going down tonight. Normally, I don't have a lot of use for the feds, but Russo—" His voice hardened. "That son of a bitch is the reason I spent ten years in prison. He framed me and I swore I'd find a way to get even with him. Tonight I got my chance."

Natalie looked at him in surprise. She'd never seen such

passion in Frank Delmontico's eyes. "So you warned Spence about the ambush?"

"Damn straight, I warned him."

"What are you doing *here?*" she asked, waving her hand at their surroundings. "How did you and Spence know where to find me?"

"I've been watching you lately," Frank admitted. "Keeping my eye on you. I know what it's like to be accused of a crime you didn't commit. I thought maybe I could find a way to help you. When I saw you leave your shop with the Bishop woman, I figured she was up to no good. I tailed the two of you out to the parking lot where I hooked up with Spence. We followed you out here."

An ex-con and an FBI agent coming to her rescue. Yet another irony in her life, Natalie thought.

"How can I ever thank you," she said, putting her hand on Frank's sleeve.

He smiled grimly. "The only thanks I want is to see Jack Russo behind bars. And Spence has already promised me that pleasure."

AT POLICE HEADQUARTERS, Natalie gave her statement and was then ushered into a small holding room. Thanks to the tape, she'd been assured that the charges against her would be dropped immediately. Natalie knew she should be ecstatic that her nightmare was finally coming to an end, but she wasn't. All she could think about was Spence and the look on his face before he'd turned and walked away from her.

The door to the room opened, and she glanced up, hoping it would be Spence. But when Blanche walked through the door, Natalie's heart dropped. She wasn't ready to face her friend yet. Not after what she'd learned tonight.

Was that how Spence felt about her? she wondered.

Blanche looked terrible. She looked as if she'd dressed in a big hurry, throwing on the first thing she found and not bothering to comb her hair or put on makeup. She approached Natalie tentatively and sat down beside her.

"I can only imagine what you must think of me," she said quietly. "You must think I'm little better than Melinda."

"You're not a murderer," Natalie said.

"No. I'm not a murderer." Her voice was filled with self-loathing. "I'm just a stupid woman who betrayed her best friend. The only real friend I've ever had. Oh, Natalie." She broke down then, weeping softly into her hands. Finally she looked up, wiping the tears from her face with the back of her hand. "The only excuse I have is that I loved him," she whispered. "I really loved him."

"Then I'm sorry for you," Natalie said softly.

Blanche glanced away, as if no longer able to meet Natalie's eyes. "When he came to me and asked for the key and alarm code to your shop, I refused at first. I couldn't imagine why he wanted them. But he said you had something of his. Something you wouldn't give back. He only needed a few moments alone in your shop to find it, and then his relationship with you would be severed forever. I thought if he got what he wanted, he'd leave you and Kyle alone."

Natalie stared at her in disbelief. "Are you saying you did it for me?"

Blanche closed her eyes briefly. "I wish I could. But I was thinking of myself. I thought if I could help him do this one thing—"

"He would be grateful enough to leave Melinda and marry you."

Blanche nodded. "As I said before, I'm a stupid woman."

Natalie let that pass without comment. "After I was charged with Anthony's murder, when the police thought that I had let him into my shop, why didn't you come forward then? Why didn't you try to clear me?"

Blanche turned back to her. "I was afraid to! Don't you see? I had a motive every bit as strong as yours. The shunned, desperate mistress. I couldn't take that chance. I was too scared."

"And so you said nothing," Natalie said coldly. "What if I had been convicted? Would you still have remained silent?"

"I don't like to think so." Blanche stared down at her hands.

"But you don't know for sure, do you? I thought you were my friend, Blanche. I thought I could trust you."

Blanche lifted her tearstained face. "Can you ever forgive me?" she whispered.

"I don't know," Natalie answered sadly, her thoughts once again turning to Spence. "Sometimes forgiveness is not that easy to come by."

DAWN HAD BROKEN BEFORE Natalie finally saw Spence again. He came to the holding room to bring her home. For that small gesture, Natalie was profoundly grateful, because she knew what it had cost him. He had found out in the cruelest way possible that Kyle was his son, and Natalie had only herself to blame.

She glanced at his silent profile as he pulled the car into her parents' driveway and killed the engine. He sat for a moment with his arms draped over the steering wheel, looking indescribably weary as he gazed out at the dawn. It was all Natalie could do not to reach out to him.

Instead she remained silent, waiting for him to speak. When he turned to her, she held her breath.

"Why didn't you tell me?" he asked at last. "Back then, when you first found out. Why didn't you tell me?"

"You don't know how much I wanted to," Natalie told him. "But you were gone. I didn't even know how to find you. And then Anthony started telling me all those lies about you, making me believe that you had never cared about me, and that you certainly wouldn't want my baby. I was alone and I was frightened and I didn't know what to do."

"So you listened to Anthony."

Natalie sighed. "He told me that he would marry me and give my baby a name. He said it was the perfect solution for everyone concerned. The baby would be taken care of, and you would never have to know. You and your...fiancée could get married, just like you'd planned. No one had to get hurt."

"You said last night that by the time I came back, you'd already found out what kind of man Anthony was. Why didn't you tell me then?"

"Because by then Anthony had made me strike a bargain with him. He made me promise I would never tell anyone the baby wasn't his. He said medical tests could be faked and doctors could be paid to say anything that he wanted them to say. He said if I made trouble for him, he would prove in court that the baby was his, and that I was an unfit mother. He would take Kyle away from me, and I would never see him again. And I believed him," she said, wiping her moist cheek with the back of her hand. "I knew what he was capable of."

"So you said nothing," Spence said, unmoved by her tears. "And all these years, I've lived without my son."

"I'm sorry," Natalie whispered. "But back then, I'd gotten myself into such a mess with Anthony, I didn't see any other way out. All I could think about was protecting Kyle.''

''What about after Anthony was dead?'' Spence demanded. ''What about last night, before we made love? Didn't you think I had a right to know then?''

''Yes. I wanted to tell you. I tried to tell you, but…so much has happened lately, to both of us. Anthony's murder, my arrest. And then your mother, threatening to take Kyle away from me. I…just didn't think the time was right.''

''Would the time ever have been right?''

She turned away from his accusing eyes. ''I…don't know.''

''You didn't trust me, did you?''

''We didn't trust each other, and just like you once told me, I had to consider every possibility.'' Natalie wasn't looking at him, but she could feel his eyes on her, boring into her, drilling her with accusation. She turned to him, her gaze pleading for understanding. ''Don't you see? Kyle means everything to me. I couldn't stand the thought of losing him. Without him—''

''Don't,'' Spence interrupted harshly. ''Don't tell me how empty your life would be without him. Because I already know, Natalie. I already know how empty a life can be.''

She had never seen eyes more bleak than Spence's at that moment. She had hurt him, more deeply than she had ever dreamed possible, and Natalie was very much afraid he would never be able to forgive her.

''Please try to see it from my point of view,'' she begged.

He shook his head. ''I'm trying to, but all I seem to be able to think about is the last six years I've spent alone. It didn't have to be that way.''

His features looked ravaged in the pale light of dawn, and Natalie could only imagine what this night had done to him.

"I'm sorry," she whispered again. "I'm so sorry."

"I'm sorry, too," he said, his eyes as hard as steel. "I'm sorry it ever had to come to this."

TWO DAYS LATER, on Christmas Eve, a cold front moved into the area, and the temperature dropped fifty degrees overnight. Suddenly the riverside tables along the Riverwalk were deserted, save for the blackbirds and pigeons who braved the cold weather to peck at a few stray bread crumbs.

Natalie stood at the front window of her shop, enjoying a lull in what had been an impossibly busy morning— thank goodness—as she stared down at the wind-tossed tree limbs overhanging the river. The last two days had been a whirlwind of activity. The charges against her had been dropped, and every newspaper and news station in the state seemed to be clamoring for a statement or an interview with her.

A picture of her and Kyle, beaming at each other, had made the front page yesterday. Right next to it, a photograph of a somber Spence leaving the courthouse after Anthea's arraignment had brought home to Natalie, once again, the differences in their circumstances. Her life was on the fast track back to normal, but Spence's life would never be the same. His brother had been killed and his sister was the murderer. How did one get over something like that? Natalie wondered, staring at the river. She had everything to be thankful for, and Spence...

Spence had nothing.

He has a son, she reminded herself. *He has me.*

But he doesn't want you.

And who could blame him? Spence's wounded voice echoed in Natalie's mind. *"What about last night, before we made love? Didn't you think I had a right to know then?"*

She closed her eyes. Yes, he'd had a right to know. She should have told him—almost had told him—but it wasn't something you could just blurt out. The time had to be right. Feelings had to be considered. Consequences had to be weighed.

At least, that was what she'd told herself.

"You didn't trust me, did you?"

She *hadn't* trusted him, Natalie realized. Not seven years ago, and not now. What did that say about her? she wondered. Why did she always allow herself to believe the very worst about Spence? About the man she loved?

Her heart thumped against her chest as the revelation hit her.

The man she loved.

She was in love with Spencer Bishop. Again. Still. She'd never stopped loving him. So why hadn't she told him? Why hadn't she told him everything when they were being so open with each other the night they'd made love?

Because she hadn't wanted to get hurt again, Natalie realized. Trusting someone completely was too risky. It meant putting yourself out there, giving as good as you got, and she'd never been quite willing to do that.

For the most part, Natalie had lived a charmed life. Her parents had loved her and protected her, but when things had gone wrong, she'd given up on Spence without so much as a question. She'd found it easier to believe Anthony's lies than to fight for the man she loved—because if she'd fought for him and lost, there would have been nothing left for her.

And what did she have now? Natalie asked herself with

brutal honesty. She had Kyle and she had her parents, but she didn't have Spence; and for the first time in seven years, she let herself feel the devastation of that loss.

It was Christmas Eve and she was a free woman, but Natalie had never felt more miserable. Or more lonely.

SPENCE STOOD AT THE WALL of windows in the airport and watched the 747 ascend into the clouds. Irene was on her way to London for an extended visit with friends. She'd escaped from San Antonio and the flurry of publicity Anthea's and Melinda's arrests had stirred, leaving Spence behind to clean up the mess.

As far as he knew, Irene had not spoken to Natalie to apologize for her unjust accusations, nor had she alleviated Natalie's fears regarding her threat to take Kyle away. But Spence knew that was over. Once Irene had learned the truth about Kyle—that he was not Anthony's son, but Spence's—her interest in the boy had vanished, along with any pretense of concern for his welfare.

She was gone, possibly for good, and Spence wished he could find it in himself to care. But Irene had never been a mother to him, and it was too late to pretend they were anything more than strangers to each other.

He couldn't help comparing her to Natalie. Natalie adored Kyle, and she showed him in a thousand ways every single day just how much she loved him. Kyle would grow up secure in that love. He wouldn't have to look back on his childhood with the same bitter emptiness that Spence had always felt about his.

Whatever Natalie had done, whatever secrets she had kept, Spence knew, deep in his heart, that she had done so to protect their son. Everything had been for Kyle. If the situation had been reversed, Spence couldn't say for sure he wouldn't have done the same thing.

The question now was, where did that leave them? With all the lies and the secrets and the years that had gone by, was there anything left for them?

To be honest, Spence didn't know. But what he did know was that the thought of returning to Washington— to that bleak, empty apartment, to that cold, meaningless life—brought a stab of pain to his heart. He already felt lonesome for Natalie and Kyle and for what they might have built together.

But it was better for a man like him not to have ties, he reminded himself grimly. A family made you care too much, made you lose your edge. And that was a dangerous thing.

Better that he should go back to Washington and let Kyle and Natalie get on with their lives without him.

Better that he should go back to his own life and forget about what might have been.

"WHEN'S SANTA COMING?" Kyle asked, as he and Natalie finished wrapping the last of the presents. Natalie had closed the shop early that evening, and she and Kyle had been busy ever since they'd gotten home, trying to get everything ready for the next day.

The house had been cleaned up, the broken glass swept away, books returned to shelves, and new slipcovers were in place to hide the slashed cushions on the sofa and chairs. New furniture would have to wait until the legal bills were all paid and Silver Bells had bounced back. This season had been costly in more ways than one, and Natalie knew that it would probably take years to recoup her losses.

But tonight was not the time to dwell on all that. She reached over and ruffled Kyle's hair. "The sooner you get into bed and go to sleep, the sooner he'll come."

"But I wanna see him!"

Natalie shook her head. "It doesn't work that way. Now scoot on off to bed. I'll be there in a minute to tuck you in."

He gave her a quick hug, then tore off toward his bedroom, his excitement an almost-tangible thing. Natalie wanted to savor this moment. Kyle was six years old. By next year, he might not even believe in Santa anymore, and once that happened, once the magic was gone, Christmas would never be the same.

She sighed, thinking about Spence. Where was he tonight? How was he spending Christmas Eve? Alone in the Bishop mansion? Alone in some hotel room?

Or had he already gone back to Washington? Had he already put Natalie out of his mind?

And Kyle? Would Spence forget him, too? Pretend that he had never learned the truth?

Or would he want to be a part of Kyle's life? Would he want to claim his son? Would he want to take Kyle away from her?

Natalie didn't think he would. He wasn't that kind of man. But the fact remained that she had had Kyle for six years and Spence hadn't. If she were in his place, what would she do?

It wasn't an easy question to answer, and when the doorbell rang, Natalie was glad for the interruption. Thinking it must be her parents, she swung the door wide, then froze.

Spence stood on her porch, one hand propped against the door frame. The black leather jacket, the dark hair, the shadow of a beard all combined to make him look a bit on the sinister side.

Natalie's heart thudded as they stood staring at each other for a moment. Then, without a word, she stepped back for him to enter. He brushed past her, bringing a cold draft into the room. Natalie shivered as she closed the door and turned to face him.

"I suppose you're wondering what I'm doing here," he said, looking grim.

"I...thought you probably came to see Kyle."

"I would like to see him."

"He's already in bed," she said, wondering if that was the real reason he'd come. The only reason.

As if reading her mind, Spence said, "I've made some decisions, and I thought you should hear them."

He looked so determined. So resolute. Natalie's heart dropped.

Before either of them could say another word, Kyle appeared in the doorway. "Mom! I thought you were going to tuck me in—" Then he saw Spence, and his eyes lit. He dashed across the room and launched himself at Spence, catching both Natalie and Spence by surprise.

For a moment, Spence seemed at a loss, then he caught Kyle in his arms and hugged him tightly. His eyes met Natalie's, and try as she might, she couldn't tear her gaze away. The sight of father and son embracing in front of the Christmas tree, just the way she had pictured it so many times, brought hot tears to her eyes.

Spence's eyes looked suspiciously bright, too. He buried his face in Kyle's hair, as if drinking in the very essence of his son. Then Kyle wiggled out of his arms and got down on all fours, gazing intently under the tree.

Natalie cleared her throat. "What are you looking for, sweetie?"

"I thought maybe Santa might have come while I wasn't looking," Kyle said.

"I told you he won't come until you fall asleep." Natalie tried to sound strict, but couldn't quite manage the stern expression to go with it. "Back to bed, young man."

"Can Uncle Spence tuck me in?"

Spence's gaze met hers again. Hurt flashed in his eyes, and Natalie felt his pain all the way to her soul.

"Can he?" Kyle demanded.

"If he wants to," Natalie said softly.

"I'd be honored," Spence said. The two of them disappeared down the hallway, and it was a long time before Spence returned alone.

Natalie had brought in a bottle of wine and two glasses and placed them on the coffee table. She motioned now for him to sit beside her on the sofa. "Would you like a drink?"

One dark eyebrow rose. "Are you trying to mellow me?"

Natalie's fingers shook slightly as she poured the wine. "Do I need to?"

"I guess that depends on how you feel about what I have to say." He took the wine from her, but set his glass aside without drinking.

Natalie left her own glass untouched as she turned to face him, her heart hammering in her throat. "You want to tell Kyle the truth," she said.

"He has a right to know."

She nodded, knowing what the truth might do to her son. To the way he felt about her. "When?"

"When the time is right," Spence said, using her own words. "I'd like to spend some time with him, get to know him better and let him get to know me. I don't want to hurt him, Natalie. That's the last thing I want. But you and I know better than anyone how badly lies can hurt. And in the end, the truth always comes out."

"So what are you suggesting?" she asked carefully. "That I allow him to visit you in Washington?" He shook his head and Natalie's heart sank. "You wouldn't—"

"Fight you for custody?" he asked.

"Please don't—"

"I wouldn't do that. I would never do anything to hurt Kyle. You're his mother, and he loves you. I can see that. You two have a very special relationship. I don't want to take that away from you, Natalie. Not for his sake and not for yours."

"Then what *do* you want?" Natalie asked, afraid to know and afraid not to.

Spence shrugged. "To be a part of that relationship. Maybe in a small way at first, but later, when Kyle gets to know me and you come to trust me, maybe then…" His words trailed away as Natalie gave a little gasp of surprise.

She put her fingertips to her lips. "Are you saying that…you want to be a part of my life, too?"

"I've never stopped loving you," he said with devastating simplicity.

Natalie closed her eyes as a wave of emotion swept over her. He loved her! After all the lies and secrets and heartache, he still loved her. It was a miracle, too much to hope for….

She felt his touch against her hair and opened her eyes to find herself gazing deeply into his.

"I've put in for a transfer to San Antonio," he said. "I don't want to rush you, Natalie. I want us both to have plenty of time." He smiled—a bittersweet, poignant smile. "After all, when you think about it, we hardly even know each other. You may not even like me."

"But I'll always love you," she said.

Something changed in his expression—a softening that took her breath away. "Well, that's something, isn't it? After all we've been through."

"It's everything," Natalie said softly.

He picked up the wineglasses and handed one to her.

"Merry Christmas," Natalie whispered.

"Happy Birthday," he said.

The crystal chimed gently as they touched glasses. Their lips met, but only briefly, as if they both were afraid the wonderful spell that had been cast upon them could be too easily broken.

"There's something I've been wondering about," Natalie said hesitantly. "But I don't know if this is the right time to ask you."

"What is it?"

"The night my house was ransacked...you told me your father had cut you out of his will."

A cloud passed over Spence's features, and Natalie reached out to take his hand, to offer him the love and support she'd had to keep hidden for so long.

"What I've been wondering," she continued softly, "is how you managed to post my bail. A quarter of a million dollars is a lot of money."

"Especially for a lowly FBI agent," he said wryly, but his eyes glinted with amusement. "Years ago I bought some land on the outskirts of San Antonio with the last of the money my grandparents left me. The property wasn't worth much then, and Anthony laughed at my investment. I guess he didn't figure on the city spreading so fast. Or that I might have a little more sense than he gave me credit for. Anyway, that same property is now a pretty valuable piece of real estate. I used it as collateral to secure a bank loan."

Natalie gazed at him in wonder. "You did that for me? What if I'd skipped town? You would have lost everything."

He looked back at her, his gaze deep and intense. "If

you'd left town, the money would have been the least of my losses.''

''Oh, Spence.'' She squeezed his hand, her eyes brimming with tears.

''Look,'' he said and pointed to the window behind her. Outside, in the glow of the porch light, something white drifted downward.

They both got up and went to the window. Snowflakes danced in the moonlight, twirling toward the still-warm ground, where they melted almost instantly.

Two days ago, it had been eighty degrees. And now it was snowing!

''I can't believe it,'' Natalie said, laughing with delight. ''When do you suppose was the last time it snowed on Christmas Eve in San Antonio?''

''I don't know,'' Spence replied. ''Maybe never. But it's only a few flurries. It'll never stick.''

''I don't care,'' Natalie said softly. ''I still think it's a miracle.''

''I've never believed in miracles.'' Spence's arm slipped around her waist and he drew her close. ''Until now...''

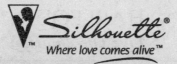

Forrester Square

LEGACIES . LIES . LOVE .

The mystery and excitement
continues in May 2004 with…

COME FLY WITH ME
by

JILL SHALVIS

Longing for a child of
her own, single day-care
owner Katherine Kinard
decides to visit a sperm
bank. But fate intervenes
en route when she meets
Alaskan pilot Nick Spencer.
He quickly offers marriage
and a ready-made family…
but what about love?

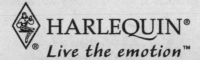

HARLEQUIN®

Live the emotion™